THE ISLAND AND THE IDOL

"My best bet," Leiria said, "is that any treaty we work out with Rhodes will be violated by spring."

Palimak laughed. "That long, huh?" Then, more seriously: "If this is the right place — the castle I saw when I was with my father that day — then all we need is a couple of weeks and a free hand. After that, King Rhodes can do whatever he wants — up to and including going to the Hells."

The airship had made a full circle and they were once again hovering just off the rear of the castle — the waterfall and the cave now in clear view. Palimak probed the atmosphere with his magical senses. Instantly, he felt a powerful force dragging at him, as if his spirit self was a bit of flotsam caught in that raging tide.

Leiria was shocked at his sudden struggle, seeing the blood drain from his already pale features. Talons emerging to cut into the rail as he gripped it. She had an urgent desire to grab him and rip him away from whatever invisible enemy he was fighting.

But she steeled herself to remain a witness, knowing there was nothing she could do to help.

Then Palimak gasped. "There it is!" he said, voice shaking with effort. "The island! And the idol, too! Just the way I remember it!"

Leiria dragged her attention away from Palimak. Below, about a hundreds yards from the cliff face, a small rocky island was emerging from the frothy waves.

Towering over the island was an immense stone image of a demon, with a long narrow face and heavy brows arching above deep-set eyes. The sculptor had given the demon a sad smile, which added to the overall effect of making the demon seem very wise.

"It's Lord Asper!" Palimak breathed.

Magical tendrils reached out to take him and suddenly he was a small boy again, gripping Safar about the waist as the great white warhorse, Khysmet, bore them both through a blinding snowstorm. Behind them an enormous ice beast was closing in fast as Safar shouted the words of a protective spell . . .

THE TIMURAS TRILOGY

When The Gods Slept (Wizard of the Winds)
Wolves of the Gods
The Gods Awaken

THE FAR KINGDOMS VOYAGES

(coming soon from Cosmos Books)

*The Far Kingdoms**
*The Warrior's Tale**
*Kingdoms of the Night**
The Warrior Returns

THE STEN CHRONICLES*

Sten
The Wolf Worlds
The Court of a Thousand Suns
Fleet of the Damned
Revenge of the Damned
The Return of the Emperor
Vortex
Empire's End

THE WARS OF THE SHANNONS*

A Reckoning for Kings: A Novel of Tet
A Daughter of Liberty

*written with Chris Bunch

THE GODS AWAKEN

THE TIMURAS TRILOGY BOOK 3

by

Allan Cole

COSMOS BOOKS

THE GODS AWAKEN

Published by
Dorchester Publishing Co., Inc.
200 Madison Ave.
New York, NY 10016
in collaboration with Wildside Press LLC

ISBN-10: 0-8439-5919-3
ISBN-13: 978-0-8439-5919-2

Printed in the United States of America.

For Cassie and Thomas Grubb
and
My friends in Washington State . . .
especially
Judy, Jon, Stormy, and Brian
and
To all my faithful friends in New Mexico
particularly
Sal, who changed my altitude

O threats of Hell and hopes of Paradise;
One thing at least is certain: this life flies.
One thing at least is certain, the rest is lies.
The flower that once has blown forever dies.

I sent my soul through the Invisible,
Some letter of that afterlife to spell,
And by and by it returned to me
To answer: I myself am Heaven and Hell.

Heaven but the vision of fulfilled desire.
Hell but the shadow of a soul on fire.
Cast onto darkness into which we—
So late emerged—shall so soon expire!

The Rubaiyat of Omar Khayyam
EDWARD FITZGERALD TRANSLATION

Part One

Syrapis

PROLOGUE

ESCAPE TO SYRAPIS

And so they flew away on bully winds blowing all the way from far Kyrania . . .

It may have been the strangest, the saddest voyage in history. The People of the Clouds mourned the loss of their leader, Safar Timura, who had guided them over thousands of miles of mountains and deserts and spell-blasted blacklands to the shores of the Great Sea of Esmir.

A paradise awaited them across that sea: the magic isle of Syrapis, where they would make their new home far away from the evil beings who had driven them from their mountain village in Kyrania.

Safar Timura — the son of a potter who had risen to become a mighty wizard and Grand Wazier to a king — had sacrificed his own life so that his people might escape.

And now a thousand villagers were packed aboard a ragtag fleet of privateers, sailing to Syrapis and safety. High above them a marvelous airship flew over the silvery seas, pointing the way.

For many days and weeks the skies remained clear, the winds steady; and at any other time there would have been cause for a grand celebration. A feast of all feasts, with roasted lamb and rare wine, playing children and sighing lovers.

The world should have been a bright place, full of promise and joy. After months of terror, the Kyranians were free of Iraj Protarus and his ravening shape-changers.

But hanging over them was the Demon Moon — an ever-present bloody shimmer in the heavens. Reminding one and all of the doom Safar had predicted would befall the world. More haunting still was the memory of Safar. The handsome young man with the dazzling blue eyes and sorrowful smile.

Everyone wept when they learned that he had been given up for dead. The mourning women scratched their cheeks and tore their hair. The men drank and regaled one another with tales of Safar's many brave deeds, shedding tears as the night grew late.

Lord Coralean, the great caravan master who had hired the ships so that they could all escape together, spoke long and memorably about the man who had been his dearest friend.

Aboard the airship the circus performers — among them Biner, the mighty dwarf, and Arlain, the dragon woman — worked listlessly at their tasks. They did only what was absolutely necessary: feeding the magic engines; adjusting the atmosphere in the twin balloons that held the ship aloft; manning the tiller to keep them on course.

Meanwhile, the decks grew shabby, the material of the balloons drab, the galley fires cold. It seemed impossible to them that Safar would no longer be at their side, amazing the circus crowds with his feats of magic.

Sadder still were Safar's parents, Khadji and Myrna, who had never imagined, even in their deepest night terrors, that they would outlive their only son. And his sisters mourned Safar so deeply they could not eat or sleep and if their husbands hadn't begged them to desist for the sake of their children, they surely would have died from sorrow.

Only four outsiders — a warrior woman, a boy and his two magical creatures — prevented the voyage from becoming a disaster.

When the privateers, seeing the poor morale of the Kyranians, conspired to seize them and their goods — planning to sell the people into slavery — the woman overpowered and slew the raiders' captain. While the boy — Safar's adopted son — combined his powers with those of the magical creatures to cast a terrifying spell that paralyzed the pirates with fear. And forced them into obedience.

The woman's name was Leiria. The boy, half human and half demon, was Palimak. And the creatures, twin Favorites who had lived in a stone turtle for a thousand years, were called Gundara and Gundaree.

Leiria and Palimak had made a promise to Safar Timura — a promise that they were determined to keep. And they would allow no one to stand in their way.

Then one day the lookout in the airship shouted the joyful news that land was in sight. And the little fleet finally came to the shores of fair Syrapis: the promised land.

Except, instead of milk and honey, they found an army waiting on those shores.

An army intent on killing them all.

But Palimak and Leiria remembered well their promise. So they roused the people and routed the army.

For three long years they fought the ferocious people who inhabited Syrapis.

And for three long years they searched for the grail Safar had urged them to seek.

They had many adventures, many setbacks, and many victories.

During that time Palimak strove mightily to educate himself. He scoured ancient tomes, quizzed witches and wizards. And he seized every spare moment to study the Book of Asper that his father had bequeathed to him.

For in those pages, his father had said, was the answer to the terrible disaster on the other side of the world — in far Hadinland — that was slowly poisoning all the land and the seas.

It was a race against extinction for humans and demons alike.

And in that race Palimak lost his childhood.

1

THE DANCE OF HADIN

Oh, how he danced.

Danced, danced, danced.

Danced to the beat of the harvest drums.

All around him a thousand others sang in joyous abandon. They were a handsome people, a glorious people; naked skin painted in fantastic, swirling colors.

And they danced — danced, danced, danced — singing praises to the Gods as shell horns blew, drums throbbed and their beautiful young Queen cried out in ecstasy. She led them, tawny breasts jouncing, smooth thighs thrusting in the ancient mating ritual of the harvest festival.

Safar danced with her, pounding his bare feet against the sand, rhythmically slapping his chest with open palms. While above him the tall trees — all heavily laden with ripe fruit — rippled in a salty breeze blowing off the sparkling sea.

But while the motions of his fellow dancers were graceful, Safar's were forced and jerky — as if he were a marionette manipulated by a cosmic puppeteer.

Madness! was his mind's silent scream. I must stop, but I cannot stop, please, pleaseplease, end this madness! Yet no matter how hard he battled the spell's grip his body jerked wildly on — and on and on — in the Dance of Hadin.

For Safar Timura was trapped in the prelude to the end of the world.

Beyond the grove, a dramatic backdrop for the beautiful Queen, was the great conical peak of a volcano. A thick black column of smoke streamed up from the cone. It was the same volcano that Safar had seen in a vision many years before. And Safar knew from his vision that at any moment the volcano would explode and he, along with the joyous dancers, would die.

Was this real? Was he truly on the shores of Hadinland, destined to be swallowed in a river of molten rock? Or was it just a night terror that would end if only he could open his eyes?

He'd had such dreams before. Once he'd dreamed of wolves and Iraj Protarus had risen from the dead to confront Safar with murder in his heart and a horde of shape changers at his back.

And, with a jolt, he thought: Iraj! Where is Iraj?

He tried to force his head around to see if Protarus was among the dancers. But his body wasn't his own and all he could do was prance with the others, slapping his chest like a fool.

He had no idea how long this had gone on. It seemed as if he'd been a barely conscious participant in a dance that went on endlessly. Yet there were moments of chilling clarity, such as now, when he would regain use of his mind enough to struggle against the mysterious force that held him.

It was a cruel clarity, because each time he knew the fight was hopeless. He'd struggle fruitlessly, then lapse into semi-consciousness.

Safar thought he heard Iraj's voice among the others and once again tried — and failed — to look.

Then he felt his senses weaken as if a drug were creeping through his veins to cloud his mind. He bit down on his lip, grabbing at the pain to keep his wits.

With the pain came a sudden memory of Iraj standing before him. Half giant wolf, half all-too-human king. Flanking him were Safar's deadliest enemies: the demons, Prince Luka and Lord Fari; and the spymaster, Lord Kalasariz. All bound to Iraj by the Spell of Four.

Yes, yes! he thought. Iraj! Remember Iraj!

And what else?

There was something else. Something that had brought him here. If only he could recall, perhaps he could escape.

The machine! That was it!

The image floated up: Iraj and the others bearing down at him;

at Safar's back the great machine of Caluz. A hunched turtle god with the fiery mark of Hadin on its shell. It was a machine whose magic was out of control and if Safar didn't stop it his beloved land of Esmir would die an early death.

He fought hard to remember the spell he'd cast then to plug the sorcerous wound between Esmir and the deathland that was Hadin.

The words kept slipping away. Think! he commanded himself. Think!

And it came to him that the words formed a poem. A poem from the Book of Asper.

Asper, yes, Asper. The ancient demon wizard whose strange book of verse had predicted the end of the world a thousand years before. And who had speculated on the means to halt the destruction.

Safar felt sudden joy as the spellwords burst from nowhere:

> *"Hellsfire burns brightest*
> *In Heaven's holy shadow.*
> *What is near*
> *Is soon forgotten;*
> *What is far*
> *Embraced as brother . . ."*

He groaned as the rest of the words fled. Safar bit his lip harder, blood trickling down his chin. Remember, dammit! Remember!

But it was hopeless. The remainder of the spell remained agonizingly just out of reach in a thick mist.

Fine, then. Forget about the verse. Think of what happened when you faced Iraj. Remember that — and perhaps the spellwords will come.

His mind threw him back to Valley of Caluz. His enemies before him, the sorcerous machine behind. He was alone: Palimak and Leiria had fled on his orders, leading the people of Kyrania to Syrapis and safety. Safar had remained to stop the machine and destroy Iraj so he couldn't pursue the villagers.

And then what?

His life, he realized instinctively, depended on recalling what had happened next. No. Not just his life — the world depended on it.

Very well. He had cast that spell. He could remember that. But, wait. Something had interfered! What, or who, had it been? Iraj? Had Iraj cast a spell of his own?

That was it! Iraj had attempted to break free from the Spell of Four, which bound him to Kalasariz and the others. Iraj had surprised Safar with that powerful bit of magic.

A collision of spells.

An explosion.

A blinding white light.

And then what?

Safar dug deep for the memory. He could recall intense heat. Then blessed coolness. Followed by a long time of floating on what seemed like billowing clouds — as if he were aboard Methydia's magic airship.

Time passed.

How much time, he couldn't say.

Then he'd heard — from far below — pipes and horns and throbbing drums. And voices — many voices — chanting a haunting song. Safar didn't have to struggle to remember *those* words, for it was the same song the beautiful Queen and her subjects were singing now:

> *"Her hair is night,*
> *Her lips the moon;*
> *Surrender. Oh, surrender.*
> *Her eyes are stars,*
> *Her heart the sun;*
> *Surrender. Oh, surrender.*
> *Her breasts are honey,*
> *Her sex a rose;*
> *Surrender. Oh, surrender.*
> *Night and moon. Stars and Sun.*
> *Honey and rose;*
> *Lady, oh Lady, surrender.*
> *Surrender. Surrender . . ."*

Safar recalled twisting around and finding himself floating above a green-jeweled isle set in a deep blue sea.

Towering over the island was the volcano. He knew in an instant this was one of the islands that made up Hadin. But how could that be? Hadin was on the other side of the world from Esmirth — e continental opposite of his homeland.

Had the violence of the spellcast hurled him so far?

Or was he only dreaming of his boyhood vision, when he'd foreseen the end of the world?

The song grew stronger, rising up to enfold him . . . *"Surrender. Oh, surrender . . ."* It drew him down like a netted fish. *"Surrender. Oh, surrender . . ."* Fear lanced his heart when he saw the dancing people of his vision and their lusty young queen. *"Surrender. Oh, surrender . . ."*

Panicking, he tried to struggle free, but the song flowed through and around him until he became a part of it. *"Surrender. Oh, surrender . . ."*

And he had no choice but let it take him. He fell into a stupor, floating downward.

Then he found himself among the dancers. Except, now he was one of them. Dumb and gaping at the nubile Queen. Warm sun on his suddenly naked back. His bare feet beating against the sand. Open palms slapping his chest in time to the music: *". . . Night and Moon./Stars and Sun./Honey and rose;/Lady, oh Lady, surrender . . ."*

Yes, that was how he came to be here. Safar suddenly felt quite calm — reassured that his mental faculties were returning. Only one small step was left. Once he retrieved the remaining words to the spell he'd cast in Caluz he could free himself.

Then excitement blossomed as another piece came: *". . . Piercing our breast with poison,/Whispering news of our deaths . . ."*

Yes! That was it! Now, there were only two more lines. Two more and the spell could be broken.

Safar heard the Queen shout and he looked up at her — dismay poisoning his resolve — and his concentration was broken.

The Queen was crying out to her subjects, pointing at the volcano. The column of smoke was thicker, blacker and pouring out more furiously. Great sparks swirled in the smoke, showering upward like blossoms from the Hells.

Any moment the volcano would explode. Just as it had in Safar's vision. Just as it had . . .

A great shock rocked Safar to the core. Not the shock of the volcano's eruption — that was still to come. But a shock of realization that he'd lived and died in this very same scene hundreds of times before.

The volcano would erupt. A deadly shower of debris driven by typhoon winds. Followed by a river of lava that would kill any who survived.

Even those who fled into the sea wouldn't be able to swim or canoe out far enough to escape. They'd be boiled alive like shellfish in a roiling pot.

In the long ago vision Safar had only been a witness to these events. But now he was one of the dancers doomed to die not once, but an endless number of deaths until the world itself was dead.

Only then would his soul be released.

Just then the last two lines came to him: "... *For she is the Viper of the Rose/ Who dwells in far Hadinland!*"

But even as he reached for them, desperate to complete the spell, he knew he was nearly out of time.

Still, he rushed on — no time to hope, much less pray. He started reciting the spell: *"Hellsfire burns brightest/In Heaven's holy shadow ..."*

Then it was too late.

And the volcano erupted.

But just before it did, he thought he heard someone calling to him: "Father! Father!"

Desperate, he cried out: "Palimak! Help me, Palimak!"

And everything vanished — except pain.

2

OF SONS AND LOVERS

Palimak peered over the railing, clutching his cloak against the damp chill as the airship slowly descended through the clouds.

Behind him he could hear Biner cautioning the crew in his rumbling baritone, "Steady, now ... Keep her steady, lads ..."

The clouds thinned and he could see the forbidding north coast of Syrapis: jagged reefs rising out of a stone-gray sea; a narrow pebbled beach ending at black cliffs that ascended to forested mountain peaks.

There came a rattle of chain mail and a faint breath of perfume as the warrior woman moved up behind him. "Over there," she indicated. "On the easternmost peak. Do you see it?"

The moment she spoke, Palimak spotted the castle. It was a black stone crown sitting atop the lowest peak, with eight turrets strategically positioned around the thick walls.

Palimak grimaced. "I see it, Aunt Leiria," he said. "But it doesn't look like how I remember it."

Leiria patted his arm. "That was more than three years ago," she soothed. "And you were on horseback, sitting behind your father."

Palimak shrugged. "I hope you're right," he said. Then he turned to the airship's bridge, where Biner held forth, directing the crew.

"Can you maneuver around the castle, Uncle Biner?" he shouted.

"Sure thing, lad," Biner called back. He barked orders and the crewmen scrambled around the airship's deck. Some tended the magical furnaces that pumped hot air into the huge twin balloons. Others checked the lines that held the ship's body suspended beneath the balloons. Still others spilled ballast to help stabilize the airship when Biner made the turn.

As they sailed around the peak, Leiria studied the fortress with a professional eye. On two sides the castle was protected by steep, rock-littered slopes. Obviously the rocks had all been piled up by the castle's human defenders.

One small stone hurled into the right place would set off an avalanche that would pour down on any ground troops foolish enough to climb the slopes.

The castle's front was just as steep and the road winding up to the gates was edged with low walls and a series of stone guard shacks, with slits for arrow holes.

The rear of the castle came right up to the edge of a sheer cliff shooting down to the hissing seas that beat against the little beach.

In the center — about twenty feet below the castle walls — a waterfall spilled out of a wide cave mouth. It fell hundreds of feet before it thundered into waves that crashed over the beach and against the base of the cliff.

"On the whole," Leiria said at last, "I'd rather defend it than attack it."

Palimak touched the hilt of his sheathed sword, eyes flickering demon-yellow. "I don't want a fight," he said. "We have more important things to do. But if that's what King Rhodes wants . . ." he grinned, displaying surprisingly sharp teeth . . . "That's what he'll get."

Leiria nodded approval. "I'm sick and tired of all these little Syrapian despots and their game playing," she replied. "They think the only purpose of a truce is to give them time to get behind you and stab you in the back."

Palimak shrugged — what would be, would be — and returned his attention to the castle.

The airship sank lower and he could make out the crowd waiting for them in the center courtyard. All eyes were turned upward to see the airship's approach.

He could imagine the amazement on their faces. The airship was a wondrous sight to behold, with the tattooed face of a beautiful woman on the front balloon. And the words "Methydia's Flying Circus" emblazoned on the other.

Methydia, dead for many years now, had been his father's lover and mentor. She'd rescued Safar from the desert and had let him join her troupe of circus performers while he had hidden from the Walarian spymaster, Lord Kalasariz.

The circus lived on in Biner, the muscular dwarf; Arlain, half fire-breathing dragon, half fabulous woman; Elgy and Rabix, the intelligent snake and the mindless flute player; and, finally, Kairo, the strange acrobat who could detach his head from his shoulders, tossing it about on the tether of his ropy neck.

In normal times, Palimak thought, they'd be preparing for a royal performance at the castle. Biner would've been stirring up excitement with his traditional bellow of: "Come one, come all! Lads and maids of All ages! I now present to you — Methydia's Flying Circus of Miracles! The Greatest Show On Syrapis!"

Palimak grimaced. The airship and circus troupe had spent more time than they liked acting as a military force, rather than entertaining. He was as sorry about that as Biner and the others. But what could be done about it?

From the moment Palimak and his fellow Kyranians had landed on Syrapis they'd been at constant odds with the violence-loving inhabitants of the island. How so many warring factions could be packed onto an island one hundred and twenty miles long and thirty miles across at its widest was a continuing and unpleasant amazement to Palimak when he was at his most depressed.

As if reading his thoughts, Leiria said, "Honestly, sometimes I think the Syrapians have got some sort of congenital war disease." She shook her head. "Remember how they greeted us at the beach that day? Olive branch in one hand, dagger up the other sleeve!"

Palimak sighed. "Poor father thought Syrapis would be a paradise for us all," he said. "A new home — maybe even a better home — than the one we left behind."

The yellow demon flecks faded from his eyes, leaving them sad and all too human. "Instead we landed right in the middle of about twenty wars all going on at the same time. Everybody in Syrapis hates each other. But now that we're here they finally have something in common — which is to hate *us.*"

His eyes misted slightly. "I guess things don't always work out the way you want," he said. "Even if you're someone as great as my father was."

Leiria wished she could give Palimak a comforting hug. But that would only make the boy feel awkward. Actually, he was a "boy" only in human reckoning.

The product of a romance between a demon princess and a human soldier, Palimak's demon side made him mature at a much faster rate than was normal for humans. At thirteen he was nearly six feet tall, although he hadn't filled out yet and was quite slender. Still, his shoulders were wider than those of most boys of his age and his broad-palmed hands had long, supple fingers. When he was angry or upset, sharp talons lanced from his finger tips like a cat's claws: a phenomenon so disconcerting that even Leiria, who'd known him since he was a babe, had never become used to it.

He also didn't act like a boy — except in rare moments when he allowed himself to relax enough to be playful. Or, blushingly so, when he was in the presence of a flirtatious maiden. Thank the Gods, Leiria thought, this part of his nature hasn't matured at the same rate as the rest of him. He had enough problems without adding sex to the equation.

Despite his youth, Palimak was the undisputed leader of the more than one thousand Kyranian villagers he and Leiria had led across the Great Sea to Syrapis and supposed safety. He had the strength of will and the charisma of his adoptive father. Backed by demon magic nearly as powerful as Safar's — who'd been the greatest wizard, demon or human, that Esmir had ever known.

During the three years since Safar's death and the Kyranians' flight from Esmir in a fleet of hired ships, Palimak had used all these attributes, plus a sometimes chilling ability for calculation, to keep the Kyranians from being overwhelmed by the fierce natives of Syrapis.

Palimak suddenly shifted. "There's the king," he said. Then he grinned. "Maybe Rhodes is going to keep his side of the bargain after all."

Leiria peered down at the courtyard. Though the airship still wasn't low enough for them to make out individual faces, there was no way she could miss Rhodes, ruler of Hanadu, the northernmost kingdom in Syrapis.

He was a giant of a man sitting on a huge, gaudy throne,

placed on a platform in the center of the courtyard. The only other people on the platform seemed to be two liveried attendants. Leiria spotted a dozen or so uniformed soldiers' but they were scattered throughout the crowd, rather than being in any sort of military formation.

"That's a scene with peace painted all over it," Leiria said dryly. "I wonder why I'm not impressed?"

Palimak curled a lip. "Maybe it's because Rhodes is the last and trickiest of the bunch," he said. "And neither one of us thinks that after all this time he's finally going to roll over on command like a dog!"

Just then the crowd stirred and the sound of fierce martial music thundered upward. Banners waved, flags were unfurled and a hundred or more colorful kites took flight.

"I think that's our official welcome," Leiria said. "Either that, or a declaration of war." She was only partly joking, knowing from bitter experience how quickly the Syrapians could turn on the unwary.

Palimak patted the fat purse hanging from his belt. "I've got enough gold here to light up even King Rhodes' scowling face," he said. "With promises of more to come for his cooperation."

He laughed. This time it wasn't forced. "My father used to always say that if you sue for peace you'd better bring both swords and money. I didn't know what he meant then, but I sure do now!"

Rhodes was notorious for his greed: Palimak was counting on this in his bid for peace, as well as on the bloody defeat the Kyranians had handed the king's forces not one month before.

"My best bet," Leiria said, "is that any treaty we work out with Rhodes will be violated by spring."

Palimak laughed. "That long, huh?" Then, more seriously: "If this is the right place — the castle I saw when I was with my father that day — then all we need is a couple of weeks and a free hand. After that, King Rhodes can do whatever he wants — up to and including going to the Hells."

The airship had made a full circle and they were once again hovering just off the rear of the castle — the waterfall and the cave now in clear view. Palimak leaned far over the rail to get a closer look. The tide was running out fast, water retreating from the bottom of the cliff face at an amazing rate.

Palimak probed the atmosphere with his magical senses. Instantly, he felt a powerful force dragging at him, as if his spirit self was a bit of flotsam caught in that raging tide.

Instead of breaking away, he fought against the force, wave after wave of sorcery smashing over him.

Leiria was shocked at his sudden struggle, seeing the blood drain from his already pale features. Talons emerging to cut into the rail as he gripped it. She had an urgent desire to grab him and rip him away from whatever invisible enemy he was fighting.

But she steeled herself to remain a witness, knowing there was nothing she could do to help.

Then Palimak gasped. "There it is!" he said, voice shaking with effort. "The island! And the idol, too! Just the way I remember it!"

Leiria dragged her attention away from Palimak. Below, about a hundreds yards from the cliff face, a small rocky island was emerging from the frothy waves.

Towering over the island was an immense stone image of a demon, with a long narrow face and heavy brows arching above deep-set eyes. The sculptor had given the demon a sad smile, which added to the overall effect of making the demon seem very wise.

"It's Lord Asper!" Palimak breathed.

Magical tendrils reached out to take him and suddenly he was a small boy again, gripping Safar about the waist as the great white warhorse, Khysmet, bore them both through a blinding snowstorm. Behind them an enormous ice beast was closing in fast as Safar shouted the words of a protective spell.

"Let me help you, father!" Palimak cried out, adding his own magic to the spell.

Safar hurled a magical jar into the beast's path and Palimak heard an explosion, followed by a shriek of agony. Then he gasped with relief as he sensed the beast falling away. But he knew instinctively that this wasn't enough and the ice beast would soon be upon them again.

He peered around his father and saw the beautiful Spirit Rider racing ahead on a black mare. She held a blazing magical torch high to guide them through the storm. They were heading for the point of a narrow peninsula, waves breaking on either side.

To Palimak's amazement, the Spirit Rider didn't stop when she reached the end of the peninsula. Instead, she rode her mare right out onto the water, leaping across the surface as it were a broad, firm king's highway.

He felt his father tense and knew he was wondering if he should follow. Then Safar relaxed — decision made — and gave

Khysmet his head. Immediately the stallion sprang across the water, running after the mare with no difficulty.

They rode like that for a time, hooves splashing in what seemed like shallow water, while on either side enormous waves boomed past. Soon the novelty wore off and Palimak dozed. He slept fitfully, waking every now and then to see the beacon still moving ahead of them.

Then Gundaree and Gundara were both shrieking in his ear. The two little magical Favorites, his ever-present guardians, were both crying out at the same time: "Beware, Little Master! Beware"

He felt a rumbling beneath him and he shouted a warning to Safar. But his father was already coming up out of his stupor, steadying them as Khysmet shrilled surprise and bounded high into the air. When he came down, his hooves skittered on slippery rock, but then the nimble-footed horse steadied himself and they were racing over stony ground.

At that moment a blast of cold winds swept in from the side, sweeping the snow away. Palimak gaped at the sight. Hunched over the little island they now found themselves on was a huge statue of a demon.

Palimak felt his father jump in shock, as if he'd been stung.

"Asper!" he said in a harsh voice. "It's Asper!"

As they rode toward the statue Palimak lifted his head and saw something loom up just beyond. About a hundred yards away was a tall, sheer cliff face, unmarked except for a wide cave mouth in the center. At the top of the cliff that was some sort of black stone structure. Palimak dully wondered what it was. Then he saw several turrets and he realized it was a castle.

Just then he heard the Spirit Rider shout and his head snapped back. He saw her poised on the mare, waiting at the steps of a wide stairway that led up to the statue's open mouth.

She shouted, "This way!" And plunged up the broken staircase to disappear into the mouth of the statue.

Safar didn't have to urge Khysmet on. The big horse leaped after the mare with such force that Palimak's grip around his father's waist was nearly torn away. A heartbeat later they were inside the idol and all was darkness.

There was a flash of light and he felt a shock shiver through his body, rattling his teeth. Dazed, he realized his father had vanished. And now Palimak was holding Khysmet's reins. More puzzling still, his hands were no longer those of a small boy, but were large and muscular.

Khysmet whinnied and Palimak instinctively leaned forward, ducking under the dim shape of a low overhang. From far ahead he heard the rhythmic pounding of drums. A great chorus of voices chanted words he couldn't quite make out.

Then, soaring over the chorus, he thought he heard a familiar voice. Recognition dawned and he shouted, "Father! Father!"

A voice full of agony cried out in reply: "Palimak. Help me, Palimak!"

At that moment a great explosion erupted, lifting him up and hurling him away on a hot fierce wind.

He burst out of the vision, gasping for air as if he had come up from the bottom of the sea itself.

And he was back on the airship again, Leiria's hand on his shoulder, eyes deep with concern.

Palimak brushed at his face, as if swatting away a fly. "By the gods," he said, hoarsely, "I swear I heard his voice!"

"Whose voice, Palimak?" Leiria asked. "Who did you hear?"

The young man's eyes were agonized. "My father's," he said. He shook his head. "It can't be possible," he said. But I think . . . somehow . . . somewhere . . . he must be alive!"

Leiria felt like the sun had suddenly decided to arise after a long, cold sleep. The ice jam broken, all the feelings she'd been holding back for so long flooded forth.

Safar! she thought.

Alive?

She clutched Palimak to her and wept.

3

THE SEA OF MISERY

All was pain.

Iraj had no body: no blood, no sinew, no muscle, no bone — much less skin to contain them.

And yet there was still pain.

In its torment, pain defined him. He was a writhing shadow of a soul on fire. A smoking stone in the guts of some howling devil dancing on the coals of the Hellfires.

If he'd had tears, Iraj would have wept them. If he'd had a tongue, he would've lapped up those tears to quench the awful thirst. And if he'd had a voice, he would've screamed for mercy. Yes, Iraj Protarus, who had never seen value in mercy, would trade his crown — and a thousand more — for one drop of pity now.

But who was there to pity him?

The gods?

Safar had once told him the gods were asleep and wouldn't answer even if the prayer were cast into the Heavens by a million voices. Safar had said many things like that and if Iraj had possessed a heart to break, or a heart to hate, he would have both loved and despised Safar now for all his wise words.

Safar Timura — enemy and friend. Friend and enemy. The one who had saved him. The one who had condemned him to this eternity of pain.

If Iraj had possessed the ability for amusement, he'd have finally known the true meaning of irony.

In his previous existence Iraj had been a shapechanger. Rabid wolf to black-hearted man, then back again.

And before that?

Images bubbled up to burst on the thick surface of his pain.

He was a boy again in Alisarrian's secret cave, swearing a blood oath of eternal loyalty to Safar. He was a young prince again, leading his armies against the demon king, Manacia, who threatened all humans with enslavement. He was King of Kings again, betraying Safar because he feared Timura would betray him first. He was a fiend again, avenging himself on Safar for the crime of uncommitted sins.

As each of these images took form, only to dissolve into a soul-searing froth, Iraj gradually emerged into an awareness that was somehow separate from the pain. It was like struggling from a molten sea to rest a moment in a world both familiar and yet alien.

He was only a lowly creature whose sole desire was to escape into death. But in his desperation to escape a more solid firmament was formed.

His first thought was: Where is Safar?

With this thought came heightened awareness: Safar was nearby! And he was also in pain. Satisfaction followed, but then he was pummeled by a further realization: Safar was not in as much pain as Iraj.

He pulled himself higher out of the sea of misery, determined to reach Safar. As he did so, Iraj sensed other creatures scuttling up behind him. Groaning things. Weeping things. Evil things.

Something like a tentacle wriggled toward him. Then a second. Then a third.

He knew who they were. When they had names, they were Kalasariz, Fari and Luka. Iraj had escaped them once, but somehow they had followed.

Not voices, but images of voices, came to him like the dry scuttling of many insects itching across his memory. "The king! Where is the king?" And, "Here, brothers!" And, "Follow him! Follow him!"

Iraj gathered all his strength and flung himself forward, humping madly like a hunted worm.

He must escape. He must reach Safar.

Crying: Safar, Safar! Wait for me, Safar!

4

THE BARBARIAN QUEEN

King Rhodes hefted the sack of gold in his big fist. "For another one of these," he rumbled, "you can be king of all Syrapis for all I care."

His bearded jaw swung open like hairy gates to make a yellow, broken-toothed smile. "'King of kings' is a title I've been hearing bandied about lately. If that's what you want, I won't stand in your way."

Rhodes was playing to his subjects, who laughed in appreciation at their king's jest, crowding closer to the platform so they could hear every word of the exchange.

Palimak snorted. "They tried that in Esmir," he said. "Didn't work."

There were angry mutters in the crowd. They didn't like Palimak's rude retort to their king.

Rhodes dug thick fingers into his beard to scratch at some irritation. "Clever answer," he said. He jerked a bejeweled thumb at a scrawny-looking nobleman at his side. "Only the other day I was telling my minister — Muundy here — what a clever young prince you are. Setting a fine example for me and my brother kings to follow."

Palimak couldn't help but notice the contrast between the rich stone set in the thumb-ring and the grime under the king's nails. He warned himself mentally to proceed with great care. It would not be wise to underestimate this man. Of all the kings of Syrapis, Rhodes was the biggest, the meanest, the most barbaric.

And yet he had more than mere cunning glinting behind those rheumy eyes. He was also obviously well-informed by his spies. His hinted knowledge of Palimak's past troubles with Iraj Protarus was firm evidence of that. One thing Palimak had learned, however, was that the only way to deal with Rhodes was from strength.

As Coralean — that canny old caravan master — liked to say, "Rhodes is either at your feet or at your throat."

"That's kind of you to say so, Majesty," Palimak replied, not bothering to hide his sarcasm.

He turned to Leiria, who was standing easy by his side, thumbs hooked over her belt. "When we get home," he said, "remind me to see about setting up a special school for the kings of Syrapis. We'll start with classes on regular bathing and grooming."

Leiria made a thin smile. She was barely conscious of the exchange, eyes flickering here and there for signs of danger.

Outwardly, Rhodes didn't take offense at Palimak's abuse. He guffawed, slapping a meaty palm against a thigh as thick as a pillar.

"What's the matter with you Kyranians?" he said. "Don't you like a good smell? A man's smell?" He frowned, pretending concern. "I worry about you, young prince. You bathe more than is healthy for you. Why, if you aren't careful, you'll catch a chill and die on us. What a pity it would be for you to let out the ghost so young. Just when we're getting to know and love you."

Palimak grinned sarcastically. "And my gold," he said. "You seem to love that as well."

Rhodes' heavy brows beetled into a frown. Another buzz of anger went through the crowd. Leiria shifted, deliberately letting her chain mail rattle in warning.

A stranger to King Rhodes' court, Leiria reflected, would've thought Palimak's impertinence foolishness of the first order. After all, the two of them were the only Kyranians on the platform with the king. And that platform — the same one they'd seen from the air not long before — was surrounded by hundreds of the king's subjects, who filled the open courtyard from wall to wall.

It was certainly an intimidating mob. Like their king, they were filthy. Food stains spotted their garments, some of which were actually quite well-made beneath the dirt. They were a large people; even some of the women were nearly six feet tall. The men sported fierce tattoos on their faces and many of the women had sharp filed teeth. Leiria suppressed a shudder.

It was rumored that Rhodes and his subjects were cannibals, although there was no real evidence of this. There was no doubt, however, that they collected the heads of their enemies. Many wore belts festooned with shrunken skulls, decorated with colorful ribbons worked into the hair.

At any other time this mob would have charged the platform and ripped Palimak and Leiria to shreds.

Leiria glanced upward. Circling overhead was the great airship. Bowmen lined the rails, arrows fixed and ready to fire. They were magical arrows, specially constructed by Palimak — with the help of Gundaree and Gundara — to strike and horribly burn any target they hit.

These, plus the other spell weapons Biner and the crew were armed with, were the only things that kept Leiria and Palimak safe. Rhodes knew from painful experience that any threatening move on his part would bring instant and massive retaliation from above.

Rhodes caught Leiria's glance and his eyes instinctively flickered upward, then back again. She noted a brief, uncontrollable twitch of fear.

Then the king recovered, placing a hairy paw of mock sincerity across his broad, mailed chest. "Here is the truth, young prince," he said to Palimak. "Spoken straight from this old heart. Despite our . . . ahem . . . difficulties in the past, I now find myself thinking of you as the son I never had."

Leiria saw a dangerous glow in Palimak's eyes: she knew he was thinking of Safar and was offended by Rhodes' remark. Sometimes she almost forgot how young Palimak really was. And with youth came a quick and deadly temper.

She broke in before things took a bad turn. "Pardon, majesty," she said to Rhodes, "but there seems to be something missing here." She looked pointedly around the platform. "Such as the matter of the hostage we agreed upon."

Rhodes turned surly. "What has this world come to?" he grumbled. "Not to trust the word of a Syrapian king! I see no reason for this hostage business. You have my personal pledge that this truce and all of its terms will stand."

"And one of the key requirements of those terms," Leiria said, "was that you would provide us with a hostage."

She turned to Palimak. "Apparently, King Rhodes still doesn't think we're serious, my lord," she said to him. "It's my advice that we leave now and allow him more time to reflect."

Palimak eyed the king. "Is that what you want?" he asked. "If you need more thinking time, I'm certainly ready to grant it. Meanwhile, the blockade will stand."

The blockade he was referring to was one of the main things that had forced Rhodes to the bargaining table. Coralean was at this moment standing off Rhodes' main port with a small but well-armed fleet of mercenary warships. Effectively bottling Rhodes' ships up and cutting off all trade with the outside world.

Rhodes sighed heavily. "Very well," he said. "If you insist." He turned and rumbled orders to one of his aides.

A few moments later there was a loud yowl — like someone had just been foolish enough grab hold of a tiger's tail! This was followed by a firestorm of shrill curses and threats.

Palimak heard someone rail, "Get your hands off me, you sons of flea-ridden curs! I'll claw your filthy eyes from your heads and your lying tongues from your mouths!"

Then he gaped as two red-faced soldiers stumbled onto the platform, dragging a biting, kicking, scratching bundle of fury between them. The men's faces and arms were dripping blood from wounds they'd already suffered in the struggle.

It took Palimak a full minute to realize that it was a woman, not a howling animal, that they were hauling before the king.

And what a woman she was! Easily as tall as Leiria, sinuously muscular like a great cat, tawny hair like a lion's and glittering diamond-hard eyes. She was half naked — someone had obviously tried to force her to dress and she wasn't having any of it.

The rich clothing, inlaid with gems and gold bead, had been ripped to shreds by her struggles, revealing an impressive expanse of shapely limbs. Only a narrow breast band and a scanty loin cloth guarded her modesty from full public view.

Not that she seemed to care. The woman was so angry, so bent on getting at the soldiers to rake them with her dagger-like nails, that the remains of her clothing were practically falling off her. Finally, after what seemed like a small eternity, the soldiers wrestled her over to the throne.

King Rhodes lumbered to his feet, drawing himself up like an angry bear. Palimak barely restrained a gulp. He knew Rhodes was big, but, by the gods, he hadn't known he was this big! Seven feet, at least. With shoulders as wide as a freight wagon.

"Stop this, daughter!" Rhodes thundered. "How dare you humiliate me in front of our friends."

Instantly, the woman ceased her struggles. But there was no fear in her as she quickly straightened up. She glared at the soldiers, who swallowed hard, gingerly let her loose and backed away.

The woman lifted her head to meet Rhodes' eyes, and sniffed imperiously, saying, "Balls to your humiliation, father dear! Balls, I say!"

She quickly and somehow regally pulled her tattered clothing around her. Making the rags seem like a royal gown.

"I am being treated like a slave hauled to market." She ran strong, slender fingers through her hair. "Worse than a slave, actually. Slaves have some value, after all. In this kingdom, it has become quickly apparent, a queen has no rights or dignity at all!"

Rhodes face went from purple to its normal drink-induced flush. He turned to Palimak and Leiria, grinning hugely and with relish.

"Allow me to introduce you, noble ones," he said, so mildly polite that they might have been at a fine dinner party, "to my daughter, Queen Jooli.

"Your hostage!"

Leiria coughed, recovered, then dipped her head. "Pleased, I'm, uh, sure."

Palimak could only stare. His entire vocabulary was stuck somewhere in the vicinity of the huge lump in his throat. Leiria jabbed an elbow into his ribs.

"Uh, yes," he croaked, "hap . . . uh . . . happy to . . . uh . . ." The rest was lost.

To Palimak's dismay, Jooli whirled about to confront him. She studied him, piercing gaze taking him in from toes to crown. Palimak suddenly felt very small and very young. Much like a minnow about to be swallowed by a large female-type fish.

At the same time a little voice whispered in his ear. "Beware, little master. She's a witch!" It was Gundaree, reduced to a flea speck on his shoulder. The moment he heard the Favorite's warning, Palimak felt a spark of sorcery leap across the space between Jooli and himself.

"So, *you* are to be my captor," Jooli said, in a voice dripping with belittlement.

Before he could react, she turned back to Rhodes. "What's happening, here, father?" she asked, equally sarcastic. "Have you been defeated by a child's army? Or is this one of your rude jests?"

Nonplused, Rhodes shrugged. "Just do what you are told for a change, daughter," he said. "Certain terms were required. And I met them. My honor is at stake here."

Eyes still on her father, Jooli stabbed a long finger at Palimak. "Bugger your honor, father," she said. "You can't really expect me to go with *him!*"

Rhodes snorted. "We've gone over this before, Jooli. As my eldest child, you are in line to succeed me. On the other hand, I'll be damned if a woman will ever take my throne."

He gave her a beseeching look. "Why wouldn't you marry any of the good and honest princes I've brought to your chamber, seeking your favor? It would've been so much simpler that way."

"They were all either boors or cowards, father," Jooli said. "What's worse, they were stupid. You expect me to confer a kingship on stupid men? And simper in their shadows, dropping dimwitted children by the dozen like a brood sow?"

Leiria struggled for self control. She felt like an unwanted witness to an intimate family fight — which this definitely was — and wanted no part of it. She wished mightily that Coralean were here. The wise old caravan master would've shut these people up with a few well-chosen phrases.

Palimak, although old in mind, was too young and out of his element for this sort of thing. Hells, Leiria knew *she* wasn't up to it and she was not only pushing the three-decade mark, but had been lover to a great king and in love with a mighty wizard. Plus a soldier commander in countless wars.

Rhodes brushed his hands together — a rare washing, if only by air. "*I'm* done with you, daughter," he said. "I've finally found you a duty you can't shirk. Your kingdom requires this sacrifice. You cannot refuse it!"

Jooli drew herself up and Leiria could tell by the narrowing of her eyes that she was about to skin her father alive verbally. It was time to stop this nonsense. There was much more important business ahead than their damned family squabble!

Leiria drew her sword — the distinctive rasp of metal riveting everyone's attention. Her steel-soled boots rang as she stomped forward, blade extended, point aimed directly at Jooli.

"What's this!" Rhodes shouted, taking a step forward. But at the same moment he looked upward at the hovering airship and all those drawn bows and hesitated.

Jooli fixed Leiria with a fierce glare. "Am I to be assassinated before my own father?" she growled. Brave as her words were, she still shrank visibly before Leiria's determined approach.

Leiria swung the blade back as if to strike, then smoothly slid it forward, turning it from razor edge to flat passiveness. She stopped the sword just short of Jooli's heart.

"Do you, Queen Jooli," she said with all the solemness she could muster, "swear to give us your royal oath that you will give yourself over to captivity? And that you will not attempt to escape, or conspire to escape, while you are in our custody?"

"This is ridiculous," Jooli protested.

"Swear it, daughter!" Rhodes thundered.

Queen Jooli made a dramatic sigh. "Oh, very well," she said. She placed her hand on the flat of the sword. "I so swear," she said. She glowered at Leiria. "There, you have my parole. Are you satisfied?"

For just a moment, Leiria imagined she saw a glint of amusement in Jooli's eyes. And she wondered, was this all an act? If so, for what purpose?

Palimak finally found his voice. "We'd better get you on board, your highness," he said to Jooli. "I have other business with your father."

He signaled to Biner and immediately a large basket, dangling from a strong cable, began its descent from the airship.

"But what about my belongings?" Jooli said. "My clothing and personal things aren't packed."

"We'll provide you with clothing," Palimak said.

"But my crossbow and my sword," Jooli protested. "I can't leave them behind."

For some reason Palimak wasn't surprised that Queen Jooli so valued her weapons. He nearly relented, then remembered Gundaree's warning. If Jooli were a witch, the last thing Palimak wanted was a chance for the queen to slip sorcerous supplies into her baggage.

"You won't need them," he said.

Before Jooli could protest some more, the basket — tended by a burly crewman — was resting on the platform.

"Get in, your highness," Leiria said with no attempt at ceremony.

Jooli sniffed, then walked toward the basket. But before she climbed in, she turned to King Rhodes. "You're going to be very sorry for this, father," she said.

And then, assisted by the crewman, she climbed into the

basket, which was raised swiftly away. There were sounds of amazement from the crowd as they saw the king's daughter disappear into the hovering airship.

In control again, Palimak swung about to address Rhodes. He slipped another bag of gold from his tunic, holding it out so the king could see.

"Before we leave," he said, "there's one other thing I want to do. And I willing to pay for it handsomely."

Rhodes' eyes glittered greedily at the proffered sack of coins. "Ask away," he said. "I'm sure we can come to some agreement."

5

THE MAGIC STALLION

The black mare pranced maddeningly just out of reach as Khysmet thundered after her across the darkening plain, heart and loins charged with *must*.

Above, gray-knuckled clouds gathered in immense lightning-charged fists. A fierce wind drove him on — so heat-charged that long blue sparks flew off his snowy back. Beneath his hooves the cloud shadows rolled past like fast-moving waves.

Behind him poured a great herd of wondrous horses, including the fifty mares who were his wives. On this magic plain he was the king of the stallions and none dared stand in his way. He'd killed attacking lions with his mighty hooves, scattered packs of jackals intent on making a meal of his colts, humbled stallion rivals for his four-legged harem.

Nothing could be denied him on this marvelous plain that spread a thousand miles between two great mountain ranges. Nothing, that is, except for the fabulous black mare who refused to acknowledge his claim on her.

The mare had appeared only a few grazing periods before:

She came like a dream — just at twilight when the insects were rising in a thick buzzing mist off the sweet grasses. Birds and bats wheeled through those clouds crying joyously as they feasted on the fat insect bodies.

Khysmet was about to shrill the signal for the herd to move to the sleeping area he'd scouted earlier in the day: a little valley — cupped between four low-slung hills — that he could easily defend against night stalkers.

But then a cloud radiant with colorful insect wings parted and the mare pranced through.

As soon as she saw him she stopped.

Steam blew through her tender nostrils as she whinnied a greeting. Then she wheeled around and looked at him enticingly over her graceful shoulders.

Khysmet neighed in astonishment, rooted for a moment by the audacity of the strange mare. Then he dimly recalled her. They'd met in the Other World, where Khysmet had once lived with his master.

Except then the mare had been ridden by a tall woman as beautiful in human terms as was the mare to Khysmet's equine senses. He'd sensed her human beauty because upon spying the woman his master had suddenly tensed, radiating a rich musk of desire. A desire just as fierce as the heat lancing Khysmet's loins as he examined the mare.

Master and horse had pursued the mare and her rider, but after a long, teasing chase, they'd vanished. Much later they'd appeared again, this time to lead Khysmet and his master through a winter storm iced with sorcery and danger. The wild ride had ended with the mare and her mistress vanishing as mysteriously as before.

And now, here the mare was once more — sans rider.

Khysmet whinnied a command for her to hold, then trotted forward to claim her.

But the mare shrilled amusement and shot away, dashing across the plain into the gathering night. Khysmet pursued her for a while, but was forced to turn back to care for his herd. He spent a long night pacing the ground, trembling with the remembered scent of her.

At dawn, the mare returned to entice him once more, rearing up to whinny her seductive challenge, then dancing off with Khysmet in pursuit. No matter how hard he ran she always managed to stay comfortably ahead, until he was forced to give up the chase and turn back.

The next time she came, however, he was prepared. His herd leaders were ready for his signal and when he charged after the mare, they gathered up his harem and followed.

The chase went on all that day into the late afternoon.

Now, with the shadows of night spilling across the wrinkled stone brows of the far range, Khysmet had the sudden thrilling knowledge that the mare was tiring.

Her steps became faltering, her breathing labored — flecks of pure white foam flying off her nostrils.

And then she stopped and he shrilled his victory cry, sprinting forward to close the gap and take her.

But there was a flash of lightning and the human woman suddenly appeared, dropping from the sky to land lightly on the mare's back.

Surprised, Khysmet skittered to a halt. And then he and the mare and the woman became a living island, the herd flowing around them like a great animal river, thundering and shrilling as they raced onward, their king forgotten.

Then all was silent, except for the distant rumble of the herd's flight.

The woman's hand lifted gracefully, a single finger bending out to point at Khysmet.

He snorted, not knowing what to do.

Khysmet felt a tingling shower of magic — familiar magic. Magic that had once carried him into and through the maw of an icy hell.

The woman shouted, "Your master awaits!"

Then she and the mare whirled and leaped upward.

Khysmet leaped after them.

Up, up, up . . . until their pathway became the gathering stars.

In the glittering distance the Demon Moon shimmered in silent, bloody challenge.

Khysmet's mighty heart thundered in anticipation.

The call he'd waited so long for had finally come.

6

WHERE DARKNESS WAITS

Palimak crouched in darkness so complete it felt like he was being smothered in a damp blanket. There was no sound other than that of his breathing and the steady drip, drip of water oozing from the unseen ceiling just overhead.

It was painfully cold — like pincers squeezing his joints where they stretched the material of his woolen costume. Icy sea water made a thin, salty sheet on the floor of the tunnel, burning through the soles of his boots. The steel cap on his head, meant to ward off blows from swords or war clubs, was a painful halo of cold.

Suddenly, he felt as if all his energy was being sucked through the cap and he swept it off. The cap fell to the floor with a heart-jolting clang. At that moment a drip of freezing water plopped down and he jumped as if an invisible monster had clutched him by the back of the neck.

"No need to be alarmed, Little Master," Gundara said. "There's no one here."

"Except for the rats," Gundaree added. "You forgot to mention the rats."

"I didn't forget anything," Gundara snapped. "I just didn't want to make our master nervous."

"Maybe he should be nervous," Gundaree argued. "They're pretty big rats."

The two Favorites were each perched on a different shoulder and although they were invisible in the darkness Palimak could tell from their weight that they were full size — about three hands high.

"I don't care how big the rats are," Gundara said. "Our master is very brave."

"Maybe so," Gundaree said, "but there sure are an awful lot of them. And they're getting closer!"

"Stop it with the rats," Palimak ordered. "And get busy making a light."

"I was only warning you," Gundaree grumbled. "No need to snarl at me, Little Master."

"Honestly," Gundara said to his brother, "you're such a quarrelsome thing. I wish Mother had eaten you, like I told her."

"Shut up about Mother!" Gundaree snapped.

"I will not shut up!" Gundara stormed back. "You're nothing but a —"

"Light, please!" Palimak broke in.

"All right! All right!" Gundara said.

There was a low muttering from the two Favorites, then a clatter of little talons as they cast the spell. *Crack!* and a glowing ball suddenly appeared, hovering some six feet off the tunnel's floor.

"There's your light, Little Master," Gundara said.

Palimak started when he saw scores of small, furry bodies dart away — seeking the cover of the darkness that loomed just beyond reach of the dim, swirling light.

"And there's your rats," Gundaree said with some satisfaction. "Told you there were a lot of them."

Palimak suppressed a shudder. "Get rid of them," he commanded.

"You're supposed to say 'please,'" Gundara sniffed, acting hurt.

"Goodness, gracious," Gundaree said. "You'd think we never taught him how to be polite."

Palimak sighed. Bequeathed to him by his father, the two Favorites had watched over him since he was an infant — a mixed blessing despite their powerful magic.

Although they were twins, they were exact opposites in appearance. Gundara had the elegant body of a man, but the head and claws of a demon. Gundaree bore the face of a darkly handsome human perched on a demon's torso. Both were fashionably dressed in tunics, tights, capes and burnished boots. They were greedy, irritating, quarrelsome and had no use for anyone other than Palimak. Although they were commanded to obey him, it was no good arguing with them when they got into one of their moods.

"*Please!*" Palimak said.

"I'm *hungry!*" Gundaree complained.

"Pleases go down better with a few treats," Gundara added.

Suppressing a groan of frustration, Palimak dug into his pocket and pulled out a handful of sweets. The two Favorites quickly gobbled them up.

Gundara burped. "Is that all?" he asked.

"We're *still* hungry," Gundaree added.

"One more word," Palimak gritted, "and I swear I'll turn the two of you into big, fat, slimy slugs!"

The Favorites gulped, then leaped into action without further delay. They jumped to the floor of the tunnel. There was a purple flash and suddenly they transformed into two very large, very deadly cats.

The cats/Favorites darted forward into the darkness. An explosion of fierce yowls and frightened squeals soon followed. A moment later Palimak found himself dodging a stream of gray bodies as the rats bolted out of the gloom and ran straight for him.

"What the hells!" he shouted, as a monster rat ran up his leg.

He swatted it away. Then he kept on swatting, kicking and

cursing as a veritable river of squealing rodent bodies flowed around him, over him and even between his legs, trying to escape the Favorites.

Then it was over and he stood angry and panting as Gundara and Gundaree calmly strolled back into the light in their original forms.

"They're gone, Little Master," Gundara piped.

Glaring, Palimak opened his mouth to give them a piece of his mind. Then he shrugged. What was the use? It was his fault for not being specific. Given more than one way to do things, the twins usually chose the route that gave their master the most trouble.

To keep the peace, he managed a "Thanks, boys," then got down to the job at hand.

Palimak motioned and the two leaped back onto his shoulders. He stalked onward, the glowing ball bobbing in front of him, lighting the way. Almost immediately, however, he was brought up short and to his dismay he learned the reason why the panicked rats had rushed him. The passage ended abruptly in a blank-faced wall

"Oh, we meant to tell you, Little Master," Gundara said, "the tunnel doesn't go any further."

Palimak was stunned. "What happened?" he croaked. "This isn't how it looked in either of the visions! There was an opening! I saw it clear as day. Both times!"

"There's one thing wrong, Little Master," Gundaree said.

"Two things, actually," Gundara added.

"Oh, shut up, you!" Gundaree demanded.

Palimak growled for silence and got it. He knew very well what his trouble was. Or he could take a damned good guess, at least. He should have realized at the start of his journey through the tunnel that it wouldn't be so easy. From the moment he'd entered the mouth of the Idol of Asper he'd sensed a wrongness. It felt like a place where the blackest of magic had been practiced a long time ago.

Although there was nothing visible present, he sensed the damp corpses of ancient castings. The sense of danger had been so strong that he'd sent Leiria and the other members of his party away while he cast his arsenal's strongest series of protective spells.

The danger had seemed to lessen. But no sooner had he and his guards advanced down the tunnel again than the feeling of danger returned, just as strong as before.

Although Leiria and the others had argued fiercely, he'd made them wait at the entrance while he explored further, casting cleansing spells as he went on so there'd be nothing to worry him when he retraced his steps.

After five hours of searching through the darkness — using up the magic in one lightball after another — he'd started to realize why King Rhodes had looked at him so strangely when he'd made his request.

"The idol?" he'd said, surprised. "No one goes into the idol!"

"Nevertheless," Palimak had responded, "that's what I want to do."

Oddly enough, King Rhodes hadn't questioned him further. And his eyes had seemed to gleam with mysterious pleasure when he'd granted permission.

As he studied the blank wall once more, Palimak again puzzled over the king's reaction. When he'd entered the tunnel and encountered the spore of the old spells, Palimak had assumed Rhodes was hoping some evil magical presence lurking within the passage would do the job the king had been attempting since the Kyranians first landed in Syrapis. Which was to kill Palimak.

But now Palimak had reached the end of the tunnel and there was nothing apparent that posed any danger.

Gundara suddenly tensed on his shoulder. "Beware, Little Master!" he said.

Palimak was startled. "What's wrong?"

"There!" Gundaree said, pointing at the wall. "It's waiting!"

"And it's really, really hungry, Little Master," Gundara added.

"Maybe we'd better get out of here," Gundaree said.

Ignoring them, Palimak drew his dagger, reversed it, and started tapping on the wall. There was a sound like the beat of a drum. The wall was hollow! And then suddenly, steam started wisping off the face of the wall.

Palimak ignored it and continued tapping.

7

QUEEN CHARIZE

On the other side of the wall Palimak's tapping echoed in a vast dark chamber.

Tap, tap. Tap, tap.

Then there was a sound of things stirring, like the dry wings of large insects disturbed in their slumber.

Tap, tap, tap.

"Listen, sisters," rasped a voice. "Someone's coming!"

Tap, tap.

"Silence, sisters," said another. So deadly in tone that if there had been human ears present the voice would have chilled the foolish bearer of those ears to the marrow.

And there was silence.

Except for: Tap, tap. Tap, tap, tap.

Echoing through the chamber.

Queen Charize stirred on her throne, examining the source of the sound. She was practically blind, but that made no difference here, since sight would have been useless in her underground kingdom of eternal night. Her senses of smell and hearing, however, were so acute that she could make out Palimak and the Favorites through solid stone.

Tap, tap. Tap, tap, tap.

The hammering produced the image of a tall, wingless creature, with two legs and two arms.

Tap, tap.

And little Gundaree and Gundara were displayed in her greedy mind. They were perched on the wingless creature's shoulders. Her nostril openings widened, sniffing the chamber's hot air. The scent carried through the pores of the stone, drifting like steam wafting through from the cold Other Side.

"I smell a human, sisters," she said.

There was a low, hungry muttering from the others. "Human! Human! Human!"

Queen Charize sniffed again. "And demon as well."

More muttering. Puzzled, instead of hungry: "Human *and* demon?"

The presence of both races together was astounding. Could it be the two beings on the creature's shoulders?

The answer came from the spoor rising through the pores of the stone. And all her highly-tuned senses told her the two beings were clearly magical. With no real form. They were creations, not true living things. Strange spirits whose origins were very ancient indeed. Charize smiled to herself. She could almost taste the presence of the long-ago sister witch who had made them.

Again she tested the air. Separating the human and demon

scents. Tap, tap, tap. Form radiating an image on her brain. And then the scent was traced back to a single source — laid over the sound image of the wingless creature.

"A feast, sisters!" she chortled. "Let him in!"

There was a hungry muttering. Broken by one voice:

"Pardon, Majesty. But what if it's Safar Timura?"

The question was a hot dagger to the huge organ that served Charize as both heart and lungs. It had been a long time since she'd truly fed on a human's spirit and her intense hunger had interfered with her memory.

"How dare you speak the name of Safar Timura?" she rasped. "It is forbidden here!"

"Just the same, sister," came the voice. It was that of Tarla, her royal rival. "I must speak it for the good of us all. It was Safar Timura who nearly destroyed us, if you recall."

Queen Charize remembered very well.

Again came the sound from the Other Side: Tap, tap. Tap, tap, tap.

And there was a slip in awareness and she found herself back at that moment — some ten sheddings ago — when her most grievous enemy, the mighty wizard Lord Timura, had confronted her. Except, in this vision, she found herself in Timura's mind. Cloaked in darkness. Danger all around. She experienced both his emotions and her own at the same time.

Charize choked in disgust as her mind merged into the filthy body of the remembered other: She *was* Safar Timura! And she was surrounded by darkness and ghastly beings. And those beings were herself and her sisters!

Safar heard heavy talons rattle on stone and a snuffling sound, like a beast following a strong scent. He knew he had to do something quickly before he was found.

The idea jumped up at Safar and he knew he couldn't wait and think it through, because with thought would come fear and fear's hesitation would be the end of him. He made a spell and clapped his hands together and roared: "Light!"

And light blasted in from all sides, nearly knocking him over with the sudden shock of it. He had been blinded by darkness before, now he was blinded by its white-hot opposite. There were awful screams of pain all around and then his vision cleared and the first thing he saw ripped his breath from his body.

The beast towered above him, enormous corpse-colored wings unfolded like a bat's. It had the stretched-out torso of a woman with long thin arms and legs that ended in taloned claws. There was no hair on its skull-like head and instead of a nose there were only nostril holes on a flat face shaped like a shovel.

Safar nearly jumped away, but then he realized the creature was too busy screaming in pain and clawing at its eyes to be a threat. He was in an enormous vaulted room, filled with blazing colors. Great columns, red and blue and green, climbed toward glaring light then disappeared beyond. The room was filled with hundreds of death-white creatures, some crouched on the floor howling pain, others hanging bat-like from long stanchions coming out of the columns. They twisted and screamed, horrid flags of misery blowing in a devil wind of conjured light.

Safar spotted the one he wanted. Again he shouted, his magically amplified voice thundering over the wails: "Silence!"

The shrieks and screams cut off at his command, and now there was only moaning and harsh pleas for "Mercy, brother, mercy!"

Safar paced forward, moving through the writhing bodies until he came to the throne. It looked like a great pile of bones — arms and legs and torsos and skulls stacked in the shape of an enormous winged chair. As he came closer he saw the 'bones' were carved from white stone. The creature who commanded that grisly throne was like the others, except much larger. A red metal band encircled her bony skull to make a crown. Unlike the others, however, the creature was silent and although she was hunched over, claws covering her eyes, she made no outward show of pain.

Safar stopped at the throne and said loudly, for all to hear: "Are you queen to this mewling lot?"

"Yes, I am queen. Queen Charize." As she answered she couldn't help but raise her royal head, carefully keeping her eyes shielded. "I command here."

"You command nothing," Safar replied, voice echoing throughout the chamber, "except what I, Lord Timura of Kyrania, might permit."

Queen Charize said nothing.

"Do you understand me?" Safar demanded.

He made a motion and the light became brighter still. The creatures shrieked as their pain intensified. Even the queen could not stop a low moan escaping through her clenched lips.

"Yes," she gasped, "I understand."

"Yes, Master," Safar corrected her. "You will address me as 'Master.'"

The queen gnashed her fangs in protest, but she got it out: "Yes . . . Master!"

Tap, tap. Tap, tap, tap.

The sound brought Charize back to awareness. It was just in time, because as her great head jerked upward she sensed danger.

Not from without, but from only a few feet away where Tarla was sidling closer. Charize could smell the hate musk on her rival's breath. Hear the faint clatter of talons reaching for her throat.

The queen slashed with her mighty claws. There was a cry, the sound of a falling body; then the heady scent of death filled the chamber. And Tarla was no more.

Excited whispers came from her subjects as word was passed on what had happened.

"Are there any others, my sisters," came Charize's deadly voice, "who wish to challenge me?"

The whispers died.

Silence.

Except for the *tap, tap, tap* from the Other Side.

And then the remembered humiliation of the incident with Timura combined with the shock of Tarla's recent bold attempt at regicide to force a decision. Charize had to show them who ruled here. A raw display of power was required to silence those who had favored Tarla.

"Let him in, sisters," she said. "And we will feast!"

Palimak pressed an ear against the wall, listening as he tapped with the haft of his dagger. *Tap, tap, tap.*

All his senses were focused on the hollow echo that came back to him. The space behind the wall was quite large, he guessed. More of a chamber than just a rift in the rock's surface. Also, it was obviously a place that was quite warm. Witness the steam rising off the stone.

Getting ready to make another sounding, he shifted and felt a scratch against his cheek. He drew back, noticing a raised ridge on the otherwise smooth wall.

"What's this?" he asked.

On one shoulder, he felt Gundara shiver. "I don't like this place, Little Master," he said.

"Maybe we should leave," Gundaree added.

"Is there danger?" Palimak asked.

Frightened as he was, Gundara could not help a snort of derision. "We said it was hungry, Master," he pointed out.

Gundaree's teeth were chattering. Still, he managed to add, "And it wants to eat *us!*"

Palimak ignored their fear. "Make the light brighter," he said.

"Are you deaf, Little Master??" Gundara said. "Didn't you hear us tell you to leave as fast as you can?"

"Do as I ask," Palimak said. Then added, "Please."

"All right, if that's what you want, Little Master," Gundaree said. "But don't blame us if you end up in the belly of some nasty thing."

"I won't," Palimak said.

The two Favorites muttered a little chant, the ball of light grew brighter and Palimak was able to see the raised area of the rock more clearly. It was a carving of a winged snake with two heads, its tongues flickering out to taste the air.

"The sign of Asper," he whispered.

At that moment the Favorites cried out in unison: "Look out, Master!"

There was a low rumble, then a loud grating noise, and as Palimak stepped back the wall began to shift in its moorings. Palimak drew his sword — double-arming himself by readying a defensive spell. But then the wall stopped moving. Foul-smelling steam hissed through an inch-wide opening between the wall and its stone frame.

He waited, whispering a spell to turn the awful odor into something more bearable. The Favorites were silent, which he supposed was a blessing. But the lack of their usual chatter was unnerving.

Palimak had rarely seen them so afraid before. During grave danger to himself their usual attitude was a cheery resignation that they'd receive a new master if the danger proved fatal to Palimak. Sure, they'd miss him. Perhaps even mourn him a little. But the fact was that after a thousand or so years they'd become fatalistic about the many short-lived creatures who had been their masters. What would be, would be. In this case, however, their attitude was far from indifferent.

Palimak probed the darkness for some sign of the danger that was worrying them. He didn't doubt its existence. Gundara and Gundaree were never wrong about such matters. But all he could sense was the spoor of the long-dead magic he'd encountered when entering the tunnel.

Once again he looked at the twin-headed snake symbol of Asper. Unconsciously he reached out to touch it. But as he did so he had a quick mental flash of something — a horrible something — leaning forward in anticipation. Its enormous fangs exposed in a wide grin.

At that moment the ball of light sputtered and died and all became darkness. There was a subterranean rumble, then the heavy grating of stone against stone: he sensed that the door was opening wider.

Palimak took a deep breath and stepped through.

And then there was a loud, echoing *boom!* as the door slammed shut behind him.

8

ESCAPE FROM HADIN

Oh, how he danced. Danced, danced, danced. Danced to the beat of the harvest drums . . .

Safar fought against the spell's fierce grip. He groaned with effort as the cosmic puppeteer manipulated the strings, forcing him through another performance on the doomed stage that was Hadin.

All around him his eternal companions pranced and sang, giving themselves over joyously to the harvest queen's song: "*Lady, O Lady, surrender! Surrender . . .*"

Smoke once again columned up from the volcano that formed a backdrop for the dancing queen. Showering sparks flitted through the black smoke in seeming time to the music.

Any moment now history would repeat its terrible cycle and Safar would once again experience the soul-searing death of flesh, bone and spirit.

But now there was a difference. And with that difference came hope. It seemed to him that he'd regained awareness more quickly than the other times he'd been resurrected in the eternal hell that was Hadinland.

And now he was armed not only with the words of Asper's

spell, but also with the memory of Palimak charging out of the mist of some Spellworld on the muscular back of Khysmet.

Of course, it could all be merely another awful manifestation of the eternal damnation that he'd been flung into when he'd first cast the spell back in Esmir. In fact, he had no proof that the original spell had worked. He had only a vague feeling of success. For all he knew the poisons might still be pouring through the magical portal that linked Hadin with Esmir.

Another worry — what about Iraj? What had happened to him? Safar had a skin-crawling suspicion that his old enemy lurked nearby. Perhaps not exactly in the Spellworld of the doomed Hadin. But close. Very close.

He tried to concentrate. Tried to push his magical senses into places where he thought Iraj might be hiding. But he was so caught up in the spelldance that he could only keep prancing like a naked clown.

"Lady, O Lady/ Surrender . . ."

Slapping his palms against his chest. Pounding time with his bare feet in the hot sand.

For a frightening second he nearly lost control — and with it his will to cast the spell that he prayed would free him.

Then he heard the distant thunder of the volcano building toward its fiery climax. The queen turned to observe the eruption and then shout her belated warning to her doomed flock. Just as she had hundreds of times before.

Grasping for all his strength, Safar quickly began to chant the words of Asper's spell:

> *"Hellsfire burns brightest*
> *In Heaven's holy shadow.*
> *What is near*
> *Is soon forgotten;*
> *What is far . . .*

Iraj struggled higher onto the rock.

Or at least he imagined it as a rock. Just as he imagined the soul-burning sea behind him to be something that could be described as a "sea." Never one for deep reflection, Iraj had no sense of the metaphysical, much less words to describe it.

All he knew was that he could hear Safar's voice. And although that voice came from a place he couldn't see, he was certain it was quite close.

There it was now:

> *". . . Embraced as brother;*
> *Piercing our breast with poison,*
> *Whispering news of our deaths . . .*

Iraj knew instinctively that his enemy was preparing to escape.

And he was determined to escape with him.

Iraj flung himself higher, ignoring the pain as he flopped onto the rough surface. At the end of the rock was a blue-gold shimmer of light. He thought he could make out movement in that light. Gigantic shadows, dancing to a rhythm he couldn't hear.

Safar was one of those shadows.

He was sure of it.

Iraj reached . . . reached . . . reached . . .

The primitive creature that was Kalasariz saw Iraj moving and cried out to the others. "The king," he rasped. "Follow the king!"

Racked by pain, he heaved closer to Iraj.

Behind him the two wormlike things who were Fari and Luka heard his call.

Desperately they forced their bodies after him.

Lava was already rolling down the sides of the volcano when Safar chanted the last lines of the spell:

> *". . .For she is the Viper of the Rose*
> *Who dwells in far Hadinland!"*

A great cloud of black smoke burst from the mouth of the volcano. The queen and the other dancers screamed in terror.

Safar braced for the mighty blast of hot breath that he knew would follow.

But just then he heard a shrill animal cry. With that cry came power over his own limbs and he sagged — nearly falling to the sand. It was as if the puppet strings had been suddenly cut.

There was another shrill trumpeting and he staggered to his feet. With difficulty, he turned on numb limbs and his blood thrilled when he saw an amazing creature charging across the beach.

It was Khysmet! White coat gleaming silver in the sun.

Safar didn't stop to think where he had come from, or how.

Somehow he got the strength to move forward. Then to run on legs that felt like dead stumps as he staggered across the sand to meet the stallion.

When he reached him, he gathered all his strength and threw himself on Khysmet's broad back.

The horse swung around and sprinted for the shoreline where the waves crashed over a tumble of black rocks.

At that moment the volcano erupted.

An enormous blast of burning hot wind smashed against them.

But instead of dying, they were flung high into the air.

Safar had a sensation of soaring. Then he felt Khysmet plunge forward. It was as if the stallion had suddenly grown wings and they were hurtling across a flame-washed sky.

Behind him he heard someone shout: "Safar!"

It was Iraj's voice.

Safar bent around, but there was nothing to see except the smoking ruins of the island.

Then he felt something sear his chest and he cried out in surprise and pain. It seemed to burn through flesh and bone, then pierce his heart like a fire arrow.

And then the pain was gone as quickly as it had come.

Khysmet trumpeted joy, surging forward with even greater speed.

Safar was too weary to feel anything now. He collapsed on the horse's back, letting his friend carry him away to wherever he wanted to go.

Still, he couldn't help whispering, "Free, free." And then he thought he heard a faint echo: "*Free, free.*"

Stupefied by exhaustion, he barely registered that echoing voice.

Then darkness seized him and he knew nothing more.

9

DEATH SONG

Palimak was surrounded by huge red eyes that glittered at him hungrily through the darkness. He couldn't move; his limbs were like stone and each breath came with great difficulty.

His mind was a chaos of half-formed thoughts. Where was he? Who were these creatures? Why had he ignored the advice of his Favorites? And what in the hells had possessed him to step through that door in the first place?

Although the inky-black chamber he found himself in was sweltering hot, a chill ran down his spine as he realized that "possession" wasn't too far off the mark.

He'd entered because he had been compelled. Some powerful force had reached through the very rock to seize him and bend him to its will. Deafening him to his survival instinct's loud clamor of alarm.

Gundara and Gundaree were silent. From the absence of weight on his shoulders, he guessed they'd shrunk to their smallest size, hoping they wouldn't be noticed.

He heard a heavy body moving toward him and he raised his eyes to see the largest of the burning orbs coming closer. By the gods, he wished he could see more!

Although, perhaps it was just as well he couldn't. From the lumbering sound of the body and the fact that the creature's eyes were several feet above his head, Palimak realized that the beast must be enormous.

With that jumble of frightened thoughts came an idea: These creatures feared light! If someone had asked him how he knew this, he couldn't have answered. The knowledge just suddenly bloomed in his consciousness: to escape, all he had to do was conjure up another ball of light.

Desperately, Palimak tried to signal the Favorites — sending his thoughts out through the well-oiled mental channel between them. Their disappointing answer came racing back. That avenue of escape had been slammed shut by the same powerful magic compelling him to enter the chamber. The spellcaster had factored in its own vulnerabilities and had made sure that no light spell at Palimak's command would work within these chamber walls.

Strong magic rippled the dank currents of sweltering air as the huge red eyes moved closer.

Palimak dug deep for strength. But with a shock he realized that merely keeping the life forces burning in the tomb of his spell-frozen body had drained his powers. He couldn't even open his mouth to speak, much less scream.

The beast paused in front of him, its breath like a foul wind issuing from an open grave. Then it moved slowly around him, as if measuring Palimak for that very same grave. Finally it returned to the front, huge eyes widening even larger — two red orbs ready to swallow him up.

Then the beast spoke. "This creature is a puzzle to me sisters," it said. Rasping though it was, Palimak detected a feminine quality in the voice. "From all outward signs it is human," the voice continued. "But there is also a demon scent to it. Demon and human and in the same body. How could this be?"

A low mutter swept the chamber — many low voices echoing: "How could this be? How could this be? How could this be?"

The beast's voice rumbled with what Palimak thought might be laughter. "No matter, sisters," it said. "Human or demon, it will taste just as fine."

"As fine . . . as fine . . . as fine," came the echoing reply.

The hungry edge in all of those voices nearly swept away Palimak's will to resist. But he strained mightily to make one last desperate effort.

Then it was like a gate opening, and power burst forth. His whole body tingled as it awakened. A burning sensation afflicted his eyes, as if they'd been struck by hot sunlight. He closed them. The pain vanished and when he opened them again the night-black darkness had dissolved into a dusky gloom.

Surprised as he was by this just-in-time return of his powers, he still didn't move. Towering over him was a nightmare figure — grave-devil white with outstretched wings so wide they seemed like they could enfold a score of Palimaks. Behind the beast were similar creatures, slightly smaller, but just as heart-stoppingly ghastly.

The beast bent its terrible head until its eyes were at Palimak's level.

It said, "Before I eat you — whether you be human or demon — I'll gift you with my name. It's none other than Queen Charize you will honor with your flesh. Queen Charize who will suck up your marrow. Queen Charize who will savor your soul. So make yourself ready, little one. As ready as you can."

As Charize spoke, Palimak's eyes flickered left and he saw a high altar with a half-dozen steps leading to the top. Resting on that altar was an enormous coffin whose lid was sculpted into the shape of a demon. Emblazoned on the sides of the coffin was a golden twin-headed snake with outstretched wings.

Immediately he knew what it was: the long-lost tomb of Lord Asper!

This was the place he had sought from the moment he'd set

foot on Syrapis. Long ago his father had told him the tale of his visionary visit to the chamber of horrors ruled by Queen Charize. And of the coffin he'd found there — a coffin containing, Safar had been certain, the body of Lord Asper, as well as many secrets.

It came to Palimak that if only he could reach the coffin he would be safe. And with that knowledge came the odd feeling that he was not fully in command of his mental faculties. It was as if some older, wiser being had entered his body. A being of cool cunning and calculation. He felt strong and coldly superior. Magical power coursed through his veins.

He spoke, a touch of sarcasm coloring his tones. "Pardon, royal one, for defiling your ears with my puny voice. But before I die I would demand a boon from you."

Surprised, Charize stepped back, barbed tail curling like a giant scorpion's.

"What's this?" she growled. "You can speak?"

A sound like mistral winds hissing through the poisoned thorns of a devil tree stirred the cavern: "He speaks, sisters, he speaks!"

Palimak shrugged, which surprised the monster queen even more. Her spell should have rendered him not only speechless, but immobile as well.

"It's a small thing," he replied. "I open my mouth and words present themselves." He glanced at the queen's horrid minions who were whispering to one another, uneasy at his ability to shake off the effects of Charize's spell. "The important thing isn't whether or not I can speak," Palimak continued, "but whether you will grant me the boon I've requested."

Queen Charize had recovered her wits. "Boon?" she said scornfully. "Why should I grant you a boon?"

Palimak frowned. "Are you the Queen Charize," he asked, "who claims to be ruler of the Sisters of Asper?"

The question surprised him as much as it did Charize. Where had it come from? And why was his voice deeper, his words formed from an experience and a knowledge beyond his ken?

"Claim!? Claim!?" Charize roared. "How dare you speak such words of doubt?" Her talons clattered angrily. "Now, your death will not be so easy, foolish one. You will linger in exquisite agony before I eat you."

Palimak's instincts begged him to scream pleas of Mercy, lady, mercy. Instead, he amazed himself by finding the courage to smile.

"If the gods will my death, so be it," he said. "Painful though that death may be."

He managed even greater nerve and wagged a finger under the queen's flaring nostril slits. "But I'll die knowing you are a great liar," he said. "Claiming a throne you don't deserve."

The queen's barbed tail shot toward him, poisoned hook aiming for his heart. Palimak wanted to jump away, but he steeled himself. A heartbeat later he was rewarded as the hook point stopped scant inches from piercing his breast.

Charize glared at him, clearly confounded by his boldness. All around her the other creatures hissed in wonder at their queen's hesitation. Whispering, "Is it true? Is it true? Does Charize lie?"

At that moment Palimak spotted the bloody corpse of one of her subjects, sprawled near what he thought might be her throne. Several of the beasts were gathered next to the corpse and it seemed to him that they were the ones leading the chorus of doubts. In his misfortune, had he in fact been fortunate enough to have stepped into the middle of a palace revolt?

"Who are you to dare brand Charize a liar?" the queen roared. "Tell me your name before I kill you."

"Why, I am Prince Timura," Palimak answered. "Perhaps you'll find that name familiar. Hmm?"

Gasps of terror echoed through the chamber. "Timura! Timura! Timura!"

Charize's great jaws unhinged, but not to attack. Instead she was in shock. Then her jaws snapped shut as she fought to recover her dignity.

"Now, you are the liar," she said. "I have met Safar Timura. And you are not him. He was fully human. There was no demon blood running through his veins."

"Actually, I'm his son," Palimak said. "Disbelieve that at your own peril."

Charize managed a sound that Palimak took for forced laughter. "What a fool you are," she said, "if you think you are a danger to me."

"Perhaps I am a fool," Palimak said. "Test me and we shall see. But I promise you this: one of us will be dead before the test is done. And I strongly doubt that it will be me." He chuckled. "My father told me what a coward you were. How he bested you with the simplest of spells."

Charize clacked her talons in annoyance. "It was a silly trick, nothing more," she said. "You will notice I didn't fall for the same trick this time. My spell made you powerless to bring light into this chamber!"

Palimak snorted derisively. "You silly creature," he scoffed. "I don't need light. I am part demon . . . as you noticed. And with my demon eyes I can see you and your sisters quite well."

He surprised himself when he said this. Until the moment he opened his mouth, Palimak hadn't realized what had happened. Raised among humans, he had kept the demon side of himself at bay for most of his young life. It was a part of him that he feared. A side that he believed was capable of shameful cruelty. However, he now realized it was the demon side that had saved him. Somehow, when fighting to win his powers back, he'd broken through to his demon self and this was what he was using to confront Charize.

As this realization ran through his mind, it also came to him that there was more to it than that. Far more than just his demon powers were available to him. Suddenly, he felt as if his father was quite near. This notion took him by such surprise that he nearly turned his head to see.

But the chamber abruptly became silent and he quickly shifted his full attention back to Charize. A moment before she'd been wavering between waiting to find out more about her new enemy and killing him on the spot.

As he looked up, he saw that indecision end as she drew back a mighty claw to gut him where he stood. Unfortunately, there was nothing Palimak could do about it. This was Charize's lair, after all. And on her own ground there was no magic he knew of that was powerful enough to do more than slightly wound her before he died.

Palimak instinctively went for the bluff. He struck quickly, conjuring up a spell that would be quite painful, but would actually do little damage.

Charize gasped as the spell hit her and jumped back. Before she had time to think, Palimak laughed at her.

"That's just a small sample of what I can do," he said. "Threaten me again and I shall turn you into ashes." He gestured at the others. "I'm sure your sisters have wearied of your rule and will thank me for killing you. So don't make the mistake of thinking I am vulnerable merely because I am outnumbered."

The other creatures muttered. From their tone, Palimak could tell that his bluff had struck the target dead center. None of them would mourn if Charize fell.

Unsure of her ground, the queen decided to play for time. "You asked a boon, small one," she said. "What is it?"

Palimak nodded, as if satisfied the danger had passed. "I entered this chamber," he said, "because I seek the tomb of Lord Asper. My father told me it was here and bade me pay homage to him."

Charize snarled. "You entered this chamber," she said, "because I compelled your obedience. There was no free will involved in your decision."

Palimak shrugged. "The more you speak," he said, "the more convinced I am that you are a liar."

He turned, as if he were about to stroll easily away through an open gate, instead of being confronted with a thick stone door. He even raised a hand, as if to cast a spell that would open it. He was mildly surprised when he saw that his hand looked barely human. His sharp claws were so fully extended that his fingers were misshapen. His tongue reflexively moved around inside his mouth and he found long sharp fangs instead of blunter human teeth.

An odd part of him wished he had a mirror to peer into, wondering what his face looked like. How much of a demon had he become?

"You didn't answer my question," Charize said. "What is your boon?"

Palimak turned back. "Why, only to pray before Lord Asper's tomb," he replied.

Charize nodded her mighty head at the dais. "Go pray," she said. "But know that you will pray your last, little one. For you will not leave this chamber alive."

Palimak felt a spark of fear. She'd finally guessed he was bluffing. And was only letting this charade play out long enough to satisfy her followers.

He hid this knowledge and strode calmly over to the dais and mounted the stairs. He didn't have the slightest idea what he was going to do next. It seemed there were two liars in this chamber. Palimak was the first — Safar had most certainly never told him to pray at Asper's tomb. He was only working off a vague notion that once he reached the tomb there might be a chance of escape.

The second liar was Charize — just as he'd claimed. Palimak had studied the ancient Book of Asper Safar had bequeathed to him long and hard. And he doubted strongly that the old master wizard had left creatures such as Charize and her sisters to guard his resting place.

If Asper had truly intended such a thing, there'd have been broad hints about it in the book — the latter pages of which were filled with the demon's thoughts on his approaching death. He'd known his illness was fatal and had worried that despite all his efforts, no one would find his tomb and the secrets it contained. Secrets that might save the world from the disaster he'd foretold.

When Safar had visited here in his vision, Asper's ghost had commanded him to come to Syrapis. Since Safar's death had prevented this, Palimak was determined to take his father's place.

As he knelt before the tomb the world shifted slightly and Palimak remembered his wild dream ride on Khysmet, his father shouting to him for help. And he thought, but is he really dead? And, if not, how can I save him? And what is it I'm supposed to save him from?

Charize rumbled, "What are you waiting for? Pray!"

Her voice jerked Palimak back to a chilling reality. If he didn't come up with something quickly he'd soon be dead himself. Palimak bent his head over the twin-headed snake that was the symbol of Asper.

In the background he heard Charize lift her monster's voice in song:

"We are the sisters of Asper,
Sweet Lady, Lady, Lady.
We guard his tomb, we guard his tomb,
Holy One . . ."

Although the sound of her voice was like broken glass scraping against stone, the song was strangely familiar. It became even more so as Charize's subjects joined her in a blood-curdling chorus:

"We take the sin, we take the sin,
Sweet Lady, Lady, Lady.
On our souls, on our souls,
Holy One."

Out of Palimak's memory crawled the courtyard scene in far-off Caluz, where Queen Hantilia and her subjects sang a similar song. In Hantilia's case the song was a call to sacrifice, a mass suicide for the greater good of Esmir and the world at large. But the same song rang shrill and evil when Charize and her devil horde sang the words in their banshee voices.

". . . On our souls, on our souls,
Holy One."

It was a harsh melody of despair that nearly ripped Palimak from his moorings. All his confidence dissolved and his life suddenly seemed like it was dangling from the slenderest of threads in the Fates' holy loom. And he thought: Help me, father! What shall I do?

At that moment what sounded like a great drum boomed from someplace close by.

And Asper's golden snake came alive.

Part Two

The Return of Safar Timura

10
BETWEEN WORLDS

Safar jarred awake, the thundering sound of an enormous drum booming in his ears. At first he thought that he was back in Hadin and the harvest drums were commanding a new performance.

Then relief flooded in along with awareness as he realized he was still astride Khysmet who was racing across a starlit sky. No more would he be forced to dance the mad dance of Hadin under the erupting volcano.

He was free!

Yes, but free for what? The question came from nowhere. And for some reason it frightened him. Where was he going, and why? What fate awaited him?

Other sensations flooded in. The first was the knowledge that he was now fully clothed. He flexed his limbs and felt a familiar weight, then glanced down and saw he was dressed in the same battle gear he'd worn when he'd faced Iraj and his minions back in Caluz. To his delight, he even felt his sheathed sword slapping against his thigh as Khysmet soared onward.

Reflexively, he touched his belt and found the small silver dagger waiting there — the magical witch's knife Coralean had given him long ago.

Then he heard the drum again and lifted his head. Off in the distance — moving at the same speed as Khysmet — was a bobbing torchlight. He whispered a sightspell and the image grew clearer. A spark of joy ran through him when he saw the glorious black mare and the familiar figure of the beautiful Spirit Rider.

Safar grinned and was pleasantly surprised how good the smile felt. It had been a long time since he'd worked those muscles, that was for certain. And now that he understood who had saved him, the "why" didn't matter as much as before. Khysmet whinnied as if in agreement.

Safar glanced around, trying to guess where he might be. The first thing he noticed was the absence of the blood-red Demon

Moon. He'd already figured that he and Khysmet were in some sorcerous betweenworld. Asper had postulated the existence of such alternate worlds in his book. He'd even performed some experiments whose results were promising, although not final proof.

Absently, Safar ran some magical calculations in his mind. Although they didn't lead him to any useful observations — much less a discovery — it was eminently satisfying to use his brain again for so elegant a purpose.

For a long while he'd felt like nothing more than an enslaved animal. Like a poor dumb ox tethered to a grain wheel, going round and round with no will save that instilled by his master's whip.

He looked out at the Spirit Rider, torch held aloft, ebony skin gleaming in the starlight. A base side of him ached to catch her and enfold her in his arms.

By the Gods, it had been ages since he'd felt such life!

Then once again he heard the thunder of the big drum. This time the sound was followed by a long hiss, like that of an angry snake. The sound continued: boom! . . . hiss . . . boom! The rhythm was vaguely familiar. And then the identity of the sound came to him. A man of the high mountains, he'd had scant experience with the sea. But that was what it sounded like: a rolling sea striking some coastline, then drawing slowly back to gather strength to strike once more.

He looked down and saw a sparkling night ocean beating against a shore. Another sightspell increased his perspective and he saw a huge stone idol rising out of the booming surf.

Safar recognized the figure immediately. It was Asper.

Syrapis was just below!

The Spirit Rider and her mare plummeted downward. The mare whinnied for them to follow and Khysmet trumpeted a note of agreement.

Down and down.

Down and down.

Down!

"Something's wrong," Leiria said. "Palimak's been gone too long."

"Aye, lass," came Biner's rumbling reply. "I was thinkin' the same thing myself."

He shifted his bulk, bringing the heavy club up. It was Biner's favorite weapon — a thick-headed club sprouting a needle-forest of horseshoe nails.

His action triggered Leiria's decision. "Let's go," she said, starting down the tunnel.

Biner followed, along with the dozen Kyranian soldiers who had volunteered for the expedition.

Leiria had been reluctantly hanging back for well over an hour. Palimak had commanded them to wait, which was something that Leiria — a woman of action — was never very good at. Except when the waiting involved ambushes, of course.

She'd always been supremely patient when it came to tarrying by a trap set for an enemy. In such cases she enjoyed herself as much as any sane person can take pleasure in the foul art of warfare. During an ambush one could visualize the enemy's approach. See the canny noncom in charge of the attacking squad pause to study the terrain ahead. But you had been so clever — and this was the greatest thrill — covering all traces of the ambush that it was as if you were a trickster ghost. And a small fire of delight would bloom in your bosom as the noncom decided to ignore the prickling hackles at the back of his neck and advance to his doom.

But there was no pleasure of any kind standing idly by while someone else went about a possibly dangerous errand. Especially since Palimak — in Leiria's professional opinion — had been a bit too quick handing out orders. He'd merely said that she and the other members of the party must wait while he explored the tunnel. No arrangements had been made for emergencies. And in Leiria's mind, Palimak's delayed return certainly fitted the definition of an emergency.

That was the trouble with having such a youthful commander. Usually Palimak listened to her soldierly advice. Also Coralean's, when it came to matters of money or diplomacy. And Biner's, when the mission involved an aerial expedition.

However, this admirable trait tended to be tossed right into the slop hole when he was confronted with a threat that required his magical powers — which was Palimak's own area of expertise. It was then that the arrogance of youth overtook native caution and he tended to rush into the sorcerous breach without further thought.

Leiria moved swiftly along the tunnel, the flickering torchlight picking up signs of Palimak's passage: boot depressions in the salty silt on the floor, or the glitter of wet marks on the wall where he'd leaned.

Otherwise, she saw nothing except the occasional lone rat that panicked at their approach and dashed through their legs. About half an hour earlier a thick swarm of rats had descended on them — frightened, Leiria guessed, because they'd been cornered by Palimak and had no other way to flee.

Leiria was not a squeamish woman, but being confronted by all those dirty, squealing little beasts had unnerved her. She had taken no satisfaction from the near-hysterical curses of Biner and the others as they had fought off the wave of rodent intruders. When it was over, she'd felt humiliated by her own instinctive reactions. Perhaps this had been the main reason she'd finally decided to wait no longer and investigate what had happened to Palimak.

They splashed onward through the cold passage for many minutes, pausing only to recharge the pitch on their torches from the wide-mouthed jars of the stuff they'd packed along for that purpose.

Then they came around a corner and were brought up short by a thick stone wall that blocked all other progress.

"What's this?" Biner barked.

He looked back along the passage, searching for other openings, even though he knew very well there were none.

"Where in the hells did he go?" he wondered.

Leiria ignored the question, scanning the wall, looking for a break.

Nothing.

Then she spotted the twin-headed snake symbol carved on the wall. It glowed in the light when she held the torch close. Leiria put an ear against the stone, listening.

Immediately, she heard someone cry out in alarm "It's Palimak!" she shouted at the others. "He's in there!"

She threw herself against the wall. She rebounded, cursing in frustration, shoulder numb where she'd struck the stone. Even so, she prepared to hurl herself against it again.

But Biner stepped in front of her. He swung the club against the wall with all his strength. There was a loud crack! as a piece of rock broke off.

He swung again.

And again . . .

The Asper snake came alive, leaping off the face of the coffin, twin jaws hissing, long fangs lancing out for the strike.

Palimak jumped back, shouting and scrabbling for his sword. But he caught a bootheel on one of the steps and tumbled awkwardly to the ground.

Still, he managed to roll to one side, drawing back his sword to strike.

"Don't, Little Master, don't!" Gundara cried.

The warning came just in time to stay his hand. The Asper snake loomed over him, growing larger and brighter. Heads striking this way and that. Long tongues of flame shooting from its mouths.

"It's on our side, master!" Gundaree shrieked in his ear. "Our side!"

Palimak heard a deep moan of pain and swiveled to see Charize holding up a huge clawed hand to shield herself from the bright light.

The Asper snake swooped about the vast cavern, sparks showering off its long tail as if from some kind of reptilian comet.

Charize's monsters howled in agony, colliding with pillars as they ran this way and that, or smashing against the vaulted ceiling itself as they flew blindly away on their huge wings in their desperate effort to escape the intense light.

Palimak heard Charize scream in fury and pain and as he came to his feet he saw her rushing toward her throne. A enormous bone-white scepter leaned against one arm. Instinctively, Palimak knew it was some kind of weapon.

And then he knew it was because Gundara shrieked, "Run, Little Master, run!"

But there was no place to run, except after Charize, so he charged her, sword outstretched.

It was an unequal contest. Despite her bulk, Charize moved with amazing speed, great wings flapping so that she was carried forward in great hops.

Still, Palimak was right on her horned heels when she reached the throne and grabbed up the scepter.

He struck, but his sword bounced off the scaly armor of her back. Her tail lashed out, sending him flying and he crashed to the ground, dazed.

If Charize had gone after him then it would have been all over. But evidently she saw him as a lesser enemy and focused her wrath on the Asper snake.

Palimak heard her roar words in a language he didn't understand and a bolt of blue flame exploded off the tip of her scepter. It struck the snake full force. The creature hung in the air for long seconds, both heads hissing and wriggling in agony.

Another blast of blue fire from the scepter crashed into the beast. This was followed by an enormous explosion of pure sorcerous energy.

Charize's sisters shrieked in pain as the blinding light burst over them.

Palimak came to his feet, rubbing burning eyes. Then his vision cleared and he saw that the Asper snake was gone and the chamber had returned to its former gloom.

Charize was the first to recover. She shouted to her subjects, "Kill Timura! Kill him!"

Slowly, they formed around her. Then they advanced, Charize at their head.

Palimak backed up, feeling like a fool as he waved his puny sword before him.

"It's been nice knowing you, Little Master," Gundara squeaked.

"Oh, shut up!" Gundaree snapped. "We're going to be eaten too, you stupid thing!"

For a change Gundara did not reply. For some reason the lack of argument between the twins frightened Palimak more than any other experience in his young life.

Then his heels bumped against the bottom of the stairs leading up to Asper's coffin. Charize's jaws widened into a terrible grin. Her sisters tittered in ghastly amusement.

"And now, little one," Charize said. "And now . . ."

11

BLOOD AND DARKNESS

Queen Charize leaned forward, one great claw stretching out to slice Palimak's life away.

He cut at her with his sword, but she only laughed and slapped it aside.

At that moment an enormous drumboom resounded from behind Charize and her army. They jolted about to see what this new threat might be. The boom was immediately followed by the trumpeting cry of what Palimak swore was a horse.

Then there was the thunder of hooves and a shouted war cry.

Palimak gaped as some invisible force burst through the line of monsters, hurling them aside.

There was a skitter of horse's hooves, another war cry, and then two more creatures fell to the ground, gutted and fountaining blood.

Then Palimak thought he heard someone shout, "Palimak! To the tomb, Palimak!"

It was Safar's voice.

His father's voice.

Without hesitation Palimak whirled and rushed up the short flight of stairs to the coffin. He was too numb to be surprised when he saw that the huge lid had been thrown open.

The mummified corpse of an enormous demon stared blankly out at him. He had time enough to see that it was dressed in black wizard's robes decorated with bejeweled symbols. Then he heard Charize hiss orders and he came about to do battle.

The beast that was Queen Charize roared at her sisters to close in on the invisible force. At the same time she struck out blindly with her scepter. A blast of blue light shot out, but she must have missed because the magical light hammered at nothingness.

Although for just a moment Palimak thought he could make out the shadowy figure of an armored warrior astride a great stallion.

Then the vision was gone and everything became a strange, violent shadow-play as Charize and her sisters battled the invisible force.

He saw a line of beasts form before Charize, saw that line bend as the force cut through them. Then the way was open and Charize clubbed at the air with her scepter.

Palimak heard a heavy thump and a groan as her scepter struck something.

There was a long pause, as if the attacker were struggling to recover, then the moment broke and Charize roared defiance, charging forward.

He heard a meaty thunk, saw Charize stop in mid-charge. And suddenly a red line jagged across her throat.

Charize toppled over, huge head falling to one side — bony skull held only by a thread of gristle — and she crashed to the floor.

There was a shocked silence as Charize's sisters stared down at their queen's lifeless body. Then that silence grew longer and more thoughtful as both Palimak and the creatures realized that the horseman and his steed were no longer present in the chamber.

First there was a shuffle — many claws and talons clicking against the stone.

Then a single whisper: "Who will be queen?"

That whisper became a chorus, "Queen? Queen? Queen?"

And the first voice began to chant:

"We are the sisters of Asper,
Sweet Lady, Lady, Lady . . .

The others took up the chant, turning on Palimak as they did so.

". . . We guard his tomb, we guard his tomb,
Holy One . . ."

And Palimak had the soul-shivering realization that the battle for royal succession would be fought over his body.

Thwack! as Biner once again assaulted the wall. His club blow did so much damage that Leiria had to shield her face against the shattered rock that exploded outward. Even so, a sharp piece of stone cut her hand and the blood started to flow.

Leiria ignored the wound. What's a little blood, even if it's your own? She studied the results of Biner's work. Strong as he was, mighty though his blows might be, he'd only managed to hammer out a shallow depression into the wall. At this rate, hours would pass before they broke through — assuming Biner didn't wear himself out first.

There was one dubious victory his efforts had won — the depression made a kind of funnel that magnified the sound on the other side. They could hear plainly the clash of battle raging in the chamber beyond.

"Dammit, Biner!" Leiria growled. "This isn't working."

Biner didn't waste his energy on a reply. Instead, he drew back the club once again — planting his feet far apart and bunching his big shoulders in readiness for the blow.

"Here, let me help you," came a woman's voice.

Startled, Leiria turned to see Jooli standing there. Flanking her were the Kyranian soldiers who were gawking at King Rhodes' daughter. Apparently they'd been so surprised to see her, that they had let her walk right through their ranks.

Biner — stopped in mid swing — glared at her. "What're you doing here?" he demanded.

Jooli gave a throaty laugh. "Not making a fool out of myself, that's for certain," she said.

Leiria was angry. "I don't know how in the hells you escaped your guard," she said, "but I don't have time for you. Get your royal behind out of here before I thin-slice it for rations!"

"I'm a witch," Jooli said, answering Leiria's unasked question. "Right now the guards on your airship think I'm tucked away nice and cozy in that tiny closet of a cabin you gave me."

Biner was furious. "I don't care if you are the witch of all witches!" he roared. "Remove yourself from my sight, woman!"

Jooli chortled. "You have more muscles in your head," she mocked, "than you'll ever get in your body."

She took a step forward. Leiria started to block her, but there was something about Jooli that gave her pause. Leiria quite liked Biner. But sometimes he *did* tend to let his brawn get in the way of cool thought process.

Just as he sometimes used his big voice — even more startling because it came from the body of a dwarf — to hammer down people it wasn't always wise for him to overpower.

Jooli plucked the club from Biner's fingers as if it were a feather. He was too surprised to react. Then she made a gesture at the wall with her free hand. And she chanted:

> *"You are stone!*
> *You were sand.*
> *You are strong!*
> *You were weak.*
> *Strong to weak.*
> *Weak to sand.*
> *Sand to dust!"*

On the last line she leaned forward and gently tapped the stone wall with the club.

With barely a sound the entire thing collapsed, making a two-foot-high pile of dust on the floor.

Leiria didn't waste any thought on Jooli's amazing feat of magic, much less her motives for being here.

The only thing she cared about was that the wall that had been barring her way was gone. And now she was staring into a deep, black emptiness.

Although sight was absent, hearing was plain. There was a whispering of many voices. Harsh voices. Alien voices. Growing louder and louder, until the words rang clear:

> *"We are the sisters of Asper,*
> *Sweet Lady, Lady, Lady . . ."*

Then she heard Palimak shout: "Get back!"

Leiria hurled her torch deep into the dark cavern. There was a flare as sparks scattered in every direction.

She caught a glimpse of nightmare creatures — enormous things, with long fangs and vampire wings — then the torch guttered down.

"More light!" she shouted to the others.

And she charged through the opening, sprinting toward the place where she'd caught a brief glimpse of Palimak's pale face.

As she ran she heard Biner bellow orders. More torches arced into the cavern. Spears of light crashed against the floor, scattering flame in every direction so that the chamber became like a night sky lit by a meteor swarm.

Ungodly screams came from all around her, as if she'd burst into a nest of banshees.

She collided with a massive body, struck out blindly with her sword. An exploding torch revealed a horrible figure towering over her. As her sword bit into flesh she had time to realize that the creature was cowering in agony.

Warm fluid splashed her arms then she stepped around the creature and kept on running — dodging or slashing at any shadow that got in her way. The images revealed by the hurled torches seemed jerky, unreal, as light gouted, then died, then gouted again.

A smaller shadow loomed up and a stab of light came just in time for her to stay her hand: she saw Palimak — eyes wild, sword stained with gore.

"Leiria!" he cried, voice full of relief.

She leaped to his side, whirling to see a shadow army of shrieking beasts advancing on them. From far across the chamber she heard Biner bellow his war cry, followed by sounds of fighting. The others had joined the battle.

"They fear light!" Palimak shouted, at the same time dodging a huge claw striking out at him from the darkness.

Leiria lopped at the claw, sharp sword cutting through flesh and bone. And she heard a satisfying howl of pain.

"All I need is a little time," Palimak cried out, "and I can stop them!"

Knowing he meant to cast a spell, Leiria tried to give him the time he needed, chopping and thrusting in every direction. But there were too many of the creatures and after a moment Palimak broke off his efforts and joined her in the fight.

Even so, the fight was clearly turning against the Kyranians. She could hear Biner and the others trying to fight their way through. But her limbs grew weary and each blow seemed to have less effect. The torches were all guttering out and the chamber seemed to grow darker and more deadly by the minute.

Then she heard a wild ululation and a tall, slender figure vaulted over a knot of beasts.

There was a blast of light and the creatures howled, shrinking back. Leiria had time to see a shattered pot of burning pitch on the floor.

The light from the fire dazzled her for a moment, but as the flames died — too quickly! too quickly! — she saw that it was Jooli who had vaulted to their side.

She'd found a pike somewhere and was jabbing at the beasts in the guttering light as they recovered and pressed forward for the kill, mad with pain and hatred.

Jooli leaped up beside her, then turned, her shrill ululating war cry sweeping away Leiria's weariness.

The two of them attacked the beasts full force and it was if they had been a fighting team for years, instead of only a few minutes.

Jooli's pike would thrust at a creature, running it through to the backbone. While at the same time Leiria's sword would slash and cut at any who dared the defensive gap Jooli's attack would leave open.

Then Leiria would dance forward, doing awful damage with her sword, Jooli at her back, lancing pike giving Leiria the room she needed to maneuver.

Even greater damage was done when they would fall back, the creatures surging forward to take them. Their very numbers making them easy targets for the steel snake-like strikes of sword and pike from the two warrior women.

Still, the numbers were so unequal that Leiria knew they

couldn't last much longer. And she could tell from Biner's shouts and the sounds of fighting across the chamber that his attack was stalled.

Just then she heard a dry crack! and a cry of alarm from Jooli.

Leiria glanced to the side, but in the stormy twilight of the chamber she couldn't see what had happened. All she knew was that suddenly she was ringed by snarling beasts, talons reaching out to take her.

Leiria struck at a shadowy claw, felt the blade bite, then she was flung back, her sword swept away.

Stone steps cut into her backbone as she fell, knocking her breath away.

And she sprawled there helpless, without even enough fight remaining to kick and bite and claw with her nails.

Two enormous red eyes loomed over her. She saw the glint of long fangs reaching for her throat.

Her mind raged in fighting fury. But she didn't even have breath enough to curse her enemy before she died.

Just then she heard Palimak shout: "Light!"

And suddenly a hot white light seared into being.

It was so bright, so blinding, that Leiria wasn't sure whether she'd been saved, or if she had been killed and her ghost was seeing the fiery entrance to the Hells.

12

SAFAR RETURNS

Light delivered victory, but it came at a terrible price.

The creatures, with their pale, death-worm skins, cowered on the floor of the vast chamber. Their howls of agony from the light were so intense that even Leiria, the most battle-hardened of soldiers, was moved by pity.

They were like flies in a cruel boy's insect collection — pierced through with needles of light. Pinned to the floor, their immense wings flapping feebly as they circled those impaling shafts on all fours, shrieking in pain and begging for mercy.

After Leiria had recovered she clambered to her feet and saw

Jooli rising from the place where she had fallen — tossing away her broken pike. Blood leaked from a shallow arm wound where a talon had caught her.

About twenty feet away she saw Biner, surrounded by the other members of the Kyranian party, transfixed by the sight of the groaning monsters. The Kyranians were covered with blood, but when they unfroze from the shock and started to move Leiria sighed in relief when she realized that little of the blood was their own.

Biner came up to her, shaking his big head. "What do we do with them, lass?" he asked. "Make them prisoners?"

Before she could form an answer out of the chaotic thoughts and feelings racing through her mind, Palimak stepped down from what Leiria realized for the first time was a dais.

Behind him she saw the great coffin sitting on the platform — the mighty sarcophagus that was also the source of all that brightness. For out of its open lid spilled a blazing river of light, filling every nook and cranny of the chamber with an intensity that forbade the existence of even the smallest shadow.

The coffin light framed Palimak, silhouetting him larger than life. As intense as that light was, Leiria could see his eyes huge and glowing with magical fires. She saw the long talons arcing out from his fingers. And when he opened his mouth to speak she shivered at the sharp teeth he revealed — almost like fangs.

His ears seemed to have points that were more pronounced than normal. And his pale skin appeared more translucent than usual, with a green cast just beneath the surface. It was as if, she thought, another Palimak were ready to burst through. His demon side. Which was a Palimak she wasn't so certain she wanted to know.

And then she thought, No, it is a trick of the magical light. He's still my little Palimak. My dear little Palimak. The strange child I carried away from Zanzair on horseback. Chortling the first rude words taught to him by Gundara and Gundaree, "Shut up, shut up, shut up!"

He had been still oblivious to the fact that his mother, Nerisa, had just been killed by Iraj Protarus. Or that Iraj and his soldiers were hunting him now, bent on putting Safar, Leiria and the child to the sword.

Palimak turned to her, blazing eyes commanding. But when he spoke, his voice was a soft, almost mournful, counterpoint.

"We have to kill them, Aunt Leiria," he said. "I'm sorry to

make you do this, but I don't think we have any choice. They're worse than any nest of vipers."

He drew in a deep breath. "Vipers, at least," he said, "have a purpose that's not so different from ours. No more terrible than ours, anyway. They have to eat, they have to breed and protect their young. And they only harm us if we threaten those needs and wants."

He gestured at the corpse of one of the beasts. It was much larger than the others, its head sheared from its body and fallen to one side. Eyes glaring hatred even in death.

"That's their queen," he said. "Queen Charize. And she was an evil thing, a hateful thing. And her purpose was something I still really don't understand."

He pointed at the open coffin. "That's Asper's tomb," he said. "I think there's promise there. Hope there. Father said there was, at any rate. And Charize was trying to subvert it. Turn it into an evil force for her own uses."

Palimak picked up his sword, which he'd dropped while making the light spell. He advanced toward one of the cowering creatures, talons retracting into his fingers. Fangs turning back into human teeth again. Eyes transforming into something more human with each step he took.

He looks so sad now, Leiria thought. And she wondered how hard it must be for him to wear a cloak of human form after living in the steel-hard skin of a demon.

He raised the sword high. "Mercy, master!" the creature shrieked. "Mercy!"

Leiria thought she heard Palimak groan in sorrow. But perhaps it was only a result of the muscular effort it took as he brought the sword down and cut off the creature's begging. Then, without pause, he went to another and took its life. Then another, and another . . .

Reluctantly, Leiria retrieved her own sword and joined in the slaughter.

After she'd killed her first victim, Biner, Jooli and the soldiers joined in. But just as hesitatingly. Whereas before they had fought and killed with a will, now they just struck out blindly, trying not to look at the poor, mewling things who were their victims.

Sometimes they stopped, sick of themselves and the gods for requiring such a thing. But Palimak urged them on, saying his light spell wouldn't last much longer.

In the end Charize's underground kingdom sank in a welter of gore. A place where the Butcher King had set up market with enough corpses to feed the greatest of cities. Except no one would ever feed on this flesh, so in their deaths Charize's subjects were denied even that most basic honor. They would putrefy here. Unwanted, unneeded, and mourned only in the nightmares of Leiria and the others who would most certainly never boast of their victory in this place. Because it was mass murder, nothing more.

So went the false Sisters of Asper. And as Leiria slew her last she remembered their refrain: "*We take the sin/ We take the sin./ Lady, Lady, Lady.*"

The words would remain with her for the rest of her life.

Palimak could feel himself transforming. Sharp pin-prickles stabbed his skin as if he'd just been caught out in a lightning storm in the High Caravans of Kyrania. Hair like barbs in his skull. Eyes so dry it was painful to blink. The air was oppressive, crackling with energy.

He felt like he was two animals stuffed into one skin. One was cold logic: what was required, must be done. The other wanted to weep in empathy for his enemy. As he struck another scaly head from its shoulders, he thought, What if this were me?

Gradually, the softer side — the human side, he realized — superseded the first. And each killing blow became more difficult. No, that wasn't correct. It wasn't harder to kill, but it took more passion. He had to conjure up hate to power his muscles as if it were a magical spell. He had to hate these things to kill them. Invest them with all the deviltry the human world could imagine that he could deliver the blow.

And when he was done and there were no more creatures left to kill, he stood panting over the last corpse. Blood singing for more. Mind horrified at what he had done.

It was then that he realized he was fully human again. It was then that he realized he'd been fully demon before.

And on the whole, he thought, he much preferred the demon state.

Palimak mentally shook himself. Appalled at that thought. He was human, dammit! More human than demon!

Wasn't he?

Palimak buried this doubt. Triggered an avalanche of excuses and rationalizations, plummeting so quickly down that mountain of emotions that all other thought was smothered.

He looked at Leiria and saw . . . what was it? . . . relief? . . . in her eyes. Glanced down at his hands and saw that the claws had retracted into . . . normal? . . . human fingers. And then the rest of him felt human as well. Body and mind. Mind and body.

And there was blood everywhere he looked. Blood that he had spilled.

He felt sick and wanted badly to flee from this place.

Then he threw his sword away. By the Gods, he didn't want that blade in his hand anymore! It felt filthy. Defiled. And he was glad to be rid of it.

He also badly wanted to get out of this chamber. To seal its horrors off from the rest of the world with the largest boulder he could find.

A small voice chattered in his ear. "The coffin, Little Master," Gundara said. "Remember Asper's tomb."

And Gundaree added, "That's why we came here, wasn't it?"

Mind swirling with weariness, Palimak turned to face the tomb. The light spilling out was so hot and bright that he had raise a hand to shield his face. He was vaguely aware that Leiria and the others were watching him; probably wondering if he were possessed, so forced were his movements. But he didn't have the strength to voice reassurance.

He made a weak gesture, but the light only barely dimmed. It was still too hot to approach and he didn't have the strength to make a better spell.

"I'm hungry!" Gundara announced. It sounded loud in his ear, but Palimak knew from experience that the others couldn't hear.

"Me too," Gundaree added. "I want something sweet to eat. Like some honey cakes."

"With syrup all over them," Gundara put in. "Yum, yum."

"I don't have any honey cakes on me at the moment," Palimak said, too tired to worry that his human friends would think he was talking to himself. He patted the pocket where he kept their treats. "Maybe some currants. But that's it."

"They probably have pocket lint on them," Gundaree sniffed. "I hate lint!"

"Besides," Gundara said, "currants give me gas. You can't imagine what it's like living in a stone turtle when you have gas all the time."

Palimak couldn't help but grin. In the middle of all this blood the twins remained true to form. They were safe now, that was all that mattered. Base needs came first, bless their greedy little souls.

"I'll get you some honey cakes when we get back to the airship," Palimak promised.

Gundara sighed. "All right. If that's how it has to be. I guess we can't do anything else."

"But I want doubles," Gundaree insisted. "You have to promise doubles. Plus some really old cheese. Smelly as you can get it."

"Doubles it is," Palimak said. "And all the smelly cheese you can eat."

Once again he gestured, but this time he felt a surge of extra power from the Favorites. The light dimmed until it was bearable enough for him to look at the coffin straight on.

He clumped up the steps, boots heavy, feeling like he was walking through mud. But as he advanced up the stairs the Favorites were giggling to themselves, as if they had a great secret. Palimak figured they had something up their sleeves to get further promises of treats.

Then he was at the coffin.

He peered inside, expecting to see the mummified remains of the demon wizard, Lord Asper.

Instead a man, wearing the very same robes Asper had been entombed in, stared blindly up at him.

And the twins chorused: "Surprise, Little Master! Surprise!"

It was his father . . .

Safar Timura!

Palimak blinked, stunned.

Then Safar's eyes came open. His lips moved, forming words.

In a haze of unreality, Palimak leaned forward to listen.

"Khysmet," Safar whispered.

Then a hand came out, gripping Palimak's tunic and drawing him down with surprising strength.

And Safar said, insistent, "Where is Khysmet?"

13

THE WITCH QUEEN

It was near the end of day when the king's spies brought him the news. Rhodes hurried out to his castle's seaward wall and clambered up onto one of the big ship-killing catapults that defended this portion of his fortress.

According to his spies, Palimak and his party had left the warrens of the Idol of Asper and were now carrying a strange burden to the airship.

The catapult — hewn from the largest timbers in Syrapis — made a difficult climb for a man of Rhodes' bulk and he gasped curses at his underlings. But the curses were really directed at himself for the sloth that had turned his once muscular body into such a wheezing mass of fat.

This was the reason, he thought, that Palimak and the Kyranians had been able to best him. He'd not only allowed his body to become larded, but his mind as well. He'd grown lax — and by example had allowed his subjects to become lax. His own mother had belabored Rhodes when he was a prince for his lazy tendencies.

Barbarian though he might be, Rhodes had a good mind and a natural instinct for strategy, plus an unerring eye for spotting his enemy's weaknesses.

He was also blessed with formidable strength and speed, especially for someone so large. At birth he'd been over fifteen pounds, which would have made for a difficult delivery if his mother had been a normal woman. But she came from a race of overly large people — not quite giants — and Rhodes' entrance to the world through her wide hips and iron womb had been rather routine. If passing a cart horse could ever be called routine.

This combination of superior size and mental acuity had made Rhodes an easy winner over the other petty kings and queens in Syrapis. That was what had made him lazy, he thought. It had been too easy. And when Palimak and the Kyranians had arrived he had not been prepared for their new forms of warfare.

Rhodes finally reached the top of the catapult and peered over the walls to see what his enemy was up to. Across from him, hovering over the little island that was home to the Idol of Asper, was the airship. Not for the first time, envy gripped him as he gazed on that remarkable machine.

It was this magical device, he thought, that had been the key to the Kyranians' many victories over him and his royal Syrapian cousins. If only he had been blessed with such a thing the tale might have had a different ending. The humiliating scene in the courtyard two days before would not have happened. Instead it would have been Palimak and that bitch warrior woman of his who would have suffered the shame of defeat.

He lapsed momentarily into a reverie in which the two of them were being dragged before his throne to be condemned to the nastiest agonies that Rhodes' best torturers could devise.

Rhodes brought himself up short. No time for imaginary pleasures. He must be stronger than ever before. He must spy out his enemies' doings and look for the weakness that might deliver them into his hands.

He saw the tide was turning below. Waves were already beginning to wash over the island. In an hour or so there would be no dry ground. An hour after that the idol itself would disappear beneath the creamy froth of the waves.

He gestured and an aide handed him a spyglass. Rhodes peered through it and made out Palimak directing four soldiers who were swaying up a large, mysterious object. What in the hells was it?

He adjusted the focus, following the object up as it rose in the net that enclosed it. Was it some sort of box? And what was that carving on the lid? Then he realized it was shaped like a coffin. If so, it was a very big coffin indeed. Large enough to hold a man twice Rhodes' size, that was for certain.

Once again he studied the carving on the lid. Just before the coffin came level with his eyes, he realized what the carving was. It was a demon! Not only that, but the demon's face had the same features that were carved into the stone idol.

It was none other than Asper! He was certain of it. Then the coffin rose out of sight and a moment later the airship crew were muscling it over the rails to the deck.

Heart thundering, mind whirling with questions, Rhodes swung his glass back down to the island. Two men were carrying a stretcher down the stairway that descended from the idol's head. On the stretcher was a tall man, dressed in black robes. Rhodes couldn't tell if the man was conscious, but he noted with interest how tenderly his stretcher bearers treated him. A man of importance, no doubt. A man beloved.

This impression was underscored when he saw Palimak and the woman general rush over to the stretcher. Palimak gripped one of the man's hands. While Leiria bent over to kiss him. Then the stretcher was placed in a net, which was swayed up to the airship.

Rhodes followed its progress, then nodded with satisfaction when he saw the dwarf who captained the airship and his first mate, the exotic dragon woman, personally assist the crew in getting the stretcher aboard. Whatever the identity of the man, he was obviously of enormous importance to the Kyranians.

Rhodes had never seen him before, but that in itself didn't mean anything. There were many Kyranians he had no knowledge of. What gnawed at him was that his spies had never brought him word of someone of such obvious importance. Did the Kyranians have a secret leader? Someone of far greater importance than Palimak, whom everyone had been led to believe was the supreme commander of the Kyranians?

Was this fellow, the object of such respect and affection, the secret power behind Palimak's throne? The reason why one so young could perform so many remarkable feats of warfare and magic? If so, what had happened to the mystery man? Why was he in the stretcher, obviously ailing or injured?

A spark of hope flared in Rhodes' chest. If his suspicions were correct — and the man *was* their secret leader, then his weakened state might weaken the Kyranians as well.

He lowered the spyglass and quickly clambered back down the catapult. Excitement made the return trip much easier. Rhodes needed advice to take advantage of this vulnerability — assuming that's what it was.

And the best person who could provide it was his mother, Clayre, the beautiful witch queen of Hanadu.

Later, Rhodes would berate himself for not tarrying a bit longer on his catapult perch. If he had, he'd have seen his daughter, Jooli, unfettered and armed, making her way out of the idol's entrance and hurrying down the stairs. And he might have wondered why the Kyranians were allowing their hostage such freedom.

Aboard the airship, so many tears of joy flowed at Safar's miraculous return that they would have filled an ocean.

"He'th alive!" Arlain sobbed, smoky rings issuing from her dragon's mouth. "Thafar hath come back to uth!"

Biner honked emotion into a kerchief, then knuckled moisture from his eyes. "Methydia would be so happy," he said, "to see the dear lad with us again."

Renor and Sinch, mere striplings when the exodus from Kyrania had begun but full-grown young men now, knelt by the stretcher, crying unashamedly.

"If only Dario could be here," Renor said. "He always insisted Lord Timura was still alive." Dario, dead two years now, had been the grizzled warrior who had trained and drilled all the young men of Kyrania.

Soon all the other crewmembers and soldiers were kneeling

around the stretcher, sobbing prayers of thanks to the Lady Felakia — goddess patron of Kyrania — for returning Safar to them.

In the background, Elgy and Rabix piped music, while Kairo did a little dance of happiness, tossing his head from one hand to the other.

Leiria and Palimak clutched each other, sobbing uncontrollably.

During all this, Safar was quite still. Eyes closed, breath coming in little gasps. Oblivious to everything around him.

Then a breeze came up, making the airship's lines buzz. Leiria shivered, feeling the sudden cold, and broke out of the cocoon of happiness.

"Let's get him into the cabin," she said. "Before we make him sick with all our affection."

She and Palimak picked up either end of the stretcher and carried Safar into the luxurious main cabin that had once been the quarters of Methydia, the long-dead witch who had created the airship and circus. And who had been Safar's lover.

Jooli, a total stranger to Kyranian affairs, watched from the outskirts of the little crowd, wondering about this man who was the cause of so much love and unashamed emotion.

The only thing she was sure of was that whoever he might be, the fellow was an immensely powerful wizard. Even unconscious, exhausted and ailing, the magical rays radiating from him were so intense that her own sorcerous abilities were nearly overcome.

He must be a good man, she thought, otherwise these people would not be so overjoyed. If he were a tyrant — like her father — they might have abased themselves, but only out of fear. Except, powerless as he now was, they would have been more likely to have cut his throat before he regained cruel consciousness.

An act Jooli had seriously contemplated herself upon occasion, when she'd come upon her father in a drunken stupor.

Then, just as the stretcher disappeared into the cabin she caught a strange eddy in the magical waves the man gave off. It was something not so good and not so kind and certainly not worthy of adulation. She tried to sniff it out, locate its source. It seemed to come from the mysterious wizard. But for some reason she couldn't fathom, it was also apart from him.

Something . . . not evil . . . not exactly that, at any rate. But redolent of fiery ambition and greedy hunger.

Then she lost the scent and by the time the cabin door closed

Jooli wondered if it had been her imagination. Nothing more than a cynical reaction to all that outpouring of love.

She sniffed the air one more time and found nothing amiss. Jooli shrugged. Yes, that was it. Only her imagination.

A moment later Biner thundered orders and the crew rushed to the lines and the engines.

Then Biner cried, "Put some muscle into it, lads! The folks at home will want to hear this glad news! Safar Timura is with us again! By the gods, from here on out it'll be, 'Damn everything but the circus!"

And the airship swept away on chilly winds, heading for the new kingdom of Kyrania.

The place Safar had spun into a dream for his people so long ago.

Rhodes tromped down many long flights of stairs to his mother's chambers.

She made her salon in the deepest reaches of the castle. Past the grain and wine stores, paltry now after the series of losing battles with Palimak Timura. Below the furthest dungeons where Rhodes imprisoned men and women who opposed his reign but who were too important in kill outright. Beneath the realm of the royal torturers, who gleefully plied rack and hot pincers in his majesty's service.

Below the treasury — which Rhodes loved even more than his harem. The treasury was guarded by his best and most loyal soldiers, who were paid three times the normal rate to ensure that loyalty.

Here he had experienced both his highest joys and deepest despair. Shuddering in pleasure during those times when he had heaped rich ransom and tribute chests into its crowded recesses. Weeping like a mourning woman as his wars with Palimak drained it to a puny thing, with only a few chests of jewels and gold left.

Only yesterday he'd deposited the two sacks of gold Palimak had given him to sweeten the treaty and to gain his favor for the Kyranian expedition into the Idol of Asper. When he'd added the fat coins to his store it had eased his humiliation a little bit. It had even given him slight hope that someday the tables might be turned: Palimak defeated, gold and gems once more flooding into the chamber.

As Rhodes walked past the treasury, guards snapping to and

saluting, he had a moment of regret that he couldn't tarry there and run Palimak's gold through his fingers. Imagining that each coin was a piece of flesh wrested from Prince Timura's body.

Scores of torches lit the marble receiving area marking the entrance to his mother's apartments. The walls were decorated with enormous murals — pastorals extolling the many beauties of Syrapis.

On their surface the compositions radiated peace and harmony with nature. But if one looked closer there were little horrors in each mural that changed their whole meaning. A seascape, with Syrapis' most picturesque shore in the foreground. A burning ship in the far background, a winged monster scooping up sailors from the sea and devouring them. A vineyard, where handsome lads and pretty maids played lusty games beneath ripe grape clusters, drunk with the joy of the harvest wine. In the distant corner, a demon king leading his fiends in an unspeakable orgy of torture of those same lads and maids.

Rhodes thought they were quite nice, although he was wise enough not to have similar murals in his own chambers. Beauty, apparently, was in the eye of the beholder. And what Rhodes beheld and loved would have given nightmares to even his cruelest soldiers.

The chief of the witch queen's eunuch guard greeted him, twitching his head in a perfunctory bow and asking him to wait while Rhodes was announced to his mother. The eunuchs were all enormous men — the chief guard was almost as large as Rhodes — thick slabs of muscle beneath even thicker slabs of fat. Except their muscles were diligently exercised, whereas Rhodes had done nothing at all for a long time except eat, drink and shed tears over his starving treasury.

When he was granted permission to enter, Rhodes walked into his mother's salon with some trepidation. Mighty ruler of Hanadu though he might be, his mother was a powerful influence over him. She wasn't exactly the power behind the throne, but what she wanted she generally got. And her son lived in fear for her favor. Something he had been out of for a long time now. Specifically, since he'd lost his first battle with Palimak.

Queen Clayre had been his father's third wife — taken to seal an alliance. Big as she was, she was perfectly constructed in proportion: long shapely legs and arms, a marvelous bosom and an hour-glass form. When Princess Clayre had wed his father that beauty — flowing out of such a large package — had made her a rather exotic bride and his father couldn't get enough of her in their early days. At least, this was what Rhodes' mother frequently told him, as her body slaves gathered round to make her up and clothe her in robes which fairly flowed over a still near-perfect form.

Rhodes doubted that she exaggerated very much. To this day Queen Clayre was considered one of the most beautiful women in Syrapis. She was also renowned for her lusty appetites and took young lovers frequently and casually. She was quite discrete, however, surrounding herself and her ladies in waiting with eunuch guards whose loyalties were fierce and unquestioning.

It was one of those guards who greeted the king as he entered the chamber. He was quickly turned over to the chief eunuch who led Rhodes into her presence. He didn't announce the king, instead putting a finger to his lips to ask the queen's son for silence. Rhodes looked across the ornate chamber and saw his mother bent over her spelltable that was littered with ancient scrolls which were piled next to little jars filled with magical potions and powders.

Only the center of the table was clear. Although Rhodes couldn't actually see, what was there, he knew very well what it contained. Set into the table was a large area with tiles of pure gold, all encrusted with gems and arranged to form a pentagram.

Clayre seemed to be studying one of the parchments, glancing once in a while at the pentagram, then nodding as if to confirm her speculations.

She was dressed in the finest robes, all decorated with the magical symbols that declared her the High Priestess of Charize. Around her neck was a many-layered necklace made of black pearls. Some years before, six men working from tide to tide — day in and day out — had shortened their lives by many years to gather the pearly parts that made up his mother's necklace.

As Rhodes dutifully waited for his mother's attention, he saw sparkling red lights leap from one strand of the necklace to the next and back again, as if the pearls were alive with some inner force. Which, of course, they were, since Queen Clayre was a powerful witch.

Rhodes worried at a hang nail, thinking about his mother. Daughter of a minor king, she should have had little influence over his father's court. But she had proved to be a genius at harem intrigue. Within a few years of her only son's birth she'd removed her two rivals.

One by hired assassination — or, at least, that was what palace rumor said. Rhodes knew for a fact that his mother had used magic, plus her feminine charms, to work her will on one of her rival's sons. And it was that son who had slain his own mother, then committed suicide after he'd come out of his trance and seen what he had done.

The other rival she'd killed herself, smothering the woman with a pillow while the rest of the harem watched. Even the big eunuchs guarding the harem didn't dare interfere, because by then everyone feared his mother.

The two murders had made Rhodes crown prince, although this claim was disputed by his half-brothers and half-sisters who had been borne by his father's other two wives. But Rhodes' mother worked hard to ensure his succession.

She put together a salon that welcomed the best athletes of the time. And she spent her money freely to buy the wisest scholar-slaves available in Syrapis. These athletes and scholars Rhodes teachers for his body and mind throughout his young years. And their wise words were backed up by his mother, who taught her son everything she knew about court politics.

At six, Rhodes could lift the fifty-pound stone shot that was favored for the mobile catapults. At eleven, he'd stalked his twenty-year-old half-brother — and his main rival to the throne — from one trysting place to another. His rival had a weakness — a fatal weakness as it turned out — for other men's wives. As a matter of fact, Rhodes had finally caught his brother at the very seaward wall he'd perched upon to spy on Palimak.

Just to the right of the base of the catapult was a little alcove. A sheltered altar to some minor god, whose name no one could remember. It was also a favorite meeting place for lovers.

As Rhodes waited nervously, he thought about that fateful day. Drawing strength from the memory. He grinned as the image rose up of the honey-tongued weakling who had opposed him so long ago. The mother of Rhodes' princely rival had been an ambitious second wife. She'd named her son Stokalo after the legendary Syrapian prince who had been banished by his cruel father but who had eventually returned from the sea to win back his rightful throne.

Stokalo was strong, but not so strong as Rhodes. He had an agile mind, a mind schooled in warfare by Rhodes' father, who favored Stokalo even after the life had been choked out of Stokalo's mother by the offending pillow. But he was not so smart as Rhodes, who as a boy used to humiliate him in games of chess.

Rhodes thought of that day when his sibling, angry over a defeat, had laid himself wide open for elimination. He'd sent a message to his most recent lover — the young wife of a great general. The message said that they were to meet at the seaward wall where the fun would commence. Naturally, a spy who favored Rhodes had gotten a glimpse of that message and had passed on the news.

So the thirteen-year-old Rhodes had raced to the alcove ahead of the sinful couple. Lurked in the shadows until Stokalo was fully engaged — his lover pinned against the wall, gown hoisted above her hips — and then had crept up behind them.

A meaty hand grasped his brother's neck and a heavy knee jammed into his backbone, breaking it as easily as if it had been a twig in a drought forest. The woman had been too panicked to scream and had only moaned, cowering against the wall, as Rhodes lifted up his brother's dead body up and hurled it over the side.

He had thought about killing the woman on the spot — eliminating the only witness to the murder. Instead, he'd given her a chance to live or die and she'd chosen the wiser course.

First, by servicing the young Prince Rhodes. Second, by claiming that she'd inadvertently witnessed Stokalo's suicide while taking an evening stroll to catch the air.

Rhodes stirred a finger in his dirty beard, aroused by the memories of the means he'd finally used to eliminate Stokalo's former lover not many months later.

But before he could relax into that treasured memory, his mother coughed. He glanced up, starting when he saw her beckoning him.

As he approached, she said, "I have news, my son. Both fair and foul."

Her eyes were glowing, full of witchy power — making her appear even more beautiful than usual. "The foul news," she went on, "is that Queen Charize is dead. Slain by Palimak Timura."

As that disaster smacked him in the gut, Clayre waved it away as if it were nothing. Chortling in her rich, deep, earthy voice.

"The fair news," she said, "is that I've found someone better to replace her. Several someones, actually.

"And what they hate, above all things, is anyone named Timura!"

14

THE COUNCIL OF ELDERS

Rhodes stared at his mother for a moment. His shock at her announcement that Queen Charize — the true source of Hanadu's strength — was dead gradually subsided as the rest of her words rang through.

The monster Charize was dead. Not so bad by half if the rest of what she had to say was true. But what was this about an alliance? With powerful figures who shared his hatred for Palimak Timura?

Rhodes grinned. "Good news, indeed," he rumbled. He looked about the room. "Where are these wise men? Bring them out so I can greet them properly."

Clayre gestured at the golden tiled pentagram in the center of the spelltable. Rhodes peered at it, as if expecting to see something. But it was empty.

"They can't be summoned so easily," she said. "They want certain assurances. Assurances, I'll warrant, that you'll be glad to grant."

"Anything!" Rhodes breathed with deep feeling. "As long as they'll deliver Timura into my hands."

Clayre stared at him a moment, as if measuring her son's commitment. Finally she said, "I'll need to cast some rather complicated spells. And there are certain sacrifices we'll need to make to appease Charize's ghost. Give me a a week or so — a month at the most — and the bargain can be sealed."

Although he was filled with curiosity, Rhodes didn't question his mother further. Magic made him nervous. It was something he had no talent for, so it was something to be distrusted. One of his secret regrets was that he hadn't inherited his mother's sorcerous abilities. Instead, they'd skipped a generation to favor his oldest child, Jooli.

He'd never liked Jooli. If it had been up to him he'd have drowned her at birth. After all, his first-born should have been a son. A male heir who no one would doubt was the rightful person to succeed him to the throne. Increasing his dislike of his daughter was the early talent she'd shown for things that only a man should have possessed. Strength, speed, skill at arms.

But what had sealed his dislike was the revelation that she was a witch. His mother had informed him of it one day and for a time had tutored the child. All went well for a while and then his mother had reported in great disgust that Jooli had suddenly turned away from her and would have nothing more to do with her grandmother.

Rhodes had chastised his daughter, but although she was quite young she spoke her mind quite plainly. And she had made it very clear that she had no intention of entering into a spell bargain with Queen Charize, much less help provide the steady stream of sacrificial victims the monster queen had required of Hanadu for time immemorial.

The reasons Rhodes and Clayre hadn't removed Jooli long ago were complicated since they involved the bloody diplomacy Syrapis was known for. Further complicating things was the fact was that Rhodes had found it necessary to not quite withhold his blessing of Jooli as his rightful successor.

This was why he'd ordered her to become a royal hostage to Palimak. And it was his heartfelt desire that when the time came to break his treaty with the Kyranians Jooli would be the very first victim of young Timura's wrath.

His mother impatiently rapped bejeweled fingers on the spell-table, snapping Rhodes out of his reflections.

"Yes, mother?" he asked.

"I didn't summon you," she pointed out, "so I assume you came here for some purpose."

Rhodes nodded and proceeded to tell his mother about what he had seen while spying on the Kyranians. The enormous coffin bearing Asper's image and the mysterious man who had been carried out of the idol on a stretcher, a man whom all the Kyranians seemed to worship.

Queen Clayre was troubled, frown lines marring her beauty. "This does not bode well," she said. "The coffin was clearly Asper's."

Rhodes frowned. "That's ridiculous," he said. "How could the Kyranians have taken it from Charize?"

"I told you she was dead," Clayre reminded him. "And that Prince Timura was the cause of her death. Which should give us even greater reason to be especially wary of him. If he could kill Charize, he is even stronger than we feared."

Again, she rapped her rings on the table. "Possibly," she said, "it has something to do with the man you saw them remove from the idol."

Rhodes didn't answer. None of this made sense to him.

"Which means," his mother added, "that this alliance with these . . . ah . . . Timura-haters I mentioned, might be a better idea than even I'd imagined. In fact, I now think their offer has everything to do with the appearance of the mysterious person you observed."

Then she sighed, as if suddenly weary. "Leave me, my son," she said. "Let me reflect on this."

She offered a cheek, which Rhodes dutifully kissed and he started for the door.

But just before he left the room a gleam of light caught his attention. He glanced over to the mural just above his mother's spelltable, which was where the glimmer had come from.

The mural was an idealized painting of Hanadu during ancient times when, legend said, Lord Asper had lived in Syrapis. There was the castle, a bit smaller, not quite so imposing as the fortifications Rhodes had built. In the foreground, riding down the winding road leading out of the castle was a troop of soldiers, wearing archaic armor. At their head was the king — a handsome man of middle age. He was flanked by women warriors — his daughters the scholars said.

Rhodes had always admired the pictures of the king's daughters. Strong, fierce, all remarkably beautiful. Many times he'd dreamed of bedding those warrior princesses. Particularly the ebony-skinned woman who rode next to the king on a stunning black mare. The two of them made a fiery, intriguing pair, so full of life they practically burst out of the mural.

He'd studied that mural many times over the years, so it came as a huge surprise to him that there was a detail present he apparently hadn't noticed before.

Just ahead of the column was a fabulous white stallion. Rearing up before the black mare and her rider. Hooves striking painted sparks in the air.

He peered closer, wondering why he hadn't seen that magnificent horse before. Something in the back of his mind also wondered if those sparks had been animated a second ago. The reason why his attention had been drawn to the familiar mural.

"Is there something else?" his mother asked.

He almost spoke. But then, as he gazed at the mural it came to him that maybe he hadn't noticed the stallion before because he had always been so intent on the king's shapely daughters.

This was not something a son discussed with his mother. "No," he said. "There's nothing more."

"Very well," she said. "I'll call for you when I know more about our new allies."

King Rhodes nodded and exited the room.

It was a strange homecoming for Safar. He was barely conscious when he arrived at New Kyrania, the mountaintop home his family and friends had carved out in their wars with the Syrapians.

Of this time he had only vague recollections of bells and pipes and songs sung in praise of someone the villagers must have loved dearly or there wouldn't have been such a grand celebration. He didn't connect that someone with himself.

He had vague impressions of his mother, Myrna, his father, Khadji, and all his sisters gathered about his bed. In the background was the tall figure of a strange person who reminded him of Palimak but who was too old and self-possessed to be the boy he remembered.

Also in this dream — for that was what he thought it was — stood Leiria. Beautiful as always. Strong and steady in her armor. A rock for his homecoming — if that was what this dream was about. And in that dream Leiria stepped through the throng and kissed him — and ah, what a kiss it was. And he felt such regret for steeling himself against that love before.

And in this odd otherworld of Safar's consciousness, he remembered their meeting. A warrior woman, one of Iraj's personal bodyguards, given to him by his former friend. He recalled his guilt about that act — which had required his acceptance. An even greater guilt, since it was against all Kyranian principles and teachings that one human being could be given to another. And he remembered their first days of lovemaking, when he was mourning Methydia's death and he had used her to soothe his grief.

What a sin that had been. Even though she'd whispered to him during their embraces that she didn't mind if he was thinking of another.

Regret upon regret as he recalled what a friend she had become. Sacrificing everything to save him from Iraj. Not once displaying jealousy about Methydia, nor especially about Nerisa, the little Walarian thief who had grown into the love of his life.

What had been wrong with him? Why hadn't he realized that Leiria was above all others?

Such a sin. Such a sin. So extreme the gods would never forgive him.

And then he thought, but the gods are dead!

And that was followed by — Every woman I've ever loved suffered tragically for knowing me.

I'm not worthy.

This is why I've been condemned to dance eternally to the deadly music of Hadin.

And then he feared that at any moment he would suddenly hear the harvest drums resume their throbbing and once again the wild spellsong would compel him to dance, dance, dance. Palms slapping naked chest. Bare feet pounding the sand. On and on while a thousand others danced beside him. The beautiful harvest queen leading them on.

And the volcano ready to erupt!

But after a while, when nothing happened, he dared to wonder if somehow the cycle had been broken.

Then one day the stranger who looked like Palimak bent over Safar, pressing cool cloths on his forehead. The smell of healing incense tickling his nose. The stranger whispered words of affection, asking if there was anything he required.

He tried to speak, but his lips were numb. There was something very important he needed to say. But the words wouldn't come.

The stranger said, "What is it, father? What do you require?"

Maybe this *was* Palimak. Although it seemed unlikely, because the Palimak he remembered had been quite small. But the terrible yearning in his heart pushed him past these doubts.

So he answered, "Khysmet! Where is Khysmet?"

And he lapsed back into unconsciousness.

The Council of Elders had not met for several years. In fact, the last time they'd been together had been in Esmir when Safar had cajoled them into entering the Blacklands. For a long time, dire circumstances — such as a dead run to escape Iraj Protarus — had prevented such a gathering of Kyrania's most prominent men.

An attempt had been made to bring that traditional ruling body together after they'd landed on Syrapis, but Palimak had blocked it. A youthful witness to their endless, and, in his view, foolish debates, he'd decided to dispense with that form of village government the first time the question had arisen.

Supported by Coralean, that canny old caravan master, as well as by Leiria and the other members of the Kyranian army, he'd not so gently pushed them aside. Forming instead a loose counsel of advisers, which included Biner, Arlain and the other members of the circus troupe.

Constant warfare, plus an unbroken string of victories, had kept the Elders quiet. These men — who'd once tried to exile Safar and Palimak — held little standing with the other villagers. And those who had occasionally dared to contest Palimak's will had found themselves in a very small minority.

Once in a great while Palimak had even used the force of magic to compel the Elders to obey his commands. Actually, it wasn't so much obedience as a sudden, magically induced desire on their part to follow where he led.

At first he'd been ashamed of these tricks. His father had drummed into him the value of village democracy, where all views were accounted for and compromises made. On the other hand, when he and Safar had separated in Caluz, another message had been delivered. It was up to Palimak, his father had said, to lead the Kyranians to safety while he remained behind to confront Iraj.

And when Palimak had pleadingly asked what he should do if they refused, Safar had answered harshly, "Then make them!"

So that was what he had done, from that moment on the Esmirian shores of the Great Sea when they had all demanded to wait for Safar's return. And Palimak, believing his father dead, had cast the greatest spell of his young life, forcing them to wait no longer and flee to Syrapis.

Since then his guilt had subsided. Now he had become accustomed to being their prince. Practically a king — although never in the history of Kyrania had its people been ruled by royalty. So when Foron, the chief of the Elders, had come to him demanding a meeting, he'd been quite irritated. Who needed these stupid old men?

But what could he do when even his grandfather, Khadji, supported Foron's request?

And so three days after they'd borne the ailing Safar to New Kyrania, Palimak convened the Council of Elders to let them have their say.

He'd expected only long windy speeches praising their native son Safar Timura and welcoming his return to the bosom of his people. Perhaps a declaration of a special feast day to celebrate it.

But that was not how it had turned out.

Masura, leader of the loyal opposition, spoke first. "I'm a blunt man," he said, "so I won't shilly-shally around the point. Which is this: The miraculous return of our beloved Safar

Timura — your *stepfather* — proves what I have always suspected. That you have been lying to us all along!"

The young man made note of the way Masura underscored Palimak's questionable status as Safar's adopted son. He reflected briefly on Masura's hypocrisy; this man had not only opposed Safar but had been the leader of the group trying to exile him.

"I really think we should use words that aren't so incendiary," Foron said, in minor admonishment. "Accusations of lying are a bit strong, if you ask me."

Palimak said nothing, only raising an eyebrow at Foron's weak defense. In the past he'd always been a strong supporter of the Timuras and certainly no friend of Masura.

Then Foron turned his gaze on Palimak. "However, in Masura's defense," he said, "I must admit there is understandable concern about *certain things.*"

"Such as?" Palimak asked.

"You told us he was dead!" Masura accused, voice shaking with emotion. "You convinced us to abandon him in Esmir. Lies! All lies, which has now been proven!"

Palimak glanced at Khadji, expecting some support from his grandfather. To his dismay, he saw the old man nod in sad agreement.

"It's true, my grandson," Khadji said. "We all protested. But you insisted."

"And that's another thing," Masura broke in. "Why was it that a boy was able to insist on anything? And why did we just nod our heads and shuffle on board the ships, leaving our beloved Safar behind?"

"You didn't leave him behind," Palimak pointed out. "We found him here in *Syrapis*. I found him, actually. So you have no point."

"It was the work of some devil," Masura insisted. "I just know it was. How else do you explain your . . . unusual . . . influence over us. You wave a hand and everyone does your bidding."

He leaned closer, face dramatically lit by the traditional council fire. "Perhaps I spoke in error," he said, a wide sneer greasing his face. "Maybe it wasn't some devil's work — but a *demon's* work!"

He glanced around at the others, smiling grimly when he saw they had taken his point — Palimak's status as a half-breed.

"I say there should be an investigation," he said. "A special committee appointed by the Council of Elders to decide once and for all if this . . . this . . . demon's spawn . . . has possessed us. To make us do terrible things, such as abandon our dear friend, Safar Timura."

"That's not unreasonable," Foron agreed. "Eliminating certain insulting terms, of course. Such as 'demon's spawn.' Palimak is one of us, despite his background. We should treat him as such."

"He's a good boy," Khadji said. "He's always been a good boy. I can attest to that." The he sighed. "However, there are certain questions I have myself."

He glanced at Palimak. "No offense, my boy." Then back to the council. "I'll support an investigation — as long as it's not biased, of course."

The others murmured . . . of course, of course. And before Palimak knew it Foron was lifting up the white kid's-leather sack that held the voting markers. He upended the bag and dozen or more tiles spilled out; half were black, indicating a no vote, while the other half were white, meaning yes.

Palimak's blood went to high boil. He'd had enough, dammit! Betrayed by his own grandfather, by the gods! Although a small part of him whispered there was some truth in what they said. But to the hells with that! He'd done it for their own good, hadn't he? Only doing what his father had asked.

On his shoulder, the speck that was Gundara whispered in his ear, "We're ready, Little Master. Just say the word!"

Palimak's fingers stole into his pocket, touching the bit of magical parchment he kept there for just such emergencies. All he had to do was withdraw it, toss it into the council fire and a heady smoke would fill the room, making the men insensible. Then, with the help of his Favorites, he'd cast the spell that would make them pliant to his will and he'd send them on their way.

The spell would make them forget the confrontation. And he could easily create some clever bit of fiction to fill the gap in their memories. Such as the festival honoring Safar, the arrangement of which he'd originally thought was their purpose.

Then sudden self-disgust rose in his gorge. And his hand was empty when he yanked it out of his pocket. He got to his feet.

"Go right ahead," he said. "Have your investigation. I'll abide by the will of the majority."

Ignoring the shock on their faces and the mutters of surprise that swept the room, he stalked out of the chamber.

It's up to my father, now, he thought. And with that thought a feeling of immense relief washed over him.

15

THE CALL OF HADIN

Leiria watched Coralean pace the room, big bearded head bent in concentration as he listened to Palimak explain what had happened at the meeting of the Council of Elders. She could hear quarrelsome voices outside, coming from the market place.

Normally, the disputes would be about the prices and quality of the goods being offered. But now — although the exact words weren't distinct — she knew the voices were lifted in heated debate about the future of the Kyranians in Syrapis.

Since Safar's return and Palimak's abdication of responsibility, politics had reared its head, showing its ugliest face. Everyone seemed to have their own strongly held opinions, with no views shared in common. It was minority against minority and as a result the only rule was that of chaos.

When Palimak was done, the wily caravan master sighed deeply and shook his shaggy head. "Coralean is not a man who easily passes judgment on another," he rumbled. "But I must confess, young Timura, that all you have told me is deeply troubling to this weary old heart." He thumped the massive structure that was his chest.

Then he fixed Palimak with his fierce eyes. "But, my headstrong friend," he went on, "it is with the greatest regret that I must tell you that a grievous error has been made. And I fear it is you who have committed it, though it pains me to point out the mistake.

"You should never have allowed the Council to convene, young Palimak. Failing that, you should have used all your wiles to prevent the outcome of that meeting. I blame myself for not being here to advise you. But, alas, I was busy with those pirates who call themselves ship captains."

"But what the Elders suspect just happens to be true," Palimak replied, voice weary from lack of sleep. "I *did* force my will on them before. I did use magic to make them see things my way. Not once, but many times."

He looked over at Leiria with sad eyes. "I even did it to you, Aunt Leiria," he said. "You would never have left Esmir if I hadn't cast a spell on you. You'd have waited there until the hells turned to ice before you abandoned my father to the Fates."

"I know that," Leiria replied. "And I can't say your actions don't bother me when I think on it. However, we now know Safar never would have showed up. The wait would have been futile."

"But he wasn't dead," Palimak said. "I was wrong."

"And he wasn't in Esmir, either, was he?" Leiria said. "It was in Syrapis that we found him. There's no doubt in my mind that if you hadn't forced us to come to Syrapis, inspired us to defeat Rhodes and the others and then led us into that horrible chamber, we never would have found him. Don't ask me how he got here. I'm no sorcerer, so I couldn't say."

Palimak smiled bitterly. "Well, I am a sorcerer," he said, "and I can't tell you, either."

He gestured at the immense coffin crammed into one side of the tower room that he used for his quarters. "The first time I looked inside I saw the remains of a demon. There was no mistaking that corpse for anything but. Not just his looks, but the sheer size of him."

Palimak shook his head. "I've never seen a demon so large," he said. "Besides that, the demon looked exactly like the pictures and statues of Lord Asper. So that's who I think was in there. Not my father, but mummified remains of Asper."

Coralean stroked his beard. "You've said that the next time you looked Asper was gone and instead you found the ailing body of my dearest friend, Safar Timura: correct?"

"Just as you say," Palimak replied.

"A mystery indeed," the caravan master said. "One designed to confound even one such as Coralean. A man who has seen more things than most."

He turned to Leiria. "How is our Safar?" he asked. "Has his condition improved?"

She brushed away the sudden moisture in her eyes. "No, it hasn't," she said.

For three weeks, Leiria had helped Safar's mother and sisters nurse him. Spoonfeeding him broth, which he instinctively swallowed without ever regaining consciousness. Bathing the body she knew so well; except it was uniformly tanned from head to toe, which was most odd. It was as if he'd been naked under a hot sun for a long time. Also, other than what grew on his head, he was completely hairless. His face, his chest, his limbs, his groin.

Then, not long ago, he'd started to sprout a beard. But instead of coming in dark, like the hair on his head, it was golden. Since Safar had always kept his features smooth she'd shaved him, puzzling over the yellow hairs.

Also, his eyebrows and the hair on his head seemed lighter. Although that might have been from the sun that had toasted his skin. Stranger still, this morning, when she'd given him his sponge bath, she'd seen a little golden nest of hair beginning to form in his groin.

She'd wanted to ask his mother and sisters about it. But Leiria had never been Safar's wife, only his former lover, so she hadn't managed to summon the nerve to ask such an intimate question of the prudish Kyranian women.

"There's no need to mourn, my beautiful Captain," Coralean said. "Safar will be back with us in spirit as well as body soon enough." He tapped his head with a strong, thick finger. "Coralean knows it here." He thumped his chest. "And here."

"He's spoken a few times," Leiria said. "So that gives me hope. Except he always says the same thing." She shook her head. "He keeps asking, 'Where's Khysmet?' I wish could answer him. I keep thinking — if I could suddenly produce Khysmet he'd recover. But of course, that's a hopeless task. The last time we saw Khysmet was with Safar in Caluz. My guess is that he was probably killed when Safar destroyed the Idol of Hadin."

She paused, reflecting on the enormous explosion they'd all witnessed from the distant shores of the Great Sea. She shuddered. "Nothing could have survived such a calamity," she said.

To her surprise Palimak said, "I'm not so sure of that. My father did." He paused, thinking. Then, "I told you what happened in Charize's chamber. How, when all seemed lost, what I thought was my father's ghost engaged those monsters. But it wasn't a ghost, was it? Because we later found my father alive in Asper's tomb."

"Yes, yes, but we were talking about the horse," the caravan master said, displaying rare impatience.

Palimak sighed. "The whole incident all seems like a terrible nightmare now. So I can't say for certain. But it seemed to me that during the battle I heard Khysmet. You all know that trumpeting sound he made whenever there was a fight?"

Leiria and Coralean nodded. They remembered it very well. Especially Leiria. She couldn't count the number of times she'd followed that wild cry into always-victorious battle.

"Well, that's what I heard," Palimak said. "Or maybe it's what I wanted to hear. I can't say."

"Are you telling us there's more to this mystery?" the caravan master asked. "Poor Coralean's brain, agile as it is, has not been able to unravel the knot of Safar's sudden resurrection, much less these other things you suggest."

"If you did hear Khysmet," Leiria said, "where is he now? Where did he go?"

Palimak groaned in frustration. "I don't know," he said harshly. "But every day that goes by, I wonder if I didn't make a big mistake by not searching Hanadu for him, instead of leaving so quickly."

Always a woman of action, Leiria said, "Let's return to Hanadu and see. It's stupid sitting around here wondering about something we can't prove unless we go there in person. And if we do find Khysmet, maybe Safar will recover."

Angry shouts echoed from the market place. Coralean peered out and saw the Elder, Masura, haranguing the villagers. His words weren't distinct, but they were obviously causing a heated debate. People were jabbing fingers at one another, defending whatever stand they had taken.

He turned back, face dark with displeasure. "Coralean is not the sort of man who usually advises delay," he said. "Direct action has always been his motto, as you both well know."

He jabbed a thumb at the window. "However, it's Coralean's considered opinion that this would not be a good time to undertake another expedition to Hanadu. There's too much discontent in our ranks. King Rhodes is no fool and would be certain to sniff out our weakness. Then we'd have another war on our hands."

He grimaced. "With so much disunity, Coralean fears that the outcome of such a war might not achieve the same happy result as before."

"I'm not sure we have anything to lose," Leiria said. "It's my guess that his spies have already informed his hairy majesty that we're at each other's throats."

"Possibly so," Coralean replied. "But to hear a thing from a spy is not the same as knowing it in your heart. Spies are notorious tellers of falsehoods. They lie for gold. Or they lie to please their master, telling him what they think he wants to hear.

"Sometimes spies do both. Fattening their purses and getting in their master's good graces at the same time. King Rhodes knows this, so he'll wait until he has absolute proof before he moves against us. And it is Coralean's view that it would be foolish for us to provide him with the proof he seeks. Let him labor for it. And if the gods are kind to us, our problems will resolved by then."

Palimak sighed. He felt like a child. Confronted by forces he didn't understand and certainly wanted no part of.

"If only my father would get well," he said. "He'd stop this squabbling. He'd know what to do!"

Coralean studied him. Then, "Although Safar has returned to us, it's still up to you, my young friend," he said. "You must act. We can't wait for your father's recovery. It saddens Coralean deeply to say this, but there's a chance Safar might never recover."

"But he has to!" Palimak moaned. "I can't force people against their wills any longer. I never liked doing it. And I don't want to start again."

Leiria fixed Palimak with a hard look. She said, "This is a rotten time, Palimak Timura, to develop a conscience."

"Our beautiful captain has hit the target in its tender center," Coralean said. "The troubles we are having now with the Council are nothing compared to the evils we will face very soon."

Palimak raised a questioning eyebrow. "What could be worse than this?"

"As you know, I've just returned from negotiations with our hired fleet," Coralean said.

"They want more money?" Palimak asked. "That's easy enough. We've plenty of gold and jewels in the treasury."

The caravan master snorted like a bull. "Of course they want more money," he said. "Mercenaries always want more money. It's in their greedy natures to wring the sponge dry, then press it again in case there's a speck of moisture left. But our new worries aren't on account of money. Coralean has had the distasteful task of dealing with such men many times during his long, illustrious career. Sea pirates, land pirates, they're all the same.

"I reasoned with them. Thumped the heads of a few captains. Slipped their lieutenants a little gold to foster insurrection. And eventually arrived at terms favorable to us."

Leiria eyed him. "So what's the problem?"

"Waterspouts," Coralean said.

Palimak and Leiria gaped at him. What in the blazes?

Coralean nodded. "Yes, indeed, my friends. Waterspouts," he continued. "'The biggest damned waterspouts in all creation,' is how one captain put it. One of them appeared right off the coast of Hanadu. According to the captain, who swears he hadn't had a drink in a week — a lie, of course, but no matter — this particular waterspout was over a mile wide. And powerful! Strong enough to pull the biggest ship under. At least, that's what the captain said."

Coralean plucked a leather-covered flask from his belt and

drank deeply of the wine it contained. He handed it to Palimak, who shook his head. Then to Leiria, who nodded absently and drank as deeply as the caravan master.

"I questioned a sampling of common seamen from the other ships," Coralean said, "and they confirmed the tale. As a point of fact, the spout forced the fleet to put out to sea for more than a week."

Coralean sighed. "Thank the gods Rhodes didn't know that, because there was a time when the blockade we have established along his coast did not exist."

"But now the fleet's back, right?" Palimak said. "So there's nothing to worry about."

"Oh, you couldn't be farther off the mark, young Timura," Coralean said. "The fleet's back. The blockade once more intact. But I fear — and more importantly those pirates fear — that new manifestations will occur. Sailors are the most superstitious of men, as you well know.

"But it seems they have reason for their nervousness. For similar waterspouts have been reported in the seas between Syrapis and Esmir. There's news that a dozen fishing boats disappeared just off Caspan. Sucked down by a waterspout, I'm told."

"But why should we worry?" Leiria wanted to know. "Waterspouts can't get us on land. And if the sea off Syrapis breaks out in them like plague rash, it doesn't matter if all the ships light out for deep water. We might not be able to land at Hanadu, but neither can Rhodes send a raiding party to our shores. Who needs ships, if Nature Herself forms a blockade?"

But Palimak immediately understood what Coralean was getting at. Ghostly fingers chilled his spine.

"It's not King Rhodes he's worried about, Aunt Leiria," he said, his voice trembling. "Or, really even the waterspouts." Then, to Coralean. "Isn't that right?"

Again, the caravan master sighed heavily. "Indeed it is, son of my dearest friend," he said. "Safar predicted the end of the world long ago. He said the gods were asleep and no longer concerned themselves with human, or demon, affairs. I didn't believe him, at first.

"But look what has happened to Esmir! Despite his valiant efforts to destroy the machine at Caluz — plugging the magical breach between Hadin and Esmir — the poison has continued to spread. The seafarers tell me much of Esmir is now uninhabitable. That people are fleeing to the coast in tremendous numbers."

He pressed his hands against his temples, as if in pain. "It is my fear," he said, "that this poison will soon spread to Syrapis. And then what will we do? The waterspouts are quite possibly the first sign of such an occurrence."

Just then they heard a rooster crow. Surprised, for it was midday, they turned their eyes to the window. Another cock joined in. Then another. Somewhere a donkey brayed and horses whinnied. Then all the dogs started to bark.

They looked at each other, wondering what was happening. Palimak opened his mouth to speak.

At that moment the earthquake struck!

There was no warning. The floor heaved under them. Coralean was flung against the window and nearly toppled out. Leiria snatched at him, pulling him back.

The floor heaved again. Leiria was hurled backward, still holding on to Coralean. They fell heavily to the ground. The massive stone fortress swayed like a fragile sailboat in a storm.

Palimak found himself lying on the floor, staring up at the ceiling as an enormous crack shot from one side of the room to the other. Stone shattered into sand and rained down on him, but he couldn't rise. It was as if a gigantic weight was holding him down. All he could do was shut his eyes against the falling debris.

He heard screams from the market place. Rock grinding against rock. Glass and clay jars bursting. Large objects hurled to the ground from great heights. Animals bawling in pain and fear.

And then, as suddenly as it had begun, the earthquake ended.

Silence hung like thick velvet drapes. The atmosphere was filled with dust, sparkling in a wide burst of sunlight streaming through the enormous hole in the wall where the window had been.

Then the silence was broken by the sound of movement from across the room. Palimak and the others turned and gaped at the sagging door, which had been half-torn from its hinges.

A wild-eyed figure staggered through the doorway. It was Safar.

"It's Hadin!" he cried. "It wants me back!"

And he collapsed to the floor.

16

UNDER THE DEMON MOON

Kalasariz floated above the golden-tiled plain, which stretched away from him on all sides for what seemed like an enormous distance.

For the first time in what seemed like eons, the spymaster was without pain. He felt strong and confident — mind as sharp and clear as it had ever been.

He knew that he was still quite small; that the plain was actually a table, with a tiled center. And that the enormous face bent over him was that of a normal-sized human woman. A witch, actually. Who at this moment was mumbling the spell that would break the last link of the magical chains that had imprisoned him for so long.

Beside him, Luka and Fari were whispering to one another. He couldn't hear what they were saying, but he had no doubt that they were conspiring against him. Prince Luka and the Lord Fari disliked one another intensely. But as demons they were united in their hatred of all humans — especially Kalasariz, who had been their rival from the beginning.

The moment the witch cast her spell, they would attack him. If Kalasariz had possessed a face, he would have smiled that thin cold smile that tens of thousands had feared for so many years.

For the spymaster had plans of his own. Plans that included Luka and Fari only in a small, but possibly delicious, sort of way.

It was a pity things had to be as they were, Kalasariz thought. Although he loathed the two demons, it wouldn't have prevented him from working with them as an equal. Unlike Luka, he'd never envied Iraj Protarus his throne. Nor had he ever shared Fari's jealousy of Safar's former title of Grand Wazier to the king.

All his adult life the spymaster had been content to remain in the background. Letting others wear the trappings of power, while he steered the course. The only person who'd ever aroused the green-eyed beast in his bosom had been Safar Timura. And that was because Safar had quite different ideas on how Iraj should rule his kingdom. Nor did Safar's plans include Kalasariz in any role — especially not that of the power behind the throne.

Complicating Kalasariz' enmity for his rival was the strange hate/love relationship between Safar and Iraj. Before they fell out the two had been boyhood friends. Blood-oath brothers. But so what? What was a blood oath when a grand kingdom was at stake?

As the spymaster thought about these things it suddenly came to him that perhaps the reason he'd failed in his fight against Timura was because of Kalasariz' own lack of ambition. Maybe he'd been a fool all those years being content to be the power behind the throne.

Perhaps by relying on kings to do his work, instead of acting directly on his own behalf, he'd sown the seeds of his own failure.

The spymaster started getting excited. What a new and interesting way of looking at things!

Above him, the witch shifted position and Kalasariz put these thoughts aside to be examined more fully later. He had to keep his wits about him for what was coming next.

Although the spy master's smallness prevented him from clearly making out what the witch was up to — all things were so enormous that he couldn't see past the immediate details in front of his face — he smelled burning incense and guessed she was moving to the next part of her spell.

Beside him, Luka and Fari stirred restlessly. They were silent now. Conspiracy completed, he suspected. Waiting their moment.

Kalasariz had no idea how he and the others had come to this place. When Iraj had grabbed onto Safar's magical robe-tails, Kalasariz had instinctively followed. Leaping into the trough of his sorcerous wake, carrying Luka and Fari with him.

Then Iraj and Safar had disappeared and Kalasariz had found himself hovering between darkness and light, Fari and Luka mere specks of existence floating nearby. For some reason they were even smaller than he was and quite weak. And so when they heard the witch's voice summoning them, it was Kalasariz who had answered. And it was Kalasariz who had negotiated with the witch.

She would give them substance. A place in this world. In return, they would join her in her struggle against her deadliest enemy — Palimak Timura. The three agreed most enthusiastically. For wherever Palimak was, they'd find Safar. And wherever Safar was, they'd find Iraj — their errant brother of the Spell of Four.

Iraj had broken the spell's link, condemning them to puny existences that the most insignificant insect would not envy. Their only hope was to find Iraj again and bring him under their power.

Fari, who had been a master wizard in his previous existence, had explained that this time the bond could be reformed differently. Since Iraj had violated the Spell of Four, it was no longer necessary to make him the kingly center.

"All we require is his essence," Fari had said.

"His essence?" Kalasariz had puzzled, not certain what he meant. "How do we accomplish that?"

If Fari had owned lips, he would have smacked them. He answered, "We eat him!"

This answer had inspired the glimmerings of what Kalasariz now believed was turning out to be the greatest plan in his career.

The witch's indistinct mumbling ended. The huge head drew back, long hair stirring like a great forest in a summer storm.

"Make yourselves ready," she commanded.

She gestured, mountain of a hand slicing downward.

But as it descended, Kalasariz whipped around to confront Luka and Fari. He had time to see them coming forward, then there was a white-hot flash that blinded him. Even so, he didn't hesitate but surged forward.

There was a slight sting, then another, as he engulfed first Luka, then Fari.

Thunder boomed and he felt an enormous weight crushing downward. The weight eased. Became . . . normal? He opened his eyes and found himself staring into the glittering eyes of the witch. They were at his level.

The spymaster looked down and saw he was kneeling on the table. The golden-tiled center almost completely covered by one knee.

He was gripped by a delight so fierce it verged on hysteria. For a moment he considered stepping off the table and removing the witch before she became too much of a bother.

Then he thought better of it. From the negotiations, she hadn't seemed the type to leave an opening.

"I can put you back the way you were with a snap of my fingers," Queen Clayre warned. "So I wouldn't move too quickly, if I were you."

"I wouldn't dream of it," Kalasariz said with a smile.

The queen grimaced. "Where are the others?" she asked.

Kalasariz covered his lips as he burped politely. He said, "I ate them."

The queen frowned at him a moment, head turning to one side, ear cocked as if she were listening. The frown turned to a smile. Then a laugh.

"Oh, that's very good," she chortled. "You've consumed your enemies, but they still exist inside you. They're your slaves now. With no will of their own."

"We didn't get along very well," Kalasariz replied. He hesitated, then decided it was best to be truthful. "Circumstances forced us together. But when you were working your spell I got the rather strong impression that they were planning to end our partnership."

"But you acted first," Clayre said.

"It seemed the prudent thing to do," Kalasariz said.

He glanced about the room, noting with mild surprise that everything was in disarray. Chairs were knocked over. Broken glass and clay jars were scattered across the rich carpets, which were also stained by spilled liquids. A shelf of books had been dumped over. And everything was covered with a thick, fine dust.

"What happened here?" he asked.

The queen shrugged. "Nothing to concern yourself about," she said. "Just an earthquake." She waved a dismissive hand. "I was anxious to work the spell, so I didn't bother getting a few slaves in to clean the mess up."

Kalasariz thought this was a very interesting admission. Obviously, time was of the essence to the witch. It was a good thing to know. If she was facing some self-imposed deadline, then he could drive a harder bargain.

"What exactly is it you want me to do?" he asked.

"Help my son regain the royal mantle he deserves," she replied.

The spymaster smiled. "You've certainly come to the right person for that," he said.

Palimak sat by his father's bedside all that night. Safar's breathing was labored. Sometimes he would twitch and moan. But mostly he was still, dragging in each breath, then letting it go in a long sigh as if there were a heavy weight on his chest.

Twice he became suddenly rigid, the pulse in his throat visibly throbbing. He'd whisper, "Khysmet!" And then his body would relax and the labored breathing would begin anew.

Outside, even the nightbirds and insects were silent. Everyone and everything had been exhausted by the earthquake. Fortunately, no one had been killed and although many had been injured, those injuries mostly consisted of cuts, scrapes and minor bruises. The damage to the buildings was spotty. Some walls had collapsed in the fortress and several homes had been destroyed.

However, the earthquake had arrived at a lucky time. It had been a fine day and most of the Kyranians had been outside. Now everyone was so weary from cleaning up the debris and treating the injured that they were fast asleep.

Palimak studied his father's sleeping form. The Demon Moon was shining through the window, bloody red light pooling on Safar's chest as if he were horribly wounded.

He thought about his father's sudden appearance in the doorway after the earthquake. His wailing cry that Hadin wanted him back. Instinctively, Palimak knew these were not the mad ravings of a sick man. If someone had asked him what Safar had meant, he couldn't have answered. Not precisely, at any rate. But he strongly sensed that Coralean's report of the waterspouts in the Great Sea and the desolation overcoming Esmir had something to do with it.

As did the earthquake.

For the eighth time that day, he withdrew the Book of Asper his father had entrusted to him when they had parted three years before. He placed the book's spine in one hand and let the pages fall open as they pleased.

He peered down at the page that had presented itself. And, just as it had seven times before, the same poem showed him its face:

There is a portal,
Through which only I can see.
There is a secret,
I dare not breathe.
Under the Demon Moon there
Is thee and me.
And then there is no more
Of me and thee.

Frustrated, Palimak snapped the book shut. The eighth appearance of the poem in as many attempts was certainly no accident. But what in the hells was that damned Asper getting at? And how could he have conjured such a reoccurrence from the distance of a thousand years or more?

If only his father would awaken and explain to him what the poem meant. A wave of self-pity swept over him. He thought, It's not fair! I'm only thirteen years old. Other children my age spend most of the day at school, or at play. Or doing minor chores, like tending the animals. He brushed away a tear. Then steadied himself. It just was, that's all.

Fate had decreed it long ago when the parents he'd never known had met and had fallen in love. A human father and a demon mother. Both dead now. Mercifully, perhaps, all things considered. At least they wouldn't be forced to witness the end of the world.

And then he thought, And they don't have a chance to save it, either.

He felt a tingling sensation and his gaze was drawn to the window which framed the evil face of the Demon Moon.

It seemed to be summoning him. Calling him. He heard a harsh voice whisper, "Pa-li-mak! Pa-li-mak! Pa-li-mak!"

The moon's pull grew stronger. So strong it felt like his scalp was being lifted from his skull.

His head ached with a rhythmic pounding hammering from within. And with each drumbeat — for that is what the hammering seemed like — the pain intensified until he thought he could bear it no longer.

Then once again he heard his father moan, "Khysmet!"

Safar shifted in his bed. There was a metallic ring as the silver witch's knife fell to the stone floor. To Palimak's pain-intensified senses it sounded like a sword clashing against a shield.

Joints aching, he retrieved the knife, then found his gaze drawn to the red moon-glitter reflecting off the blade.

They'd found the knife while undressing him and had placed it under his pillow. It was Safar's most prized possession — given to him by Coralean for saving the caravan master's life. Palimak started to slip it back under the pillow, then hesitated when an image caught his eye.

Once again he peered at the shiny surface of the blade. He saw eyes staring back in the dagger-shaped reflection. For some reason they didn't appear like his own. Still, they seemed familiar.

The pain in his head was so intense it was difficult to think. His emotions were as dull as his thoughts. The rhythmic pounding made everything seem distant, unreal. He turned the blade and saw other portions of the reflection. A slash of a wide forehead. Another of what seemed to be a square, bearded chin.

How strange!

He blinked and the reflection seemed to shift and then became a mirror image of himself.

The pain vanished. It was as if all the agony had been contained in a cask of water and then someone had knocked out the plug and it had quickly drained away.

Now the knife shone silver instead of red. Palimak looked up and saw the Demon Moon had risen above the top of the window frame. The soft glow of the morning sun gleamed through.

Palimak was surprised he hadn't noticed the passing of so many hours. One moment it had been late night. Then he'd stared into the knife's surface and all that time had collapsed.

He didn't remember falling asleep. How could he have, with all that pain — and its sudden, blissful release? But it seemed to be the simplest and therefore the most logical explanation. It also accounted for the strange image he'd thought he'd seen reflected in the knife blade.

Yes, that was the answer. He'd fallen asleep.

With dawn's arrival, Palimak started putting his plan into action.

First he got out the little stone idol and summoned the Favorites. The boys were usually cranky in the morning, but he had some sweets ready for Gundara and some very old cheese for Gundaree. They munched on the treats, quarreling with one another between bites, but he kept pulling tasty bits from his pockets until they were more or less settled down.

Palimak turned his attention to the task at hand, fishing various magical items from a leather purse: six tiny pots filled with special oils; small packets of sorcerous powders, each of a different color; a jar of an alcohol-based elixir, in which he'd dissolved powder made from ground ferret bones; and finally, a little mirror.

He drew magical symbols on the floor, using a quick-drying paint for ink. While he worked, Gundara and Gundaree hopped up on Safar's bed.

"The old master looks pretty sick," Gundara observed in cheerful tones.

"Maybe he'll die," Gundaree put in, partly stifling a yawn with his hand.

"You two are such ungrateful wretches," Palimak said. "Three weeks ago he saved your worthless lives. Now you're all but getting ready to bury him."

"I only said he looked sick," Gundara protested. "Gundaree was the one who talked about dying."

Gundaree put hands on his slender hips. "What's wrong with that?" he demanded. "Death happens, you know. When you get to the bottom of the Scroll of Life, that's it!"

He made a cutting motion across his throat. "Finished. End of story. It's the same for everything that lives. Fish do it. Sheep do it. People do it. And demons do it. Although I suppose fish and sheep don't have very interesting stories on their Scrolls."

Gundara leaned against Safar, relaxing. "I don't know about that," he said. "I met a fish once who had a pretty interesting life. It was maybe six or seven hundred years ago, not long after we were stolen by that witch."

Gundaree shuddered. "Why do you have to bring her up?" he protested. "That witch was a terrible mistress. Maybe the worst ever. You're going to spoil my whole day by making me think about her."

"I was talking about a fish, not the witch," Gundara said. "That great big fish they served up at her birthday banquet. It was still alive, remember? And they were cutting off strips to make fish bacon."

Gundaree grinned. "That was great bacon," he said, licking his chops as he fondly recalled those fishy snacks.

"I wish you'd stop interrupting my story," Gundara grumped. "While you were eating that poor fish, I was talking to him. About how he used to live at the bottom of the sea and had more female fishes than you could shake a fin at. And all the adventures he had fooling the sharks and the sea snakes."

He shook his head, marveling at the memory. "What a fish he was!" he said. "A fish above all fishes."

"You ate him too," Gundaree said. "After you made friends with him and promised you'd free him. You got in there too and ate the fish bacon as fast as the cooks could fry it up."

"It seemed like the polite thing to do at the time," Gundara said. "I didn't want to insult him. Let him think he didn't taste good."

Gundaree hopped up on the bed with Gundara. He studied Safar's face for a moment. "I still think he looks like he might die," he said. Another yawn. "If I weren't so sleepy, I'd feel bad about it."

Palimak did his best to ignore them. They were what they were and there was no way anyone would ever change them, much less warm up their cold little hearts. Usually they didn't bother him that much. In fact, their dark humor appealed to the demon side of him.

He couldn't help but smile at his own hypocrisy. The truth

was, if they hadn't been talking about his own father, he might have found their conversation pretty damned funny.

The rueful smile made him relax. He arranged the pots on the floor, making a six-pointed star with the mirror in the center. He sprinkled powder from each of the packets into the oil pots, then lit them with a candle.

Multi-colored smoke hissed up, filling the chamber with a sweet, heady odor. Gundara and Gundaree made gagging sounds of protest, but he paid them no mind.

Next, he took out his father's dagger, reversed it, and rapped the mirror with the butt. The mirror shattered. He rapped again, breaking it into smaller pieces. Then he stirred the glass bits with the tip of the knife, mixing them up.

Palimak squatted back on his haunches. "All right, boys," he said. "I'm ready for you now."

Grumbling, Gundara and Gundaree hopped back down on the floor.

"This isn't going to work," Gundara said. "He's too sick."

"You might kill him," Gundaree added. "Did you ever think of that?"

"Besides," Gundara said, patting his little belly, "I'm too full to work."

"Enough!" Palimak barked, finally letting his weariness get the better of him. "I've fed you, pampered you, and listened patiently to your mewling."

His eyes glowed demon yellow. "If you don't want to work, then by the gods I'll seal you in your stone house and throw it into the deepest part of the sea I can find. And you can argue with each other and the damned fishes for a thousand years, for all I care!"

The two Favorites went through an instant change in attitude.

"We were only jesting, young master," Gundara said, flashing his white fangs.

"Yes, yes, only a joke," Gundaree put in. "We'll help you all we can."

"And, I must say," Gundara added, "the old master really is looking much better."

Palimak motioned, and the Favorites leaped up on his shoulder and shrank to flea-size specks.

He concentrated on the bits of shattered glass, breathing deeply, taking the incense smoke deep into his lungs. The spell he'd chosen came from a poem of Asper's his father had recited to him long ago.

Palimak chanted:

"Wherein my heart abides
This dark-horsed destiny I ride?
Hooves of steel, breath of fire —
Soul's revenge, or heart's desire?"

Suddenly, the shattered glass reformed into a mirror. A swirling image appeared on its surface.

Palimak felt dizzy and he gripped his knees as if he were about to fall.

He heard his father whisper, "Khysmet! Where is Khysmet?"

There came a thunder of hooves.

And Palimak was swept away.

17

DEADLY BARGAIN

Rhodes was in an ugly mood when he tromped down the stairs leading to Queen Clayre's chamber. Who in the Hells was king here, anyway? So what if she was a witch? So what if she was his mother? How dared she think she could summon him with an imperious snap of the fingers. Didn't she know he was busy?

The earthquake had done extensive damage and he'd spent half the previous day and the entire night, plus most of today, overseeing the clean-up and rescue work. Twenty-two dead. Fifty-three more buried in rubble and possibly dead. No matter that they were only slaves. They were valuable, dammit! Brawny workers and comely women all; plus half the women were pregnant, and therefore worth double.

Rhodes did not deem himself fortunate because there had been no deaths among the citizenry. They'd only suffered injuries — two hundred minor, forty-six, serious. Pity some of his courtiers hadn't been killed instead of the slaves. In his estimation they were all a needless drain on the kingdom's treasury.

He would tell his mother all this, then give her a good piece of his mind for interrupting his labors digging out the collapsed slave quarters.

But when he came to the closed door leading into his mother's rooms, the king paused, stricken first by doubt, then by weakening resolve. Feared by thousands — no, tens of thousands — Rhodes always found himself undergoing a transformation in Clayre's presence. He was a brave man. A king who always led his troops from the front even in the fiercest battle. But when his mother spoke his nerve fled like kitchen beetles when a torch was lit.

Adding tension to this particular visit was the knowledge that his mother had been working on the plan they both had agreed would turn the tables on Palimak Timura and the Kyranians. He thought it was a good plan. Fortuitous circumstances had delivered the means into their hands. Three powerful devils who had appeared the moment after Queen Charize was killed by Palimak. Devils they could enslave and use against the Kyranians.

Still, he had grave doubts about the part he was supposed to play. Then Rhodes thought, be damned to magic! Why can't we just do things the old, honest way? Such as slipping a spy into Palimak's quarters and slitting his throat?

His mother, sensing his presence, called out: "Come in, my son. We're waiting for you." Cursing under his breath, Rhodes entered.

Across the room — looking more beautiful than ever — his mother was regally ensconced in her wide-backed, pillowed throne. Standing in front of her was a tall man, who turned as Rhodes entered. The man had features as pale as death and he was so thin that his long face looked like a skull. His eyes were flat black — giving away nothing. He smiled when he saw Rhodes and the king thought he'd never seen such a terrible smile. Thin lips made a long red gash in the pale face.

The man nodded his head in what could have been taken for a slight and oh, so imperious bow.

"Good afternoon, majesty," the man said in deep tones. "It's a great honor to finally meet you." He held out his hand.

Rhodes was furious at this gesture. How dare this . . . this . . . common creature . . . offer such an intimate exchange as touching hands with the King of Hanadu!?

"Go ahead, son," his mother said. "Take his hand."

Rhodes was not only going to refuse, but his hand instantly went to the hilt of his sword. By the gods he'd cut this swine's heart out and have it roasted for supper! But, strangely, his hand swept past the hilt, rising of its own accord to find the stranger's.

"My name is Kalasariz, majesty," the spymaster said as their fingers touched. "And I understand we're about to have a great deal in common."

And then he laughed. Rhodes nearly balled up his fist to smash that laugh out of the man's head, when a shock ran up his fingers — lanced along his arm, then burst into his heart.

The king clutched his chest, but then the pain was gone. And he found himself staring into empty air.

Kalasariz had vanished!

The astonished king scanned the room. "What in the hells!" he exclaimed. "What happened to that son of a whoremaster?"

Clayre smiled gently. "Don't you remember our plan, my son?" she asked. "He's inside you now. A supremely powerful force at your instant command."

Kalasariz stared out at the queen through Rhodes' startled eyes. He could feel the king's throat constrict in fear. His heart trip hammering, his veins and nerves running with ice.

The spymaster experienced the king's shudder of agony. The licking of dry lips, then an embarrassing stutter, as Rhodes said, "I . . . I . . . You didn't warn me, mother!"

"I thought it would be less of a shock, my dear," Kalasariz heard Clayre reply through the king's ears.

This is a good body, the spymaster thought. And he quite liked the mind. Although it was filled with confusion now — shot with more fears than a brutally violated maiden. But he sensed the sharpness of the king's brain, and the cunning, oh, the cunning, it was like finding a honeycomb in a bitter wilderness. It wasn't so cunning as the thinking organ that Kalasariz had himself been blessed with. But it would do. It would do.

He whispered to Rhodes, *Do not trouble yourself, majesty. I am a very discreet fellow. I will do nothing to interfere with your natural functions. I'm only here to advise. And to add to your already inestimable powers.*

To his surprise, the heart he shared with Rhodes went from trip-hammer to hysterical pounding. The ice in the king's veins switched to shocking fire. And he realized that his "voice" had unnerved Rhodes, coming from within as it did. Funny, came a thought as an aside. Funny, how Kalasariz had imagined his own lips moving, his vocal apparatus making words, but the entire process had been mental. Much faster than real speech.

So fast, in fact, that he could react and suggest new things with a speed that outpaced the sudden relaxed feeling growing in

Rhodes' bladder. There was no way Kalasariz would permit the shared embarrassment of Rhodes pissing their pants.

So he said, *When the time comes, majesty, I'll help you kill your mother.* Various of Rhodes' organs became calmer. Kalasariz went on: *She's been telling you what to do for far too long now. Using her magic to keep you under her thumb. It's not fair, you know. A mother should allow her child to be the man he truly is. I saw it right off. The instant I entered your body.*

There was a tremble when he mentioned the part about body entering so Kalasariz hastened to add, *This is a temporary solution for both our problems, majesty. Your mother forced me into this situation. But rest assured, as soon as we accomplish our common goals, I have a plan to properly separate us into two delightful human beings again.*

Unconsciously, Rhodes opened his mouth to reply. Kalasariz quickly jumped in. *Say nothing to me now,* he advised. *Wait until we are in private and we can learn to communicate together without giving our conversations away.*

Rhodes nodded. He got the message. His heartbeat calmed and his breathing became more gentle.

Queen Clayre glared at Rhodes. "Why are you nodding your head like a fool?" she demanded. "Are you listening to me? Have you heard a word I've said?"

And to Kalasariz' immense satisfaction, Rhodes replied with the utmost calmness:

"Yes, mother. I hear."

Then Kalasariz internal "sight" was jarred as the king's eyes moved to the side and focused on a large mural. The spymaster saw an army marching out of a mountaintop castle. And at the head of that army was a mounted warrior armored like a king. On either side of him were women warriors — princess generals, Kalasariz guessed by the banners they flew. One of the princesses was dark-skinned and rode the most magnificent black mare Kalasariz had ever seen.

It's just a painting, he thought. Why is the king so interested? Is he a lover of fine art? Or horseflesh? Or both? He quickly became bored with Rhodes' attention to the mural and attempted to turn his thoughts away to some proper planning. Maybe he'd snoop around this new body a bit to see just how well things worked. Maybe he'd talk the king into visiting his harem tonight. It had been a long time since Kalasariz had enjoyed the embrace of a woman.

But the king's fixation with the mural was so strong that Kalasariz couldn't tear his own mind away.

He felt Rhodes' vocal chords open and once again experienced the rumble of the king's voice.

"What happened to the horse, mother?" Rhodes asked, finger lifting to point at the mural.

Queen Clayre turned her head to look. Nothing caught her attention, much less caused her any surprise. She turned back to her son.

"What horse?" she asked.

Kalasariz felt the king's heart quicken. "I saw a white stallion there," he said, still pointing. "Right in front of the black mare. It was rearing up on its hind legs."

The queen snorted impatiently. "I've lived with that mural my entire adult life," she said. "And there was never a white stallion in it."

"But I only saw it a few days ago!" Rhodes protested.

"You were imagining things," Clayre replied. "It comes from drinking too much. Which I've warned you about many times. It doesn't do for a king to lose his wits to wine."

Rhodes opened his mouth to argue, but Kalasariz moved in. *Never mind the horse, he advised. We can talk about it later.*

The king suddenly relaxed. "I'm sorry, mother," Kalasariz heard him say. "I was obviously thinking of a different mural."

But in his mind was a blazing image of his mother tied to a stake, flames leaping up around her as she writhed in agony.

Very good, majesty, Kalasariz thought-whispered. *A most appropriate image. And I'd be pleased to help you make that dream come true. But only at the proper time, hmm? We have other business to attend to first.*

As if she had been listening in, Clayre said, "We have pressing business to attend to, my son. Business I think you will quite enjoy."

With a flourish she placed a small wooden container on the table. It was made of some kind of rare dark wood — polished and giving off a pleasing scent. It had hinges made of white gold, with a tiny lock also of white gold.

"I made this two years or so ago," the queen mother said, eyes narrow as she poked something into the lock — a minuscule key, Rhodes supposed. "About the time you lost your first battle to the Kyranians." Her voice dripped with accusation.

The king flushed at the humiliating memory. The Kyranians

had presented a much smaller force than had the Syrapians. But as Rhodes and his army had marched into the valley the Kyranians had occupied, the airship had appeared overhead.

It was Rhodes' first experience of aerial bombardment and on nights when memory of the incident kept him awake until dawn, he recalled in vivid and frightening detail the fire raining from the sky. The screams of his men set ablaze. The smell of burning flesh. The shock of realization that his army had turned tail and was running down the hill. Men hurling their shields and weapons away in their haste to escape.

"It wasn't my fault," he muttered.

"Of course it wasn't, my son," Clayre said, waving her hand airily, as if the notion had never entered her head.

Then her voice hardened. "I can understand it happening the first time," she said. "There was the surprise of a new and mighty weapon. But it kept on happening, didn't it? Every time you faced Palimak Timura in battle. It was the same old story. He'd draw you into a trap. The airship would show up.

"And once again the Kingdom of Hanadu would suffer a humiliating defeat because the king was too stupid — or too cowardly — to come up with a solution."

Rhodes burned with fury and embarrassment. Kalasariz said nothing to soothe him, curling himself up in a little ball of indifference just beneath the king's heart. Wisely staying out of the confrontation.

Clayre opened the box and took out a strange multi-colored object. She placed it on the golden tiles in the center of the table.

Rhodes puzzled over it for a moment, then realized it was a diorama of the Kyranian stronghold. It was a perfect replica, from the forested peak it sat upon to the old stone fortress his spies had identified as the place where Palimak and his key people were ensconced. Below the fortress was the village proper, market place in the center, slant-roofed homes spread out on either side.

Rhodes studied the terrain with a professional military eye, searching out the weak points.

Then his frown deepened. "If this model was made two years ago, mother," he said, "then how have you managed to put in details my spies didn't map out until several weeks ago?"

He pointed at the turreted gatehouse guarding the entrance to the fortress. "That's where Palimak has set up his command post and sleeping quarters. Two years ago it was in ruins. And my spies have only just reported its reconstruction."

The witch queen chuckled, in that maddeningly condescending manner she had. "Either my spies are better than yours, my son," she said. "Or your spies work for me first — and you — second."

Clayre gave him an amused look. "If I were you I'd decide in favor of the former, because the latter would only put you to unnecessary anguish and work. This is not the time to dispose of all your spies, you know. You'd have to train a whole new crew."

Another chortle. "And you still wouldn't know if they were yours or mine."

Rhodes lost all patience. "What exactly do you want, mother?" he snapped. "All my young life you said your greatest desire was for me to be king. But now that I'm king you seem to do everything to subvert me."

Clayre pretended to be shocked at his charges. "Me?" she mocked. "Subvert you? My only son? My heart's desire?"

She placed an insincere palm across her shapely bosom. "Why, I only want what is best for you. I have no other ambition but to see you become king of all Syrapis. Is that not our family's destiny? A destiny I have sought from the moment I learned the story behind that painting?"

She indicated the mural of the mounted king and princesses. The gesture took some of the heat out of Rhodes. Clayre supposed it was because of the strength of her argument. Actually, it was because Rhodes had remembered the white stallion.

Where had it gone? Dammit, he hadn't been drunk when he'd first spotted it! His brow wrinkled as he wondered if his mother had commanded one of her artist slaves to paint the horse out, just to bedevil him.

Kalasariz stirred. Something was going on. Rhodes was thinking about that horse again. And what was this about mural-painting slaves?

Clayre asked, "Do you recall the tale, my son?"

Rhodes shrugged. "Yes, mother," he said. "I remember it very well."

"Even so, perhaps I should tell it again to refresh your memory," she said. "And also for the benefit of our new friend who resides within you."

But to Kalasariz' disappointment, Rhodes chose this time to dig his heels in. "If you please, mother," he said, "let's leave it for another time. I've much to do, what with the earthquake. Besides,

I'm far more interested in what you intend to accomplish with that."

He pointed at the diorama. "How will it help in our fight against Palimak Timura?"

Clayre frowned, clearly irritated at her son's impatience. Then she shrugged, "Very well," she said. "I'll leave the story for another day. As for that model, I'd intended to use it as a focal point for a spell I cooked up with Charize. A bit of magic that would cause the Kyranians no end of trouble and more than a few deaths. With luck, it might have even resulted in the rather gruesome demise of Palimak Timura himself."

The witch queen sighed. "But Charize's own death put paid to that plan. As I said before, alone I don't have enough magical strength to perform the necessary sorcery."

She smiled. "But that was yesterday's disappointment. Today, the sun is shining brightly and our hopes are reborn. For now we not only have the assistance we require, but a whole new plan to bedevil our enemies."

"When do you want to start?" Rhodes asked, assuming correctly that his role as host to Kalasariz meant his presence would be needed.

Clayre motioned at the table. "I'm never one to put off a devilish deed that needs to be done," she said. "So why don't we begin now?" She gestured for him to approach the table.

Rhodes obediently moved forward. Then he hesitated. "There's only one thing," he said.

"And that is?" Clayre asked.

"Have you forgotten your granddaughter is being held hostage by the Kyranians?" He pointed at the model. "What if this spell endangers Jooli?"

The witch queen raised an eyebrow. "Do you really care?" she asked.

Rhodes shrugged. "Not particularly," he replied. "She's always been more of a bother than she's worth."

"My sentiments exactly," Clayre said. "As granddaughters go, she certainly lacks a certain . . . well, reverence." Her attention returned to the model. "Now, let us begin."

And she started to weave her spell. Inside the king, Kalasariz wriggled with delight. It was good to be back on a winning side again.

The only thing troubling him was that Rhodes didn't seem very enthusiastic. Was it because of this Jooli person? The one Kalasariz guessed might be the king's daughter?

If so, perhaps his reluctance was understandable, even though Rhodes plainly disliked his own child. Although Kalasariz had little empathy for people stricken with parental love, he had a professional understanding of that all-too-human malady. The spymaster had relied on it many times as a lever to get his own way.

Then he caught a stray thought from Rhodes. And, dammit, he was still wondering about that horse! That's the trouble with kings, Kalasariz thought. They can't seem to keep their minds on the job at hand. Important tasks. Like killing people!

A blue light formed over the model of the Kyranian stronghold. Tiny figures began to appear. Men and women. Children and animals. And then the figures came to life!

Clayre said, "One thing I noticed about Palimak and his friends when they were visiting Charize was that they absolutely hate and fear rats."

She placed a cage next to the now-living model of the Kyranian stronghold. Inside was a large gray rat. She poked it with a long needle and it squealed in pain and fury.

Clayre laughed as it attacked the bars of the cage. "I'll give them rats," she said, "like they've never seen rats before!"

And then she opened the cage and the enraged rodent leaped onto the model.

18

HORSE MAGIC

Leiria watched the crowd of angry villagers march up the hill from the market place. She leaned easily on her spear, smiling as if they were only a few friends coming to call for dinner, instead of an unruly mob in the making.

She whistled a casual little tune. Behind her Renor and Sinch took her signal and slipped through the gatehouse entrance. They shut and barred the door. As planned, they would take up position inside in case things really got out of hand and the crowd took it into its minuscule group mind to break through.

Besides herself, she had only Coralean — who stood at her

right — and five other soldiers loyal to Palimak.

"I think we can manage well enough," she said to Coralean. "There's only a hundred or so of them."

"Sometimes there's profit in violence," the caravan master said. "Although, as all who know Coralean would confirm, I loathe to engage in that sort of business. Unless, of course, there's no other way of conducting one's affairs. After all, a good family man must consider the well-being of his wives and children. And only the greatest liar in the world would cast doubt on Coralean's dedication to his family."

Leiria nodded at the approaching crowd. "Do you see any profit there?" she asked.

Coralean stroked his beard, considering. Then he shook his mighty head. "They have nothing of value," he said. "Only their own foolish thoughts."

Leiria sighed. "I'm afraid this is turning out to be one of my least favorite days," she said. She glanced up at the empty sky. "I wish Biner and Arlain were here with the airship," she said. "That'd sure keep this group peaceful."

The circus troupe had taken the airship out on a routine surveying expedition. There were no decent maps of Syrapis and Leiria had been intent on filling that gap since their arrival on the island. Unfortunately, the latest mission had coincided with what appeared to be turning into an uprising.

"It is probably for the best they aren't here," Coralean said. "Our Kyranian friends hold the circus folk in awe. And if Biner was forced to act against them on our behalf, they'd lose all influence over them."

He shrugged his massive shoulders. "Only two people can truly help us in these circumstances. Safar, who is ill. And Palimak, who is unavailable."

When Leiria had risen this morning she'd found a note waiting for her from Palimak. He'd said he was involved in a long and dangerous job of spellcasting. Under no circumstances was anyone to disturb him or enter Safar's room.

Leiria had checked the door to the room and found it barred. She'd smelled the faint scent of magical incense and ozone wafting through the crack under the door. She knew from things that Safar had said in the past that if she ignored Palimak's wishes, it might result in the deaths of her two friends.

Then she'd received a much more disturbing message from Masura — who'd apparently overthrown Foron as chief of the

Council of Elders. The new headman said that he and the other villagers demanded an immediate hearing. Since she didn't dare disturb Palimak to get help, she'd politely asked Masura for a delay.

The headman, however, was evidently so intent on a confrontation that he'd sent back a note refusing her request. He'd even had the temerity to threaten herself and Coralean with immediate expulsion.

The result of this heated exchange of paper was presently being played out in the mass march on Palimak's headquarters.

Leiria heard a faint scraping noise and turned to see Jooli climbing out through one of the fortress's windows. The royal hostage dangled by her fingertips for a moment, then dropped lightly to the ground. She casually brushed herself off and strode over to join Leiria and the others.

"You shouldn't be here, majesty," Leiria said.

"Just call me Jooli," the young queen said. She nodded at the crowd coming up the hill. "This doesn't look like the best time to stand on court formalities."

Leiria looked at her through narrowed eyes. "Whatever I call you," she said, "the point is that you are supposed to remain in your quarters. We're responsible for your safety."

Jooli chuckled. "How safe will I be if your friends have their way? I doubt if those people will honor any agreement you have with my father."

"She does have logic on her side, Captain," Coralean pointed out.

"I'm also bored to tears," Jooli put in.

She stretched her long arms and worked her shoulders, getting the stiffness out of her muscles.

"I could use a bit of exercise," she said. "And I thought perhaps your fellow Kyranians would provide it."

Then she indicated Leiria's sword. "Loan me your blade," she said, "and I'll stand with you."

Leiria hesitated. Queen Jooli had mystified her from the very first meeting. She clearly despised her father. Had been instrumental in freeing Palimak and Safar from the monsters in the cavern. And had spent her short term as a hostage acting more like one of Leiria's warrior companions than the daughter of their greatest enemy.

At that moment Leiria realized she'd grown to like Jooli. And was possibly even beginning to trust her.

She drew the sword and handed it over. "Have at it," she said.

Jooli smiled, took the sword and gave it a few experimental swings. "Nice balance," she said. Then she turned to face the villagers, who were nearing the top of the hill.

Naturally, Masura was leading the crowd. But Leiria noted with extreme interest that only four other members of the Council of Elders were present. Foron, the ousted former headman was notably absent. Obviously, Masura's victory was far from unanimous.

Then she heard a commotion and saw another group approaching the crowd — angling in from a path that village boys used when taking the goats to pasture. It was a much smaller group, but it included Khadji Timura, Safar's father, and Foron. Several other influential villagers were also present.

"With fortune," Coralean observed, "wiser heads might prevail."

Jooli snorted. "If not, I'd be happy to lift a few of the stupider ones from their shoulders."

Leiria said nothing. The prospect of killing people she'd fought beside and had lived with for several years was depressing, to say the least.

The two groups met. Although she couldn't make out what he was saying, Leiria caught the gentle sound of Khadji's voice. A renowned potter, Khadji had been much respected long before his son's accomplishments had won him so many honors. Foron joined in, as did the others, and the conversation grew animated — much hand-waving and point-making gestures.

Then Masura's voice rose above the others. "We're through listening to the Timuras! I say we drag Palimak out here and make him answer for his crimes!"

There was a roar of approval from Masura's followers. They shoved Khadji and the others aside and continued their march up the hill. The crowd was working itself up, shouting oaths, sliding over into mass hysteria.

"Get ready," Leiria warned.

And there was a creak of leather battle harness and a rattle of metal as her people braced for the onslaught.

Queen Clayre chuckled at the scene before her — the tiny figures of Foron's mob charging toward Leiria's small group.

"Well, well," she said. "Apparently we have some new friends among the Kyranians to assist us. It's so much easier to make magical mischief if people hate each other!"

King Rhodes' attention was riveted on the drama unfolding in the model of the Kyranian stronghold. He'd never realized the Kyranians were so divided. By the gods, if only he had a few troops present, he'd wipe them out with ease!

Then he frowned. Where was Palimak? He peered closer and couldn't find a trace of his enemy. Then he spotted his daughter lined up with Captain Leiria and Lord Coralean, waiting to hurl back the mob.

"What's Jooli doing helping them?" he rumbled.

"Never mind that now, son," Clayre advised. "I need your full attention to cast this spell."

"Be damned to her!" Rhodes growled. "She has no business getting involved."

The soothing voice of Kalasariz came from within. *Don't trouble yourself, majesty. All who betray you will be punished. This I swear to you.*

With Kalasariz sending out calm feelings, Rhodes relaxed and once more started concentrating on the spell.

Meanwhile, Kalasariz was loving every minute of this new and most powerful experience. He could feel the tingling of Clayre's magical energy coursing through the king's veins. And within his spirit self he could sense the agony of the creatures that were Fari and Luka as they leaped about to do his bidding. It was a delicious feeling to witness his enemies humbled so. They were less than insects in this new world he'd carved out for himself.

Clayre muttered spell words, sprinkling powders over the model.

The blue light intensified as she continued to weave her deadly spell.

As the crowd approached, Coralean made one more attempt to settle things peacefully. He stepped forward, raising his hands high. So powerful was his personality that the crowd came to an immediate halt and fell into silence.

"People of Kyrania," he said, his big voice carrying to the most distant edges of the crowd. "All of you know in your heart of hearts that Coralean is your oldest and dearest friend. And I call upon your affection for me — and upon our long and profitable association — to hear Coralean's words."

There were murmurs of agreement in the crowd. Masura glowered, furious at the caravan master's effect on the others.

"Please, my dear friends," Coralean continued, "do not shame yourselves this day. Do not sully Kyrania's long tradition of peaceful discussion and compromise. It is this quality of yours that has most endeared you to me over the years. A quality that I hold in the highest esteem."

Masura shouted: "The time for talk is over! We've had enough Timura trickery."

Coralean looked hurt. "Do you accuse me, Coralean, of anything but honest intentions, my friend?"

"You're no friend of mine!" Masura shouted. "You're nothing but a paid toady of Palimak Timura!"

There was a flash of steel as Masura suddenly drew a blade from beneath his cloak and leaped forward to strike the caravan master down. So unexpected was his attack that even Coralean, an experienced fighter and agile despite his size, was caught unaware.

He threw up an arm in surprise and Masura aimed his blade at the caravan master's exposed heart.

But Leiria was quicker, jumping between Masura and Coralean. She felt a hot, stinging sensation as Masura's short sword cut into her arm. But she turned with the blow, catching the main force on her body armor. Then she grabbed Masura by the throat and hurled him backwards.

"Assassins!" Masura screamed. "Assassins!"

Only a few people had seen his attack. Most believed it was Leiria who had struck first.

Chaos erupted and the screaming mob surged forward.

Rhodes watched in joy as the Kyranian mob attacked his most hated enemies. He burned in even greater delight in anticipation of what would come next.

Kalasariz shared his delight, soaking up the hot juices flowing through the king's veins. Meanwhile, he whipped his little slaves into a frenzy, driving Fari and Luka to greater heights of pain. Drawing on the powerful magic their agony produced.

Queen Clayre shouted, "Now!" and stabbed an elegant finger at the model of the Kyranian fortress.

Kalasariz felt the pull of her powerful magic and delivered his own pent-up sorcery in twin hammer blows of energy that blasted through the king's eyes.

The blue light hovering over the model turned white hot, then burst. Fiery particles rained down on the melee below.

It was Jooli who caught the first hint of danger. A man was lunging toward her and she parried his sword thrust and kicked his legs out from under him.

But as she turned to confront the next attacker her hackles suddenly rose and her hair stood up on her scalp like hot needles.

Instinctively she looked upward and saw an enormous blue cloud floating overhead. The cloud was shaped like the face of a beautiful woman — a familiar face with two enormous eyes that glowed with evil power.

"Beware!" Jooli shouted. "It's my grandmother!"

No one heeded her warning. They were too busy fighting.

In the next instant all that changed. A lightning bolt shot from cloud to ground.

There was an enormous, ear-bursting crash and suddenly the air was filled with fiery particles raining out of the sky.

Someone screamed in pain as a particle settled on his flesh. Then another person cried out as his hair caught on fire.

The two victims broke from the crowd, running wildly, blindly away. Shouting, "I'm on fire! I'm on fire!"

The crowd scattered under the deadly rain, people diving for any shelter they could find.

"With me!" Jooli shouted, whirling and running for the shelter of the stone overhang that protected the door.

Leiria, Coralean and the others knotted in beside her. Pounding at the door for Renor and Sinch to let them in. Mistaking the hammering for the mob trying to get in, the two young guards ignored their entreaty.

Then, as suddenly as it had started, the hot rain stopped. People peered out from their hiding places — farm carts, trees, big clay jars they'd upended.

"What in the Hells —" Leiria began.

"She's not done with us yet," Jooli broke in, cutting her off.

"Who are you talking about?" asked a bewildered Leiria.

"I told you — my grandmother," Jooli snapped. "Queen Clayre." Then, as if it would explain everything, "She's a witch."

"What do we do?" Leiria asked.

"Wait and see what happens next," Jooli advised.

But even as she answered she was digging through her own mental book of spells, searching for a defense. Feeling helpless even as she did so. The power of her grandmother's attack had surprised her, humbled her. She'd had no idea that Queen Clayre possessed such abilities.

At that moment the ground turned spongy under her feet. It started to crumble and she jumped away, shouting a warning to the others.

She whipped around to confront whatever new threat Clayre had in store for them and saw a large dark hole in the ground where she and the others had been standing. Then glowing red dots appeared in the hole. The air suddenly took on a sharp, foul scent of rodent droppings. There was a scurrying and a squeaking — and then hundreds of large rats poured out of the hole.

Coralean booted one rat and slashed at another with his sword. Shouting in surprise as it dodged his cut and leaped onto the blade itself and ran up his arm. He hurled it away, splattering its body against the fortress walls.

But then others swarmed up at him and he cursed and swatted at the squeaking tide. Leiria and the soldiers fared no better. The numbers were overwhelming and they soon found themselves being driven back, dripping with blood from the many bites they suffered.

Jooli cast the only spell she thought might prove effective, but it flattened in the air like a burst goatskin bag.

Screams came from every direction and she could see where other holes had suddenly appeared, pocking the hill like an ugly skin disease. Thousands upon thousands of rats poured out of the holes, attacking the Kyranians with a stunning ferocity.

Fleeing people stumbled, then were quickly overwhelmed by the rodents who went for the most vulnerable parts — snapping at eyes and throats and lips. Slashing ears into bloody ribbons.

Jooli leaped up onto a low wall, clubbing rats away with the flat of her blade. Leiria used her spear to vault onto the wall and they stood back to back, protecting one another against the horrid tide.

But the rats kept coming and Jooli felt her strength slipping away at a frightening rate.

She knew she couldn't last much longer.

Rhodes danced up and down, shouting in glee as the rats overwhelmed the Kyranians. Kalasariz did his own little ghost dance inside the king, thrilled at this easy victory.

Even the inscrutable Queen Clayre let some true emotion leak through, saying "Good show!" as a big rat leaped over Leiria's head and sank its teeth into the back of Jooli's neck.

But then there came a sound like a thunderclap and the fortress door boomed open.

And now it was Queen Clayre's turn to cry, "What's happening?"

Leiria heard Jooli shout in pain and she whirled about, plucked the rat from Jooli's back, snapped its neck and threw it away. A rodent jumped on Leiria's leg, digging in sharp claws and teeth. She smashed it off with her fist, then caught another in mid-leap on her spear point.

It was then that she heard the thunderclap, followed by the crash of the big fortress door slamming open. She looked up, dazed. And beheld a most wondrous sight.

Charging out of the fortress was Safar, mounted on Khysmet! Palimak was seated behind his father, gripping his waist. Safar was waving a long curving sword that glowed like a golden beacon.

And he shouted in a great voice: "Come the winds! North and South! East and West! Come! Come the winds!"

There was a roaring sound, like a distant sea gathering its strength. Then the roar became a wail, then a giant banshee shriek.

The next thing Leiria knew, she was being hammered by fierce winds blasting over her from all sides. She grabbed Jooli and the two women toppled off the wall to take shelter behind the stonework.

Leiria raised her head to see — wind-borne grit lashing her face and scouring her helmet like a sanding machine gone mad.

At first all she could see was the glowing tip of Safar's sword. Then the atmosphere seemed to steady and she could make out the dark, funneling cloud that swirled around man and horse and boy. The banshee sound suddenly changed to shrill squeaks and she saw the rats being lifted off the ground and hurled into the sky.

Thousand upon thousands of them, swept into the heavens, to disappear into the great blue cloud that had a woman's face.

Then the cloud tore apart and was gone.

The wind ceased. And all was silent.

Rhodes shouted in surprise as the model of the Kyranian fortress exploded.

And then thousands of rats were falling from the vaulted ceiling of his mother's chambers. Squealing in fear and anger.

It was as if a rodent hell had opened its gates and let loose a vicious tide of fur and claws and teeth.

Clayre stood frozen in fear as the first of the rats went for her.

Then she screamed in terror.

Quickly, Rhodes grabbed his mother, lifting her off the ground. Then he rushed up the stairs, Clayre under one arm, smashing rodents under his heavy boots.

He got her through the door, turned, and slammed and barred it, squashing several rats as they tried to slip past.

The king set his mother on her feet. "What a mess!" he said, then turned his back on her and staggered to his chambers where he collapsed on his bed.

He slept for three days straight and not even Kalasariz could arouse him.

Then he got up, called for food and ate like a war horse. When he was satisfied, Kalasariz spoke to him from within, saying, *You seem quite calm, majesty, considering all that has happened.*

Instead of answering the question, Rhodes said, "Was that Safar Timura? The big man on the white horse?"

Yes, Kalasariz replied. *You can see why he's given me so much trouble over the years. He's a very powerful wizard.*

Rhodes thought a moment, then nodded as he made up his mind. "I want that power," he said."

Then you shall have it, Kalasariz vowed. *We'll just consider your mother's first effort a noble but failed experiment.*

"I have no problem with that," Rhodes said. "I'm not one to give up easily."

He paused, then, "That stallion Safar was riding?"

Yes, what about it?

"That's the steed I was talking about," Rhodes said. "The horse I saw in the mural when I last visited my mother. And then it was gone. Vanished!"

Perhaps we should examine that mural more closely, Kalasariz suggested.

And so Rhodes revisited his mother's chambers. While he'd slept, the rats had been exterminated by poisonous spells. Their bodies were still being hauled away by slaves when he entered his mother's rooms. Clayre was nowhere to be seen. She was probably off somewhere in borrowed quarters, nursing her wounded pride.

"The mural's just over here," Rhodes said, lighting a torch and carrying it to his mother's throne.

But when he looked up his jaw dropped in astonishment.

There was no sign of the mural. The wall was completely blank.

19

HOMECOMING

Safar's homecoming was a glorious celebration that lasted a full week. There was much singing, feasting and sacrifice to the Goddess Felakia. Sparkling fireworks filled the nights, dazzling kites of many colors the days. The whole mountaintop was thick with the heady scent of roasting kabobs and spiced fruits and perfumed rice. Wine flowed in rivers and everyone was drunk from dawn to dawn.

His parents and sisters fussed over Safar, weeping and laughing in relief that he was with them once again. Men thumped his back and called him brother and hero. Women offered themselves, swearing they would do anything he desired — with no betrothals asked in return. Coralean gave him a treasure chest filled with exotic gems and rare coins struck by kings in distant lands.

His circus friends staged a fabulous performance in his honor. Biner dressed in his best ringmaster's uniform to direct from the ground as Arlain and Kairo performed many wondrous feats on wires strung from the high-floating airship to the ground. Arlain in her skimpiest costume, breathing long tongues of fire. Kairo juggling his detachable head along with a flaming sword. While Elgy and Rabix played stirring music specially composed for the show.

During all these events Khysmet was always nearby, flowers woven into his mane and tail by pretty Kyranian maids. Palimak sat at Safar's feet, feeling light as a feather, now that he no longer had to wear the heavy mantle of leadership.

Leiria was perhaps the happiest of them all, standing permanent guard at his side. Her burnished armor shining almost as strongly as the internal glow of her overflowing heart. She was joined by the fiercely loyal Renor and Sinch who made certain Safar was safe from all who approached.

With no discussion, Jooli made herself part of this group. She appeared one morning and took up position beside Leiria. It seemed so natural that no one questioned her right.

Safar made only one speech during this time. On the first day he called all the villagers together to purify the mountaintop of the last vestiges of Clayre' sorcery. Afterward, he told them how overjoyed he was to be home again. Although he didn't say where he had been, it was understood by all that Lord Timura had suffered much for them. He congratulated his friends and family for successfully negotiating the Great Sea and making a new home in Syrapis, despite many difficulties and personal sacrifice.

Finally, he begged them to pardon Masura and his supporters for their actions. Left unsaid was that until Safar's miraculous appearance the majority of the villagers had sided with Masura. Everyone seemed quite anxious to forget that ugly little truth.

Safar said he understood and even agreed with the concerns of the Council of Elders. However, these were perilous times that called for extraordinary measures when it came to leadership.

Here he drew Palimak close to him, praising him before the entire assemblage for all that he had done to protect the people of Kyrania. And for so faithfully carrying out all Safar had commanded.

This simple and loving declaration banished any doubts that might have remained among the villagers about Palimak's role since their flight from Esmir. Coupled with the pardon of Masura and his supporters, everyone was so relieved that they wiped their minds of all grievances, real or imagined.

Yet all that gladness was an illusion. Safar knew he would soon have to make his people face a terrible truth: all they had suffered and all they had endured was nothing compared to with the dark days to come.

But he allowed them this brief time. Let them dance, dance, dance, as he had in the endless nightmare of Hadin.

Meanwhile, he would marshal his strength and resources and play the deadly waiting game.

Deep in the wine-dark night, Safar paced the room. Filling one whole side was the great empty coffin of Lord Asper. On the wall above the coffin was the mural that had once graced Queen Clayre's chambers.

Here was the glittering castle and the mysterious King of the Spirit Riders leading his army into battle. There were his warrior daughters, each more beautiful than the other. In front of them was the most beautiful of all — the ebony-skinned princess on the midnight-black mare who had appeared several times over the years to warn Safar, or lead him to safety.

It was all a maddening puzzle. A labyrinth of hidden meanings. Safar had little memory of what had happened since his escape from the past and future dreamworld of Hadinland. There were only impressions, swirling like stars in a drunken sky. There was the wild ride on Khysmet. Quick snatches of the battle with the monster queen in her underground lair. A hazy period of illness, when he sensed he had been knocking on Death's door. Then Palimak had appeared astride Khysmet and they were hammering together at a stony surface.

The surface finally gave way and he suddenly found himself bursting out of the wall of this very room. And then he was charging out of the fortress on Khysmet to meet and defeat the plague of rodents attacking his people.

Safar stared at the mural. He remembered being a momentary part of the ancient painting — sitting astride Khysmet with Palimak, whispering for him to remain quite still while the spell he'd cast continued its course.

He was peering out into the room of the witch queen, Clayre. Nearby was her son, King Rhodes — ruler of Hunan. They were bent over a table, concentrating on something. What it was, he couldn't see. But he could feel the intense flow of magic arcing back and forth between them.

Then it came to him that Rhodes wasn't a true part of that magic. He was only a vessel, with a sorcerous something within.

Safar dug deeper, investigating this oddity. He caught the whiff of a familiar scent. It carried him all the way back to his student days in old Walaria. By the gods, it was Kalasariz!

He'd defeated the canny spymaster several times before, but he kept arising like a vengeful ghost to bedevil him. Somehow he'd taken up residence within the king.

There was still more. What was it? Who was it? Then he sensed the lesser presences of Prince Luka and Lord Fari — Iraj's old demon companions of the Spell of Four. Kalasariz had somehow turned the tables on them. Now they were his much-abused slaves.

However, that left a major question unanswered. There was Kalasariz, Luka and Fari. That made only three.

What had happened to the all-important fourth — Iraj Protarus?

Safar had strained mightily, but couldn't find a single trace of the man who had once been his dearest friend but was now his bitterest enemy. Had Kalasariz managed to kill Iraj as well? That didn't seem possible. Wily as Kalasariz was, Iraj was not one to go so easily.

As Safar had pondered this, Palimak had cast the remaining portion of his spell and they'd been hurled across a spectral world into the Kyranian fortress.

Safar sighed heavily, still caught on the horns of the dilemma of Iraj. He turned away from the mural, which Palimak's spell had transported with them. There were too many questions, each requiring him to follow completely different roads, so it was unlikely a single answer could be found that would satisfy everything.

A line from the Book of Asper crawled into memory: *"All that is Without is Within . . . And all that is Within, is Without . . ."* Safar smiled. Once again he was confronted with another murky verse from Asper that seemed to have meaning. But the meaning defied penetration. No help there.

He strode over to a mirror, and for the first time in what seemed an eternity, viewed his own face. There were the familiar features. The blue eyes, the long chin, the strong nose. He was richly tanned from his time under the hot Hadin sun. No answers there, either, my friend.

Safar touched his chin. There was a bit of a morning stubble. Safar got out his razor, stropping it keen for a shave. Idly, he noticed the stubble was golden instead of its usual dark shadow.

When he'd bathed last night he'd noticed the same was true of the hair on his chest and privates. There were also several wide golden streaks running through the dark hair on his head. Obviously, so much time being naked under that burning sky had bleached him out — possibly forever.

The rest of his body seemed unaffected, except he was more muscular than before. Some good had come from his time in Hadin. He'd always been strongly built, but now his chest and limbs were heavier, more defined. And now that he was well he felt like he was filled with a never-ending supply of energy. This was a definite bonus. For he'd need all the strength he could summon for the hard days ahead.

Safar soaped his face and started shaving. He paused a moment, staring into his own eyes as if they belonged to another, wiser man. And he asked that other man, *Where is Iraj?* But no answer came from this silly exercise.

He chuckled at his foolishness and continued his ablutions.

In his hiding place, Iraj suppressed outright laughter.

He was so close to his enemy that if he had a knife he could catch him unaware and kill him. Of course, he'd need hands to hold that knife — which was something he lacked at the moment. In fact, he had no body at all. And wasn't it odd that he didn't miss it?

Then again, maybe it wasn't so strange. In Iraj's previous existence as a shapechanger he'd known constant pain. Especially as he moved through the agony of assuming one form or another. Bones cracking. Skin stretching and transforming. Internal organs boiling in a sorcerous cauldron. Brain and nerves on fire as they were bombarded by over-intensified sensations.

No, this was much better. The spirit form was a perfect container for the hate he felt for his enemy. What was more, as a spirit he could be patient in the extreme. And patience was a quality that Iraj had never possessed before.

Here he would wait — just out of his enemy's sight. He would watch all that occurred and,at the proper time and the proper place, he'd strike.

Poor Safar.

Sentence had already been passed and he didn't know it.

20

STORM OVER SYRAPIS

The monsoon season struck Syrapis full force. Even the natives said it was the worst in recent memory.

First came the stultifying atmosphere, settling over the island like a thick, uncomfortable blanket. Breathing was accompanied by a wet rattling of the lungs. Old people and babes were most affected by this and Safar and Palimak were kept busy night and day treating a host of respiratory ailments.

This was accompanied by a series of heavy rainstorms that drenched everyone to the bone. Clothes never seemed to dry. Small wounds became huge weeping sores. The animals developed mange and other skin diseases. Goat milk and cheese became a precious commodity as the mother goats' teats dried up.

Next came the crops. The Kyranians had brought seeds and cuttings from their high-mountain homeland. Over the past few years the Esmirian plants had done well in the mountain fortress the Kyranians had chosen for a home. But the monsoon brought a dampening sickness with it. Roots of young plants were pinched off by the disease. The older plants were stricken with a mysterious fungus. Gray patches would suddenly appear on the leaves and within only a few days the plants would wither and die.

Lightning was a constant peril. Striking without warning even on those rare days when the skies were blue and empty. Parents taught their children to make a small presence if they were caught out in a lightning storm.

They were taught to crouch down, head between their legs, being sure to keep their weight balanced only on their toes. The idea being to make as little contact with the ground as possible. They were also told to stay away from fences during a lightning strike. And if caught out in a wooded area, to get under the shortest tree. For some reason the Lightning Gods favored the tallest objects on which to concentrate their wrath.

The airship was grounded the whole time and there was no surveillance while the monsoon storms lasted. Safar and Palimak weren't too concerned about this vulnerability, reasoning their enemies were just as hampered by the storms as they were.

Safar, however, was concerned about the mercenary fleet they'd hired. Besides the airship, it was this sea force that had kept King Rhodes bottled up. Coralean was dispatched, along with a strong guard, to make certain the pirate captains remained loyal.

Meanwhile, Safar spent all his spare time pondering his next move. He told Palimak and Leiria about his enslavement to the spell of Hadin, his escape and the subsequent disappearance of Iraj.

"I suppose we'll unravel those mysteries in good time," Safar said one night. "But at the moment the thing that intrigues me most is that mural."

He indicated the painting on the wall. "I wonder mightily what the story is behind that. Who was the king? And what of his daughters? Especially the dark-skinned woman on the black mare. When her ghost visited me she said she was a Spirit Rider. And that she was commanded to lead me to Syrapis. For what purpose, I don't know."

"Maybe it has something to do with Lord Asper's coffin, father," Palimak said. "To me, that's as big a mystery as the mural. One moment I saw his mummified corpse. And then he was gone. To be replaced by your living body."

"I have an inkling of what happened to Asper," Safar replied. "It's my theory that the coffin is a gateway between here and Hadin. Unless I'm in grievous error, we basically traded places."

He thought a moment, then added, "At least, it is was a gateway. It's closed now. And there's no way of reopening it again."

Outside, the intensity of the rainstorm increased, furiously pounding on the shuttered windows.

Leiria shivered. "Give me a sword, a spear and a shield and I'll fight any enemy you put in my way," she said. "But all this talk of magical gateways, missing corpses and Spirit Riders is unnerving."

Palimak said, "About the mural, father . . ."

"Yes?"

"Why don't we talk to Queen Jooli?" he asked. "Maybe she can tell us its history."

Safar considered his suggestion. Jooli was nearly as big a puzzle to him as the magical mysteries he was attempting to unravel. He still thought it odd that a hostage should so completely switch her loyalties.

Yet he sensed he could trust her implicitly. She clearly hated her father, just as her sympathies were clearly with the Kyranians. Perhaps it had something to do with her witch's powers. Had she learned something through magic that had opened her eyes?

There was only one way to find out.

"Send for her," Safar said.

A few minutes later Jooli came into the room, still sleepy-eyed from her bed. Twin lightning spears crashed outside, light flaring through the shutter panels. Mixing with the wavery light of the torches sputtering in their brackets on the wall.

Jooli was wearing a long, soft gown and in the sudden intensity of light her slender figure was outlined through the rich cloth. At the same time Safar caught the scent of her perfume — delicate flower blossom. He was startled at her beauty, realizing this was the first time he'd seen her out of armor.

He started to speak and found his voice had grown husky. It had been a long time since he'd been with a woman and she'd caught him off guard with her earthy presence. He cleared his throat to cover his embarrassment and bade her to sit and take some wine with them.

They talked casually for a time, drinking wine and remarking that the storm seemed to be subsiding. Safar noticed that Jooli was eyeing him speculatively, no doubt wondering why she'd been called here. He felt a gentle touch of magic as she sniffed about to see if there was any danger. When none was found, the subtle probing quickly vanished.

Jooli spoke first, going directly to the heart of things. "I suppose you're all wondering about me," she said. "Wanting to know why I'm acting like such a willing hostage. And why I seem so disloyal to my father.

"I suppose you're even asking yourselves if it's some sort of trick. Suspecting, maybe, that any day now I'll reveal my true colors and stab someone in the back."

The rain made a gentle patter now and Safar smiled. "No one thinks that of you, Jooli," he said. "It's apparent to us all that when we found you, we found a friend. Although I must admit that I'm mystified how we came to be so fortunate. Until you came here to live, you knew nothing about us."

"That's not quite true," Jooli said. "You see, Safar Timura, I've been waiting for your arrival ever since I was a girl."

There was a long silence as everyone in the room wondered at this startling remark. A sudden wind blew up, crashing against the shutters.

Palimak's eyes jerked toward the mural, then toward Jooli. His demon senses prickling with awareness. He muttered, "Yes, it makes sense."

Safar said, "Apparently my son is much more astute than I am, Jooli. Which doesn't surprise me. In not too many years our roles are sure to be reversed. And he will be the teacher and I his willing student. But please enlighten me. So I'll possess the same knowledge as my son."

"I'm only guessing, father," Palimak said, blushing. Safar was his hero and he didn't want to discover any chinks in his armor, much less think of himself as superior in any way.

Once again, the storm's fury lessened. The pounding at the shutters became a faint, tap, tap, tap.

Safar chuckled. "Let's see how good a guess it was, son," he said. "Go on, Jooli. Please explain."

Jooli nodded. "Gladly. I've been waiting for the right moment and it's finally here. However, first I need to tell you a little about myself. So, if you'll forgive a rather lengthy approach . . ."

"We have all the time in the world, Jooli," Safar said. Then he grimaced, rueful. "Although that might not be as long as we wished."

"I know something about that, too," Jooli said. "The gods asleep. The Demon Moon. Hadin. The end of the world."

As if on cue one of the shutters came loose, crashing back and forth with the wind. Palimak jumped up to fix it back into place.

Safar acted as if nothing had happened to disturb them. "This is getting more and more interesting," he said mildly. "Go on."

Without preamble, Jooli said, "I am the oldest of my father's children. I am also the best warrior in Hunan. This is no boast, merely a statement of what is so. I have natural abilities, plus I've trained long and hard at the art of warfare. As you've no doubt noticed, in Syrapis a leader must be a noteworthy warrior, or she wouldn't be able to hold her kingdom much past the coronation.

"Regardless, in my view I am the rightful successor to the throne of Hunan. There is no law in our land forbidding a woman ruler, so my claim to the crown is certainly not without merit."

The wind took on a sighing note, whispering many sad things. And Leiria murmured, "But your father is reluctant."

Jooli laughed, not without bitterness. "When it comes to my father," she said, "*reluctant* is such a mild term. 'Over my dead body' is more the way he puts it. Although lately he's dropped that phrase. Imagining, I suppose, that I might take him up on it. Anyway, he's done his best over the years to marry me off to one prince or another. Hoping to get me out of the way and make a key alliance to boot.

"He's also tossed me a royal bone by giving me the title of 'Queen,' and a few hundred acres of farmland to rule so I can have an independent income and satisfy my cravings for leadership by ordering the cows and harvest crews about."

Outside, there was a lull in the storm and everything became very quiet.

Safar frowned, then said, "You don't seem the sort of person to be ruled by overweening ambition. Do you really want the crown of Hunan so badly you'd take up with your father's enemies? Or is there another, much deeper reason?"

Jooli gave him a long look. Then she hoisted her wine cup, drained it, hooked the jug and refilled her cup. She gave a long sigh.

"Yes, Safar Timura," she said, "I do have a deeper reason. And as it so happens, I'm driven by the same foolish desires as you. In short, I want to wake up the gods and save the world!"

Safar nodded, then said, "Good. Now, tell us about the mural."

Palimak gaped in surprise. Leiria stifled laughter when she saw his expression. The poor boy had really believed he had guessed something his father was too slow to realize. She didn't say anything to him, but she thought, It's time you understood, little one, that Safar always knows! Then a sad caveat came to her: Except when it's a personal matter. When it came to love, Safar was as ignorant as a splay-footed plowboy.

Jooli said, "Yes, the mural. I've just about reached that point in my story. But one moment more, please."

"You can have as many moments as you desire," Safar said.

"You can't fully understand," Jooli said, "until I tell you about my grandmother — Queen Clayre. Queen Mother Clayre, to be more exact."

The lull ended with a loud crash of lightning, followed by a torrent of rain that slammed into the old stone fortress, shaking it.

Jooli glanced at the trembling shutters, then back at Safar. She said, "My grandmother's a witch, as I told Leiria before — rather alarmingly when all those damned rats appeared. And I've made no secret that I'm a witch as well."

She smiled first at Safar, then at Palimak. "As if I could keep such a thing from two such powerful wizards."

Palimak blushed. Safar's face remained a bland, albeit friendly shield. Leiria's eyes narrowed. The flattery wasn't called for. Then her features relaxed as she realized that Jooli was nervous. The female artifice was only reflexive. She thought, As if you haven't foolishly reacted that way yourself upon occasion! Then she saw Jooli's eyes darken as she realized her error and gave herself a mental kick. It made her like the woman even more.

The slip seemed to make Jooli concentrate more on her tale. She bowed her head, speaking so low her words could barely be heard over the storm.

She said, "At one time my grandmother was training me to take her place as Queen Witch of Hunan. I was about five years old when she first brought me into her chamber. It was shortly after my mother died."

Jooli stopped speaking for a moment. Then she shook her head, saying, "I've often thought she poisoned my mother. But that's another tale that has nothing to do with what has occurred since."

Safar gently picked up her wine cup and gave it to Jooli to drink. She sipped the wine, nodded her thanks, and continued.

"My grandmother introduced me to all the mysteries over the next few years," she said. "I was a good little girl who never gave her elders cause for concern. I did what I was told, when I was told. And then one day I saw the mural."

She gestured, indicating the painting on the wall. "Oh, I'd seen it before, of course. Even wondered about it. It's such a romantic scene. A noble king. Warrior daughters at his side. Marching off to do battle against what you instinctively knew was a very powerful and evil enemy. I was especially struck by the dark-skinned princess who led the procession. She was so beautiful, so brave, on that great black mare!

"I made up heroic little stories about her in my mind, substituting myself in her place. Once I asked grandmother about the mural, but she became very angry and said I was asking too many stupid questions. That it was just a painting, nothing more.

"But on this particular day I was alone in her chambers. She was off about some sort of business, I don't recall what. And as I gazed at the mural I started thinking that it couldn't be just a painting. It had to have some special meaning. I got up and went into the hallway, where there were other murals. They're still there, as a matter of fact. And they are frightening things! Ugly things! You've never seen them, but if you had you'd know what I mean when I say they look like they were created by some devil from the hells.

"I learned later that this description wasn't so far off the mark. The originals were done long ago by a great artist — a wizard — in the employ of that ancient king." She motioned at the golden-mailed king in the mural.

"But my grandmother used those murals for her own purposes," Jooli continued, voice harsh. "At one time they were all beautiful pastorals that lifted the spirit. But she painted over portions of them, inserting nightmarish, sinful scenes. Despicable things. They make me ill just thinking of them. And then she used the altered murals to create black spells against her enemies. I learned later that her bargain with Charize, the monster queen, made all this possible.

"For some reason, she never touched the mural that now sits in this room. I don't know why. But I think she's afraid of it."

Safar asked, "Can you tell us anything about the people depicted in the mural?"

Jooli smiled. "I certainly can. In fact, I met the dark woman. She is a creature of the mural. It was she who told me about you and your holy mission. She bade me to wait for your appearance in Syrapis. And to do everything I could to ensure that your mission is successful."

Safar was stunned. "You mean she only exists in that painting?"

"Quite so. Now, at any rate," Jooli said. "She and her family lived hundreds of years ago. They were rulers of Syrapis when Lord Asper arrived here from Hadin. They watched over him while he labored over his books, seeking an answer to the disaster that would someday overtake the world. And when he died, they created the idol and the death chamber you found his coffin in. Asper made the coffin with his own hands when he knew his death was near."

"What about Queen Charize?" Palimak asked. "How did she and her monsters end up ruling Asper's chamber?"

"My grandmother said that she was Asper's Favorite. He came upon her in Hadin and although she was evil, her magic was so strong that he used her to help cast his most difficult spells. Before he died, he enslaved her and set her to guard his tomb.

"But over much time she managed to break his spell and free herself. There are some who say that Charize is responsible for all the warfare in Syrapis. That she and her minions set human against human to feed on our misery."

Jooli shrugged. "I don't know how true that is," she said. "In my experience people don't need that much of a reason to kill one another. I do know this, however. In order to live and create her sisters she required someone in the outside world to help her. And, in recent years, my grandmother was that person."

Palimak grinned, demon eyes glittering in delight. "Now that Charize is dead," he said, "it'll make it damned hard for your grandmother."

Safar sighed. "Maybe so," he said. But his tone was doubtful.

He was thinking of the new being Queen Clayre could now rely upon. The creature that was Kalasariz who dwelt in King Rhodes. He didn't say anything, because he was loath to tell Jooli what Rhodes had become. Even though she disliked him — perhaps even hated him — it would be a difficult thing for a daughter to bear.

He decided to wait for a more appropriate time. The tale Jooli was telling was already having a great effect on her. Her features had become pale and drawn, eyes sitting in bruised hollows. He changed the subject.

"What of the Spirit Rider?" he asked. "Could you tell us of your meeting with her?"

Jooli nodded. She was growing weary. Not so much because of the talk, but because of all the memories that had come flooding back as she spoke to her new friends.

Somewhere far off a dog howled and she realized the storm had finally ended. Silence cloaked the room as she gathered her strength.

And then she drank down her wine and began the tale . . .

21

JOOLI'S SONG

She was a lonely girl of less than ten years. Her limbs were long and lanky like a young colt's, and she could scamper up a tree like a mountain goat. And she could run like the winds, sprinting past even the fastest boys in the Kingdom of Hunan.

Jooli was full of fire and curiosity, but inside there was an emptiness created by the loss of her mother. An emptiness made deeper and sadder still because of her father's neglect. And so it was that when her grandmother took Jooli under her wing, at first she went gladly. Looking for love even more than the knowledge of the world that she so craved.

The Queen Mother's chambers were a frightening place for a child. The light was dim and wavery, with guttering torches sending off a greasy smoke. There were little scratching and squeaking noises coming from the moving shadows produced by the light.

Shelves were lined with books marked with strange witch's symbols — red scorpions, fanged snakes and pinched monster's faces. Glass jars filled with preserved animals and human body parts added to the grave-like feeling of the chilly room. And there was the heavy scent of sorcerous ozone, mixed with the torch smoke and heady incense that left the metallic taste of old blood in her mouth.

But she put a brave face on it, going eagerly to her grandmother's chambers every time she was called. Doing her best to ignore the fearsome atmosphere. Paying close attention to all her grandmother taught her.

Although Clayre was a cold, unfeeling woman, the child simply thought this was merely her grandmother's way and believed in her heart that she was loved. Why else would the Queen Mother pay so much attention to her?

Jooli was thrilled by the gradual exploration of her magical side. Her grandmother said she had talents no one else in Hunan had — other than Clayre, of course. And she boasted that there were few people in all Syrapis who could perform any magic — and most of them were very weak.

Only Clayre and Jooli were so blessed, the queen mother said. She said it was a talent passed by blood through the women of their family, but always skipping a generation. Clayre's own daughter — dead many years now — never displayed magical abilities. And neither Clayre's mother. It was Clayre's own grandmother who had introduced her to the witching arts.

She said that although there were years between them, she and Jooli were like sisters. "Sisters of the Oath," as she put it. Exactly what oath, she didn't explain. Then one day her grandmother summoned her and put her to the test.

Clayre placed a small doll on the table. It was dressed in the clothes of a courtier and had a pinched little face carved from an apple that had then been dried in an oven, painted and lacquered.

Jooli giggled when she examined the face and realized it was modeled after her father's cranky old Grand Wazier. King Rhodes thought highly of the man — he was as parsimonious as the king and always looking for ways to add coin to the royal treasury. Lately, he'd complained of the "unwarranted expenditures" that went to pay for the Queen Mother's care.

Clayre loved her luxuries and was constantly adding to her collection of jewels and fine clothing. Goat's milk and expensive oils were used in her bath. The purest henna and rarest powders for her make-up. These things, along with the high prices for her witch's potions, had caused the Wazier to question the money she spent. Her son fervently supported the old man.

"Why, I could pay for a month's rations for a battalion with what it costs to keep you, mother," he'd said.

Jooli'd heard her grandmother complain about the Wazier, but hadn't thought about the controversy very much. She only knew the old courtier didn't seem to like children and complained bitterly when she got underfoot. Once she'd dropped a sweetmeat on the floor, getting it grimy. So she'd thrown it away. The Wazier had seen this and had berated her for wasting food. He'd lectured her for a half-turn of the glass, making her cry.

And so when she saw the doll with the Wazier's funny face and her grandmother had said they were going to play a little joke on him, she'd giggled and eagerly agreed to help.

"We're going to try something very special together, dear," Clayre said, drawing the child to her magical table. "But I'll need you to concentrate with me, ever so hard. Can you do that for your grandmother, my sweet?"

Jooli agreed without hesitation. Her grandmother's voice was so gentle, so loving, she thought she'd never been so happy since her mother died.

On the table was a toy executioner's platform, complete with a masked doll bearing an ax, and a little bench for the victim to kneel over and expose his neck.

This didn't bother Jooli very much. Executions were quite common in Hunan and there was always a fantastic party atmosphere at them, with treats for the children and puppet shows and all sorts of wondrous things to get the crowds in the mood to witness the evildoer receiving his just punishment.

Jooli clapped her hands in delight. "We're going to give him a pain in the neck!" she crowed. "That's perfect, because that's what he's always calling me."

She frowned. "Although once he said a bad word, instead of 'neck.'"

Clayre smiled and Jooli noticed an odd glitter in her eyes. "That's exactly what we're going to do, my sweet," she said. "Give him a pain in the neck!"

Jooli frowned, suddenly concerned. "But it won't hurt too much, will it?" she asked. "He is pretty old, after all, and maybe that's why he gets so cranky. Maybe his bones hurt or something."

"Don't worry, dear," Clayre said, "it'll only hurt a little bit. And after that — why, he'll never suffer again." She chuckled. "You won't find him so cranky after we play our little trick on him."

Mollified, Jooli helped her grandmother prepare the spell. Following Clayre's directions, she set four gray candles, pebbled with black, around the toy platform. When Jooli lit them with a taper, they gave off a purplish, sweet-smelling smoke.

She sprinkled a white powder up the little steps that led to the executioner's bench. More powder was dribbled on the bench, then smeared on the tiny ax held by the toy executioner. Finally, using a pen dipped in glistening black ink, Clayre had Jooli draw a circle around the Grand Wazier doll's neck.

She got a little of the ink on her fingers and Clayre made her stop and wash them carefully with vinegar before they proceeded.

"Otherwise it will make your fingers burn when we cast the spell," her grandmother explained.

Jooli's eyes widened. "Will it make his neck burn too?" she wanted to know. "I wouldn't want to really, really hurt him, or anything."

"No more than a sunburn, dear," Clayre replied. But she said it a little quickly, although Jooli didn't think about that until later.

When all was ready, Clayre gave Jooli the doll. She told her to pretend it was the real Grand Wazier and to make the doll walk up the steps, then bend over the executioner's bench. Four tiny cuffs fixed to the bench were locked around the doll's hands and feet.

Jooli did as she was told, but after she arranged the doll, Clayre wasn't satisfied, saying, "We need to stretch his neck a bit, dear."

As she spoke, she tugged on the doll's dried apple head, drawing out more of the cloth neck and tucking in the collar of the robe so the inky mark Jooli had made was fully exposed. She told Jooli to focus all her attention on the task at hand. And to repeat everything Clayre said.

Then she sang:

"We are the sisters of Asper,
Sweet Lady, Lady, Lady . . ."

In her high, piping voice, Jooli chanted:

"We are the sisters of Asper,
Sweet Lady, Lady, Lady . . ."

Then Clayre sang:

We guard his tomb, we guard his tomb,
Holy One . . ."

And Jooli repeated:

We guard his tomb, we guard his tomb,
Holy One . . ."

Then the chamber's dim light faded even more until it became quite dark. The golden tiles glowed into life, bathing the executioner's platform in an eerie light. A ghastly face formed on the tiles, floating there as if caught in a watery mirror.

"Welcome, Sister Charize," Queen Clayre intoned.

Jooli was frightened and started to draw away. But Clayre pulled her back.

"Speak with me, child!" she commanded. "Repeat all I say!"

Then Clayre said again, "Welcome, Sister Charize." And she tugged at Jooli's arm to do the same.

Jooli quavered, "Welcome, Sister Charize."

Although she certainly didn't mean it! This horrible creature with its long glistening fangs and scaly face was certainly not welcome anywhere near her, as far as she was concerned.

"We have a boon to ask, dear Sister," Clayre said, tugging once again at Jooli's arm to prompt her.

And so, against her will, Jooli repeated, "We have a boon to ask, dear Sister."

The beast's jaws opened and a voice like rough sand on a washboard said, "Is this the girl we spoke of, Sister Clayre?"

Jooli's racing heart skipped a beat. Was this . . . this . . . Thing! . . . speaking of her?

Then she knew the answer, because her grandmother said, "None other, Sister. She goes by the human name of Jooli."

Red eyes turned on little Jooli, who felt as if they were boring holes into her soul. "And is she ready to take the oath, Sister?" Charize asked in that terrible voice.

"Indeed she is," Clayre replied. "And the boon I ask is her initiation into the Sisterhood." Clayre indicated the toy platform and dolls. "All is prepared. We only need your assistance to complete the spell."

There was a silence as the face floated over the scene. Then Charize chuckled. It was an awful sound.

She said, "Ah, I see. The king's Grand Wazier. What a nasty little man. I'd be pleased to grant your boon and welcome the girl into the Sisterhood. Proceed."

"Thank you, Sister Charize," Clayre said. Then to Jooli: "Concentrate, my sweet. And we'll all cast the spell together."

And she sang:

"O, join us together who now are apart.
Make us an arrow aimed for his heart.
We are his pain, we are his hot blood.
Spilled on the ground in a great raging flood!"

Charize joined in, rasping:

". . . O, join us together who now are apart.
Make us an arrow aimed for his heart . . ."

Trembling, Jooli piped in her clear voice:

". . . We are his pain, we are his hot blood.
Spilled on the ground in a great raging flood!"

To Jooli's horror the dolls on the bench suddenly came alive. The wazier doll screaming and struggling against his bonds. The executioner doll running forward, lifting his blade high to strike. And *whack!*, the head came off! And the white powder was transformed into a torrent of blood flowing across the platform and down the steps.

Jooli shrieked in horror. She broke away from her grandmother and bolted from the room, Clayre angrily calling after her to come back. But Jooli closed her ears to her grandmother's commands and ran to her room where she hid under her bed all day and all night.

The next morning, Clayre sent a burly slave to fetch her. Jooli protested, but it was no use. The slave grabbed her by the feet and dragged her out from under the bed. On the way to Clayre's chambers they passed the Grand Wazier's room. To Jooli's relief, she heard him groaning in pain. At least he was alive! She got a peek into the room and saw him sprawled on his bed, a bloody bandage around his throat. Puzzled doctors were in attendance.

As she was rushed down the stairs to her grandmother's sanctum, the ghastly murals on the walls took on new meaning to Jooli and she was even more terrified when she entered the chambers. Thankfully, her grandmother was absent — off on some errand. The slave told her to sit and wait Clayre's return. He disappeared up the stairs, leaving her alone. Suddenly, she gripped her neck — wondering if her grandmother was making a Jooli doll. Was her head about to be lopped off?

Just then, a soft, sweet voice called to her: "Joo-lii! Joo-lii!"

Startled, she looked around. But there was no one else in the room.

Again: "Joo-lii! Joo-lii!"

There! It came from behind her. She turned, but all she could see was the beautiful mural of the King and his warrior daughters. Then a light glittered in the armor of one of the princesses. It was the dark-skinned woman on the black mare! Jooli leaned closer. Her eyes widened and she saw the woman's hand move. The princess of the mural was waving to her! Beckoning?

And she saw the lips move and heard: "Come to us, Jooli!"

The child stretched out her hand. There was a gentle tingling sensation and suddenly there was a roaring in her ears. The ground heaved under her, but she wasn't afraid. And then she was flying through the air, her arms around the narrow waist of the Sprit Rider. The wind blasting in her face as they rode the black mare through a starry sky.

She peered around the Spirit Rider's shoulder. Far away she saw a glorious golden city. The city of the mural: The ancient Kingdom of Hunan!

Jooli lived there for a year. It was the happiest year of her life.

She paused in the telling of her tale. A mischievous smile graced her lips.

"While I was there," she said, "they taught me a song. They called it the 'Song of Safar Timura.' Would you like to hear it?"

Everyone said they would. And this was the song she sang, in a high clear voice that made her audience laugh and cry and sigh:

Colored lights play, smoky mist swirling low;
Two indistinct figures catch spotlight's glow,
Bow in the center as breathless crowd waits
For the fates to decree, On with the Show!

On gyring wheel 'neath Kyranian sky
Vessels take shape under artisan's eye.
Master's young son laughs to magic the clay;
'Cross Black Land afar spins circle awry.

In wizard's den on high mountain tor,
Protarus unveiled, mighty conqueror.
Demon-fang casting the perils disclose
That brothers of spirit must stand before.

The road divides, leads to glory or doom
Writ by silver stars and the crimson moon.
One to Walaria, wizardly school'd
By generous caravan master's boon.

Protarus, the bloodier path does take
Crush spirit and flesh, an empire to make.
Victor triumphant, but victim of war
Honor held captive for cruelty's sake.

Spell-magic and wisdom the potter gain,
While dancers of death whirl 'neath burning rain.
Swift thief, young girl, bears a talisman strong
A gift to fight fire with love's brighter flame.

Upon the ages-blackened turtle's dome
The map of journey's danger, fiery home
Of Hadin's mountain; hell of earthly end?
Can valor save what Asper saw to come?

Within, the Favorites sleep, then wake to see
Their master, strong Safar, whose prophecy
Demands they heed Iraj's deadly call
The wizard's vision calls relentlessly.

Which high-born son's path must evil beware,
Child of the mountain or war chieftain's heir?
Both stride with power, yet wisdom's undone;
The gyre off-balance, the gods unaware.

Above! Converge the signs of Khysmet's paths:
Demon moon portends empires' bloody clash,
Sky-borne circus, star-crossed, young wizard bears,
While Hadin's bellows raise the fiery ash.

Iraj, icon of Alissarian
To restore the kingdoms of Two to One
Ensorcels his soul to confound Safar
Can brothers' blood oath be ever undone?

Demons, cold allies, he marches before
By compact with hell, now bound evermore.
The potter's dreams shaped like clay on the wheel
Lie shattered in pieces by the Unholy Four.

Desert sands to mystic Caluz soon lead,
Place of Hantilia's astonishing deed.
Great turtle, apostate, artifice bent,
The wheel of Hadin's malevolence, Heed!

The wolf's stride lengthens, the chase faster make,
Speed sorcery's evil and sword's bright hate
Sharp as the arrow in Nerisa's breast
And will doom be sealed when the gods awake?

Two paths, divergent, 'cross sinister seas
Might alchemy meld to one Destiny.
A race to gain mighty Asper's abode
Syrapis' secrets behind fierce Charize.

Three for the quest to battle Esmir's woe
Banner'd with courage against demon foe
Wizard, warrioress, and magical child
Will only the three be allies enow?

But wait! Now Four! Joins a mysterious queen
Once hostage, once ally, spirit-realm seen;
Her journey now meet, now merge with the One
All to quench Hadin and birth Asper's dream!

Leave mem'ry of past, and future esteem
Soul forfeit if need, the champions deem
To leap to battle, by honor full-armed,
By courage and love, the world to redeem.

And now, tent brightens, the spells lightly fall;
The next act awaits the ringmaster's call.
Biner steps forth, gleaming eye and sly grin:
"Damn everything else, the circus is all!"

22

TRUMPET OF DOOM

Jooli paused at the end of the song, weary from reliving the memories of her youth.

Safar and the others applauded her, which did much to lessen her weariness.

"If you let Biner hear your voice," Safar said, making Jooli blush, "he'll recruit you for the circus and make you a star performer."

When they were settled again, Jooli said, "As I mentioned, the time I spent in that magical kingdom was the happiest year of my life."

She took a long drink of wine to restore her energies. "Actually," she said, correcting herself, "it was only a few minutes in real time. If anything in this world can be called real, that is. But in the spirit world of the mural it was a year. And in that year I was not only healed, but armored against my grandmother's designs."

She shook her head. "I wouldn't have survived if the Spirit Rider hadn't rescued me."

Safar stared at the mural, his mind a meteor shower of thoughts, ideas, questions. Although the mural was only a thin wash of paint on stone, the people portrayed seemed full-bodied and alive. Especially the Spirit Rider, with her haunting beauty and beckoning hand. Posed on the fabulous black mare as if she were about to fly away.

He forced calm on his spirit and turned to Jooli. She was staring at him with an odd look of expectation in her eyes.

"Tell me her name, please," he said.

Jooli nodded, as if she knew he'd ask this. "Princess Alsahna," she said. "And her father's name was King Zaman. The last king to rule all Syrapis. And the grandson of the great Alisarrian."

Safar felt like he'd been hit by a chariot-wheel spanner. "By the gods," he said, "can this be true?"

Jooli started to protest, but he stopped her with a raised hand. "I don't doubt your word, Jooli. Of course it's true. It's only that this revelation makes things so clear, so simple that it . . ."

He let the rest trail off. Excitement building. Then: "Alisarrian was Asper's student, correct?"

"Correct," Jooli said, surprised at Safar's intuition. "His

teachings were the foundation of Alisarrian's greatness. Not only as a general — a conqueror — but as a sorcerer.

"But later, Alisarrian spurned Asper's ideas. King Zaman said this was the reason for the break-up of Alisarrian's kingdom after his death."

Safar boiled with excitement. He'd learned as a schoolboy that Alisarrian's death had led to the bloody human-versus-demon wars in Esmir. And that Lord Asper, the old demon master wizard, had been part of the committee of wizards who ended those wars by creating the Forbidden Desert that divided the two species for centuries. Ended only in Safar's time when the demon king, Manacia, broke the spell and invaded the human lands. Which led, in turn, to the rise and fall of Iraj Protarus. Who worshipped and emulated Alisarrian as if he were a god.

But then Safar came full circle and his excitement ended with a great emotional crash, plunging him into depression.

What did any of this matter? It only confirmed what the histories already hinted at. Of interest to scholars, to be sure. Except in a short time there would be no scholars, much less history for them to ponder.

Jooli said, "It was while I was with Princess Alsahna that I learned about Hadin. About the end of the world. And about you, Safar Timura."

"I noticed she used my name — and many other names familiar to us all in the song she taught you," Safar said.

Jooli nodded. "But it was you she mainly spoke of. The princess said you were the only one who could change the course of history. That someday you would come to Syrapis to learn Lord Asper's secret. And that I was to help you find it."

Palimak snorted. "Which secret?" he said sarcastically. "My father's had me studying Asper's secrets since I was a toddler. Why, the first words I learned to read were from the Book of Asper. He might have been a mighty wizard and all. But he makes everything so mysterious that there's literally thousands of secrets. And it's not even that big a book!"

Safar smiled, remembering Palimak's long-ago complaint that the world of magic was unnecessarily vague and complicated.

"If I ever write a Book of Palimak," the young man said, echoing Safar's thoughts, "every word will be as plain as the nose on your face. And it won't be written in poetry, that's for certain. Why, I'll bet Asper spent more time and energy looking for a rhyme than he did putting down his thoughts."

"You could very well be right, son," Safar said fondly. "I've often thought the same thing, especially when studying Asper. Whose words are murky, to say the least. The only thing is, poetry does reduce a complicated thought into something more manageable. And as for magic, verse helps focus your mind on the spell."

"If you two don't stop it, I'm going to scream!" Leiria broke in, disgusted. "Debating the merits of verse in magic isn't going to get us anywhere. Except dead from boredom!"

She pointed at Jooli. "The woman just told you something that to my poor, dull, soldierly mind is pretty damned important. So ask her, please! What secret was she supposed to help you find?"

Jooli rose. "It's easier to show you than tell you," she said.

She went to the huge coffin of Asper, beckoning the others to join her. She positioned them around the coffin: Safar at the carved head, Palimak at the feet, herself and Leiria on either side.

Jooli grinned at Palimak. "I'm afraid you're going to have to put up with a little more murky poetry," she teased.

Palimak only nodded. He could feel the magic radiating from the coffin. But it was a very strange sort of magic — whether for good or ill, he couldn't say.

Safar had a different reaction to the magic. To him it seemed amazingly familiar — as if he'd come upon his own footprints in the snow.

He studied the carved features of Asper. They seemed almost lifelike — the long demon fangs, pointed ears, heavy horn over a much-wrinkled brow. Deep-set eyes made of rare red gems that glittered in the torchlight. He seemed so incredibly wise and sad — contemplating a grim future.

Then Jooli raised her hands to cast the spell and Safar bent closer, eager to see what happened next.

Jooli chanted:

"The Gods dream awhile of me and thee:
Demon and Man alike in our Hate.
Come sound the trumpet for all to see:
Darkness and Light, twin rulers of Fate!"

Safar heard a long, deep sigh, like that of an old ghost set free of his bonds. The torchlight dimmed, then flared anew — much brighter than before. Asper's gemstone eyes became two ruby-red spears of light.

Jooli leaned forward, passing her hand through the beams, chanting:

> *"Yes, come sound the trumpet*
> *Before the Castle of Fate.*
> *And there you'll find Asper*
> *At Hadin's last gate!"*

Safar heard a sound like the tumblers of a enormous lock turning over. Then a click! And the red beams vanished and the carved jaws gaped wide. For a brief moment Safar thought the demon had come alive and was about to speak. Then he saw that the open mouth offered a passageway.

He started to reach, then hesitated — looking up at Jooli.

She nodded, encouraging him. "Go ahead. Reach inside."

Safar slipped his hand into the opening, felt something there, and drew it out. Puzzled, he held the object up for all to see.

It was some sort of seashell. About eighteen inches long, spiraling from its finger-wide tip to its bell-shaped opening. Its colors were various shades of orange and white, all very glossy as if the shell had been fired in a pottery kiln. He thumped it experimentally and found that it was hollow.

Then he realized the shell was very much like the conch shell horns the musicians played in Hadin. Except long and narrow like a . . .

"A kind of trumpet?" he asked Jooli. "Like the one in the spell verse?"

"The very same," Jooli replied.

Safar started to raise it to his lips, then hesitated. "Shall I try it?" he asked.

"I don't see why not," Jooli said. Then she laughed. "I've been waiting for this moment since I was a girl at Princess Alsahna's knee!"

In his hiding place, Iraj burned with curiosity. He was anxious to get on with whatever was going to happen next.

Palimak caught a whiff of strangeness. He sniffed the atmosphere with his magical senses, but couldn't trace the source. It must be the coffin, he thought. And turned his attention back to his father, who was lifting the shell trumpet to his lips.

Safar blew and the most wondrous music issued forth. It was as if a whole orchestra of musicians were playing — pipes and horns and silver-stringed lyres. With a single wild wailing trumpet swooping above and through and below all the notes like a glad hawk set free on the winds after a long period of captivity.

On the wall the mural shimmered. Then not only the painting but the entire wall dissolved. Except instead of looking out on a Syrapian night, they were gazing across bright rolling seas.

A tall ship danced over the waves, graceful sails billowing in a balmy breeze. Playful dolphins and flying fishes leaped high in its wake, making the whole a joyous scene. The ship flew a flag bearing the symbol of Asper: a twin-headed serpent, borne on jagged-edged wings. And soaring above it all was the unmistakable silhouette of the circus airship, suspended beneath its two painted balloons.

Safar lowered the shell trumpet, but the music kept playing — growing more haunting, more compelling. Each note beckoning them to follow.

Palimak saw familiar figures moving about the tall ship's bridge.

"Look, father!" he said in awestruck tones. "Don't you recognize them?"

"It's us!" Safar said.

Jooli pointed at a slender figure in armor. "I'm there, too," she said, pleased and amazed at the same time.

"I wonder where we're going?" Leiria marveled.

Safar indicated the red moon hanging low on the horizon. "There's only one course that puts the Demon Moon so low," he said. "We're bound for Hadin."

Leiria was startled at how grim he sounded. She looked at him. His face was pale, blue eyes hollowed and bruised.

Then the scene vanished to be replaced by the hard, blank surface of the fortress wall. And the mural of the Spirit Rider was gone.

Safar turned to them, slowly straightening his shoulders as if steadying a weighty burden. "Oh, well," he said, smiling brightly. "It's not as if I didn't know that I had to go back."

Palimak caught the worry hiding beneath the false surface of cheer. "It'll be different this time, father," he said. "You were in some kind of spellworld before. It's wasn't the real Hadin."

"I know," Safar said. But he was shaking his head slowly, uneasy.

"Maybe we're looking at this the wrong way," Leiria offered.

The world and everything in it could go to the Hells, as far as she was concerned. She'd do anything to spare Safar further agonies.

"How do we know that wasn't a false vision? Something concocted by Charize and her monsters?"

"It wasn't," Safar said. "To begin with, Charize had nothing to do with the mural. That's clearly Asper's work. Just as it was clearly Lord Asper's intent for Princess Alsahna — whom I've always thought of as the 'Spirit Rider' — to help me discover a way to keep the world from destroying itself.

"As you can plainly see there is no sense denying — or fighting — our fate." He drew in a long breath. "We must go to Hadin. And as quickly as possible."

Palimak became frightened. Not for himself, but for his father. Suddenly he saw him as a driven, tragic character. Doom was written all over his features.

"Let's not be so hasty, father," he said. "I think we ought to look into this some more. You know . . . Study the auguries . . . Reread the Book of Asper. After all, Hadin is on the other side of the world! Thirteen thousand miles away. We need to look for other answers before we decide to do something so drastic."

"Palimak's right," Leiria said. "We can't just abandon everything and everybody in Syrapis. Think of your family and friends. You brought them so far. And now you're going to leave them again."

Desperate, she turned to Jooli. "Tell him," she said. "Tell him there must be another way. Another answer!"

Jooli gave a sad shrug. She quite liked Leiria and Palimak and was loath to disappoint them. But what could she do?

"Princess Alsahna was quite clear," she replied. "The only one who can decide is Safar Timura."

At that moment the floor heaved under them. The earth shock was so great that they were hurled flat.

It was like riding a giant bucking horse and they found themselves clinging to any surface they could dig their nails into.

Objects crashed to the ground, shattering. Plaster and stone rained around their ears.

Outside, people and animals panicked, screaming and bellowing in fear.

Then, as suddenly as it had begun, the earthquake ended. And all was still and all was silent as they braced for another shock.

Finally, they realized it was over.

Safar was the first to his feet. He looked around, surveying the damage. Furniture smashed, stone walls cracked, the floor split right down the middle.

"There's your answer," he said. "We go to Hadin!"

In his hiding place, Iraj knew fear. He'd just escaped from that awful place. He fought for calm.

Safar was right. There was no other choice: they had to return to Hadin.

Part Three

Bound for Hadinland

23

THE CRY OF THE TURTLE

Safar stood on the bridge of the tall ship watching the green rolling seas froth into white spume as they parted before the wooden prow. Hungry birds followed in their wake, filling the air with their gleeful cries as they swooped on fish stunned by the ship's swift passage.

From above he could hear Biner shouting orders to the airship crew. And — more faintly — the roar of the magical engines that kept the balloons taut and the airship aloft. He smiled, remembering just how much fun it was to be a member of the airship's crew. Everyone would be rushing to perform the tasks Biner set, laughing and joking with one another as they sailed through azure skies.

The atmosphere would be the direct opposite of what he'd experienced thus far on the tall ship. The vessel — named the *Nepenthe* — was the best that Coralean could provide from the mercenary fleet. Although Safar was no sailor, it certainly seemed sound enough.

But the crew was sullen, the captain harsh and when orders were given the sailors were slow to act. To Safar they also seemed deliberately clumsy — fouling lines, tangling sails and generally making an unnecessary mess of things.

Sooner or later he would have to do something about this state of affairs. However, at the moment he was content just to get the voyage started. He consoled himself, thinking he had thirteen thousand or more miles to bend matters — and the captain — to his will.

Some consolation! By the gods, if there were any other choice he would've taken it. To begin with, he dreaded the voyage's goal. Of all the becursed lands in this becursed world, Hadin was the last place he wanted to visit. Secondly, as far as he knew such a voyage had only been accomplished once before: by Lord Asper many centuries ago when he'd journeyed to Hadin and back again.

No wonder the captain was moody and the sailors unwilling. Safar was paying them handsomely — many times more than they'd ever received before in their seafaring careers. He'd also promised rich bonuses when the voyage was complete.

However, these men had never strayed far from Esmir. Venturing only to the not-so-distant islands, such as Syrapis. They were ignorant men, had sometimes even worked as pirates, and had little knowledge of the wider world. But, ignorant as they were, in their many voyages they'd experienced first-hand what the scholars of Esmir had only speculated about.

Safar watched a great sea turtle swim frantically away from the path of the ship. It was a huge creature — big enough to seat a large man on its broad shell. Possibly a hundred years or more in age.

He smiled ruefully, thinking this was how all but the wisest scholars and priests saw the world they lived in. According to Esmirian myth, the world was borne on the back of a sea-turtle god. In turn, the continents that made up the world were carried by lesser turtle gods.

There were four such continents — confirmed in Asper's voyages. First there was Esmir — which in the language of the ancients simply meant The Land, or The Earth. Then Aroborus, the place of the forests. The third continent was Raptor, the land of the birds. A place they wouldn't visit until their return voyage.

Last of all was Hadin, land of the fires: a continent shattered by the forces at work there into a vast island chain that crouched at the bottom of the world.

The place, Asper said, where he waited at "Hadin's last gate."

Of course, Safar didn't think Asper would actually be waiting there. The old demon had been dead for a thousand years, after all.

Nor was Safar certain that he'd truly find a solution to the world's ills once he reached Hadin.

However, despite his uncertainties Safar was driven to act. His entire adult life had been devoted to this mission. And many had suffered and died as a result of his obsession to halt the poisonous cloud that was slowly killing the world.

And he had no doubt many more would meet similar fates before he was through.

To accomplish his goal, Asper said Safar would have to awaken the gods. Exactly what this meant, or how he'd go about it, Safar was far from certain. He'd have to wait until he arrived in Hadin to find out.

Safar wondered how his people would fare during his absence. Even if he were successful it was unlikely he'd survive the experience and return to Syrapis to find out. Would they prosper? Would they find happiness again? The happiness lost to them when he'd led them from their ancestral home, Kyrania — the Valley of the Clouds.

As he pondered these unanswerable questions his mind floated back to the last night he'd spent with his family, friends and fellow Kyranians.

Safar had invited all the Kyranians to a farewell feast, although only his closest confidants were aware of its purpose.

Long tables were set up in the main courtyard of the mountain fortress. Colorful lanterns were hung all around giving everything a cheerful atmosphere. The tables were heaped with every dish and delicacy he could manage to assemble in the short time he'd had to prepare. And the finest Timura jugs were set out, full of wine and beer and cold goat's milk sweetened with honey — this last for the children.

First Safar put on a little show to entertain the Kyranians and brighten their spirits. With the help of Biner and the other circus folk he performed many astounding acrobatic feats, spiced with glittering displays of magic.

Biner and Arlain put on their clown costumes and wowed the crowd with their most humorous antics. Safar also performed horse tricks with Khysmet, showing off the stallion's uncanny abilities.

Finally, when he thought the moment right, he asked them all to gather round for an announcement. There were more than a thousand Kyranians, so he had to stand on a table for all to see. He cracked a magical amplifying pellet so that no one would miss his words.

"My dear friends," he said, "the time has come to speak to you on a matter of the utmost importance."

Immediately his mother and sisters burst into tears. His father, face pale, straightened his shoulders and tried to look stoic. But it was hopeless, for several tears could be seen running down his cheeks. Safar's family had been told of his plans and could no longer hold back their emotions.

Everyone looked at them, a sense of dread chilling the air.

"I stand here before you with a grieving heart," Safar said. "I've known all of you my entire life. And we have been through so much together — good times and ill. So it is with great sadness and much reluctance that I now tell you that I must take my leave.

"Perhaps forever."

There was a stunned silence. Followed by shouts of, "No, Safar! It can't be! Stay with us! We love you, Safar! We love you!"

Safar bowed his head, letting the outpour flow over him until it was spent.

"Thank you, my friends," he said, eyes glistening with barely checked emotion. "But you must understand this isn't something I want to do. When I was a boy herding the village flock through the passes of the Gods' Divide I was given a sacred trust. And I cannot refuse what I have been called to do."

Foron leaped onto the table with him. "Please, Safar," he said. "You must listen to us. You are a great man. Still, you are only a man. You cannot prevent what the gods desire. Forget the outside world. Remain with us."

He made a sweeping gesture that took in the fortress and the mountains beyond. "This is a paradise, Safar. Just as you promised back in Kyrania. We had to fight for it, to be sure. But this is a wonderful place.

"Look about you, my friend. Look at all the plenty. There are fish in the sea begging to be netted. Forests full of game, rich earth eager for seed and fat herds of goats to be milked or slaughtered. And the mountain air is so clear and clean and sweet it's like drinking wine when you breathe."

"All you say is true," Safar replied. "But there are forces at work that will soon end this paradise. It will be destroyed, just as Kyrania was destroyed."

Foron shook his head. "No one doubts your wisdom, Safar," he said. "But in this one thing I must tell you that you are wrong. I can't believe it's necessary for you to leave us in order to fight whatever evil it is that threatens us all. Again, I beg you — remain with us.

"Allow us to fight with you. And if we win, what gladness. And if we lose, so be it. At least we'll all die together."

The crowd took up a chant: "Fight, fight, fight. Fight together!"

Safar let them chant for a time, then raised his hand for silence. When he got it, he said, "I wish with all my heart that what you said was true. But it isn't. Please let me show you so you can see for yourselves."

He gestured for Foron to step down. When he'd done so Safar

said, "First, I beg you to send the children away. What you are about to witness is not a sight for young eyes."

After the children had gone — the babes borne away by the village grannies — Safar called again for everyone's attention. When he had it, he drew the shell trumpet from beneath his cloak. People gaped at it. They'd couldn't imagine the sea creature that had once inhabited the marvelous shell.

As he raised the trumpet to his lips Safar took a deep breath. And then he blew, long and hard.

Once again the sounds of the wondrous magical orchestra filled the air. The Kyranians murmured at the beauty of the music. Then they gasped when they saw the Spirit Rider suddenly appear on the fortress wall, shimmering like an apparition. Then, once again, the mural and the wall dissolved into nothingness.

As the solid stone dissolved there were loud cries of alarm as the Kyranians found themselves looking *down* on a yawning emptiness. It was as if they were at the edge of a sloping cliff and were about to fall into a terrible abyss.

People clutched each other, the tables, the benches — anything to prevent themselves from plunging into the unknown.

Safar himself didn't know what was going to happen next. And when the music and then the scene changed his nails dug into his palms until they bled.

First came the familiar throb of the harvest drums. The conch shells wailing. The rhythmic slap of bare feet on sand and open palms on naked chests. And then they were looking down on the beautiful people of Hadin dancing before the smoking volcano. Their lovely harvest queen leading them in song:

"Her hair is night,
Her lips the moon;
Surrender. Oh, surrender.
Her eyes are stars,
Her heart the sun;
Surrender. Oh, surrender.

Her breasts are honey,
Her sex a rose;
Surrender. Oh, surrender.
Night and moon. Stars and Sun.
Honey and rose;
Lady, oh Lady, surrender.
Surrender. Surrender . . ."

Then the volcano erupted and the Kyranians screamed and turned their eyes away as the island people died their agonizing deaths.

Thankfully, the scene finally dissolved, giving way to a myriad of bubbling lights of many colors. The music took on a playful note and when the living picture realized itself, they saw an old sea turtle swimming comically over and through rolling waves of dark emerald.

There were a few giggles of relief. Some of the younger men and women cheered loudly for the turtle.

Another shift in the music occurred as the turtle came to land and painfully climbed onto a black rocky shore. There were birds everywhere, birds of all possible varieties.

A studious young Kyranian made an educated guess and shouted the name of this country: "It's Raptor — the land of the birds!"

Several scholarly men and women in the crowd murmured agreement.

The instruments took on the musical personalities of birds they saw. Some soaring with haunting cries. Some whistling melodious mating tunes. Some hawking and chattering over rocky nests. And everywhere there was the peep-peep-peep, of new life. Nestlings calling for their mothers and fathers to "feedmeloveme, feedme-loveme, feedmeloveme . . ."

But just as people were smiling, nodding in empathy at this feathered life, a huge green poisonous cloud swept over Raptor. Enormous ghostbats, shrilling and hungry flew out of the cloud. Followed by shrieking reptiles on leather wings.

Once again the Kyranians had to turn away at the killing horror that was visited upon the land.

This time no one laughed when the turtle paddled frantically away.

Now came the music of forests and rivers. Innocent song of clear-flowing creeks, mossy ponds and flowered paths that wound through an exotic jungle. Sweet pipes carried cooling breezes through the branches of every sort of tree imaginable. Wise oaks, foolish pines, swaying willows and forest giants lifting their aged heads into the very clouds.

They saw all the things the music spoke of and more. The scholarly youth proclaimed the land as Aroborus, the place of the forests. But no one had to hear him to know the answer.

Their attention was riveted on the turtle, pausing just off a gentle, sandy beach. Its blunt head and sad eyes lifted to the skies. Then the Kyranians groaned as the poisonous cloud swept in, bearing all the horrors they'd seen before.

The turtle paddled away, so weak she could barely negotiate the slow-rolling seas.

Now the music took on a hard, desperately driving note. Shimmering scene dissolved into shimmering scene, one after the other. But each one had the same subject: the turtle swimming and bobbing on endless seas. Sometimes the water was the deep green that indicated of enormous depths. Sometimes it was bright blue and cheery. And sometimes it was slate-gray and forbidding, with glistening icebergs shot with eerie rainbow colors: layers of purple and pink and green and sapphire-blue.

And always, in the background, was the poisonous cloud sweeping over the endless oceans. Fish turning up white-bellied, dead in its passage. Seals and otters and even enormous whales shriveling to the bone as they breathed their last.

Dead birds plummeting from the sky in such numbers that it seemed the heavens had become an avian graveyard, opening up to rain a torrent of feathered corpses.

Finally, the turtle climbed up on a pebbled beach. It barely had the strength to pull itself from the foaming surf. By now, no one was surprised when they recognized the long, curving shoreline. It was the same place where the Kyranians had landed three years before.

Someone — it wasn't the student — voiced the name in a low, drawn-out hiss: Syrapis!

The turtle struggled, using the last of its strength to dig a shallow nest with its flippers. Then it squatted over the hole and began to lay its eggs. Each one membrane-white, turning to ivory as it met the air and fell into the hole. The shadow of an embryo turtle showed through the thin shell.

The turtle covered the eggs as best she could, shoveling pebbles and sand. Then she lifted her head and saw the killing cloud drifting overhead.

A single tear formed, then fell.

And the turtle died.

The music stopped and the fortress wall re-formed itself. Leaving a silence moist and thick and twisted like the rough blankets kicked off in a nightmare that refuses to end. As before, there was no sign of the mural.

All eyes turned to Safar. He thought he'd never seen such

haunted looks. Such fearful looks. So much begging and pleading for rescue — for deliverance.

Although not one word was said, the silence was like a shout.

Safar said: "Do you see? Do you finally see?"

And they did.

Safar leaned against the rail, the *Nepenthe* leaping and bucking under him as it turned and caught the wind for Hadin.

He saw the turtle paddle over a ten-foot wave. Disappear into its trough, then climb the watery incline on the other side.

A light hand touched his shoulder. It was Leiria's.

She watched the turtle's progress with him for awhile. And just as it became a dot on the horizon she whispered, "Gods speed, my friend. Gods speed!"

24

THE KING'S SPIES

The old goat strained wearily at the harness, hauling a little cart over the broken pavement. Aboard the cart was a legless beggar dressed in the rags of a soldier. Crying, "Baksheesh! Baksheesh for the blessing of the gods!"

The beggar was moving through the tawdry harbor district of the Syrapian town of Xiap, so his pleas for alms went unheeded. A drunken sailor spat at the beggar when he offered his bowl, a single coin rattling against the battered tin sides. A syphilitic whore mocked his injuries, wondering aloud what else he had lost besides his legs.

But the scar-faced beggar ignored the insults, switching the goat's flanks to keep moving. And all the while he cried his plaintive, "Baksheesh! Baksheesh for the blessing of the gods!"

He was making his way along a pot-holed freight road that ran alongside the docks. Out in the Bay of Xiap were twelve of the thirteen tall ships that made up the Kyranian naval force. Several lighters were moving toward the docks, ferrying sailors on liberty to a night of debauchery.

If a suspicious man had been following the beggar he might —

just might — have caught the slight jerk of the wounded veteran's head when he noted the missing ship.

And if that same distrustful fellow had stayed close to the cart after that he'd have seen the beggar switch the goat into a quicker pace. Making straight for a seedy waterfront tavern — still rattling his bowl, still crying his cry, but with much less intensity.

The beggar pulled up in front of the tavern, anchored the goat with a rope tied to a heavy stone and hoisted himself off the cart onto knee stumps padded with leather. He had brawny arms and muscular shoulders, so he hopped up onto the porch with ease — bearing his weight on blocks of wood clutched in each fist.

A moment later he was through the door and swinging himself familiarly along a narrow passage between the rough, ale-stained tables.

The place was nearly empty and he had no trouble picking out his favorite spot. He grabbed the edge of the bar and swung himself up onto a stool with acrobatic agility.

The laconic barkeep grinned at him through blackened stumps of teeth. "Mornin', Tabusir. Bit early for the grog today, ain'tcha?"

"Thirst don't know th' time o' day, Hazan," Tabusir said. "'Sides, th' pickin's been sweeter'n a whore's smile on payday."

He slapped a silver coin on the bar. "Got this one right off," he said. Tabusir shook his purse. Hazan's eyes glittered at the jingling music of minted coin. "Primed th' pump for six, seven more."

Hazan grew friendlier still, filling a tankard to the brim and planting it before Tabusir. "Yer the luckiest beggar I ever seed," he said in most respectful tones. "Most of the lads get nothin' but empty bellies in these parts."

"It's me charmin' ways," Tabusir laughed. "Plus I spin a good yarn 'bout how I lost me legs in th' service of th' good King Rhodes. Fightin' Hanadu's enemies and all."

He shrugged. "Course, it don't hurt that th' yarns be mostly true."

Tabusir rapped the coin on the bar. "Yer lookin' thirsty, too, Hazan. Buy one fer yerself outta this."

Hazan poured one for himself with pleasure. "Yeah, yer sure did yer share, Tabusir," he agreed. "Nobody can deny it. Least, not in front of me, they can't. I'd box their ears for insultin' such a good friend."

Tabusir nodded toward the open door — and the harbor

waters beyond. "Speakin' of th' enemy," he said, "better start waterin' down the ale. Saw a whole mess of 'em headin' out from th' fleet."

Hazan grinned broadly. "Music to a hard-workin' barkeep's ears," he said. "Lads musta got bonuses, or somethin'."

The barkeep shouted up the stairs to wake the whores and bargirls. Then he turned back to Tabusir. "I wouldn't tell this to nobody else, Tabusir," he said in low tones. "But bein' as yer such a good friend . . . I ain't *that* sorry that the Kyranians took over this here port.

"We was sewer-dirt poor when Rhodes was still runnin' things in Xiap. But ever since the blockade, why, times have shined, they have. Paid all the bills, got a nice line of credit with them tight-fists suppliers. And I'm even thinkin' of knockin' out some walls and puttin' in more tables."

He nodded at the stairs, where the women were already tromping down, sleepy-eyed and cranky at being awakened so early. "And some more beds, too. Lots more beds!"

Tabusir pounded the bar and laughed as if Hazan had just told the greatest jest. "Ain't that th' truth," he said. "Only goes to show that sometimes it pays to lose th' war!"

Hazan joined in the laughter. Then they heard the loud voices approaching and a moment later the first wave of enemy sailors burst into the room. And they kept coming. And coming. Until Hazan and the women were hard pressed to keep up with the various desires of all the lusty, thirsty sailors.

Tabusir made himself companionable. Buying drinks, telling jokes, nodding in sympathy when the sailors griped about their officers who overworked them without mercy. Most of them said they preferred their previous lives as pirates. Although they allowed the pay in their former careers wasn't as good — and was certainly more chancy.

"But at least a pirate's a free man," one sailor said. "And he's got a say in how the ship's run. But all we do is drill and train and patrol. Like we was in a *real navy, or somethin'.*"

The name that seemed to come up the most was that of Lord Coralean — a name well-known to Tabusir. And the drunker the sailors got the more they cursed the caravan master. As near as Tabusir could make out, Coralean was generous with his gold, but was entirely too domineering for these men — all criminals who'd fled Coralean's brand of regimentation long ago.

"It's even worse since he cut out the *Nepenthe* and sent it off on some godsforsaken mission," said one sailor, who sounded a little more educated than the others. "Now we have more area to patrol and they're working us like slaves."

Although he didn't show it, Tabusir was most interested in this bit of information. It answered the question about the missing ship. He plied the man with more drink and when the fellow tried to hire the services of a pretty whore and came up short of cash, Tabusir kindly made up the difference.

In return, he learned some things that turned those few coppers into a fat purse of gold.

Miser though he was, King Rhodes did not begrudge a single coin of the eventual reward he gave the handsome young spy. Why, it was easily worth half his treasury.

Although he certainly didn't tell Tabusir that when he stood tall and straight before him, delivering his news.

"I confirmed the report in several other taverns," Your Majesty," Tabusir assured him. "And then I went up the coast to visit some other ports and the story was the same."

Kalasariz stirred in his nesting place within the king. *Press him some more,* the spymaster said to Rhodes. *Safar Timura is a very cunning man. It could be one of his tricks.*

"My only hesitation," Rhodes said to Tabusir, "is that you seem to have come by this information so easily. This isn't just a leak of the Kyranian plans, but a damned big floodgate you have opened."

Tabusir nodded. "That's a good caution, Your Majesty. And I thought the same thing myself. Which is why I visited those other places, instead of coming directly here. The thing is, Majesty, these sailors have no loyalties. They're for hire to the highest bidder. And no matter what their superiors might say, they don't feel beholden to any master or cause."

Kalasariz mental-whispered: *Even so . . .*

Rhodes took the cue. "Even so, the events you described could have been staged for our benefit. And purposely leaked to the sailors."

Tabusir shook his head. "Forgive me, Majesty, but I don't believe so. The story was given out by Lord Coralean that *Nepenthe* was only assigned a different mission — a mission that still involved the blockade. The idea was that the *Nepenthe* would become a roving ship, going wherever the captain thought necessary to stop any supplies or weapons getting through to us.

"However, one of the *Nepenthe*'s crew was badly injured shortly after she took sail. The captain thought the sailor was dying anyway and sent him back."

Kalasariz wasn't satisfied. *That's pretty damned humane, of the captain, don't you think, majesty?*

Rhodes agreed. "Why didn't the captain just let him die?" he asked Tabusir. "And throw the body over the side. That's what I'd do, rather than risk security."

"So would I, Your Majesty," Tabusir said. "But sailors are very superstitious. Especially this lot. I think the captain didn't want to spook the rest of the crew. Or, maybe it was Coralean. In either case, they thought it best to accept the risk. The injured man looked *near* as dead. How could they know he'd have a miraculous — and, for them, unlucky — recovery?

"In fact, Majesty, the man was a malingerer and a coward. First, he hears that the *Nepenthe* is sailing away from Syrapis for parts unknown. Then the Kyranian airship joins them. Coward though he might be, the man's no fool. It's obvious to him that if the Kyranian land forces are willing to part with the airship, something desperate — and quite dangerous — must be in the wind.

"So he injures himself — but not that badly — and takes a potion to give him a fever. So he'd look like he was at death's door. It's an old sailor's trick — well-known to this band of criminals.

"Then the moment he's returned to the fleet he takes an antidote. Recovers. And then goes off with his companions to drink and talk like, well . . . like a drunken sailor, Majesty!"

Kalasariz mental whispered: *Admirable logic!*

Rhodes nodded. "Well done!" he said to Tabusir. He took a heavy, gem-encrusted ring from his finger and gave it to the young spy. "Take this to the Treasurer," he said with a wide smile. "And turn it in for whatever it's worth."

Tabusir was well pleased. He dropped to the floor and knocked his head against the pavement, thanking Rhodes profusely. Then he took his leave.

But just before the guards escorted him out, he turned back.

"Pardon, Majesty, but there's one other thing . . ."

"Yes?" Rhodes asked.

"There's a tavern at the port run by a man named Hazan."

"What of him?" Rhodes wanted to know.

"He's a traitor, Majesty," Tabusir said. "And no friend of Hanadu's."

Rhodes shrugged. "What do I care what a lowly tavern keeper thinks, or does?"

Tabusir nodded. "I understand, Majesty. Only . . . I was thinking . . . if you were to quietly do away with him . . . then substitute one of your spies . . . Well, the tavern is an excellent place for intelligence, Majesty, and . . ."

He let the rest drift away. It was too obvious, in to his mind, and might bore the king.

"That's good advice, young Tabusir," Rhodes said. "I'll think on it." And he waved a hand, dismissing him.

Tabusir bowed low and exited.

Kalasariz said: *I quite like the cut of that fellow. Reminds me of myself when I was just getting started in the spy business.*

Rhodes said, "Should I promote him?"

Yes, yes, Kalasariz replied. *An excellent idea. But we should keep him close to us, hmm? He'd be useful for, shall we say, very personal errands?*

The king thought this excellent advice. Then, armed with Tabusir's intelligence, he descended the long dark stairs to consult his mother.

25

THE IMPS OF FOREBODING

for several weeks all was peaceful aboard the *Nepenthe*. The ocean was calm, the wind a sailor's dream. Brutar, the aptly-named captain of the ship, eased off on his men and the crew became less surly and settled into a somewhat more orderly routine.

The sea teemed with life. They sailed through enormous schools of fish, some of which were quite exotic and so colorful it was like sailing through a magical artist's pallet. Reds and greens and yellows flowing by in an endless stream.

Once they saw a huge crocodile chasing the fish and the colors spurted in all directions as they fled its gaping jaws.

The birds became so used to the *Nepenthe* that they grew quite tame — settling on the rails and mast spars within easy reach. The sailors thought this a good omen and started feeding them by hand.

It became a common but always comical sight to see a burly, scarred ex-pirate cooing over a seahawk as he tenderly fed it bits of biscuit and salt-beef.

Leiria and Jooli kept busy exercising the young Kyranian soldiers who had joined the expedition. Leiria and Palimak had handpicked the lads, being sure to include Renor and Sinch who had proved themselves in many battles and were corporals now. She'd also brought along Sergeant. Hamyr, a grizzled old warrior with much experience to keep all the lads in line.

There'd been so many volunteers that Safar had assembled the entire army to console all those being left behind. And to remind them that the safety of their families and friends was at stake.

Safar suspected the sight of the twenty crack soldiers being put through their paces by the two magnificent warrior women had a little to do with the more friendly attitude of Captain Brutar and his crew.

Not only was the Kyranian equipment the best they'd seen, but the fighting tricks that the Kyranians displayed were enough to give any potential mutineer pause.

And, of course, there was the ever-present airship hovering over the *Nepenthe*. Some of the sailors had witnessed Biner and his circus folk in battle in the past — raining death from the sky — and word soon spread that they were to be feared even more than the soldiers.

Every once in a while Safar trotted Khysmet out of the comfortable stable he'd had specially constructed for him. First he'd have the men create a small arena on the main deck, covering the wood with a thick layer of sand to make the footing easier for the stallion. Then, with the help of Leiria and a few of the soldiers, he'd put on a thrilling one-horse cavalry display.

Weaving and bobbing in the saddle, while wielding a wooden sword. Ducking completely beneath Khysmet and coming up on the other side, like a warrior from the great plains of Esmir. Or rearing the stallion back onto his hind legs and letting him paw the air with his steel-shod hooves as if Khysmet were fighting off attacking infantrymen.

It always made for a good show and further strengthened the wary respect the sailors had for the Kyranians.

After awhile Safar felt confident enough to leave the *Nepenthe* and spend some time with his old friends aboard the airship. Sometimes Palimak came with him, sometimes Leiria or Jooli. But he always made certain that at least two of his commanders remained on the ship to keep watch on the seamen.

Traveling in the airship took him back to the carefree days of his youth when Methydia had rescued him from the desert. He recalled those times while scudding through empty skies like a cloud, watching the world pass beneath his feet. Standing at the rail, looking down at the small, sea-bound figures aboard the *Nepenthe*. Or simply sprawling on the deck, surrounded by friends and talking over old times and adventures.

The circus folk never forgot their true life's purpose, which was entertainment. They were always rehearsing or trying out new tricks. Sometimes Safar would join them and for an hour or so he could imagine he was one of them again. Sailing across Esmir, staging shows at festivals, fairs, small towns . . . wherever the winds took them.

It was only during these impromptu moments that Safar could forget the nature of his mission and the heavy responsibility he had to all those who'd agreed to help him. But more than anything, it made him forget how alone he was.

It was a state of being that was entirely his own fault. Ever since his escape from the spellworld he'd kept a careful emotional distance from everyone. Especially from Palimak and Leiria. He made sure he was never alone with either one of them. He wasn't certain why he found this necessary, except that he was edgy about engaging in talk that went beneath the surface.

Safar could tell they were both a little bewildered by this, although they hadn't had a chance as yet to think on it and be hurt.

Sometimes, late at night, he'd think about his dilemma. Pick and poke at it like a child toying with a small wound.

Oh, he loved them both, there was no doubt about that. And there was nothing he wanted more than to embrace his son and be a father to him once again. Or to draw Leiria close and seek her kisses and warm comfort again as he had so many years before when they had been lovers.

But for some reason he felt awkward with them — no, not awkward. That was definitely the wrong word. What was it then?

And then one night the answer came to him: He felt as if he'd somehow betrayed them.

But why? This made no sense. He'd never done anything to harm them. And would never dream of doing so.

Or would he?

When he thought that, he became fearful. Alien to himself. As if there were another part of him — a part he'd never known about before — that lurked in the shadows . . . waiting. To do what, he couldn't say. Except this other part had no love for Palimak and Leiria. And did not want the best for them.

As soon as he thought that he suddenly became very calm. The strangeness vanished and he drank down his wine, feeling whole again.

Odd, how the mind played tricks on itself when the wine was deep and the hour late.

Other people noted Safar's forced solitude. One of them was Jooli.

She found herself powerfully attracted to this strange man with eyes as blue as the seas they sailed upon. Back at the Kyranian fortress she'd seen the young women approach him, but to no avail.

At the time it had puzzled her that Safar was able to resist their advances. On the other hand, she didn't sense that he preferred men or boys over women.

Not that this would've seemed odd to her. In Syrapis, there were many men who quoted the old saying: "Women are for babies, boys are for pleasure."

Just as there were many women who sang the merry little tune: *"It is our duty, misses,/ to breed a mighty army;/ but we save our best kisses/ for our sisters who bliss us;/ and know all men to be barmy!"*

Since they'd met, Jooli had given Safar no indication of her interest. After all, it would be unseemly for a royal person to express such sentiments — unless she was certain they'd be returned.

However, during the early weeks of the voyage, when she'd consumed more wine than normal, Jooli had found herself pacing the deck outside her stateroom as restless as a she-tiger in season.

She kept thinking how handsome Safar was. The dark, curly hair. The boyish grin. The startling blue eyes beneath mysterious brows. The ripened lips. The strong neck and torso. And those cursedly graceful legs, revealed when he carelessly crossed them and his tunic rode high.

Adding even stronger spice was the magnetic aura of his wizardry. She'd never met anyone who possessed such powers. To embrace a man like that would be like embracing a storm. Witch joined to wizard loin to loin. The images were a sleep-disturbing aphrodisiac of the worst sort.

One night she encountered Leiria on the deck, who was doing

a bit of pacing of her own. Immersed in her own hot-blooded thoughts, Jooli at first didn't recognize the similarities of Leiria's symptoms.

Casual talk soon turned more personal. "I'm not one who impresses easily," Jooli said. "But I've certainly grown to admire Lord Timura."

"There's much to admire," Leiria agreed. "Good people are never disappointed when they come to know him better. You can't go wrong if he gives you his friendship."

Jooli nodded. "I thought as much." She hesitated, then, "I'll be blunt," she said. "Woman to woman, I find it strange that no one shares his bed. Is he some sort of priest who has taken a vow of celibacy?"

Leiria smiled. "Nothing like that," she said.

Jooli frowned. "He has no wife?"

"No."

"No one he's betrothed to?"

"Never in his life."

Jooli hissed with exasperation. "What's wrong, then?" she asked. "Every man of his rank and prestige I've ever known had whole harems to pleasure them."

Leiria's eyes took on a faraway look as she thought about this. Absently, she said, "Safar could have that as well." Then she nodded, as if coming to a conclusion. "But he's definitely a one-woman man."

Then Jooli noticed moisture forming in her friend's eyes when Leiria added, "He found that woman a long time ago. But she died."

"If you mean Methydia," Jooli said, "I've heard that tale from the circus folk. But I also got the idea that although he loved her — and she loved him — it wasn't a permanent thing. An older woman . . . a sorcerous mentor . . . a passing fancy for the two of them."

"That's true," Leiria said. Her voice was soft, memory going back over the years to her first meeting with Safar. Then, so faint Jooli could bare hear her: "Although I didn't realize that in the beginning."

Leiria's eyes hazed over as her mind flashed back to that time so many years ago . . .

* * *

When Leiria awoke she found herself nestled in the crook of Safar's arm. Ever so gently, he was trying to disentangle that arm.

Feeling warm and loving, she smiled at him. Pulling him closer, wanting to give him more of what they'd enjoyed all night. But Safar was tense. She sensed that he felt like he was betraying another.

Safar disengaged from her politely, but firmly. "I have duties to attend to," he said.

At first Leiria pouted. Then she giggled and got up, saying, "I mustn't be selfish and take all your strength, my lord."

Faint as his answering smile was, Leiria loved it. The intensity of her feelings surprised her. Not long before she'd been the warrior concubine of King Protarus. How could she fall in love with another so quickly? Embarrassed, and confused, Leiria arose hastily and pulled on her clothes.

But she couldn't help but comment, letting words flow without guard. "You called out another woman's name in the night," she said.

Leiria made certain her tones were light, but she couldn't hide the hurt. She saw Safar's eyes flicker, sensing her pain. And she loved him all the more because of that.

Safar said, "I'm sorry."

Leiria forced an oh-so-casual shrug. "I don't mind," she said. "It's good that your heart is faithful."

She kept her head down to hide emotion, pretending to concentrate on her harness and weapons. She said, "The king has ordered me to comfort you and guard you with my life."

Then Leiria raised her head and she couldn't help revealing the tears welling in her eyes. "The king orders," she said with deeply felt conviction, "but I do it gladly."

She straightened, every inch a royal warrior. She said, with all the conviction she could muster: "I will guard you and I will be this other woman for you for as long as you like."

Leiria almost took her leave with that. But she found there was one more thing it was important for her to say. "Perhaps someday," she said, desperately fighting to keep her voice from trembling, "It will be my name you speak instead of . . . hers."

And then Leiria fled.

Leiria came back to the present, feeling Jooli's eyes on her. "The woman's name was Nerisa," she said. "Safar loved her and she died tragically."

She shrugged. "What's more tragic is that Safar believes it was his fault. Just as he thinks that he is to blame for Methydia's death."

"Is there any truth to it?" Jooli asked.

"None at all," Leiria said. "But Safar's like that. He takes on guilt faster than anyone I've ever met."

Jooli eyed her. "You're in love with him, too," she said.

Leiria blushed. She said, low, "Yes. We were . . . lovers once."

"And he sent you away," Jooli asked, "because of his guilt?"

Leiria wiped an eye. "No, I sent him away," she said. "Or I left, at any rate. But it was because of his guilt, yes."

"And now you wished you hadn't?" Jooli asked.

Leiria only nodded.

"What are you going to do about it?" Jooli prodded.

Leiria shook her head. "Nothing," she said. "What's done is done."

Jooli put a hand on her shoulder. "Sister," she said, "thank you for keeping me from making a big mistake."

She looked Leiria straight in the eye. "Let me return the favor by giving you a word of advice. You are wrong, sister. You were wrong then and are wrong now. And when the right time comes, be sure to correct the mistake. And you'll both be happier for it."

Then she turned and walked back to her cabin. Leiria stared after her, too surprised to answer.

"Something's wrong with my father," Palimak said.

He was lying on his bunk, arms behind his head, the two Favorites perched on his chest nibbling sugar rolls and cheese.

Gundara belched. "Of course there's something wrong with him," he said. "He's a master, isn't he? Masters always have worms in their brains." Another belch. "Present company not included, of course."

"Speaking of worms," Gundaree said. "I found a nice fat one in a biscuit the other day. It was dee-lish-shous! Better than old cheese."

"You're such a disgusting thing," Gundara sneered. "How can you stand yourself?"

"Worms, worms, worms," Gundaree said.

"Stop it!" Gundara shouted. "You're making me sick!"

"Big fat juicy ones," Gundaree continued. "Worms in your sweets. Worms in your sugar buns. Worms, worms, worms!"

"Shut up, you!"

"Don't you say shut up! You shut up!"

"Shut up, shut up, shut — Ouch!"

Gundara rubbed his backside. Palimak had just given it a

stinging flick with his finger. "Why'd you do that?" he whined. "I wasn't the one talking about worms."

"And I didn't say shut up first! You — ouch!"

Now it was Gundaree's turn to rub his tender behind.

"Do I have your attention now, boys?" Palimak asked.

The twins muttered, "Yes, Little Master," while rubbing their rears.

"Now, I was talking about my father," Palimak said. "There's something wrong, but I can't figure out what it is. Ever since he got back, he's been acting . . . well . . . I don't know . . ." He shrugged . . . "Strange, I guess."

"Seems the same to me," Gundara said.

"Me too," Gundaree agreed.

"Why are you asking *us*, Little Master?" Gundara wanted to know. "We don't care how people act. People are people, which is pretty stupid."

"Yeah," Gundaree said. "People are sometimes stupid one way. Sometimes stupid another. So it's all the same to us. Stupid is stupid. What more is there to know?"

Palimak sighed, trying not to become impatient. He fed them more sugar buns and cheese to shut them up.

"I was talking about magic," he said. "Could something have happened to him in that spellworld that somehow affected him?"

Gundara shrugged. "Sure, it could have," he said. "But it didn't."

"How do you know?" Palimak asked.

Gundaree snickered. "There he goes, just like people. Acting stupid."

"I'm also part demon," Palimak reminded him.

Gundara belched loudly. "What's the difference?" he said. "Stupid with fingers, or stupid with talons. Still stupid."

"All right," Palimak said. "I'm being stupid. But if I'm so stupid, how am I supposed to know unless somebody tells me."

Gundaree giggled. "That's our job," he said. "Stay with you always and tell you when you're being stupid."

"Not that you ever listen," Gundara said. "Lots of times we say, 'Run, Palimak, run! Run for your life!'" He gave Palimak an admonishing look. "But you don't run. And someday they're going to catch you. Mark my words!"

"I'm marking them," Palimak said. "But you still didn't answer my question. Why am I being stupid about my father?"

Gundaree gave a long and weary sigh. "Because, Little

Master," he said, "if something magic was going on we'd *know it, right? And so would you. You're a wizard!"*

"But you're both better at that kind of thing than I am," Palimak said. "Much better. The witch who made you gave you heightened powers so you could protect your masters." He pointed at the door. "Why, if something that meant me harm was walking toward this at cabin this very minute, you'd both know. And warn me. Right?"

Gundara shuddered. "Something's coming, Little Master!" he suddenly squealed.

"Stop fooling around," Palimak said, getting irritated. "I'm serious about this!"

"And so are we!" Gundaree cried. "Look out, Little Master, here it comes!"

And at that moment Palimak heard a heavy body thump against his cabin door.

26

CORALEAN

Coralean was tossing fitfully in his bunk when he heard the scratching at his cabin door.

He'd spent a miserable day both cajoling and threatening his fleet captains, all of whom had been stricken with jealousy over the handsome sums paid to the crew of the *Nepenthe.*

Never mind that none of them had actually wanted to join Safar on his mysterious mission. Never mind that the camel had been let out of the stable and now everyone knew Safar's mission was a dangerous around-the-world voyage with minimal chance of success.

The mere thought that other men were enjoying fatter purses than theirs was more than those pirates could bear. They wanted more money, they wanted it now, or they would lift the blockade on King Rhodes.

In the end, Coralean had used all his persuasive powers to get them to agree upon a lesser sum. Although he'd sweetened the contracts with promises of bonuses for every month spent on station patrolling the Syrapian coast.

The problem was that Coralean was uncertain how successful he'd actually been. Blockade work was incredibly boring, sailing up and down one sector day and night with only occasional breaks for debauchery at free ports such as Xiap.

These men were used to action and now that Syrapis was more or less pacified they were all yearning for their former lives — lives that had been spent plying their trade as thieving cutthroats.

In a way, he didn't blame them. Coralean was just as bored. He was also bitterly disappointed that he couldn't have sailed with Safar. That's where the action would be, no doubt about it. Moreover, he worried that without his skills as a negotiator — won through many years of running caravans across the wilds of Esmir — Safar's chances of success would be much less.

But, he thought, what other choice did his dear friend have? Safar needed wise old Coralean at home in Syrapis commanding the naval fleet that kept the Kyranians safe from the quarrelsome kings and queens of Hunan. Especially that devil Rhodes. That eater of camel dung. That intestinal worm of deceit.

There was no telling when and where Rhodes would strike next.

The caravan master snorted. Just let him try! Coralean, former bull of the land, was now the bull of the sea. If Rhodes launched an attack he wouldn't stand a chance against wily old Coralean!

That thought alone should have sweetened the caravan master's sleep. But he had other, more immediate, frustrations. He ached for the comfort of one his wives. Unfortunately, of the twenty-three women who constantly praised him as husband and lover, he'd only taken Eeda with him on this trip to the fleet.

Eeda was his newest bride. Barely eighteen, she was younger than many of Coralean's fifty children. Lusty and adventurous in bed, Eeda was so sweet-tempered that only one or two of his wives appeared jealous. And he had no doubt he could cure that jealousy when he returned home, bearing gifts of jewels, rich cloth and his ardent attention.

At the moment, however, Coralean wished mightily he hadn't delayed his husbandly duties. Upon his arrival at the fleet, Eeda, poor thing, had taken ill. Apparently she was newly with child and suffered from that sickness of early pregnancy. The result was that she had taken to her bed — leaving Coralean alone in his.

Not that he begrudged her the rest.

Was not Coralean the most understanding of husbands, who

doted on his wives? Did he not see to their every need, even anticipating such niceties as insisting that each one should always have a private room that they could retreat to in times such as these?

Coralean groaned and turned uncomfortably in his bunk. Wishing that sometimes, just sometimes, he wasn't such a mighty bull of a man. Whose powerful seed took root so swiftly and easily that he had to deny himself the most important of all his pleasures.

It was at that moment he heard the scratching at his door.

Ah ha! he thought. It must be Eeda. Her sickness had passed and now she longed for the strong, lusty arms of her bull, her Coralean.

Eagerly he rose from his bunk and went to the door, white sleeping shirt swirling around his massive frame like a tent battered by the desert winds. His hand went to the latch, but just before he threw back the lock he hesitated.

What if it wasn't Eeda? What if it was someone who meant Coralean harm? One of Rhodes' spies, perhaps. It would be difficult, but not impossible, for an assassin to swim or row the two miles from Xiap and slip on board under the cover of night.

How would the assassin know which cabin was Coralean's? Again, a not impossible task. Perhaps the killer had a colleague aboard. These men were pirates, after all. To them, Coralean's life was worth no more than the coin he could keep heaping into their palms.

One of them might not have been completely satisfied with Coralean's bargain and high have decided to get as much as he could all at once by betraying the caravan master to Rhodes' hired killers.

Coralean's lust turned to anger. A man of many enemies — none of which he believed he deserved — he had not lived so long by ignoring his instincts.

Again, he heard the scratching. But this time, instead of sweet Eeda, he imagined a sharp-faced killer with a dagger poised on the other side of the door.

Coralean snatched up his sword and at the same time ripped the door wide. A figure was crouched on the floor and the caravan master's blade was swinging down, ready to split the assassin in two, when he heard a small cry of terror.

"Lord and master!"

It was Eeda!

Coralean caught himself just in time and stayed the blow.

His heart hammering from what he'd almost done, Coralean

leaned down and drew the girl to her feet.

"I'm so sorry, little one," he said, embracing her. "I didn't mean to frighten you. How can you ever forgive your Coralean? Who believed his dearest wife was an assassin at his door."

To his surprise, Eeda hissed, "Silence," and pushed him back into the room. She whirled, softly shut and latched the door, then turned back.

"They're not at the door yet, my lord husband," she whispered. "But they'll be here soon!"

Coralean frowned. Lovely and young as Eeda might be, she was the daughter of a wild Syrapian chieftain. And was well-experienced in matters of the assassin's knife. Taking her word that danger was afoot, he hastily drew on his clothes.

"Who are these men, dear one?" he rumbled. "And how do you know what they plan?"

"Earlier my illness chilled me, lord husband," she said. "And so I had closed the little round window in my cabin. But then I began to feel feverish and longed for fresh air. So I opened the window, hoping there might be a sea breeze. The window was so small, however, that the breeze was faint. So I put my face close to get all the air I could."

The caravan master slipped his boots on. "Go on, dear one," he said. "Tell Coralean what happened next."

"As you know, lord husband," she continued, "my cabin is below the captain's. And his little round window was open too."

"It's called a porthole, dear one," Coralean corrected her. Eeda was very much a landswoman and had no experience with terms of the sea.

Eeda shrugged. "Thank you for instructing me, lord husband," she said.

But her tone was just sharp enough for Coralean to realize she wasn't thanking him at all. The caravan master warmed even more to her. What a sassy wench she was!

"Pray continue, little one," Coralean urged.

Eeda nodded, catching the implication of an apology. Which was as far as Coralean would ever go with one of his wives.

"I heard the captain speaking to some other men," she said. "I don't know who the other men were, but I could tell right off they weren't crewmen. And from their barbaric accents I was positive they were from Hunan."

"Rhodes' men!" Coralean growled, buckling on his sword.

"None other, my lord husband," Eeda said. "My dear lord

father was a prince unsurpassed by any in the number of men he hated. But of all his enemies, he despised King Rhodes the most."

"Another reason for Coralean to admire your father," the caravan master said. "Now, tell me, dear one. Did you hear what these men planned?"

"Yes, lord husband," Eeda replied. "They intend to kill your soldiers. Then capture you and hold you for ransom."

"Let them try," Coralean growled, hand going to the hilt of his sword.

"I believe I said they intend to," Eeda pointed out. Poking at Coralean's manly pride a little harder than perhaps a good wife should. The caravan master frowned, but said nothing. "You should also know that this isn't the only ship in danger. Several of the other captains have also thrown in with Rhodes. Or at least that's what I heard one of the men claim."

Her pretty brow furrowed as she thought of something else. "About that man, lord husband," she said. "The captain used his name. It was Tabusir. Lord Tabusir. And it was my impression that this conspiracy was his idea. And that he has much at stake with King Rhodes to see it's carried out properly."

Just then, Coralean heard bootsteps thundering overhead. Then the wild cries of surprised, brutally awakened soldiers as Tabusir's assassins attacked them in their sleep.

He started to buckle on his armor, preparing to rush up on deck and join the fray. But then he heard the sound of many men coming down the stairway, then along to corridor to his door.

Overhead, the sounds of the fighting had ceased. He could be of no help there.

"Pardon, lord husband," Eeda said.

And he looked down to see that she'd found his battle ax. She pointed at the porthole.

"Perhaps you could make the little round window bigger with this," she said.

"By the gods, woman, you are a wonder!" Coralean roared, not bothering to hide his voice from his enemies.

Eeda blushed and bobbed her head. "Thank you, my lord husband," she said prettily.

Then she drew a dagger from her bodice and stood guard at the door while Coralean hacked at the "little round window" until it was large enough for him to pass through.

The men were breaking down the door when he grabbed Eeda by the waist and hurled her through the enlarged porthole.

And just as the last door plank exploded inward and the men poured into the cabin, Coralean forced his own bulk through the hole and fell into the dark waters below.

As he emerged sputtering to the surface two small, strong hands grabbed him by the collar, pulling him under again.

Coralean kicked up, trying to get a breath, only to be pulled under again.

Finally, he yanked the hands away, grabbed a slim figure about the waist and got his head above water to drag in a shuddering breath.

"Forgive, me lord husband!" Eeda cried. "But I cannot swim."

Above, he could hear men shouting in the cabin from which he'd just escaped. "He's gotten away! After him!"

There was a thunder of boots on the lower deck.

"Take a breath!" Coralean commanded Eeda.

The moment he felt her chest fill with air he dived back under the water, pulling a frantic Eeda with him.

Arrows and spears rained into the water after him.

Coralean held Eeda tight with one arm and kicked deeper. Following the bow, he swam under the ship to emerge on the other side.

"Get on my back," he whispered to Eeda.

Quickly, she did as he directed and he kicked away from the ship, strong arms powering them through the waves.

Behind him he heard the cries of his enemies as they spotted him again. But he ignored them and kept swimming, heading for another ship about a quarter-mile away.

He prayed they wouldn't have sense enough to lower boats and pursue him until it was too late.

His prayers were answered as he heard the splash of arrows falling nearby. They were going for the quick kill, but it was night and the glowing red Demon Moon made the light tricky.

If Dame Fortune smiled they'd keep missing until he was out of range.

She must have had two heads that night, because while one smiled, the other frowned. For although he and Eeda escaped the arrows, they heard the sounds of fighting as they approached the other ship. Obviously, there was no refuge to be found there.

Coralean stopped, treading water, while he looked around to see what his next move ought to be. There was a fire burning on the next closest ship, so he knew that was no good.

Be damned, this meant three ships had gone over to the enemy!

Eeda gently tugged his collar for attention. "Look, lord husband," she whispered. "To the left!"

Coralean paddled around and saw an empty boat bobbing about fifty yards away. Apparently it had broken loose from the ship during the early stages of the fight.

He struck out for it and soon he and Eeda were hauling themselves over the side. Coralean didn't waste any time. Quickly, he found the oars and started rowing. Big muscles bunching and easing, sea-water and kelp streaming from his head and beard as from some burly god arisen from the depths of the ocean.

A half-hour later he was crouched under the broad stern of the *Tegula*, straining to hear what was happening on deck. He heard men talking, but their voices were so low that he couldn't make out whether they were friend or foe. Whoever they were, the boarding nets were in place so they obviously knew something was happening.

Eeda tugged at his sleeve, signaling. Coralean turned to see that the flames aboard the ship that had been on fire had been put out. Now its sails were going up and it was moving away — heading out to sea. The other two ships were already under way and were nearly clear of the bay.

Cursing and so angry he was prepared to face alone whatever foe awaited him aboard the *Tegula*, Coralean started to draw his sword. But the scabbard was empty, the sword lost in the long swim.

Just then, Coralean heard the splash of oars and he lumbered about in the small boat, grabbing up an oar for a weapon. Eeda had her dagger out, ready to fight beside him.

Then a harsh voice called out: "Make one move, you flea-bitten Rhodesman, and you'll be eating my arrow for supper!"

Coralean's heart leaped with joy when he heard the broad accent of a Kyranian soldier.

"We're safe, lord husband!" Eeda cried.

And she threw her arms around him, nearly toppling them both into the sea.

Several hours later, Rhodes and his three ships were standing just off the narrow tip of Syrapis. A stream of boats churned out to meet them. Each carried an oil lamp hoisted on a pole and the effect was like a rare string of pearls from his treasury bobbing on dark waters.

These boats, however, were more valuable to Rhodes than a

whole chest of pearls. For each was loaded with soldiers, weapons and stores enough for many months.

The king strode happily up and down the deck of his command ship — the *Kray*. Within a few hours he'd have five hundred crack troops crammed into his ships. And then he'd be off well before the Kyranians sniffed out his plan.

His only disappointment was that he hadn't been able to capture Coralean. But that didn't matter now. Even that canny old devil wouldn't suspect what Rhodes was up to until it was too late.

When they heard the news of the king's raid on their ships, the Kyranians would think Rhodes was planning an invasion of their territory by sea. They'd scramble as fast as they could to bolster their defenses. And then they'd send all their ships and men down to meet him.

Only to find he wasn't there.

Thinking of their bewildered faces when they finally learned what he was up to, Rhodes couldn't contain a chuckle. By the gods, sometimes it was good to be king!

Within him, Kalasariz shared his pleasure — reveling in the hot juices of victory. *Brilliant, Majesty, brilliant*, he said in that whispered inner voice that Rhodes had become quite at ease with.

And it won't be long, Majesty, Kalasariz added, *before you'll shine with even greater brilliance. When we've cornered and crushed Safar Timura and that fiend he calls his son!*

Rhodes nodded vigorously, oblivious to the nearby Tabusir and his other officers who wondered what the king was doing, muttering and nodding to himself. Was he drunk?

Then Clayre's voice cut through, spoiling the king's good mood. "Son, son! Come at once. I have need of you."

"The old bitch!" Rhodes growled low.

Do not trouble yourself, Majesty, Kalasariz soothed. *Once we have the Timuras, we won't need her anymore.*

And Clayre shouted, "Did you hear me, son? I'm calling you!"

Mood restored, Rhodes chuckled again and started for the Queen Witch's stateroom.

And he cried brightly, "Coming, mother!"

27

CREATURE COMFORTS

"Don't open the door, Little Master!" Gundara whispered.

"It's *definitely* not a good idea!" Gundaree chimed in.

Once again, Palimak heard a heavy thump against his cabin wall.

"What is it?" he asked.

"Something really, really mean," Gundara replied.

"And hungry," Gundaree added. "You forgot to mention that."

"You *always* say that," Gundara sniffed. "Mean things usually are hungry. That's what makes them so mean."

Palimak put a finger to his lips, shushing them. He motioned and the two Favorites leaped up on his shoulders and perched on either side of his head.

He put his ear against the door, listening. Nothing.

No, wait! He thought he could make out a creaking noise. It reminded him of thick boughs settling in a tree. Very strange.

Palimak opened mental gates to his demon side and his senses became more acute. Beneath the sound of the settling boughs he heard a slight clicking. Like a beetle? No, not that. Then more clicking. Was there more than one?

Cautiously, he sent out a magical feeler. He caught the vibrating aura of a single being. But what kind of a being, he couldn't tell.

He slipped the astral tentacle out further, gently feeling around.

First there was a warning buzz of magic. Then suddenly something white-hot burned his senses and he snatched the probe back.

"It still doesn't know you're awake, Little Master," Gundara whispered.

"That was just its armor," Gundaree explained.

Palimak noticed he was dripping with sweat. And it wasn't from fear or tension. The cabin was definitely getting warmer.

Then his demon hearing picked up a rustling sound, like a breeze disturbing an old pine. Followed by more clicking sounds. All very faint.

"It's trying to talk to me and Gundaree," Gundara said.

"But it doesn't want us to wake you up," Gundaree said.

"Go ahead and answer," Palimak said.

Evidently they did, because he felt a tingling sensation run up his spine and his hair stood on end. Followed by another heavy thump against the wall. And the sound of the whispering pines and insect-like clicking.

Then silence — the waiting kind where stillness takes on a shadowy presence. The room grew warmer, the atmosphere dank from the sweat pouring off Palimak in rivulets. Finally:

"He doesn't seem so mean now, Little Master," Gundara said.

"Not mean at all," Gundaree added.

"But he's still hungry," Gundara said.

"So what?" Gundaree said. "You can't blame somebody for being hungry."

"That's true," Gundaree said in singular agreement. "I'm hungry right now, as a matter of fact. And it's making me feel mean."

"What does he want?" Palimak said, paying no attention to the last.

"Oh, nothing much, Little Master," Gundara said. And Palimak could almost hear the shrug in his voice.

"Except he wants us to help kill you," Gundara added.

Palimak raised his eyebrows. But said nothing.

"He promised us all sorts of nice things if we agreed," Gundaree said.

"And he also said we wouldn't have to work so hard all the time," Gundara put in.

"He sure sounded like a pretty nice new master to me," Gundaree said.

"What did you tell him?" Palimak asked.

"Oh, that we'd think about it," Gundara said.

"Good," Palimak said. "We need to stall for time."

"Except, maybe we really will think about it," Gundaree threatened.

"The snacks around here haven't been too good lately," Gundara said.

Palimak ignored this last exchange. The Favorites had been his lifelong companions. And although they could be nasty, quarrelsome little things, in their thousand years of existence he was the only friend they'd ever had. Besides, their loyalties were bound to whoever possessed the stone turtle that was their home.

He wiped perspiration from his eyes and looked around the

cabin, trying to figure out what to do. Magic was out. The intense heat, he realized, was the by-product of a spell meant to smother his abilities.

And it was doing a good job of it, too! Even the idea of sorcery made him feel weary.

A direct physical attack would also be doomed. Whatever the thing was, it was huge and most certainly prepared to deal with Palimak on a one-on-one basis.

"Why doesn't he just break down the door and kill me himself?" Palimak asked. "Why does he need you?"

"Because you can still use us to make magic and fight him," Gundara said.

This surprised Palimak. "Aren't you two affected by his spell?"

"Little Master's being stupid again," Gundaree said.

"He certainly is," Gundara said.

"Stop it!" Palimak hissed. The heat and tension were making him impatient. "Just answer my question."

Gundara gave a long sigh, like a child pressed by an adult to explain the painfully obvious.

"Magic is what we're made of, Little Master," he said. "Don't you know that?"

"Oh," Palimak said, feeling very stupid indeed.

The Favorites were spirit folk, composed entirely of magical particles. Safar had explained this to him years ago. He'd used the analogy of a clay jar filled with water. A human or demon wizard was a jar containing a certain amount of sorcerous "liquid." Whereas spirit folk were the jar itself, plus all it contained.

"If his spell could take away our magic," Gundaree continued for his brother, "then we wouldn't be here. We'd be dead."

"Sorry," Palimak said. "I didn't mean to get angry."

"That's all right, Little Master," Gundara allowed in a rather grand manner. "We know you can't always be perfect like us."

There was another thump at the door. Then a cracking sound as something heavy leaned against it. He could see the planks bending inward under the weight.

"He's getting mad, Little Master," Gundaree said. "He wants our answer now, or he's going to come in anyway."

"Stall him some more," Palimak said.

The twins resumed their odd communication with the creature, filling the air with whispering and clicking noises.

Whatever lies they told seemed to work, because soon the

planks groaned as the weight was removed and they resumed their original shape.

Even with the help of the Favorites, Palimak knew he didn't have enough sorcerous strength to live through an encounter with the creature. Which meant the only avenue open was escape.

He glanced at the open porthole — the only exit from the cabin, other than the door. Steam from the overheated room was wisping out into the night like a fog.

For a moment, he considered climbing out and dropping into the sea. Then he dismissed that idea. The ship was under full sail and Palimak would swiftly be left behind to drown.

It was starting to come down to a choice between a watery grave or being eaten alive.

As if on cue, Gundara whispered, "I'm hungry!"

"Me too!" Gundaree said.

Absently, Palimak fished a biscuit from his pocket and broke it in half. A wriggling worm fell to the floor. Palimak looked at the worm, then at the two biscuit halves, then at the door. A hazy idea started to take form.

"What kind of a creature is he?" Palimak asked the twins.

"Oh, he's sort of like a tree," Gundara said. "Except he doesn't have any leaves."

"And he's sort of like an animal," Gundaree said. "Except he doesn't have any skin or bones."

"But he's got ever so many teeth," Gundara said.

"They're all over his branches," Gundaree added. "Lots and lots of teeth in lots and lots of little mouths, all with long, sharp tongues."

"I'm sorry we can't be more helpful, Little Master," Gundaree said. "But it's hard to describe something that's both an animal and a tree."

"And we really wouldn't help him kill you," Gundara said.

"Never!" Gundaree agreed.

A slight pause, then: "Now can we eat?" Gundara asked plaintively.

"I want the worm!" Gundaree said, smacking his lips.

"Not this time," Palimak said. "I need that worm."

He squatted, took out his dagger and cut the worm in half.

"Poor thing," Gundara observed.

Gundaree sneered at his twin. "What's wrong with you?" he asked. "It's only a stupid worm."

Gundara wiped away a solitary tear. "But she seemed so happy in that biscuit," he said. "And now look at her. One part's a head without a tail. And the other's a tail without a head."

"I'll soon fix that," Palimak said, placing a wriggling piece on each side of the door.

Then he crept silently to his bedside and fetched a pitcher of water back to the door. He crumbled up the biscuit halves, mixed them with the water and made two lumps of dough. From these he formed two credible dough men, complete with legs, arms, heads and faces with simple features.

"I get it," Gundara said. "They're sort of like the cheese monster!"

He was referring to one of Palimak's boyhood experiments that had worked well enough to get them all into trouble with Safar.

"Something like that," Palimak agreed.

Then he indicated the still-moving worm halves. "Get in," he ordered the twins.

"Yuk!" Gundara said.

"Yum!" said Gundaree.

Palimak pointed at Gundara. "Just do as you're told."

Pouting and muttering under his breath, Gundara stomped over to his worm half, held his nose, then vanished inside.

"You next," Palimak said to the lip-smacking Gundaree. "But don't you dare eat it!"

The Favorite's smile was replaced by a look of outrage. He kicked at the floor, grumbling, "I never get to have any fun!"

But he did as he was told and vanished into the piece reserved for him. Palimak pressed a worm half into each doughman and set them on either side of the door.

Then, very slowly and quietly he slipped the latch.

Heart hammering so hard he was sure the creature could hear it, he tiptoed to his bunk, stripped off the blanket and tied one end to a stool.

He placed the stool under the porthole and grasped the free end of the blanket.

Then he said to the twins: "All right. Tell him to come in!"

28

ATTACK ON THE *NEPENTHE*

Safar was surrounded by four enormous wolves with glowing eyes and slavering jaws. They were reared back on their hind legs, towering nearly two feet over him. Their front legs ended in long, sharp, demon-like claws.

He was pinned by powerful magic and couldn't move as they stalked in for the kill. His mind gibbered, How can this be? I destroyed them, dammit! I destroyed them all!

From somewhere nearby he heard beasts ravaging flesh and breaking bones between strong jaws. He could smell the stench of blood and offal from their victim. And then a shiver of helpless agony shook him to the core as he heard the victim scream:

"Help me, father! Help me!"

It was Palimak. Crying and flailing as the beasts ate him alive.

The wolves were so close now that Safar could smell the carrion on their breath. If only he could break free. If only he could fling himself at them. Or sear them with a spell. The battle would be brief and would end in his death. But that was far more preferable than living and hearing Palimak's tormented cries.

The king wolf — the largest of the four — rasped laughter at Safar's predicament. And then he spoke with Iraj's voice.

He said, "Here we are, together again, old friend."

The wolf that was Iraj gestured and a goblet appeared in his claws. It was a fragile thing with such beautiful designs carved into its surface that Safar shuddered to see such artistry despoiled. It was like being forced to watch some piece of filth ravish your sister.

The king wolf raised the goblet in a mocking toast. "To my blood brother, Safar Timura," he said. "Long may he die!"

Then he drank the contents down and hurled the goblet away to shatter on the ground. The other wolves growled in satisfaction.

And Palimak screamed, "Help me, father!"

The king wolf chuckled, then mimicked the cry, "Help me, father!"

His head snaked down until his eyes were at Safar's level. Huge and afire with hate. "What's wrong, Safar?" he asked. "Why don't you help him?"

He gestured back into the darkness. "There's still some of him left. If you act quickly, you might be able to save an arm or a leg."

Safar tried to speak, but no words would come.

The king wolf tilted his head. "What's that?" he asked. "I can't hear you."

Safar gathered all his strength and, gasping with effort, he croaked, "Stop!"

The king wolf acted surprised. He said, "Is that all you can say after all these years? Stop? Why should I? You're the one who started this. Why don't you stop? Then perhaps we can be friends again."

And Safar croaked, "Please!"

Instantly, the wolf started to transform. There was an awful popping of joints as his limbs moved violently in their sockets. His snout retreated, his eyes and ears shifted position, his gray fur dissolved.

And Safar found himself staring into the handsome human face of Iraj Protarus.

"You see, Safar?" Iraj said, hands sweeping down to indicate his transformed body. "You see what I'm willing to endure for you? And a simple 'please' was all it took."

He turned to the other wolves. "Am I a reasonable king, or am I not?" he asked.

The other wolves growled agreement that His Majesty was the soul of gentility and kindness.

Iraj grinned at Safar, dark eyes flashing with amusement. Golden hair and shapely beard beaming in a sudden shaft of sunlight.

"Do you really want to save Palimak, brother?" he asked. "What would you do to spare him?"

And Safar groaned, "Anything!"

Iraj nodded, sharp. "Good," he said. "Now that we've agreed on a price, shall we start again?"

And he waved a hand and suddenly Safar found himself standing above a snowy pass. He was back in Esmir, high in the mountains called the Gods' Divide. He could hear caravan bells jingling and could see a wagon train — Coralean's wagon train — winding toward the white peaks known as the Bride and Six Maids.

Iraj was beside him and he was young again, a boy of seventeen. And Safar was young too, with supple limbs and a heart like a lion's. Iraj pointed at two canyons that bisected the caravan track.

"The demons," he said.

And Safar saw the two forces of mounted demons waiting to ambush the wagons.

"What shall we do?" Safar asked.

Iraj laughed, drawing his sword. "Warn the caravan," he said. And he started running down the mountainside.

But in midflight he turned his head and shouted back. "Oh, I almost forgot. This time Palimak is with them!"

And he ran on, leaping over icy boulders, crying, "Follow me, brother! Follow me!"

Safar ran after him. Bounding down the steep slope, heart bursting, mouth full of ashes. He had to reach the caravan. He had to warn Coralean.

But most of all, he had to reach Palimak in time.

Except the harder he ran, the more distant became the caravan. His legs grew weary, his breath short. But he struggled on, slipping in the snow. Desperately fighting to keep on his feet. But then falling, falling . . . hearing the war cries of demon bandits as they attacked. And it was too late, too late, and he could hear Palimak scream:

"Help me, father. Please!"

And the last thing he heard was Iraj laughing.

* * *

Safar shot up in bed, clawing at the blankets, Iraj's laughter still echoing eerily from his dream. He was soaked to the skin with sweat and he shivered in the cold night air.

He could hear the low rumble of the magical furnaces that powered the airship and the fluttering of the balloons in the wind. But he didn't make the mistake of thinking what he'd experienced was only a dream and sagging back in relief.

To be sure, some of it was a dream: The wolves, Iraj, plus the repeated caravan incident from his boyhood.

He had no doubt, however, that Palimak really was in great danger. The atmosphere fairly crackled with a dark, brooding force. He had a sudden sense of looking into a huge demonic eye and seeing Palimak reflected in the surface of its iris.

Safar leaped from his bunk, hastily pulling on clothes. He rushed outside, buckling his sword belt as he ran. There were only a few crewmen about — the rest were asleep. But on the bridge he spotted Biner at the wheel. Safar raced up the stairs to his side.

"Where's the ship?" he shouted. "Where's the *Nepenthe?*"

Biner knew at once something was wrong and didn't waste time asking for details.

"About a mile back," he said. "On the lee side."

Safar bolted to the rail to look. The seas were running like an incoming tide over a sandbar. Short, frothy waves speeding past; foam faintly pink under the bright Demon Moon. He made out the billowing sails of the *Nepenthe* just where Biner had said she'd be.

"Get back to the *Nepenthe!*" he shouted to Biner. "And get everybody up."

Biner went into instant action, roaring, "All hands! All hands!"

Other orders followed and the night crew got busy adjusting the steering sails as Biner muscled the wheel over — turning the airship in a wide arc.

The soldiers and the rest of the crew poured out onto the deck. Leiria, followed by Arlain, rushed up to the bridge. Professional that she was, Leiria was already dressed to fight — boots, buckler, short tunic with a weapons belt buckled about her small waist, a bow in one hand and a quiver of arrows thrown over one shoulder.

Arlain, who never wore that much in the way of clothing except in the coldest of weather, wore only a revealing sleeping gown thrown over her startling-beautiful body. But she was wide awake and prepared for battle. Claws extended. Sparks and smoke leaking from her dragon's mouth.

"What's wrong, Safar?" Leiria shouted over the wind.

"I'm not sure," he replied. "Except that Palimak's in some kind of trouble."

Leiria didn't ask any more questions. She only nodded and raced over to the soldiers. Barking orders for them to get into position. The long days of drilling paid off and everyone moved like well-oiled clockwork. Within a few scant minutes, they were all ready.

Arlain's great eyes glowed in fury. She loved Palimak like a doting older sister. Both the product of inter-species mating, they'd been close friends from the moment they'd met.

"If anybody hurth him," she said, "I'll roatht them in their thkinth!"

Safar only hoped they had skins to roast. Other than the fact that powerful sorcery was involved, he didn't have the faintest idea what he was up against.

But all he said was, "Make sure the boarding lines are ready."

Leaking smoke through her nostrils, Arlain hurried off to do his bidding.

Safar leaned far out over the rail, patience barely under control as they tacked toward the *Nepenthe*. Biner bellowed orders as they fought the wind.

Finally they were hovering directly over the tall ship.

"Let's bring her down, Biner," Safar said. "But keep it quiet, please."

Biner nodded. The airship's best defense *and* offense was surprise. After all, who would ever imagine an attack from the skies? He signaled for runners and started a relay of whispered orders. The magical engines were cut so the only sound was the gentle buffeting of the wind against the big balloons.

Then, slowly, cautiously, the crew started bleeding air from the balloons and the airship drifted down toward the *Nepenthe*.

Safar peered at the shadowy deck as it rose toward him. He could only see a few small figures moving about. With the weather so mild, night watches on both the *Nepenthe* and the airship were kept to a minimum so everyone would be fresh in an emergency.

Everything seemed quite peaceful. The crewmen's movements were leisurely. And only the most necessary lanterns were lit — a normal practice aimed at conserving oil for the long journey.

Then Leiria was at his side again. "I don't see anything," Safar said. "But I know they're there!"

Leiria remained silent, running experienced eyes over the ship and the surrounding seas.

Then she pointed. "There's something odd along the port bow," she said.

At first all he could make out were eight dark, twisted shapes hanging off the ship. They looked inanimate, like logs of stressed timber with the branches still intact.

Then he saw thirty — possibly forty — other similar shapes bobbing in the ocean next to the ship. It was if the *Nepenthe* were sailing through debris from a lumber mill. Although there was no land for miles, it was entirely possible the cast-off wood had been carried far out to sea by a swift-moving river.

Safar wondered why the crew couldn't hear the ship bumping into the logs. They ought to be fending off the debris with poles before the hull was damaged.

Leiria said, "Did you notice how the ones in the water are moving *with the ship?*"

At first he didn't understand what she meant. But as the airship drifted lower he realized the logs seemed to be clinging to the sides of the *Nepenthe.*

Then he noticed movement from two of the eight shapes hanging from the bow. And it wasn't in reaction to the ship heaving through the waves.

Safar slid his dagger out. Whispering a spell of clarity, he cut a wide circle in the air. The area he'd inscribed began to glisten in the Demon Moonlight as if it were window glass coated with a thin film of oil.

Looking through it, everything became magnified as if through the overly large lens of a ship's telescope.

"What in the Hells?!" Leiria blurted.

Which was Safar's exact reaction. For what they both saw with startling clarity were devils' spawn incarnate. Clinging to the sides of the *Nepenthe* were huge living creatures with bodies that looked like dead, twisted tree trunks.

He increased the magnification and could see that each trunk had scores of arms and legs with the appearance of fire-blasted branches and twigs. And each woody limb was pocked with dozens of small mouths, like leeches. And each mouth contained a long barbed tongue and was rimmed with several rows of sharp fangs.

At that moment Safar heard a chorus of clicking sounds, like an army of hungry land crabs advancing across a beach. It was apparently some sort of signal, because the eight creatures hanging from the bow suddenly swarmed onto the deck of the *Nepenthe*, while the platoon of beasts still in the sea scrabbled up the sides of the hull to join their leaders.

The air magnifier collapsed as Safar raced over to Biner to whisper the news. The were so close to the *Nepenthe* that the slightest sound might have given them away.

Biner signaled his runners and swiftly the word went out for everyone to "Prepare for boarding." All over the airship the soldiers and crewmen tensed for the final order.

Safar hurried back to the rail, where Leiria waited. She'd drawn her sword and wore an odd grin on her face that looked like she thought something was amusing, but it was actually her fighting expression. He'd seen that same grin remain on her face during the bloodiest of battles as she cut down the charging enemy.

Before readying his own sword, he slipped an amplifying pellet from his pocket. He had to warn the *Nepenthe*. Unfortunately, that warning couldn't come until the last possible moment. Otherwise their surprise counter-attack would be spoiled.

Safar waited, nerves taut as lyre strings. Heart pounding against his ribs. He could see the first group of tree creatures closing in on the unsuspecting crewmen. The second, much larger group was starting to climb over the railing to the deck.

Then, as the ends of the airship's boarding ropes brushed along the *Nepenthe*'s deck, he cracked the pellet, and shouted: *"All hands! All hands! We're under attack!"*

The amplifying spell made his shout into that of a giant's. The words thundered into the night and were repeated over and over again:

"All hands! All hands! We're under attack!"

Safar didn't wait to see the effect of his warning, but leaped immediately for a boarding rope. He caught it and slipped several feet, burning his hands. The pain went unnoticed. He only let go and plummeted to the deck, landing in a crouch and coming up swift as a cat.

His sword came out and he charged the creatures, some of whom were whirling about to face this unexpected attack from the rear.

Leiria was at his side, shrilling her wild battle cry.

Behind him, he heard the shouts of his soldiers as they plunged off the airship into battle. Biner's roar of fury sounding over all but Arlain's blood-chilling dragon shriek.

Safar felt incredibly powerful and fast, as if he suddenly possessed the strength of two men. He leaped for the nearest tree beast, his jump carrying him twenty feet.

The creature towered over him by at least four feet. Long, gnarled branches filled with gnashing teeth lashed out at him, but he slashed them off with his sword.

A greenish white liquid splattered on the deck, where it hissed and bubbled. A few drops splashed his sword hand. He could feel it sear his flesh but his bloodlust was so hot he didn't care.

He chopped at the main body, felt his blade sink deep. The creature toppled to the deck, limbs and branches flailing, all the teeth chattering wildly.

Except it didn't die! Somehow the creature fought on, lashing out with its deadly branches!

A shadow reared up behind him. He turned, knowing it was too late, but desperately striking out at his attacker.

Branches enfolded him, pulling him down onto the deck. They held him there, sharp teeth ravaging his back.

Then the creature suddenly let go, falling away and he rolled over to see Leiria hacking it with her sword. Leather armor hissing as it took the brunt of the spurting acid sap.

From far off he heard Khysmet shrill his battle cry and the sound of splintering wood as the big stallion broke through the walls of his stable to join the fight.

Then he heard Jooli's shout and the cries of the Nepenthe's crew as they boiled up onto the deck.

Leiria jerked Safar to his feet and they stood side by side as an enormous tree beast scrabbled for them, huge roots serving as feet. All its branches lashing out like thick, nail-studded whips.

The fury of its assault drove them back and it was all they could do to keep out of the way of its flesh-eating limbs.

Then Khysmet suddenly appeared behind the creature, rearing up on his hind legs then plunging down with his sharp hooves.

There was a crack! as the beast split in two.

Safar vaulted onto Khysmet's back and held out a hand for Leiria. She jumped up behind them and they plunged into the fray, striking out in every direction.

The *Nepenthe* was still under full sail and the ship's deck made a heaving, slippery battlefield. It made no difference to Khysmet who launched himself like a mighty lion, biting with his great teeth and raking the creatures with his hooves.

However, even with the entire crew and all the soldiers of both ships engaged, the fight was not going well for the Kyranians. The tree beasts simply wouldn't die, but fought on with undiminished ferocity no matter how many wounds they suffered.

Even their hacked-off branches remained deadly, whipping around men's legs and tearing into them with their teeth.

And the only cries of pain Safar could hear were human.

And the only dead he saw were his own.

29

WITCH WORLD

King Rhodes and his mother were quite enjoying the battle for the *Nepenthe*.

Floating just above her golden-tiled table was an exact duplicate of the events taking place hundreds of miles from their own ship. Shimmering on her table was the night sea with the choppy waves, foam tinted pink by the Demon Moon.

A miniature of the *Nepenthe* boomed through those waves under full sail. Hovering over it was the airship, boarding lines dangling down to the deck. And all along the *Nepenthe*'s deck were the tiny figures of the Kyranians struggling valiantly but hopelessly against the tree beasts.

They could even see Safar and Leiria, swords slashing this way and that, rage across the deck on the broad back of Khysmet.

"Oh, good show, good show!" Rhodes declared as one of the creatures swept Leiria off the stallion and onto the glistening boards.

Peering at the scene through the king's eyes, Kalasariz reacted with equal glee. Of all the many people and demons he hated, Leiria was quite high on his list.

He'd been unsure of the plan when Clayre had proposed it only a few days before. Now that it was coming to fruition — with the deaths of Safar and Palimak apparently imminent — he liked it so much he was beginning to become a little envious that it wasn't a plan of his own making.

As the battle for the *Nepenthe* raged, Kalasariz reflected back on the day Clayre had had her sudden inspiration.

Stealing the ships was his idea, of course. It was the kind of sneak attack Kalasariz had mastered many years before when he was one of the three rulers of Walaria.

The pursuit of Safar was also his idea and it had taken all his cunning to convince Rhodes and Clayre this was a goal superior to their own.

The king and his mother would have been content to use the ships to launch a new invasion of the Kyranian fortress in Syrapis. Life long island dwellers, their idea of empire fitted exactly the shoreline boundaries set by the Great Sea.

And so when Kalasariz offered them the world as their kingdom, they were at first hard put to stretch their imagination beyond the spit of sand and rock that was Syrapis.

Eventually his silky powers of persuasion had fired their ambitions. All they had to do was get their hands on Safar and Palimak — it didn't matter if they were dead or alive — and supreme power would be theirs. Power that even the gods might envy.

The only worm in the apple — and this he hadn't mentioned —

was that he also needed Iraj Protarus. Kalasariz was only guessing that wherever Safar was, Iraj would be nearby.

One thing he was fairly sure of was that once he got his hands on Safar's corpse some sort of spell could be devised to locate his former king.

With Iraj in the spymaster's power, Kalasariz could rid himself of his two barbarian allies. And then he would rule absolutely. And alone. Once he had been content to share power, or even to manipulate from the shadows behind a throne.

But since he'd arrived in Syrapis to take up residence in Rhodes he'd undergone a spiritual transformation that quite excited him.

Kalasariz now truly understood that kings and allies could not be trusted — unless your boot was firmly planted on their throats. And the only way to assure himself of that happy state of affairs was to wear the royal mantle himself.

As for his plan, in the beginning the only trouble was that Safar would be difficult to catch. The *Nepenthe* had a head start of many days and it would require more luck than skill to corner the Kyranians. Once that was accomplished, however, defeating the Timuras would be simple. It would be three ships, all packed with crack troops, against the *Nepenthe*'s puny forces.

Even the airship wouldn't give Safar much of an advantage, because Kalasariz fully intended to strike when all the Kyranians were on land, taking on supplies and water.

But to surprise Safar, they needed to catch him first. Kalasariz hadn't known how go about this, but thought it best to sail after the *Nepenthe* as fast as they could and hope for some storm or other accident to delay the Kyranians long enough to overtake them.

It was his experience that good fortune usually tended to favor the hunter rather than the hunted.

Clayre, however, had other ideas. Such as creating a delay through sorcery, rather than trusting to chance. Even with the newly-won magical powers that Kalasariz now possessed — thanks to the meal he'd made out of Fari and Luka — he didn't see how it could be done.

The distance was too great, he reasoned. Plus, they didn't know the exact position of the *Nepenthe*.

The beautiful Queen Witch solved that soon enough. First she dug out a roll of ancient parchment. It was a copy of Asper's hand-drawn map of the world, which the demon wizard had composed during his travels. She'd gotten it from Charize, the false guardian of Asper's tomb.

"I never thought I'd have any use for this," she said. "However, there are some faint traces of magic in it left over from Asper. Enough to cure a wart, perhaps, but no more. Regardless, I make a habit of never throwing anything magical away, so I put it aside just in case."

She also had another surprise up her sleeve. "Bring me the gold Palimak Timura gave you," she commanded her son.

This stung Rhodes' most vulnerable part — his greedy heart.

"That gold is mine," he said. "If you want to buy something, use your own funds. I give you a large enough allowance, the gods and my treasurer know. Besides, I earned that gold the hard way."

His face darkened at the memory of Palimak and Leiria standing before him, gloating at his defeat.

"It was the most humiliating thing that's ever happened in my life," he said. "And there isn't gold enough in the world to make me forget it."

This, of course, was a gross exaggeration. Rhodes would do anything for money and power.

As witness his eager willingness to sacrifice his own daughter, Jooli.

However, Kalasariz quite understood his point. Although gold itself had never been that important to him — except for the power it contained — he was equally avaricious in other ways.

Kalasariz also knew what it was like to suffer humiliation at the hands of a Timura. He had several scores to settle with Safar on that account.

Even so, Kalasariz suspected there was more to Clayre's request than a need to buy magical supplies. She'd been quite specific, as a matter of fact. It was Palimak's gold she wanted. Not just a random purse of the stuff from the king's treasury.

He stirred in his nest, signaling Rhodes that he was about to communicate. When he had the king's attention, he said, *I know she's a greedy bitch, Majesty, but perhaps there's more to her request than meets the eye.*

Rhodes' frown deepened, but Kalasariz felt the king's nerve cords relax and knew he'd gotten through. But first Rhodes had to hear his mother out.

"Why do you always insist on arguing with me about ever little detail, son?" she said. "Your father was of the same quarrelsome nature and look what it got him."

"Dead," Rhodes replied, a little nastily.

"That's right, dead," Clayre agreed.

She sighed, thinking about her former husband. "I swear," she continued, "no matter what I said, your father had an argument against it. Why, we could have been talking about a haunch of venison and if I said it was gamy, he'd claim it was sweet. And he never listened to me. Never! It was as if he had his ears plugged with wax every time I came into his presence."

Clayre smiled in gentle reflection. "But in the end, I certainly unstopped his ears, didn't I? Unfortunately, a corpse can't hear. Still, I made my point clear to his ghost."

Rhodes barely suppressed a shudder. Curious, Kalasariz tapped into his memories. He caught an image of Clayre pouring hot poisoned oil into the ears of her sleeping husband. Immediately, his admiration for Clayre increased.

A difficult woman she might be, but one couldn't deny she had a sense of humor.

Clayre gazed on her stubborn son. "So, I ask you again, my son," she said, "to kindly bring me Palimak Timura's gold. Hmm?"

Rhodes bristled at the implied threat. "Or what?" he asked.

And Clayre replied, "Or I can't help you find the ship, that's all. What else did you think I meant?"

"Never mind," Rhodes said. "I'll get the gold."

When he returned with the purse, Clayre dumped the gold out on her magical table. She sorted through the coins, eyes narrowed in concentration. Finally, she held one up.

"This will do," she said. Then she dismissed the others with a wave. "You can have these back."

Puzzled, but relieved, Rhodes quickly scooped up the coins and returned them to the purse. One fell to the floor so he got down on his hands and knees and crawled about until he found it.

Kalasariz was irritated to the extreme. This was not proper behavior for a king. But he said nothing. His object was to make Rhodes think of him as his dearest friend and he had to be careful not to appear judgmental. Ah, well, he thought. Living inside another person certainly had its burdens — even though the host did do all the physical work.

"Why did you choose just that one coin, mother?" Rhodes asked after he'd tucked the purse away.

"Because it carries the strongest scent," she replied. "Apparently young Palimak held it more than the others. Perhaps he even bit the coin when he first received it to make sure it was pure gold.

In any event, he's left very heavy traces of his aura behind for us to make use of."

Then, with no further explanation, she unrolled the parchment map and placed it across the golden tiles. Four stubby black candles were stuck at each corner to hold it down. The gold coin went in the center.

"Now, help me with this," she said.

Rhodes obediently approached the table. While she concentrated, Kalasariz stoked up his own magical fires, lashing the imps that were Fari and Luka with red-hot whips until their sorcerous energies boiled over and flowed into his own.

This was Kalasariz' favorite part of his new-found skills at performing the business of magic. The two demons were hateful creatures who had worked long and hard to bring him down. Their agonies gave him pleasure of such extremes that it bordered on the sexual. Which in his present form was the best he could do, since the only way he could enjoy the mating act these days was through Rhodes' activities.

And the king was such a rutting brute, with no style at all, that his amorous exploits only whetted Kalasariz' appetite.

As he focused his powers, adding them to Clayre's considerable strength, he saw the coin begin to move. The movement was hesitant at first — a barely perceptible tremble. Then it shifted left a few inches, then right, then to the center again.

Another trembling hesitation, then it shot below the center point and came to rest.

Clayre waved a hand at the coin and it slowly transformed in shape, size and color until it became an exact duplicate of the *Nepenthe*, sails billowing in a spirit-world wind.

Then she broke the sorcerous connection and Kalasariz relaxed.

Rhodes leaned over the table to get a closer look, and through the king's eyes Kalasariz could see that the ship sat a little south of a large land mass, with small tree-like squiggles inked in.

"They're just off Aroborus," Clayre said. "The land of the forests."

"Now that we know where they are," Rhodes asked, "how do we delay them?"

"Never fear, my son," Clayre said with supreme confidence. "I'll think of something."

* * *

Kalasariz gazed fondly at the tiny figures of the tree beasts as they ravaged the Kyranian forces, driving them across the deck of the *Nepenthe.*

Clayre had been as good as her word and then some. Drawing on the Land of the Forests for inspiration, she'd created a unique and cunning enemy to delay and perhaps even destroy Safar Timura and his allies.

Kalasariz noted that Leiria was still down, barely holding off one creature, while Safar — seated on his white stallion — fought desperately but futilely to reach her.

Suddenly, he saw Jooli burst onto the scene, armed with a spear. She set the butt onto the deck and vaulted over several beasts to land at Leiria's side.

Then she jabbed at the beast that was attacking the Kyranian warrior, driving it back long enough for Leiria to come up and hack it down with her blade.

"You have to admit," Rhodes rumbled in fatherly admiration, "that my daughter is one hells of a soldier. Too bad the bitch whelp turned traitor and joined the other side."

But Clayre did not share his pride, grudging though it might have been. She became furious at the sight of her granddaughter.

"I'll fix her," she snarled.

She drew a long, sharp pin from her hair and rubbed it vigorously on the sleeve of her silken witch's gown. Kalasariz could feel the energy growing until magical sparks shot off.

Then Clayre jabbed the pin down at the tiny figure of Jooli.

But as the needle point descended, Kalasariz, whose attention had been fixed on his old enemy, saw Safar sheathe his sword. He pulled an object from his cloak that the spymaster couldn't quite make out.

When he raised it to his lips, however, Kalasariz realized it was some sort of horn.

And just as Clayre thrust the needle at Jooli, Safar blew through the horn. The sound blasted through Clayre's cabin as if it were made by some gigantic trumpet.

The Queen Witch gasped in shock as she saw two strange apparitions rise up through the golden tiles. The figures were vaguely familiar, but she didn't have time to think where she'd seen them before.

Then something was lofted up at her.

Instinctively, she ducked.

And then a great white light flared, blinding everyone in the cabin.

A moment later, when their vision cleared, the living seascape had vanished.

Only a dark smudge on the golden tiles remained to mark the spot where the battle for the *Nepenthe* had raged.

Rhodes whirled to face the witch. His features were swollen and red with anger. He'd seen exactly who those two magical creatures were.

"Dammit, mother," he roared. "I told you so! Maybe it's about time you started listening to me!"

Clayre was astounded. "Why, whatever are you talking about, son?" she asked.

"The mural, mother!" he snarled. "You said not to worry about it. But by the gods who torment us, it's come back to haunt us again!"

30

IN THE DARK SEAS

When Safar realized Leiria was gone it was as if his heart had been pierced by an arrow. One of the enormous creatures loomed up, deadly branches slashing in to take him. But he didn't care. In that terrible moment of agony only Leiria mattered.

It was Khysmet who saved him, wheeling about and kicking through all those chattering teeth and thorny tongues to knock the tree beast away.

Coming out of his shock, Safar saw Leiria lying on the deck, desperately cutting and jabbing at the huge creature towering over her. One blood-smeared leg was caught in a slender, snake-like branch and she was being drawn slowly toward the beast's twisted trunk.

Safar kicked Khysmet and they charged forward, only to be hurled back by three other creatures who moved in to block the way.

Hard as he and Khysmet fought, they kept losing ground to the living wall of pain.

Then he saw Jooli vault to Leiria's rescue. As she jabbed at the tree beast with her spear, Leiria slashed away the branch gripping her leg and then the two women joined together to drive the creature off.

It was then that a strange sensation came over him. To Safar it seemed as if he split in two and another part of him — a spirit self — was standing off at a great distance watching the progress of the battle. He could even see himself, astride Khysmet, fighting along with the others.

Although the view was godlike, his emotions were intensely human — frightened that all his friends would soon die unspeakably horrible deaths.

Then his spirit self heard a voice whisper, *Safar, Safar.*

It came from quite close — just at his ear. He even imagined he could feel warm breath stir his hair.

And then the voice came again, whispering, *Look to the heavens, brother!*

He looked up and saw nothing but the night sky. A cloud bank partly obscured the Demon Moon, dimming its red light. Surrounding it were only the stars — cold and pitiless as always.

Then he noticed a faint golden shimmer beyond the night. As if the darkness was a thin black veil drawn over a sheen of some ethereal surface.

Reflected in that sheen was the dim outline of two enormous faces. He couldn't make out who they were, only that they were watching.

And then there was motion. A disturbance. First it pierced the golden surface. Then the black veil that was the night.

A long, slender needle of flame pushed through and descended toward the *Nepenthe.* His eyes followed its course, the needle growing thinner, sharper, hotter.

And then, with a jolt, he realized it was aimed directly at Jooli!

Suddenly, his spirit self vanished and he was back in the midst of the battle. Slashing and cutting as the three creatures closed in on him and Khysmet.

But now he knew why he was losing this battle.

Fighting all natural instinct, he ignored the long tendrils of death reaching for him and sheathed his sword.

With forced calm he drew out Asper's shell trumpet. And lifted it to his lips and blew.

The sound was world-shattering. As if a thousand war trumpets — set close by — blared all at once. Everyone on the ship —

including the creatures — froze, as if they'd been suddenly turned to stone.

Floating high above the *Nepenthe* he saw the mural of the Spirit Rider. It was hazy, ghost-like and of enormous size. Then he saw the beautiful Princess Alsahna and her black mare come alive.

The Princess shouted, "For Safar!" and horse and rider soared out of the mural into the night sky. They charged, up and up — Alsahna pulling a javelin from a loop on her saddle.

And then, just before they reached the golden shimmer, the Princess hurled it at the Watchers.

An intense white light flared, then was gone. Taking with it the faces of the Watchers, the shimmering gold surface and the ghostly mural.

Now there were only the cold stars and the grinning Demon Moon to observe what followed.

Immediately, Safar sensed a subtle shift in the atmosphere. And then a settling. It was as if the very particles that made up the air had rearranged themselves into a more normal pattern.

But he could still hear the sounds of battle and human cries of pain and defiance all around him.

A long, thick branch filled with chattering teeth reached for him. Safar roared in a fury and slashed it away. Then he kicked Khysmet forward, cutting at the beast's trunk with his sword.

But this time, when the blade bit the creature screamed and died!

All over the ship the besieged humans experienced similar results.

Biner, spattered with blood from dozens of cuts, swung his great club, bursting a tree-beast in two. He shouted in glee as it writhed in agony, then grew still.

Arlain hissed a long tongue of fire at one of the creatures. To her delight it burst into flames, then toppled over the rail into the sea.

Kairo the acrobat clung to a boarding rope and swung along the deck, slashing at the creatures with a sword. Amazed that this time they remained where they fell and didn't get up again.

Renor and Sinch netted their attacker, then slung it over the side.

Leiria and Jooli had found ropes. Together they lassoed one of the creatures, toppling it. Then, with sword and spear, they slew it where it fell.

But even without the magical assistance of Clayre and Kalasariz, the beasts were not easily defeated. It took an hour of furious fighting and many tricks before the humans had killed them all and hurled them into the sea.

As Leiria and Jooli dealt with the last one, Safar and Khysmet thundered up to them.

Safar shouted, "Have you seen Palimak?"

Leiria's heart jumped as his question sunk in like a wide-bladed spear. Dismayed, she shook her head: no.

Safar leaped off Khysmet and raced toward the stairwell leading down to Palimak's cabin, Leiria and Jooli at his heels.

He didn't bother with the stairs, but jumped ten feet to the passageway below. Immediately he saw a large, ragged hole where the door to Palimak's cabin had been. He also heard movement — a dry scraping sound — and knew another of the tree-creatures lurked inside.

Leiria and Jooli had joined him by now and he signaled silence. Then the three of them crept down the passageway, weapons ready.

When he reached the cabin he peered inside. Lying in the wreckage of the room was one of the beasts. Many of its branches had been ripped away and its trunk had enormous chunks torn from it. The creature was weak and dying.

Heart racing, Safar looked about the cabin and saw no sign of Palimak. He sagged against the broken doorway, overcome by grief.

It was Jooli who finally killed the beast, running it through with her spear. Leiria called for help and several crewmen came to drag the thing away and dispose of it.

By the time it was gone, Safar had recovered some of his sensibilities. And with them came hope.

"Palimak wouldn't die so easily," he said.

"Of course not," Leiria agreed, soothing herself as much as Safar. "Perhaps he managed to get out of the cabin."

Safar winced and shook his head. "I heard one of the crewmen say that no one has seen him since he went to bed."

He studied the cabin, looking for some sign. At first all he could see was the broken debris — smashed furniture, shattered bunk, scarred walls and deck. Then he spotted something peeping out from under a ruined plank.

Safar lifted the plank away, revealing a strange little object in the shape of a man. He squatted down to examine it more closely.

"It's been molded from dough or something," he said to Leiria, who was looking over his shoulder. He touched it. "It's still wet," he said.

There was an impression in the belly of the dough man where a navel might be. There was slight movement in the depression so Safar gently pulled the dough away from the edges. To his surprise he found what appeared to be part of a still-living worm. At the same time his magical senses caught a faint spark of sorcery.

Safar grinned. This was Palimak's work.

"It's a cheese beast," he said.

"What?" Leiria asked. "I thought you said it was made from dough."

"Never mind," Safar said.

He moved some other planks and found another dough man, but this one was missing a leg. However, he found the worm's other half wriggling within. An idea of what Palimak had intended started to come to him.

"Over here!" Jooli said.

Safar turned to see her pulling a blanket through the porthole. She held it up and he saw that one end of the blanket was tied to a broken stool. Jooli placed it across the porthole, measuring. The stool was larger by several inches than the opening.

"He used the blanket to hang outside the cabin," she said, "so the creature couldn't get at him."

Safar came to his feet. "Go tell the captain to turn the ship about," he said to Jooli.

Then, to Leiria: "Ask Biner to get into the air as fast as he can. Palimak is out there someplace — and I mean to find him if I have to search every inch of sea from here to Aroborus!"

Palimak tightened his grip on the blanket. He said to the twins, "All right. Tell him to come in!" And he dived head-first through the porthole.

Slender though he was, he stuck at the hips and found himself in the ridiculous position of hanging half in and half out of the cabin, his posterior facing the monster as it burst through the door.

A fit of hysterical laughter nearly overcame him when he had a sudden vision of the creature gaping in astonishment when confronted with such a rude view of his victim.

But the chattering sound of many teeth spurred him onward and he kicked himself through the rest of the way.

Palimak plunged out into the night, then was brought up short by the blanket rope as the stool rose up to slam across the porthole.

He hung there a moment to recover, swaying with the motion of the ship. Then he spun about, got his feet against the hull and pulled himself up hand over hand until he could see through the porthole.

His first sight of the creature took his breath away. Its twisted, blackened trunk. Scores of branches and minor limbs waving madly about. All pockmarked with hundreds of little mouths filled with sharp, chattering teeth. And it was huge. Standing just inside the cabin — the wreckage of the door hurled to one side — its jagged-edged top was jammed against the ceiling.

It was also looking for him — turning slowly, first this way, then the other. Long barbed tongues tasting the air like a nest of snakes hunting their prey. Any minute now, it would make the connection between the stool jammed against the porthole and the whereabouts of its intended victim.

Palimak concentrated, drawing on all his powers. Opening the gates to his demon side and feeling the strength pour in. His nails grew into talons, cutting through the blanket, making his grip catlike and more assured.

He felt his canine teeth lengthen until the sharp points hooked over his lower lip. And his eyes burned in their sockets, turning a blazing yellow that cast twin beams of light onto the hull.

He hissed the spell words remembered from his boyhood. Foolish words, composed by a child. But the moment he said them he felt a surge of magical energy well up. He called out to the twins, using his mental "voice" to urge them to join him in the spell.

They replied in unison, their spirit voices like little bells — We're here, Little Master! We're here!

And boom! he cast it. Thunder crashing against his spirit ears as he hurled it into the cabin. And boom! boom! the little dough men containing Gundara and Gundaree jumped to their feet, swinging around to confront the beast. They were on either side of him, so small and made only of moistened bread crumbs that it would be laughable even to think the word "surrounded," much less use it.

But then they started growing and growing until they were the same size as the monster. And they were strong, so strong — dough flesh hardening into the consistency of steel — that they weren't laughable any longer.

And there was nothing funny at all when the creature realized it had been tricked and closed with them. All those deadly branches whipping out to embrace and kill the Favorites.

The three strange beings locked in battle. Crashing about the cabin, shattering everything in sight. The only sound was the destruction. There was not one roar of fury or agony from any of the creatures.

For Palimak it was like watching three mute giants fighting it out in an arena too small for any of them to escape.

As the fight raged, Palimak tried to shout a warning to the crewmen on deck. But his shouts were swept away by the heavy sound of the wind and crashing waves.

Even so, it didn't seem to matter. Because, ever so slowly, the twins gained the advantage. Hardened flesh impervious to all those teeth, they ripped off limbs and gouged out hunks from the beast's thick trunk. Greenish-gray acid splattering everywhere to hiss and burn wood and cloth.

Finally they had the creature pinned to the floor and were tearing at the jagged top Palimak imagined as a head. He thought it was over. The beast's movements growing weak, as if it were dying.

Then, suddenly, it surged up. Strong and fresh as when the fight had begun. And the furious battle commenced again.

And again.

And again.

Each time the twins got the creature down it somehow found new strength to fight on. The minutes dragged on like each was a year. And slowly Palimak and the twins began to weaken.

He dug deep for more strength, finding just enough to make one last desperate attempt to call for help. But this time he made the shout magical, calling for Safar:

"Help me, father! Help!"

For a brief moment Palimak thought there was an ethereal connection. A stirring of the magical atmosphere. So he clung to the blanket harder, directing the twins to continue the fight as long as they could.

After what seemed like an eternity he heard his father's voice raised in a thunderous cry:

"All hands! We're under attack!"

And Palimak laughed. Help was on the way. But then from the deck he heard cries of pain and the sounds of battle. Khysmet shrilling his battle cry, shattering the walls of his stable with his powerful hooves. And then the shouts of Leiria and Jooli and Biner and Arlain.

All of them fighting just as desperately as he.

Then the twins cried out, Help us, Little Master! Help us, please!

And that was the end of it.

Clinging with one hand, Palimak fished the stone turtle from his pocket and raised it high. He called for the twins and the turtle suddenly glowed as they fled into it.

Through bleary eyes he saw the doughmen collapse, then shrink to their original size. And the monster started turning again, hunting him with those flickering snake tongues.

Palimak returned the turtle to his pocket. And let go of the blanket.

Cold, salty water enveloped him. He kicked his way to the surface and when his head emerged he could see the *Nepenthe* moving away from him.

He saw a rope dangling from the side, trailing in the water and he swam after it. Arms and legs churning furiously. He nearly caught the rope. But then, weary, so weary from the battle, he slowly fell behind.

Then he could swim no more.

Palimak rolled over on his back and floated. The sounds of the fight on the *Nepenthe* growing fainter and more distant by the minute.

Finally, there was silence — and he knew he was alone.

Then he heard a stirring and Gundara and Gundaree hopped up on his chest.

"Please, Little Master, don't give up!" Gundara said.

"It would be awful if you drowned, Little Master," Gundaree added.

Palimak couldn't help but smile. "It's nice to finally know you care," he said.

"Of course we care, Little Master," Gundara said.

"If you drown," added Gundaree, "then we'll sink with you."

"And then we'd have to live on the bottom of the sea for ever and ever," Gundara said.

"I can't think of anything more boring," Gundaree put in. "Although it might not be so bad if we could find some nice fat sea worms."

"That's disgusting," Gundara said. "You stupid worm eater!"

"Shut up, Gundara!"

"No, you shut up!"

Palimak was too tired to intervene. And he floated along under the Demon Moon, wondering how long it would be before he drowned.

The twins voices echoed across the empty sea like strange gulls that cried, "Shut up, shut up, shutup!"

31

BLOOD AND MAGIC

When the king is unhappy, the sages say, all must suffer. And Rhodes was not a happy king. Standing on the bridge of the *Kray*, lashed by wind and rain, he watched grimly as his chief executioner applied an ax to the exposed neck of an unfortunate sailor.

The offense: laughing at the king's clumsiness. Oh, the fellow protested he hadn't seen Rhodes slip and fall on the slick deck and was only laughing at a comrade's jest. And never mind that the comrade had supported his friend's innocence, swearing that neither had witnessed the royal mishap; and that the jesting and the laughter it drew was a mere coincidence.

If the king's mood had been brighter he might have shown mercy and spared the friend's life. After all, Rhodes appreciated loyalty to a comrade as much as any man. A tongue plucked from the liar's mouth with hot pincers would've sufficed as punishment.

On a feast day, or his birthday, he might even have reduced that sentence to a hundred lashes with the cat, followed by a bath in vinegar and salt.

However, Rhodes had just come from a quarrel with his mother and there was never any question that both men would have to die.

Usually, he would've enjoyed the proceedings: various tortures, performed by the executioner, so ingenious that both men were brought to the brink of death. Then their revival by a special elixir whose recipe had been the executioner's family secret for several generations.

And, finally, two satisfying whacks of the ax, with the cutoff heads posted on stakes as a warning to all potential transgressors that the king's dignity must be preserved at all costs.

Sadly, Rhodes' heart was so troubled that not even these delights moved him.

All hands had been ordered on deck to view the executions. Soldiers and crewmen, ship's officers and royal aides standing silent and miserable in the rain as first one, then the other head was removed.

When the second head fell and rolled across the deck, Rhodes saw one of his men turn away and retch.

"That soldier!" Rhodes snapped at Tabusir, who hovered nearby. "I want his head as well!"

"Which one, Majesty?" Tabusir inquired mildly.

The king stabbed out with a bejeweled finger, indicating a uniformed drummer's lad. Too young to grow a beard or to steel his heart against the troubles of another.

"I'll have no man in my army," the king said, "who can't stand the sight of a little spilled blood."

Tabusir didn't point out that the soldier was probably no more than thirteen summers old. And after two beheadings the pitching deck was running with so much blood mixed with rainwater, that it splashed over the men's boots like spillage in a heaving slaughterhouse with stopped-up gutters.

Perhaps there was just a twinge of sympathy for the lad in the spy's heart. Or perhaps it was a pang of doubt at the king's judgment. In either case it was apparent from their gloom that none of the assembled men were happy about the executions. And maybe it was merely due to a spot of indigestion. After all, he'd eaten a hearty, heavily-spiced meal just before the day's bloody entertainment.

Whatever the reason, Tabusir swallowed his rising bile and snapped a salute so military-perfect that even in a drenched uniform he looked crisp and professionally eager.

"Immediately, Majesty!" he said.

Then he strode briskly off to collect two guardsmen. Moments later the surprised drummer's lad was dragged from the ranks and delivered to the executioner.

A mutinous murmur swept across the ship, silenced by growls from sergeants and bosons. Only to be aroused again by the lad's screams as he was forced to kneel on the gory deck.

"Please! Please!" the boy cried. "I did nothing! Nothing!"

Both the pleading cries and the angry muttering stopped abruptly when the ax fell and the boy's head plopped to the deck.

Immediately, Rhodes felt much better. "Three's a charm against all harm," he murmured to himself, reciting an old nursery jingle. He smiled, trying to remember the rest.

From inside him, Kalasariz spoke up, finishing the doggerel: . . . Four's a chore and to all a bore;/ Five's a sty, not a pig alive;/ But six is a trick of the very best mix!

Rhodes chuckled, to the vast relief of all the aides gathered about him. Even these battle-hardened men worried that the executions were an ill omen and bad for morale.

"That's good!" the king said aloud. "That's very, very good!"

Thinking he was speaking to them, his aides all murmured that, indeed, Majesty, the executions had been a remarkable performance.

Inside him, Kalasariz said, *Thank you, Majesty. But it is you who deserves the greatest credit for thinking of these executions. I always found that a mass beheading was a lucky way to start a new venture. It both pleases the gods and chastens the men.*

Rhodes nodded agreement, but this time he used his internal voice to reply, saying: *It's amazing how much wisdom can be found in a nursery rhyme. From a child's mouth, etc.*

At that moment, Tabusir came trotting up. "All has been done as you commanded, Majesty," he said, snapping another crisp salute.

"Excellent work, Tabusir," Rhodes said.

He pulled the smallest ring from the collection on his fingers and tossed it to the spy as a reward. Tabusir caught it and bowed low, murmuring artful words of appreciation.

"Now go fetch three more," the king said. "And deliver them to the executioner with my compliments."

Skilled as he was in covering his true feelings, Tabusir's gaze flickered. "Pardon, Majesty," he said. "But which three do you desire?"

Rhodes shrugged. "Doesn't matter," he said. "Choose who you like. The main thing is that I want six heads posted on the main deck."

Then the king turned and strode from the bridge, saying, "Lucky number, six." Then, in a sing-song voice, he added, "Six is a trick of the very best mix!"

And he roared with laughter, stomping down the passageway to his mother's quarters. As if on cue, the squall suddenly ended when he disappeared from view.

Stunned by the king's behavior, all the men were careful to keep blank faces and did their best not to meet each other's eyes. One of the aides, a jowly, red-faced colonel named Olaf, tried to pretend for all of them that everything was quite normal.

"It's good to see the king in such high spirits again," he said to Tabusir. "You are to be congratulated for such excellent service to His Majesty."

His smile was friendly, but jealousy glittered in his eyes. Seeing it, Tabusir only bowed his head slightly in thanks.

Olaf made the mistake of continuing. "Although I certainly don't envy you your next task," he said with a smirk. "It's not going to make you very popular with the men."

He turned to the others. "Isn't that so, gentlemen?"

There were murmured agreements, some louder than others.

He turned back to Tabusir. Laughing, he said, "Tell me, young man, how do you plan to choose three more victims? By lot? Or will you make them draw straws?"

Tabusir pretended honest puzzlement. "I'm not sure," he said, his face worried. "But I'll come up with something."

"You'd better think fast," Olaf said, amused at Tabusir's predicament. "When the king wants heads he tends to be most impatient."

"Is that so?" Tabusir replied. Then he frowned, as if musing. "I've been trying to place your face for some time, Colonel," he said. "Then it came to me. Weren't you the officer who refused my commission a few years ago?"

Olaf's eyes widened in sudden fear. Jowls trembling, he said, "Oh, it most certainly wasn't me!"

Tabusir examined the man's face with deliberate slowness. Olaf couldn't help but let one hand steal up his chest to touch his fat throat.

"Are you sure about that?" Tabusir asked. "I'd swear you were the man. I rarely forget a face."

"No! Truly!" Olaf squeaked.

Tabusir made an elaborate shrug. "Ah, well, then," he said. "I suppose it's a case of mistaken identity." Then he bowed low. "My apologies, Colonel for begging an end to this most delightful conversation. But I must be off to find the king his heads."

Another bow. "With your permission, of course."

Olaf made a weak-fingered wave, babbling, "Yes, yes. You must not tarry. You have the king's commission!"

Tabusir strolled away, leaving a group of very shaken officers in his wake.

He looked up at the clearing skies, thinking, What an excellent day this has turned out to be.

In his mother's quarters, Rhodes was thinking the same thing as Clayre made an apology so rare that no matter how hard he racked his brains, he couldn't recall another such incident.

"I humbly beg your pardon, my son," she said, "for being the cause of our quarrel. You were right to worry about the mural and I should have listened to your concerns."

Rhodes was about to press his advantage and make her grovel more before accepting her apology, but Kalasariz hissed a warning and he thought better of it.

"It's a thing of the past, mother," he said, forcing magnanimity. "We'll not speak of it again."

He paused, giving Kalasariz time to suggest how to proceed. Then he said, "Have you figured out how the mural disappeared from your chambers, mother?"

Clayre sighed. "I'm afraid not, my son," she said. "Nor do I know how it came into Safar Timura's possession, much less how he managed to use it against us."

She raised a golden wine cup to her beautiful lips and drank sparingly. Then she said, "The trouble is that the mural was there for so long that I'd quite forgotten it. Oh, I had heard stories. Stories that I believed were myths. That the mural depicted the first great king of Syrapis and his daughters. One taleteller even had it that the king portrayed was the grandfather of Alisarrian."

Clayre took another sip of wine. After a moment of reflection, she said, "Although I thought these tales were only myths, I must have sensed some truth in them. For it is the only one of the ancient murals in my chambers that I did not use or alter in any way for my magical purposes. And although it does not excuse my forgetfulness, it does explain why I put it from my mind."

The Queen Witch placed the goblet down quite firmly, her eyes growing fierce. Her fabulous looks so intensified by the emotions roiling within that even Rhodes was stricken by his mother's beauty.

"But I promise you this, my son," she said. "Before this journey is done I will find a way either to nullify the power of the mural or use it to use it our own advantage."

Both Rhodes and Kalasariz were relieved to hear this. "Do you think we can continue the expedition with some hope of success?" the king asked.

"Without a doubt," Clayre said.

Then she waved at her gilded table, where the map was still pinned against the tiles by the four black candles. The replica of the

Nepenthe now sitting a few hair's breadths from the coast of Aroborus.

"I can also report that our efforts were not completely unsuccessful," she said.

Rhodes looked carefully at the scene and gradually he detected slight movements in the ship. A little fluttering of the sails. An almost imperceptible pitch and roll of the hull. Then he realized that the ship was not quite touching the parchment of the map. And that it actually rested on seas so faint that a flicker of the eye would make them vanish.

"The last time," Clayre said, "my only mistake was that I tried to interfere. It was Jooli's fault, really. Honestly, that girl could drive the most patient of people mad. Still, I shouldn't have tried to kill her. That's what alerted Safar Timura to our presence."

Again, she raised the chalice and sipped. And she said, "I won't make that same mistake again. As you can see, I've got a very weak spell working for us now. One that's impossible for our enemies to detect and yet we'll still be able to follow them."

"That's certainly good to hear, mother," Rhodes said. "But don't we still have the problem of catching them? I mean, our delaying tactics didn't work, correct?"

Clayre smiled, her perfect features glowing with delight. "Actually, they worked quite well," she said. "Naturally, it would've been nice if we could have ended the race quickly by killing them. On the other hand, we've accomplished the next best thing."

"Which is?" Rhodes asked.

The Queen Witch's lovely smile twisted into an ugly, gloating expression.

"Which is that they've lost that little bastard, Palimak," she said. "He fell off the ship and fools that they are, they're searching for him now."

She pointed at the miniature *Nepenthe*, which had moved half an inch down the coast of Aroborus.

"If the winds stay with us," she said, "we ought to catch them within a week!"

The prospect of victory excited Rhodes. But the hope that Palimak might be dead made him positively tingle.

But then Kalasariz spoke, his mental whispers dousing Rhodes' joy as effectively as a large pail of cold water. He said, *Remember, we need the boy's body. Just as we require Safar Timura's. Otherwise you will not achieve your dream of taking their powers to overwhelm your enemies — especially your mother.*

The king's mouth went dry. He grabbed up the wine flask and drank down half its contents. His mother observed this with barely concealed disgust.

"But what if he has drowned, mother?" he asked, voice thinning with tension. "What if he fell into the sea and sank to the bottom? That'll do us no good!"

"Corpses don't sink, they float," she said. "And if he floats, I'll find him, never fear. And if he didn't drown . . ."

She paused, turning to gaze upon the *Nepenthe* with eyes as fierce as a demon's.

"If Palimak didn't drown," she said, picking up where she'd left off, "by the time I'm done with him he'll curse the gods he holds most holy for sparing him from the sea!"

32

EEDA'S SECRET

Coralean had never felt so sick in his life. From the shelter of the bridge he could see the storm-driven waves boom under the *Tegula*, lifting her up, up, up, then dropping her down so far his stomach thought it had found a new home, lodged at the back of his throat.

Torrents of rain lashed the ship in a never-ending fury. Great seas burst over the sides, flooding the decks until they were waist-high and the men had to go about their duties with safety lines tied about their waists.

Captain Drakis checked the sails with a critical eye to make certain there was just enough canvas spread, but not too much. Then he studied the compass heading and nodded in satisfaction.

"She's right on course, me lord," he said. "Lucky thing we caught this storm. If she holds, we'll cut the lead that scurvy dog Rhodes has over us by half or more."

Coralean gulped back bile and forced a smile. "Surely the gods must love the name of Drakis," he said with false cheer. "Considering the bonus I'll be blessing you with when we overhaul the king."

"Aye, that be the truth, me lord," Drakis replied. "Luck's favored the Drakis family far back as even me granny can remember. Even when we was lubbers not one of us ever went hungry more'n a day or three.

"Just when we'd be down to thinkin' old boot leather'd make a lovely meal, the gods'd send along a drunk with a fat purse and a skinny neck, if ya know what I mean."

Coralean's stomach did a somersault that was only partially inspired by the heaving deck. Seasick as he was, his imagination seized on some poor sod staggering out of a tavern to spew his guts and having his throat cut by one of Drakis' relatives.

I must be getting old, he thought, to let such flights of cutthroat fancy affect me. The Coralean fortune, after all, was not built by men who shrank at the idea of spilled blood. How many bandit heads have you cut off yourself to post on the caravan trail as a warning to others? And how many murderous competitors were buried by the trail after they tried to ambush you?

In all honesty he had to admit the difference between deaths caused through honest commerce and outright theft was slight. His mind started to wobble further down that disturbing path and he pulled himself up, realizing it was a by product of his illness. Besides, Drakis was looking at him, wondering why he hadn't answered.

"Coralean knows from personal experience what you mean, Captain," the caravan master replied. "In fact I was just reflecting on my youthful career as a raider. One day in particular stands out. It was when I won my first big stake into the caravan business. Why, we cut so many throats that day we . . ."

And he went on to spin a marvelous and detailed lie. Sick as he was, Coralean told such an artful tale of murder and deceit that the pirate captain's eyes shone with admiration. Believing himself fortunate to be admitted into the awesome presence of such a cold-hearted thief as the great Lord Coralean.

All of the captains and sailors in the fleet thought Coralean was not only as much a rogue as they were but was actually better than themselves at the craft of crime. And certainly far more cunning.

It was one of the ways he'd kept his hold over them. A steely grip he had to keep more secure than ever if he were to save Safar from being overtaken and ambushed at sea by Rhodes and his three stolen ships.

Coralean had not been fooled by the Hunanian king's ruse. A

man who had won several fortunes by never underestimating his enemies, he'd not wasted one minute thinking Rhodes' intentions were to use the ships to stage an attack on the Kyranian stronghold.

Which was what the Council of Elders had believed when he'd brought the news to them of the betrayal off the port of Xiap. They were all for rushing the army down to the beach where Rhodes was most likely to come ashore.

Fortunately, Safar's father, Khadji, quickly saw Coralean's logic. Especially after the caravan master revealed that their old enemy Kalasariz — who had once seized Kyrania with a horde of demons — had shown up in Syrapis and joined Rhodes.

Leaving Coralean to argue with the Council, Khadji had led a lighting raid on Hunan and brought back several captured officers. Rhode's men were as greedy as their king and all it took was a little creative bribery to get them to spill the details of his plan.

Immediately all opposition to Coralean's proposal to chase down the king and rescue Safar and Palimak had collapsed.

Now he was only three or four days behind Rhodes. He had all nine remaining ships at his disposal, plus a large force of Kyranian soldiers spread through the fleet. All of them well-warned and alert to the possibility of another attempt at betrayal.

If even a single sailor showed mutinous intent, he'd be cut down and thrown over the side to the sharks.

The image of sharp teeth tearing into human flesh and blood-frothed water rose up in Coralean's mind and his belly staged another rebellion.

"Is somethin' wrong, me lord?" Drakis asked, concern in his voice and a gleam of something quite different in his eyes. "Are you feelin' under the weather this day?" He waved at the straining sails. "It's only a little blow. Nothin' to set a *real sailor's belly to quarrelin'.*"

The last thing Coralean wanted was a display of weakness in front of Drakis, the most respected of the pirate captains in the fleet. Especially a weakness of the seagoing variety.

"It's not my innards that are rebelling, captain," the caravan master lied. "As all men know, Coralean has a belly worthy of a cast-iron pot. Why, a fellow once tried to poison me with lye and I drank it down and called for more."

He gripped his forehead between mighty fingers and squeezed. "It's my poor head. I blame it on that keg of brandy my wife served me last night. I only drank a gallon or so for a nightcap before bed.

Still, it seems to have given me a fierce headache."

He sighed. "The price of getting old, I warrant," he said. "I used to drink a whole keg without effect and sleep like a babe in his mother's arms."

Drakis was instantly and honestly sympathetic. Under the pirate's rules of manly behavior too much drink was a completely acceptable excuse for any number of things, up to and including taking an ax to your own family.

"It musta been a bad batch of brandy, me lord," he said. "Or maybe the keg was broached and some sea-water got in. Hells, I've gotten sick meself from that sort of thing!"

"It did taste a little salty," Coralean said, frowning.

Drakis nodded vigorously. "See, what'd I tell you? It's the brine that's makin' your head hurt!"

He placed a hand on one of Coralean's massive shoulders. "Whyn't you go below and take a rest, me lord?" he suggested. "I'll send you a keg of my own private reserve to help you sleep. Couple quarters of that, mixed with a little sugar, and you'll sleep like that babe you was talkin' about and wake up feelin' right as rain. That's my prescription."

Coralean grinned. "Thank you very much, Doctor Drakis," he jested. "I'll take your good advice and go below to my cabin."

Then, calling on his last reserves of willpower, he fought down another wave of seasickness and took his leave, reputation intact.

Eeda was waiting for Coralean when he entered the spacious cabin.

"Oh, my poor, dear lord husband," she said when she saw his pale face, "you don't have your sea legs under you yet, do you?"

The caravan master groaned, letting all pretense vanish. For reasons not quite clear to him yet, he felt more comfortable in Eeda's presence than in that of any of his other wives.

"I fear not, my pretty one," he admitted. "At this moment, your beloved bull, Coralean, feels more like a foundling calf, sick from wanting his mother."

"Here, my lord husband," she said, handing him a steaming goblet. "Drink this and you'll feel much better."

Coralean sniffed the fumes. It was brandy laced with fragrant spices. Still he hesitated, saying "I don't know if I can, little one," he said. "Even brandy may not sit well on this traitorous belly of mine."

Eeda put on a charming pout. "Oh, please trust me, lord husband," she said. "I used to make this for my father when he was feeling less than himself. And it always worked such wonders that he called it a miracle potion direct from the gods."

"I doubt if even a miracle can help me, sweetness" Coralean said. Then, moved by her pout, he relented, saying, "But I can refuse you nothing, pretty one. Although it might result in the God of Death, himself, paying a visit to carry poor Coralean away."

He drank the potion down, shuddering as it hit bottom and bounced several times. Then he smiled as the bouncing stopped and warmth and good cheer flooded through his body, banishing the sickness.

"Why, I feel better already," he said, surprised. He looked at the dregs in the cup. "What was in that marvelous elixir, my precious one?"

Eeda smiled prettily. "Oh, a little of this and a little of that," she said. "Along with a large dose of magic."

Then she gently pushed him to his bunk, unbuckling his belt and helping him with the fastenings of his clothing. A moment later he was seated and she pulled off his boots, then his breeches and shirt. Like a helpless child he submitted to her tender ministrations, letting her pull a sleeping gown over his head to cover his massive body.

He sighed blissfully. She'd even warmed the gown with a hot iron.

"You're not sorry you brought me with you, lord husband?" she asked as she pressed him down onto the bunk and pulled up the blanket.

"Even though it nearly caused a revolt in my harem out of jealousy," he said, "I've yet to regret my decision."

"And a wise decision it was, my lord husband," Eeda said. "Although your other wives are paragons of character and strength — and beauty, of course, since all your wives are perfection itself. Reflecting your good taste in women. But as it turned out, only I had the good fortune to be born blessed with the means of assisting you."

Coralean chuckled. "What a surprise that was," he said. "I never dreamed when I married you that you were a witch. Why didn't you tell me before?"

Eeda blushed. And somehow, although she was sitting on the bunk and her head was above his, she managed to look at him through lowered eyes, charming him through and through.

"Oh, I'm only a little witch, lord husband," she said. "Nothing to boast about. I can cure minor ailments, such as your sickness. And cast one or two spells that don't amount to much, but which you might find useful in your mission."

"Pardon, my sweetness," Coralean said, "but you didn't answer my question. I asked why you didn't tell me about this ability before — never mind your opinion of its worth."

Eeda hung her head. "You promise you won't be angry with me, lord husband?" she asked. "I couldn't bear it if I disturbed your serenity by being the cause of any irritation."

"How could I be angry with such a pretty thing as you?" Coralean said. "Go on — tell all. And I, Coralean, swear upon my children's souls that I won't become even slightly angry."

After a moment's hesitation, Eeda said, "Well, my lord husband, I was afraid if I said anything you wouldn't marry me. Most men are not so generous and forgiving of their wives. Just as most men would — dare I say it? — feel intimidated by having a wife who had powers they themselves did not possess."

"Bah!" the caravan master exclaimed. "Other men are not like Coralean." He thumped his big chest. "As all know, I have the strength and wisdom of many. How could I ever feel my manhood was being called into question by mere magic? Which, as you say, doesn't amount to much in any case."

"I must confess it is stronger than it was before," Eeda said. She patted her still-flat belly. "I think it's because I am with child. There are those who say a pregnant witch comes to possess abilities far above her normal state."

Coralean frowned. "Your delicate condition was one thing that almost made me decide against your request to accompany me," he said. "This is a perilous mission, there's no denying. But Coralean has faced such dangers before — too many times to enumerate. However, not once did I risk one of my wives. Who are all dear to me. Why, Coralean holds his wives and children as his most precious possessions!"

Perhaps Coralean caught Eeda's quick flash of irritation at his description of his women and children as possessions. Or perhaps he only sensed it without consciously realizing. At any rate, he instinctively corrected himself.

"Not that a human being — at least one not born or sold into slavery — can truly be called a possession," he said magnanimously. "A treasure, perhaps. But not a possession."

He smiled broadly, feeling good about himself. As if he'd given her a rare gift by all but admitting an error.

Eeda smiled as if in appreciation, but he noted the smile vanished a shade too quickly. She plucked at a loose thread on the blanket and he got the idea that she hadn't taken kindly to his admission.

Finally, she murmured, "You are most gracious, lord husband."

But she said it without feeling, as if speaking words she did not mean. And for the first time in his active career as husband and lover, Coralean became unsure of himself. What, pray, had he done to offend her?

Then, changing the subject, Eeda said, "I've nearly completed my project for you, lord husband. Are you still too ill or weary to examine it?"

"No, sweetness," he replied. "I'm feeling much better, thanks to your tender care — and your miracle potion, of course. Why, it's a wonder your father ever allowed a daughter as valued and useful as yourself to depart his household."

Another quick, cold smile and Eeda rose and went to the writing table to fetch back a piece of parchment. Coralean examined it with exaggerated interest, wondering how he could climb out of the hole he'd dug, instead of deepening it with every word he said.

The parchment had once contained only a dashed-off and highly inaccurate sketch of Safar's intended journey. Safar had drawn it absently while describing his plans to Coralean and Khadji just before he'd left. There were scratched-in mileage figures on the side — all guesses — meant mainly to help determine the type and quantity of the supplies Safar would need.

He'd thrown it away when the meeting was over, but Myrna, Safar's mother, had saved it as a souvenir — just as she saved all of her scholar son's cast-off scribblings.

She'd remembered it when Eeda had asked if there was something personal of Safar's she could have as an aid in casting a spell to locate his position. Armed with the sketch, Eeda had labored hard in the days that followed. Making many false starts, but gradually working out a magical method.

At first, as Coralean studied the parchment he could see little difference from the original. Then he noticed faint lines — appearing like the marks of an artist's brush moistened only with water, which had since dried.

Still, he was bewildered — uncertain of Eeda's intent. "You'll have to explain this to me, my sweet," he said. He shook his mighty head. "Sometimes, I must confess, your beloved husband — sage that he might appear to be — is not as wise as he makes out."

The caravan master immediately became alarmed at this admission of weakness. "But only *sometimes*," he hastened to add. "Such as when I'm weary, or have not regained my sea legs. For as even Coralean's enemies will admit, lying jackals that they are, when it comes to wisdom, no man —"

Eeda put a slender finger to his lips, shushing him. Coralean saw the coldness had vanished from her eyes and her smile was once again tender and loving.

"Say no more, please, lord husband," she said softly. "Lest you spoil the gift you have just given me."

Coralean didn't have the faintest idea what she meant, but he took her advice and said no more. Although he was not always wise he was never a fool, and so he let it rest, thinking understanding would most likely come later.

Then she plucked the parchment from his fingers, saying, "Here, let me show you, lord husband, what I have done."

Eeda took a small pouch from an inside pocket in her robe. She dipped two fingers into the pouch and drew out a pinch of glittering green dust. This she carefully sprinkled on the parchment.

"As you know, dear lord husband," she said, "I've tried many spells, but all have failed. Partly because I was afraid to spoil the parchment, making it useless to us forever. And partly because I am young and lack experience in such things. However, this morning I attempted something new. A spell of my own invention. I was only waiting for your return to test it."

Eagerly, Coralean sat up in his bunk, pushing pillows behind him. "Pray, continue, O wisest of women," he said. "Coralean is but a young, ardent student crouched humbly at your pretty feet."

Eeda gave him a sharp look, but then saw he was not attempting to make a feeble jest at her expense. It was only his way of speaking and there were no hidden meanings or insults. Once again her eyes softened and her smile became gentle.

She held the parchment up to her lips and blew. Coralean heard a sound like temple chimes swaying in the breeze. The green dust flew away, sparkling in the cabin's dim light, and hung suspended in a cloud.

Then faintly, ever so faintly, Coralean could see Safar's face forming in the cloud. He looked sad and careworn. His lips moved, forming a word, but no sound issued forth.

However, the canny old caravan master, a past master at eavesdropping on his competitors, was quite skilled at reading lips.

"Safar said, 'Palimak'," Coralean whispered. "Palimak!"

Then Safar's face — and the green cloud — vanished.

Eeda held up the parchment for Coralean to see. A thin green line was now etched on its surface. It ran in a long arc, following the trade winds from Syrapis all the way to Aroborus, where it stopped.

"That's where he is now, lord husband," Eeda said, tapping the place where the line ended.

She glanced at the mileage figures Safar had scratched on the side. "Shouldn't he have made better progress than this?" she asked.

Coralean nodded, brow knotted in worry. "Yes," he replied. "His plan was to bypass there and strike for the islands beyond, where he would take on water and replenish his provisions. His thinking was that there was so little known about Aroborus it wouldn't be wise, or safe, to tarry there."

"I wonder why he stopped?" Eeda said.

Coralean shook his big head. "There must be something wrong," he said. "And whatever that wrongness is — it has to do with Palimak!"

33

IRAJ'S SONG

The search for Palimak was stalled half the night by a swift-moving rainstorm that first reduced visibility to only a few yards, then became so strong they were forced to heave to and lay out a sea anchor to hold position.

As Brutar, the captain of the *Nepenthe*, said: "If we let the blow take us, we'll never find the place where the lad went off."

Biner took the airship above the storm, circling in the cold, thin air until just before dawn when the storm passed on to bedevil the lands beyond.

Then they resumed the search, retracing their path beyond the point where the battle with the tree-creatures had begun. Safar sent out two longboats to help scour the area, with Leiria and Jooli taking command of each of them.

Although he had little experience at sea, Safar was a skilled hunter — as were all Kyranians — and he used an old trick the mountaineers used to employ when speed was paramount — such as finding a lost child after a blizzard had passed, obliterating all trail signs.

But instead of human trackers he used the *Nepenthe* and the airship. The tall ship started in the center and circled outward, while Biner started at the most distant point and circled inward toward the center. This way the same area was scoured twice in a very brief time period and there was little chance of missing Palimak if he were still afloat.

Although he didn't say anything, Safar could tell by Captain Brutar's dark expression that he thought the search was pointless after so many hours had passed. Like most sailors, Brutar and his crew could barely swim — if at all — and thought Palimak had most probably drowned not long after he had jumped from the ship to escape his pursuer.

Brutar's expression became darker still when he saw how infested the area was with sharks and sea crocodiles. Fins constantly criss-crossed the calm seas, while hungry reptilian eyes poked just above the surface, looking for opportunity.

Once they came upon an enormous crocodile fighting with two equally huge sharks over bloody remains.

Leiria and Jooli moved up in the longboats as the terrible fight raged. Then dispatched all three of the creatures with their longbows.

To Safar's relief, the remains proved to be not human but the corpse of a serpent whose body was twice the girth of a man's.

Finally, Captain Brutar made bold to approach Safar. Embarrassed, he hawked and spat over the rail.

Then he said, "Beggin' yer pardon, me lord, and it pains me somethin' awful to say this to a father what's boy has gone missin'. In this old salt's opinion the lad's a goner and that's for certain. We can hunt 'til the Hellsfires burn themselves out and we won't find nothin' but what we already found — which is nothin'!"

Safar shook his head. "He's still alive," he said. "And if I have to, I'll turn the sea upside down and shake it out to find him!"

Brutar sighed. "Dammit, man," he said, "yer talkin' like we was lookin' fer a worm in a biscuit. Knock it 'gainst a table and the worm falls out, real easy like."

He made a wide gesture, taking in the long, empty horizon.

"The sea ain't no biscuit. And the lad, bless his soul, ain't no worm livin' and eatin' in its natural born home. This is the sea, man. Which means she'll even kill her own!"

The captain braced for an argument, but was prepared to stand fast. Personally, he didn't give a thin fishbone about Palimak, much less about Safar's tender fatherly feelings. He wanted to get on with the voyage and either collect his promised bonus or toss Safar and the Kyranians over the side if for some reason the bonus wasn't forthcoming.

Actually, it was his cherished dream to accomplish both — collecting the money and ridding himself and his crew of this pesky lot once and for all. And get back to honest pirating, instead of fighting another man's enemies for pay.

However, instead of arguing, Safar's eyes lit up. He slapped the captain on the shoulder, saying, "Thanks, Captain! You may have just solved the problem!"

And he rushed away, leaving a bewildered Brutar staring after him. What in the hells had he said to be thanked for?

Safar burst into Palimak's ruined cabin and quickly found the doughmen as well as the two pieces of worm, which still showed faint signs of life. Then he sped to his own quarters where he dug out a wine jar, emptied the contents into a basin and knocked off the jar's narrow mouth with the blade of his silver witch's dagger.

Next, he waved the dagger over the worm parts and cast a regeneration spell. Sparks leaped off the point and each piece grew the part it was missing. A moment later there were two whole worms wriggling across the table. Safar imprisoned them with an overturned cup, then went on to the rest of his preparations.

After moistening the doughmen with wine, he formed them into a single ball. Then, with his skillful potter's fingers, he sculpted a single doughman of his own. Except, instead of Palimak's rather clumsy figures, this one looked like a tall, slender, broad-shouldered youth.

Using the dagger point Safar pricked in the features and in scant minutes Palimak's face appeared like magic — although it was art, not sorcery, that Safar used.

He slit the belly, pressed the worms inside, then smoothed over the wound. The Palimak doughman went into the wine jar, whose mouth was sealed with wax. He paused, taking in a deep breath to clear his mind. Now he was ready for the spell.

He went up to the main deck, the jar cradled in one arm. Leiria was already there, face pale as death, thinking the search had been called off. Jooli was just clambering on board from the longboat. Safar signaled the airship for Biner and Arlain to join him. And when all were gathered at the bow he asked their assistance in casting the spell to find the lad they all loved.

When he thought their minds were all fixed on the single goal he gestured, and burning incense appeared in his hand, filling the air with its heady scent. He heard murmurs from behind him, where Brutar and the crewmen watched, fearful of the wizardry he was about to perform.

Then, drawing on Asper for inspiration, he whispered:

"When in your mother's womb
You did dwell;
Tarrying between love's tomb
And life's Hell;
Did you ever wonder if the fearful Path
Where you tarried
Was close or distant from Fate's wrath?
Or were you carried,
Into this world not knowing
From whence you came
Or where you were going;
Bound for Nowhere on winds of pain?"

Then he threw the jar into the rolling waves. It bobbed about for a moment, then retreated swiftly as the ship sailed on. A great shark's fin cut in front of it. Everyone held their breath, whether from the sight of the shark or in anticipation of the spell, Safar couldn't say.

Suddenly, the jar reversed course. As if powered by a mighty sail it shot forward against the waves, moving past the ship's bow, then heading steadily away to the thin green line on the horizon.

Safar pointed. "That's where he is," he said. "In Aroborus."

And then he gave orders to set sail and follow the magical device to wherever it might lead.

The shores of Aroborus were a dazzling green, as if some wastrel god had cast emeralds from Heaven's treasure house into the sea. The wind blew fragrant, carrying the heady scent of spices and fruited vines. Clouds of birds wheeled in the sky, filling the air with their mournful cries.

The wine jar came to rest on a wide beach of white sand, pebbled with broken shells of many colors — swept up from the sharp coral reefs that ringed the narrow-mouthed bay. Somehow the jar had been swept over the reefs unscathed. But at no point was there a place the longboats could get through, much less a tall ship the size of the *Nepenthe*.

Safar could see the wine jar bobbing in a tidepool and for the life of him couldn't imagine the circumstances that would have allowed Palimak to reach the beach unscathed.

Brutar said as much, pointing out that common reason said if the lad had made it this far alive, he surely would've died when he was hurled against the reefs to be shredded by their razor edges.

"Makes me shiver just to think about it, me lord," he said gloomily. "The poor boy comin' so close to safety, like. Gettin' his hopes up when he saw dry land. Then bein' 'et up alive by them reefs, like he'd run into a school of sharks."

He sighed. "And ain't it a wicked world we was born to, me lord," he said, "to allow such an innocent lad — a lad loved by all — to come to such a terrible end? Makes a simple man like meself question his faith, it does.

"Damned priests are al'ays sayin' the gods smile on the good folk who mind their laws. But if truth be known it's the bad 'uns who al'ays get through this life the easy way, ain't it?"

Worried as he was, Safar had to bury a smile at this speech, coming as it did from the lips of a committed cutthroat and pirate. Not that he entirely disagreed with Brutar's philosophy. Which was that under the unspoken laws of the heavens, it was the wicked, not the meek, who endured and prospered. While priests made themselves and their client kings rich and powerful by preaching the opposite to the masses.

It reminded him of a blasphemous drinking song from his days as a rebellious student in Walaria. He'd taught it to Iraj after they'd joined up again and it had become Protarus' favorite ditty.

He sang it whenever they got together in private to drink and talk as equals. As young brothers of the blood oath, whose sworn common goal was for the good of all.

An image rose up in his mind — so strong, so real, that it swept away the terrible present and replaced it with the pleasant past. In his mind's eye he could see Iraj sprawled on thick pillows. The slender waist of a nubile wench clasped in one hand, a cup of cheer lifted in the other.

And he was singing, the remembered voice so real it strummed

Safar's own vocal chords. He had the odd feeling that if he opened his mouth it would be Iraj's voice that came forth, instead of his own.

Although he didn't humiliate himself in front of the others, he let the scene play out in his mind. Then suddenly he lost all sense of time and place, waves of peace and half-drunken joy thrilling his imagination as the man who was once his friend sang:

"Rich man, poor man,
holy man, thief.
The rich get heaven,
the poor man grief.
Alms for the holy man,
To the thief, baksheesh!"

Then the other Safar — the Safar of the vision — joined in, slapping his knee in rhythmic time and singing the chorus:

"Oh, there's dancing on the altar
For those who do not falter.
Sin and gold for the bold.
To the meek, lash and halter . . ."

And then Leiria's voice cut through, bursting the vision like a knife thrust into a swollen bag of wine. And all the images spilled out, weakening him as if they were his life's blood.

"Are you all right, Safar?" she was saying.

He gasped, sucking in air like a man rising from watery depths, and emerged into the painful present. The wine jar still bobbed in the tidepool, but with Brutar nowhere to be seen. Instead of the captain, it was Leiria standing before him, looking up at him with worried eyes.

Safar coughed. Then he managed to nod, but the movement was jerky, clumsy. "Yes," he croaked. "I'm fine."

He glanced about and saw that Brutar was some twenty feet distant, standing with some of his officers. Safar had no recollection that they'd parted.

"Are you sure?" Leiria asked. And for the first time, Safar realized she was whispering so the others couldn't hear.

"A few minutes ago," she continued, "you were talking to the captain, then you suddenly turned and walked off as if he'd angered you."

"I'm not angry at anyone," Safar said, puzzled. "Why should I be?"

Leiria put a gentle hand on his arm. Its loving warmth seeming to act as a catalyst to cleanse the remaining dregs of unreality from his mind.

"Actually," she said, "when I came up to see what was wrong, you were smiling. You looked so peaceful I hated to disturb you."

She made a faint motion with her head to indicate Brutar. "But I didn't want them to get the idea their commander had suddenly gone mad."

"I was only thinking," Safar said. "About . . . well, it doesn't matter now."

He knew this was an insufficient explanation, but was uncomfortable about saying more. Especially since it involved Iraj, whom Leiria hated with a passion.

"Whatever it was you were thinking about," she said, "I'm glad it made you smile. It's been a long time since I've seen you look so happy."

She moved closer, soft breasts brushing against him. Familiar perfume and fragrant breath rising to fill him up like wine.

And they were suddenly just a man and a woman — lovers from another time and place come together once more.

Safar had the overpowering urge to embrace her and kiss her. To carry them both away to the bower of joy they'd once shared together.

Only the presence of Brutar and the crew kept him from acting on his impulse.

Leiria shuddered, aching for the embrace. "You can come to me anytime you like," she whispered. "I won't send you away again."

"I know," Safar said, voice rasping with effort.

Hurt came into her eyes. "But you won't," she said, nearly weeping.

"I want to," Safar said. "But I can't."

The hurt softened. And she recovered, smiling sadly. "For the old reasons?" she asked.

Safar nodded. "And more," he said. "There's . . . there's . . . something that . . ." and he gave up the struggle and broke off the rest. "I can't explain," he said again.

"Will you ever tell me?" she whispered.

"Yes," he said. The answer started as a lie but, brief as his reply was, by the time he spoke the word it became a promise.

Leiria smiled and, hidden from the sight of the others by his body, she blew him a kiss.

Then she turned and for the benefit of the onlookers laughed loudly as if he'd just told a fine jest. It must have worked for Brutar was visibly relieved.

The pirate captain turned to his officers, chuckling as if he'd overheard the joke, saying, "You see. Lord Timura was only a bit tired from worryin' and bein' up all night lookin' for his boy."

Safar squared his shoulders, again accepting the weight of all the burdens he'd escaped, however briefly.

"We'd better get going," he said to Leiria.

"Yes, we'd best," she said, but her tone was regretful.

Safar pushed emotions aside and got to work. He'd already decided how to proceed and immediately signaled for Biner to prepare to take him away. A moment later a large basket was cranked down from the skies.

Before he ascended to the airship with Leiria and Jooli, Safar sent for Renor. The young soldier approached, his ever-present companion, Sinch, at his heels.

"Biner's going to land us on the beach with the airship," Safar said. "I don't know how long it's going to take to find Palimak, or what dangers we might encounter, but I want you to be on the alert for my signal."

"Don't worry, Lord Timura," Renor said. "We'll come running the moment you send for us."

Safar patted his shoulder. He was quite fond of the young Kyranian, who had suffered and borne up under much since the days when they had all been forced from their homeland. His little brother had been the first victim of Iraj's assault — slaughtered in a high mountain meadow in the Gods' Divide.

"I never worry about you, Renor," Safar said. He grinned at Sinch. "Or you either, Sinch. Except for your tasteless jokes, of course."

Sinch blushed, pleased that the great Lord Timura remembered such a personal thing about him.

"I'll have a dozen more ready, my lord," he said, "for when you get back. I know you love a good joke."

Safar smiled in appreciation. Then he said, "The only thing that really worries me is Captain Brutar and his pirates. I want you both to be on your guard in case they decide to forgo the bonus and play the traitor."

Renor nodded. "I'll get all our boys together," he said. "Drill them in full armor and all. That ought to put the fear of the gods into those pirates. They're just rabble and they know they can't stand up to real soldiers. And if that doesn't work, we'll already have our weapons at hand to teach them some lessons about loyalty."

Safar approved this plan, issued a few more orders to cover details they hadn't discussed before, then took his leave.

Half an hour later Safar was retrieving the wine jar from the tidepool. A squad of Kyranian soldiers stood by for his orders, while Leiria and Jooli scoured the beach for some sign of Palimak.

From above came a whoosh of air and the throb of the magical engines as Biner took the airship aloft. The plan had been thoroughly discussed and the system of signals worked out. Now all Safar had to do was find Palimak.

"Over here, Safar," Jooli shouted.

He hurried to her side, Leiria joining him.

Jooli pointed at several impressions in the sand "Footprints," she said. "Although they're too faint for me to make out who they belong to."

Safar knelt, fishing out his silver dagger. He waved it over the impressions, muttering a spell. The sand shifted, moving only a few grains at a time and gradually the footprints took form, standing out deep and clear.

They were human prints — long and narrow with well-formed toes. The only thing out of the ordinary were tiny marks like hooks springing from the toes. Not hooks but talons, Safar thought. Which could only mean one thing. Relief flooded in.

"It's Palimak," he said.

Safar looked up at the forest bordering the beach. The trees were so dense they might as well have been castle walls. Then he saw the break of a narrow avenue leading into the woods.

"He went that way," he said, rising.

They followed the footprints a short distance along the beach, Safar stopping every now and again to work his magic.

Then, suddenly, the distances between the tracks started lengthening. Each footprint far in front of the other.

"He's running!" Leiria said.

"Yes, but from what?" Safar said.

Heart racing, he looked about the beach, but saw no other signs.

"I don't know what's happening," he said, "but we'd better hurry."

Then he called for the soldiers and they all plunged into the dark, ancient forest of Aroborus.

34

THE RAVENOUS SEAS

"Little Master's getting tired," Gundara observed from his perch on Palimak's shoulders.

"That's too bad," Gundaree said. "We still have a long way to go."

"I'm all right," Palimak gasped. "I'm just thirsty, that's all."

He was lying more to himself than to the Favorites. Trying to stay afloat in the increasingly choppy surf was difficult. Palimak only had his tunic, which he'd turned into water wings, to support him. He'd kept his breeches on, although their weight made things more difficult. But, except as a last resort, he was loath to shed them as he had his boots.

It had nothing to do with modesty. Naked and alive was better than clothed and dead in even the shyest person's rule book. He had a few items in his pockets and hanging from his belt that might better his chances of survival once he reached land. Such as a knife and his waterproof wizard's purse, which contained all sorts of useful things.

More importantly, he needed a pocket to hold the stone turtle, otherwise the Favorites would be lost to him. Even if he could do without them, as irritating and cold-hearted as they could sometimes be, Palimak would never condemn his mischievous friends to an eternal prison at the bottom of the sea.

"You should have told us you were thirsty, Little Master," Gundara said.

"We can do something about that!" Gundaree put in.

"Then do it, please!" Palimak croaked, throat sore and raspy from all the salt-water he'd taken in.

The Favorites directed him to put his head back as far as he could. Then they hopped onto his forehead and crouched down to suck up sea-water. To his surprise they drew in enormous quantities, blowing up like little toads.

Gundara signaled for him to open his mouth and then both of

them expelled the water in a torrent so heavy he had to swallow fast to avoid choking. Transformed in their bodies, the water was amazingly clear and sweet, like fresh spring water mixed with honey.

"Enough!" Palimak finally sputtered and they stopped, resuming their perch on either shoulder.

He took in a few deep breaths and suddenly felt his strength coming back. Most likely from the nectar the Favorites had expelled along with the water. He wondered idly if perhaps spirit folk were like bees, processing what they ate into honey.

"Thanks," Palimak said. "I didn't know you could do that."

"You never asked," Gundara pointed out.

"There's lots of things we can do," Gundaree added, "that you've never asked about."

"If any of them include a way of getting us out of this fix," Palimak said, "now's the time to speak up."

The Favorites thought for a moment.

Then Gundara said, "Well, if we could make you small enough, maybe we could fit you into the turtle with us."

"But first we'd have to make the turtle float, like a little boat," Gundaree pointed out.

"I already thought of that!" Gundara sniffed. "I'm not stupid, you know."

"That's not what our mother said," Gundaree replied.

"She never!" Gundara protested.

"Sure, she did," Gundaree said. "The last time we saw her she said Gundara was the stupidest —"

"Please, please, please!" Palimak broke in. "I'm dying here, in case you've forgotten. And if I go, both of you go!"

"Little master has a good point," Gundara said.

"I'll stop if you do," Gundaree said.

"Truce?"

"Truce!"

When they were quiet, Palimak said, "We were talking about getting me into the turtle and then making it float."

"Two very good ideas, if I do say so myself," Gundara said.

"The tide's going in," Gundaree said. "So that means we'd end up on dry land in no time."

Hopes stirring, Palimak said, "Let's get started, then. What do you want me to do?"

This was greeted by dead silence. Frustrated, Palimak said, "Come on! We're wasting time!"

"There's nothing to start, Little Master," Gundara said.

"But you both said they were good ideas," Palimak pointed out.

"They are," Gundara said. "But they were only theories."

"And, unfortunately, we can't actually do either one," Gundaree said.

Palimak groaned. Some day the Favorites were going to be the death of him — literally.

"The best thing to do is keep swimming, Little Master," Gundaree advised.

"Except maybe a bit faster, before the shark catches up to us," Gundara put in.

"Shark!" Palimak exclaimed.

He stopped treading water, paddling about to look. He saw nothing but the empty Demon Moon-lit seas.

"There's two of them, actually," Gundaree said.

"And a crocodile," Gundara added. "Don't forget that."

"I didn't want to scare the Little Master," Gundaree said. "Two sharks seemed bad enough."

"What should I do?" Palimak gasped, trying to hold back panic. "I can't outswim any of them!"

"That's certainly true," Gundaree admitted.

"We have such a smart Little Master," Gundara said. "Too bad he can't swim as fast as he thinks."

"Even if he could," Gundaree said, "he'd never get away from the sea serpent."

"Sea serpent!" Palimak cried. "Where?"

"Oh, he's about thirty feet below us," Gundara said.

"He's not sure yet if you're food," Gundaree said. "But he's starting to get the idea."

Just then, off in the distance, Palimak saw a huge fin break the surface. It started to circle him — slowly, almost lazily. A moment later another popped up, circling in the opposite direction.

He couldn't see the crocodile, but he knew it'd remain so low on the surface that his first sight would be its jaws opening wide to take him.

As for the sea serpent, he'd never spot it. The thing would probably just wriggle up to grab him by the legs and pull him under.

Palimak had been in trouble many times before, but never had he been so thoroughly trapped. His panicky mind churned for inspiration but was continually interrupted by images of being eaten alive by one — or all — of the big sea carnivores closing in on him.

Meanwhile, the Favorites were conferring. Palimak was too frightened to make out what they were saying, but he supposed it was a discussion of the dubious merits of being trapped beneath the sea, with no possibility of a new master coming along to rescue them for several thousand years — if ever.

Finally, Gundara said, "We have an idea."

"Not another damned theory!" Palimak groaned, imagining the sea serpent examining his dangling legs with hungry interest.

"Oh, no," Gundaree said. "It's not a theory. This idea we can actually do something about."

"Maybe," Gundara cautioned.

"All right . . . maybe," Gundaree grudgingly admitted.

"But it's worth a try, at least," Gundara said.

"I suppose so," Gundaree agreed. "And if it doesn't work we could always try the other idea."

"What other idea?" Palimak asked.

He felt as if he'd been cast into some other world, a surreal world. A world where his impending death could be discussed so casually. While less than fifty feet away the circling sharks were closing slowly in.

And although it might only have been his imagination, Palimak thought he could see the knobbed eyes of the sea crocodile poking up a few feet within the circles.

And the serpent — oh, damn the serpent! Let him eat the leftovers! Palimak suppressed an hysterical giggle.

"Never mind the other idea," Gundara said.

"Absolutely!" Gundaree agreed. "It'll only make you mad."

"Fine, fine!" Palimak moaned. "It's forgotten. Now, please do something! I wasn't born to be somebody's dinner."

"That's not quite true, Little Master," Gundara said.

"Yes," Gundaree said. "Don't you know that *everybody* is somebody's food?"

"Not necessarily right away, you understand," Gundara said. "But eventually. It's life's most important lesson, you know."

"Our mother used to sing us the most wonderful lullaby that sums it all up," Gundaree said. And he sang:

> *"Everybody's somebody's food.*
> *Everybody's somebody's slaything.*

And though it's very, very rude,
Everybody's somebody's food!"

Gundara wiped away a tear at the memory. "Mother was such a marvelous teacher," he said.

"Oh, gods!" Palimak groaned, seeing one of the sharks make a short dash toward him. "Please, hurry and do something!"

Perhaps it was because they saw the shark make its dash, or perhaps it was only because they'd run out of things to say. Whatever the case, to Palimak's massive relief he sensed the comforting buzz of a powerful spell being cast.

He suffered one more moment of fear as suddenly there was a surge just beneath his feet — so strong it rocked him in the water. In reaction, Palimak's body spasmed and talons shot out from his fingers *and* his toes — ready to do futile battle.

There was another surge and a huge slime-covered body bumped against his, tossing him to the side.

The water boiled and he paddled furiously to keep afloat. Then an incredibly long and thick snakelike body burst from the water. It kept coming and coming like a wagon train all tied together.

He heard a wild howl of fear and caught a glimpse of the sea serpent's head as it leaped over him — fang-rimmed mouth so wide it could swallow a small boat whole.

Then several other bodies collided with his and he went under, pawing madly to regain the surface. The tunic water wings were ripped away. His talons lashed out in every direction in a desperate, instinctual, defensive effort.

The claws caught on something — he didn't know what — then ripped along dense flesh as the creature powered past him without pause.

A moment later he was on the surface, vomiting brine, too overcome to see what was happening.

"We did it, Little Master!" Gundara cried. "We did it!"

Palimak steadied himself enough to see the sea serpent racing away. A wave hit him and he went under again. But when he resurfaced he had time to catch sight of the two sharks leaping high into the air as they pursued the serpent.

Then a strong eddy rocked him as the crocodile swam past, its muscular tail slashing through the water, barely missing Palimak.

He was so astonished at not being attacked that he forgot to tread water and went under once more. But this time when he pulled himself up he did it slowly and without panic.

Palimak started treading water, clearing his eyes. To his astonishment and supreme delight he saw the sharks and crocodile speeding away after the panicked sea serpent. All jumping high out of the water to achieve maximum speed.

"What did you do?" Palimak gasped.

"It was easy, Little Master," Gundara said.

"We made the sea serpent think he was food," Gundaree explained.

"And we made the sharks and the crocodile think he'd taste better than you," Gundara continued.

"Like the song we just made up," Gundaree said. "You know: 'Everybody's somebody's food . . .'"

"I wish you'd shut up," Gundara said. "You're making me hungry and everything the Little Master has in his pockets for us to eat has been spoiled by the water."

"I won't say, 'You shut up, too,'" Gundaree replied in a surprisingly reasonable voice. "We still have that truce, right?"

"I'm sorry," Gundara said to his twin. "I forgot about the truce. Which we really need right now."

"That's all right," Gundaree said. "I know you didn't really mean it. You were just distracted because of the storm and all."

This time Palimak's heart descended to his bowels, forming an embarrassing lump of fear.

"What storm?" he asked.

At that moment rain pelted down. And a strong wind exploded the calm, whipping up waves of fearful height.

"That storm, Little Master," Gundara answered.

"What with the sharks and the crocodile and the sea serpent," Gundaree said, "we didn't think it was a good time to mention it."

"But there's still good news, Little Master," Gundara said. "We're really, really close to land right now."

From a distance, Palimak could hear the sound of waves booming across an obstruction.

"Is that a reef I hear?" he asked.

"You're so smart, Little Master!" Gundaree said. "That's exactly what it is. A big, sharp coral reef."

"You'll probably be torn to pieces by it," Gundara said. "But at least you won't have to worry about us."

"That's right," Gundaree said. "This time when you're killed we won't be stuck at the bottom of the ocean."

"We'll be washed up on the reef," Gundara further explained.

"And only have to wait maybe a hundred years or so before a new master finds us."

"Doesn't that make you happy, Little Master?" Gundaree asked. "Knowing we won't get bored?"

Palimak's heart jumped as realization sank in.

"You mean," he said, "that you don't have the faintest idea on how to get me over that reef?"

"Well," Gundaree said, "we *do* have some theories . . ."

35

JUNGLE MAGIC

The moment Safar plunged into the jungle he knew he'd made a potentially fatal error.

Biting insects swarmed up all around him. Above, there was an explosion of wings and a chorus of shrill warning cries as birds took flight.

There was a scatter of motion in the trees, like errant winds bursting forth in every direction and he saw enormous apes swinging away from his entry point, jabbering simian curses.

A huge snake fell in his path, rising up on threatening coils, spitting poison at his eyes.

But all his alarm bells were already ringing and he brought his shield up just in time for the poison to splatter against it.

Jooli shouted something he couldn't make out, but he instinctively leaped to the side and an arrow from her bow pinned the snake to the ground.

Leiria rushed in, severing the snake's head with her sword. It fell on the black leafy ground, hissing and spitting its poisonous hate.

Safar heard shouts of dismay from the soldiers and whirled around to see thorny vines and branches shooting forth to bar the entrance into the jungle.

Somewhere not far off an ape hooted in triumphant glee.

Safar raced to the closing gap, hacking at the vines with his sword. Leiria and Jooli crowded in to help. But as fast as they cut, the vines grew back at double the speed and thickness.

Then he heard an explosive *pop!* and two large insect eyes appeared out of nowhere, only inches from his face.

Crying a warning to the others he stumbled back, only to find himself caught in the sticky tendrils of a frighteningly strong web.

He fought his way out, then slashed at the thick strands entangling Leiria and Jooli.

Freed, they dashed out of the gap, which healed itself with such blinding speed that soon there was no sign of the path by which they'd entered.

Instead, Safar found himself confronted by an enormous black spider — big as a royal banquet platter. Poison oozed from large fangs set in a mouth large enough to grip a child's head.

Several strands of web shot out of tubes along its bloated body. The thick threads wrapped around branches on either side of Safar and the spider rushed along them to attack.

Jooli's arrow hissed past Safar's ear, knocking the spider to the ground and killing it. But then other spiders — just as big and fierce — popped out of nothingness and scuttled toward them.

Safar ordered a hasty but orderly retreat along the narrow path. The squad of soldiers led the way, wary of new dangers. Jooli acted as rearguard, firing arrow after arrow into the spiders, while Leiria and Safar used their swords on those that got through.

Gradually, the number of spiders diminished and then they seemed to vanish altogether. Safar called a halt to reconnoiter but, as far as he or any of the others could tell, there were no other paths except the one they'd taken.

The trees were so tall and dense it seemed like twilight under their canopy instead of the middle of the day. The forest was strangely silent. There were no bird or insect sounds. Even the apes were quiet. It was hot and humid and the air smelled of rotting things.

The Kyranians moved on, treading lightly and keeping their voices to a whisper.

Then Sergeant Hamyr, who was a bit older than the other soldiers and a skilled tracker, found Palimak's footprints in the carpet of decaying leaves.

"At least we know we're on the right trail," Leiria observed.

"The question, of course," Jooli said, "is whether it'll eventually take us out of this place. After we find Palimak, that is."

Safar shrugged. "If we can't find a way to walk out," he said, "all we have to do is start climbing." He gestured at the towering trees. "Biner is ready to pick us up with the airship anytime we're ready."

There were murmurs of relief from Sergeant Hamyr and the others. Rattled by the events of the past hour, they'd forgotten the fall-back plan.

"We can also rely on Biner to send us reinforcements if we need them," Safar added — further comforting his soldiers.

He patted a hefty pouch on his belt. "I have plenty of signal powder. So I only have to find an open space, or get high enough into the trees, to let Biner know what's happening."

Everyone felt much better after that, talking in normal voices and enjoying a quick meal of parched corn and dried goat flesh which they washed down with good Kyranian wine mixed with honey and water.

Refreshed and with their spirits restored, the expedition continued — following the narrow path that wound through the gloom like an uncoiling snake.

However, Safar was not as unconcerned about their situation as he'd made out. Dead magic permeated the forest. Rather than coming from a single source, the magic seemed to radiate from all sides as if the very trees were inhabited by unfriendly spirit folk.

Quietly, he cast some warding spells and hoped for the best. Moments after he'd finished, Jooli slipped up to his side.

"You can feel it, too?" she whispered so the others wouldn't hear.

Safar nodded. "But I've taken some precautions," he said.

"As have I," Jooli said. "Except I don't think any of our spells are strong enough."

"That's because we don't know who or what we're guarding against," Safar said. "We're both working blind."

He gestured ahead, where the path curved around a vine-choked tree, saying, "Unless I'm well off my mark, I think we'll find out soon enough. There's something waiting for us just past that point."

Jooli's eyes narrowed as she concentrated. Then she nodded. "You're right," she said. "But I can't make out what it is. Everything seems . . . I don't know, scattered."

That was exactly how Safar would have described the strange waves of magic he sensed. It was as if they were made up of many sorcerous particles with no particular center or purpose, but had only been brought together by coincidence.

"We'd better investigate before we walk right into some sort of trap," Safar said.

"Why don't I go ahead," Jooli asked, "while you watch my back?"

Safar agreed and called another halt. He told the group there were some unexplained disturbances he and Jooli needed to investigate, playing down the danger and making it seem like a routine precaution.

Leiria knew what he was up to. They'd fought together so many times that even the subtle system of signals they'd worked out over the years was unnecessary. She sensed what was happening before he had a chance to tug his earlobe or straighten his sword belt.

Instantly, she took appropriate action. "If Jooli's going to play witch when she takes point," she said, "we'll need plenty of hard steel behind her, not just more magic."

Leiria spread the men out along the trail, spears and swords at ready. When Jooli signaled to begin, they all moved forward — Safar lagging back, alert to magical attack from both the front and the rear.

When she reached the tree that marked the bend in the trail Safar saw Jooli hesitate, then lean forward to concentrate. He'd become familiar with her sorcerous spoor and caught the tingle of her magic as she probed the area beyond.

Safar added his own powers to her work and found nothing to be alarmed about.

The he saw her shrug and step forward.

Immediately, the air around her began to glow. Although he caught no scent of magic — threatening or otherwise — Safar opened his mouth to call a warning.

Then the glow became a cloud of colorful butterflies that circled her for a moment, then swept along the path just above the soldiers' heads. Except for quick glances, no one paid them the slightest attention — not even pausing to admire this swirling rainbow of flying insects.

Leiria and the soldiers were so tensed for possible danger that the butterflies' beauty escaped them.

Jooli turned her head and called back, "Everything's fine. I'm going on." Then she disappeared around the bend.

Leiria was the next to cross and once again a cloud of butterflies appeared, circling her briefly before flying down the trail. She too signaled that all was well and that she was proceeding.

Sergeant Hamyr followed, leading the soldiers around the bend, absently brushing at a third swarm of the marvelous butterflies.

Safar paused at the tree. He studied the ground, then examined the massive roots that rose twenty feet or more before they joined the trunk.

He saw a large snake, thick as a man's body, moving slowly up one of the roots. But its attention was fixed on a monkey, sitting silently and peacefully on a limb, grooming itself.

Other than the snake, he could see nothing that might endanger him. Nor could he see where the butterflies had come from.

He heard Leiria call to him, her voice calm and reassuring. So he stepped forward, alert for the slightest disturbance.

And nothing happened. No odd shimmer of the atmosphere. Not even a single butterfly rising up, much less a colorful swarm.

He went around the bend and some distance away saw Leiria and the others squatting on the trail, peacefully munching on rations and slaking their thirst.

Leiria waved to him. "It's all right, Safar," she cried. "Come and have something to eat and drink."

Then Jooli called out. "We found more of Palimak's footprints."

Safar hurried forward, anxious to see.

Without warning, the ground shifted under him. He fell heavily, hands shooting out to catch himself.

But when he landed, instead of the leafy jungle trail he found himself gripping hot, bare ground.

And all around him he heard hundreds of voices roar: "Kill, kill, kill! Death to Safar Timura!"

Safar came up, bewildered — but automatically reaching for his sword. He found himself standing in a large arena made of hard-packed red earth.

And instead of the jungle and his waiting friends he saw hundreds upon hundreds of shouting, painted savages — all pounding the ground with the butts of their spears. Horns blared, drums thundered and somewhere a big cat screamed in fury.

From behind he heard the heavy slap of feet racing toward him and he whirled, sword coming up. But then he froze, gaping.

For charging toward him was a half-naked youth. Brandishing a long spear aimed straight at Safar's heart.

It was Palimak!

And the crowd roared: "Kill, kill, kill! Death to Safar Timura!"

36

THE FOREST OF FORGETFULNESS

Even over the whistling wind and hard-driven rain, Palimak could hear the waves boom against the reef. Dimly he made out their jagged line — the boiling surf dyed pink by the grinning Demon Moon.

He tried to back-paddle, but the tidal current was too strong, sucking him inexorably toward the reef.

"To your right, Little Master!" Gundara cried.

Palimak obediently turned his head and saw a thick black object lifting up in the curl of a wave.

"Swim for it!" shouted Gundaree.

Palimak struck out for the object. One stroke. Two. Three. And then he was drawing close and could see it was a gnarled, twisted log, with a dozen or more limp branches trailing behind.

Palimak reached for it, then caught a glimpse of a horribly familiar set of teeth grinning out of the trunk.

Fear lanced his heart and he snatched his hand back, nearly drowning as he went under in a desperate effort to kick away from the tree-beast.

He came up, choking and sputtering, pawing at the water to stay afloat.

"Don't worry, Little Master," Gundara cried. "It's dead!"

"Well, it's almost dead, anyway," Gundaree quibbled.

"Never mind that!" Gundara said. "Get up on it before you drown, Little Master."

It took all of Palimak's faith in the Favorites to comply. Gingerly, he caught hold of the tree creature. He felt a faint flutter of life and heard the weak clicking of teeth.

Doing his best to still his quaking nerves, he flung himself across the trunk. He dangled there for a moment, skin instinctively shrinking where it touched the creature's rough surface.

"Sit up on it," Gundaree ordered.

Shuddering, Palimak did as he was told — throwing a leg on

either side until he was straddling the dying beast. Then he saw one of the fang-rimmed mouths snap open near his crotch and almost flung himself off into the sea again.

But Gundara hopped down onto the trunk, pulling a kerchief from his tunic pocket. He stuffed it into the gaping mouth.

"Eat that, you stupid thing," he said. The Favorite turned back to Palimak. "See, we told you it would be all right," he said.

"Sort of all right," Gundaree cautioned.

"Well, I guess we still have to get him over that reef," Gundara admitted.

Palimak shivered. "You mean, we're not done yet?" he asked.

"Oh, no," Gundaree said. "That was just the first part of the idea."

"The easiest part," Gundara added.

If crawling up onto one of these awful monsters was the twins' idea of easy, Palimak didn't even want to think about what was coming next.

Then he flinched as one of the tree creature's trailing limbs thrashed back to life. It rose from the water, hung there for a moment, then started to curl toward him — several small mouths opening to expose chattering fangs.

"Oh, pooh!" Gundaree said. "Honestly, some *things don't know when they're dead.*"

"Cut it off with your knife, Little Master," Gundara advised. "It's hard to concentrate with all that chewing noise."

"The stupid thing's making me hungry," Gundaree complained.

Numb, Palimak pulled out his knife and lopped the branch off. It fell into the sea and sank out of sight.

"Let's get on with it, please," Palimak said, returning his knife to its sheath. He nodded at the reef. "We're getting awfully close."

"I don't know," Gundara said doubtfully. "Are you sure you can stand up that long?"

"Maybe it'd be better to wait until the last minute," Gundaree put in.

"Stand up?" Palimak croaked. "What do you mean, stand up?"

"Well, how else are you going to jump over the reef?" Gundara asked.

"Maybe he knows how to jump sitting down," Gundaree said to his twin.

"Well, maybe he can," Gundara said doubtfully, pulling on his chin. "Although I've never seen him do it. Even in the circus."

Palimak was aghast. "Have you two lost your tiny wits?" he demanded. "I thought you were going to use magic. Not have me do something that's not only impossible but ridiculous to even think about."

"Of course, we're going to use magic," Gundaree said.

"That's what we *do*, remember?" Gundara put in.

"Except you have to help a little bit," Gundaree said.

"By standing up on the tree-creature . . ." Gundara began.

". . . And jumping when we say so," Gundaree finished.

"Trust us," Gundara said. "It'll work."

"And even if it doesn't," Gundaree added, "you were going to die anyway. So what's the harm in trying?"

"We'll be all right either way," Gundara said. "Since we're so close to the beach we won't be stuck at the bottom of the sea like we would've been before."

"That makes me feel a whole lot better," Palimak said sarcastically.

"Such a kind Little Master," Gundaree replied. "Always thinking of us!"

Palimak was a hair's breadth from saying to the hells with it and revolting. But then he thought, what else can I do but trust them? He also remembered their trick with the four sea carnivores. If they could pull that off, why not this?

"All right," Palimak said grudgingly. "I'll do it."

"Isn't he brave?" Gundaree said to his twin.

"He sure is," Gundara said. "Bravest master we've ever had."

"Except Sakyah, the demon," Gundaree said. "He was *awfully brave.*"

"That's true," Gundara said. "He just couldn't jump very well."

Alarmed, Palimak asked, "You mean you've tried this trick before?"

"Sure we did," Gundaree said. "And it almost worked, too."

"Poor Sakyah," Gundara said. "He wasn't such a bad master."

"Better than that witch who got us next, at any rate," Gundaree said. He sighed. "If only Sakyah could have jumped a little better. It would've saved us *so much trouble!*"

"Never mind Sakyah," Palimak snapped. "In case you haven't noticed, it's my tender skin you need to start worrying about."

Both Favorites took note of the reefs, now no more than fifty feet away. Huge waves crashed over them, then withdrew to reveal a vast expanse of sharp coral.

"Maybe you should try standing up now, Little Master," Gundara said.

"That way you'll have a few seconds to get used to the balancing part," Gundaree added helpfully.

Heart pounding, Palimak gingerly climbed to his feet. The tree-beast swayed in the water, but he managed to steady it, thanking the gods for Arlain's lessons in acrobatics.

"That's very, very good, Little Master," Gundara said.

"Now, get the turtle out of your pocket," Gundaree said.

"What am I going to do with that?" Palimak asked, bewildered by this new instruction.

"Well, just as you jump," Gundara said, "you have to throw it."

"We'll be inside, so don't worry about losing us," Gundaree added.

Burying his suspicions about this last instruction, Palimak dutifully got the stone turtle out of his pocket. Immediately, the two Favorites disappeared inside the talisman.

The reef loomed up, the storm-driven sea thundering against it. Then hissing like an enormous nest of disturbed snakes as the water retreated, revealing a massive, dripping cliff face studded with spears of coral.

Palimak fought for balance as he was drawn up, up and up. And then a huge wave flung him forward.

He plummeted down the side of the wave, heading directly for the coral reef! Feet skittering on the slippery surface of the tree-beast, outstretched arms wavering, the stone turtle clutched tightly in his right hand.

Then he was rising, surf boiling up to his waist, the reef top coming first to eye level, then higher until he could see a small bay on the other side — edged by a broad, rain-battered beach.

For a brief moment he thought he was going to make it. That the dead tree-beast, with him upon it, would be flung to safety on the other side.

But then he saw jagged rock rushing forward and knew he was going to be slammed against it.

"Throw the turtle, Little Master!" Gundara shouted.

"And jump!" Gundaree cried.

Palimak hurled the turtle as far as he could. Then closed his eyes and leaped.

He was never quite sure exactly what happened next. The moment he jumped, the trunk of the tree-beast struck the rocks. He had a brief sensation of flying through the air. Then of falling to his certain doom.

But just before he struck, what felt like an elastic tether suddenly jerked him forward. He heard Gundara and Gundaree shouting at him, but he couldn't tell what they were saying.

Then he was plunging into the water on the other side of the reef, desperately striking for the bottom where he thought the voices of the Favorites were coming from. Clutching onto the magical tether as a guide.

Suddenly the stone turtle was in his hand again and he struck out and up for the surface. He had time to suck in air before another wave caught him, hurling him toward the beach.

Then his head struck something hard and all became shooting stars of pain against a black, velvety night.

When he came to, Palimak didn't know how long he'd been unconscious. He was lying face down in wet sand, mouth full of grit, hot sun scorching his back, the stone turtle gripped in his right hand.

And the Favorites were jumping up and down on his shoulders, shouting hysterically:

"Get up, Little Master! Get up! Get up! Get up!"

Palimak spat sand and moaned, "I can't. Gods, I hurt all over!"

"You have to get up, Little Master!" Gundara pleaded.

"It's coming, it's coming!" Gundaree cried.

He groaned and forced himself to his knees, brushing sand from his face. Then he heard a furious roar and sudden fear swept away all feelings of pain and weariness.

Hurtling along the beach toward him was an enormous lion's head. Seemingly supported by an invisible body that left no tracks in the sand, the maned head was carried about five feet off the ground.

The lion's eyes were fixed on Palimak and it was roaring in fury, exposing fangs the length and breadth of heavy spear blades.

Palimak needed no further persuasion from the Favorites. He jumped to his feet and ran for the jungle.

A narrow opening through the dense trees seemed to promise safety and he swerved toward it, practically diving through the leafy portal when he reached it.

Palimak stumbled, heard another roar — this one seeming to

come practically at his heels — and he recovered, sprinting along the dimly-lit path as fast as his demon-powered muscles would carry him.

The lion was so close that he didn't have time to stop and climb a tree. He ran onward, praying his strength and breath would hold out.

Then he came to a sharp bend in the trail, forced by a great tree surrounded by thick roots that towered many feet above him.

"Stop, Little Master, stop!" the twins shouted in unison. "It's a trap!"

But the lion roared at the same time, its foul breath washing over his shoulders.

Naked fear spurred a panicked leap and in less than a heartbeat he was hurtling past the sharpest part of the path's bend.

There was a burst of colorful lights, then a tingling sensation that shivered up his body from toes to crown. He fell heavily, landing on hard-packed ground.

Palimak remained there, hot sun scorching his bare torso. And he wondered why his heart was beating so hard and why his breath was so labored — as if he'd run a great distance at top speed.

But he had no memory of this, much less of the reason for it.

Many other questions came flooding in. He heard hundreds, possibly thousands of people cheering all around him.

Who were they? And why were they cheering?

There was also this shrill chattering noise in his ears. What was that all about?

And then he felt a stone-hard object in his pocket — jammed between the ground and his upper thigh. For some reason the object was important to him, although he couldn't say why, only that he was relieved it was still there.

Palimak thought, I wonder where I am?

And then came another, most disturbing thought: I wonder *who I am?*

Confusion mixed with growing alarm. For the life of him, he couldn't think of his name. It didn't help that all those people were shouting and those two hysterical voices chattering alien words in his ear wouldn't stop. He just wished everyone would shut up and give him a chance to figure it out.

Shut up, shut up, shut up, he thought. Odd, how those words seemed so familiar and served to make him feel better. He mouthed them: *Shut up, shut up, shut up! It was like a tonic, settling his nerves.*

Then a strong hand clutched his. And a deep voice said, "Rise, Honored One."

Palimak let himself be drawn to his feet. He found himself facing a broad, sun-blackened chest. He looked up — then up some more, neck craning back — until he saw a huge lion's head sitting upon on a man's thick, muscular shoulders.

"Good day, honored sir," Palimak said mildly, feeling not one twinge of fear at this oddity. "Who might you be?"

"I am King Felino," the lionman said.

"Very nice to meet you," Palimak replied. Then, frowning, he asked, "Pardon, Majesty, but am I supposed to know you? I hope you don't mind my rude question, but I seem to have lost my memory."

Instead of answering, the lionman handed Palimak a spear. Red ribbons were hung from its haft, looking like streams of blood.

"This is for you, Honored One," King Felino said.

Palimak nodded. "If that's my name," he said, "I quite like it: Honored One. So much better than the only other name I can think of, which is Little Master."

He grimaced. "I keep hearing that name in my head. 'Little Master, Little Master' these voices keep saying. And I do wish they'd stop."

Palimak looked around and noted he was in a broad arena made of hard-packed red earth. Surrounding the arena were hundreds of half-naked people. Faces painted with gaudy colors, teeth filed to points.

And they were all shouting: "Kill, kill, kill, kill!" as they slammed their spear butts against the ground.

Palimak looked at his own spear, then at the lionman. "Am I supposed to kill somebody with this?" he asked.

"It is your duty, Honored One," King Felino answered. "You must save your people."

Palimak nodded. "That's a pretty good reason," he said. "First sensible one I've heard all day."

Then he wrinkled his brow. "A little earlier somebody advised me to jump and although that seemed like a terrible idea at the moment, I did it anyway. And I guess it must've worked out. Because here I am, ready to do my duty and all."

Just then the voices in his ear rang louder and this time he could make out the words: "It's a trap, Little Master! A trap!"

Reflexively he glanced around the arena. "I don't see a trap," he said to the voices. Then, to the lionman, "Do you see one?"

"It is time, Honored One," King Felino said.

"That's good," Palimak said. "Because I'm starting to get tired of just standing here and doing nothing but listen to these crazy voices."

Again, he scanned the arena. "If you don't mind me asking, Majesty," he said, "exactly who and where is this person I'm supposed to kill?"

The lionman lifted his long, brawny arm, pointing. "There," he said.

Obediently, Palimak looked where the lionman pointed. At first he didn't see anything except empty arena.

Then, in the center, there was a burst of bright light. Followed by an enormous swarm of colorful butterflies exploding out of nothingness.

Puzzled, he thought, I don't see anything but butterflies and they hardly seem worth killing.

And the voices in his ear jabbered, "It's a trap, Little Master. A trap!"

"Oh, shut up with your trap," Palimak said, getting really irritated. "Can't you see I'm busy looking for somebody to kill?"

At that moment a man popped out of thin air and plunged to the ground. He remained there for a moment, as if recovering from shock.

The crowd's shouts grew louder: "Kill, kill, kill!"

"There's the villain, Honored One!" King Felino thundered. "The black-hearted enemy of your people — Safar Timura!"

Then he roared his lion's roar, quickening instant hate in Palimak's heart.

As the enemy rose to his feet, Palimak lifted the spear and charged.

And Palimak thought, Die, damn you! Die, Safar Timura!

37

WITCHCRAFT

Ordering Jooli and the others to remain in place, Leiria rushed back along the trail to the point where they'd seen Safar vanish.

She cursed herself as a fool for not remaining at Safar's side at all times, no matter what the circumstances. Leiria had watched him come around the bend, then pause as if something was troubling him. She'd even called to him to say there was nothing to worry about.

Then — right before her eyes — he'd mysteriously disappeared. There'd been no disturbance or hint whatsoever that something was going to happen. He'd just vanished into thin air.

Now, bared sword ready, Leiria was determined to take on a whole army if necessary to wrest Safar from the clutches of whatever threatened him.

But when she came to the place where she'd last seen him there was no sign of what had occurred.

Cautiously, she retraced Safar's steps — the prints of which were mingled with hers and the others — about a hundred feet back down the trail. Still nothing. She returned to the bend where they'd lost sight of him and examined the area more closely.

The only thing she found were the scattered bodies of scores of dead butterflies. This was quite puzzling. As far as Leiria could recall she hadn't seen a single butterfly since they'd entered the jungle. More determined then ever, she once again retraced the trail. Studying every inch of the ground for some sign of Safar.

Meanwhile, Sergeant Hamyr had stumbled on a new mystery.

"Look here, Your Highness," he called to Jooli. "Young Lord Palimak's footprints ain't here no more!"

Jooli strode over to Hamyr who crouched, studying the ground. He looked up at her, bewildered.

"They were here, plain as day, a couple of minutes ago," he said, making a wide circle with his finger to surround an empty spot on the path.

He tapped the center with heavy emphasis. "Right damned here, they were," he said.

"And there were others, too," he continued, pointing down the trail ahead. "But those bastards ain't there, either! You saw them, right? Or has some son of a flea-bitten goat snuck up to steal my wits?"

Grim-faced, Jooli absorbed the news. "Yes, I saw them," she said. "Unless my wits have been stolen as well."

"Where'n the hells did they go, then, Your Highness?" he asked, voice pleading. "Nothing but damn, rotted jungle trash far as the eye can see!"

"Let me take a look, sergeant," Jooli said, motioning Hamyr

aside. "And then maybe I can answer the question for both of us."

Sergeant Hamyr made room and Jooli crouched before the circle he'd scratched in the leaves. She fumbled in her witch's pouch, which hung from her belt, and found a small oilcloth packet, marked with magical symbols.

Jooli opened it and sprinkled a small quantity of purple dust into one palm. Then she blew gently across her open hand, the dust streaming out to settle on the circle.

"There it is! Right where it was before!" Sergeant Hamyr exclaimed as Palimak's distinctive footprint faded into view, thinly painted purple by the magical dust.

It remained there a moment, the dust stirring into motion as if bringing the footprint to life. Then it vanished, dust and all.

"It's gone again, by damn!" Sergeant Hamyr cursed. He looked at Jooli, scratching his head. "Do you know what in the hells is happening, Your Highness?" he asked.

Jooli nodded, face grave. "It's a false trail, sergeant," she said. "Laid by witchcraft."

Sergeant Hamyr was aghast. "You mean some wrinkle-teated witch played us the fool?" he said.

Then he reddened as he remembered Jooli's abilities and made a hasty apology. "Beggin' your pardon, highness," he said. "I guess I stuffed my boot in my mouth, heel and all!"

"No apology necessary, sergeant," Jooli said. Despite the circumstances, she couldn't help smiling. "Although I can't speak for the witch, who may or may not possess a wrinkled bosom. As a matter of fact, this witch could be a wrinkle-teated he, instead of a she."

The sergeant goggled. "I thought a witch was just a wizard in female dress," he said.

The other men had gathered around and were listening in. Although this was hardly the moment for a general discussion on gender sorcery, Jooli noted that their interest was taking their minds off their current problems.

So she said, "The difference is in power, plus the source of the magic. Witches generally get their power solely from nature and make greater use of plants, animal matter and talismans. Wizards rely somewhat on nature, but they can also draw energy from the spirit world."

She shrugged. "Generally speaking, this makes wizards like Safar and Palimak much more powerful than witches. But not always. And not in all cases."

Jooli gestured, taking in the surrounding jungle. "In this place a witch would be very strong indeed."

She started to explain that the jungle was full of animal spirits and magical plant life, but decided not to.

No sense frightening them so much they'd need a change of breeches the next time an ape hooted.

"Anyway, that's the theory," Jooli said, rather weakly.

Just then Leiria strode up, interrupting the conversation. Jooli's immediate reaction was relief that she'd be able to avoid some uncomfortable questions. But when she saw Leiria's expression all the worry returned.

"No sign of Safar?" Jooli asked, praying that her guess was wide of the mark.

Leiria shook her head — so much for the power of prayer.

"Not a trace," she said. "I couldn't find a clue about what happened."

She hesitated, frowning. "Except for one small thing. And maybe I'm just a drowning woman grabbing at straws. But I did find some dead butterflies on the trail. Hundreds of them. At the very spot where he vanished."

Sergeant Hammer said, "That don't seem right. Ain't seen a butterfly since we walked into this godsforsaken forest. And I got pretty sharp eyes."

He turned to the other soldiers. "How about you men? Seen any butterflies lately?" All the soldiers said they hadn't.

Jooli's eyes lit up with excitement at Leiria's news. "Show me," she said to her friend.

Leiria led them all back to the place where Safar had been seen last. She took the precaution of posting the men on both sides of the curving trail so they couldn't be taken unaware.

Jooli, meanwhile, was studying the heaps of dead butterflies. After she got over the surprise of their numbers, the first thing she noticed was the amazing variety of colors.

In her experience, butterfly swarms were always composed of the same shade. And if there *were differences, they were so minor that they went almost unnoticed.*

She started to sort them by color — reds, blues, greens and so on. Which was when she came upon her second discovery. No two seemed to be quite the same! Butterflies that were mainly blue might have touches of orange, or purple or red. While those that were red might be tinged or spotted with green, or brown or yellow.

And the more the she tried to break down the colors further, the more it became apparent that each individual butterfly was startlingly different from the others.

"If I hadn't seen it with my own eyes, I wouldn't have believed it possible," Leiria said after Jooli had demonstrated her discovery.

"It isn't," Jooli said. "Except through magic."

"Surely either you or Safar would have noticed if someone had cast a spell," Leiria said. "Safar's always told me that he can, well, feel it happening. Like the hackles going up on the back of his neck, or something."

Jooli nodded agreement, saying, "When Safar and I first entered the jungle we both cast spells to alert us to sorcerous danger."

She sighed. "Except we both agreed that since we didn't know what we were up against, the spells might not do us much good."

Jooli grimaced. "But this was a complete failure!" she went on. "I've never experienced anything like that!"

"Apparently, neither had Safar," Leiria said. "And yet it happened."

As the hopelessness of the situation sank its barbs deeper into them, Leiria was overcome by angry frustration. "By all that's holy," she said, "when I find out who is responsible for this, I'll spill their guts on the ground and serve up them up on a platter!"

"There's a slim chance," Jooli said, "that I might be able to grant your wish."

"How?" Leiria asked.

"By recreating the spell," Jooli said.

Leiria eyes burned with fury. "Then do it!" she demanded. "Show me this villain's face!"

"That's exactly my intention," Jooli said.

And she immediately got busy with her preparations.

First, she swept all the butterflies into a large pile. Then she spread her cloak out on the ground and upended her witch's pouch so that she could sort through the contents. As she worked, Leiria paced next to her like an angry she cat.

To calm her friend, and also to relieve her own tension, Jooli talked while she worked.

"When I was a girl learning the basics of magic from my grandmother," she said, "the whole thing seemed like such a huge, complex mystery that it was a long time before I could do even the simplest spell."

Jooli smiled, reflecting. "But my grandmother was a very patient woman," she said. "And an excellent teacher. Strange, isn't it? That even someone as evil as she is could still have good qualities?"

Leiria snorted. "Reminds me of a certain king I used to know," she said. "Iraj Protarus! King of Kings. Brutal lord of all he surveyed. And yet, he was a dreamer once. A man of good intentions, I think. And sometimes he could be quite gentle and forgiving."

She sighed. "It was greed that changed him. Not greed for money, but for power. And a man who thinks like that can't understand others might not want the same thing. That's why he ended up hating Safar so much. He couldn't believe that Safar — who in many ways had once shared his vision — had never ceased being a dreamer."

Jooli laughed. "Similar to my grandmother," she said, "but not quite the same. I think she caught the greed disease while still in her mother's womb."

Leiria shuddered. "It almost makes me feel sorry for her," she said.

Jooli looked up at her. "Don't," she said. "That's another thing she's good at. Making people feel sorry for her so she can gain the upper hand."

Then she returned to her work, choosing certain little packets and vials and putting them aside.

"Anyway, I was talking about the complexity of magic," she said. "What my grandmother taught was that witchcraft was really quite simple and logical. Almost childishly so. In fact, sometimes it helps to think like a child and not let adult narrow-mindedness infect you."

She got out a small cup and started measuring various powders and liquids into it. "The first thing I learned was to truly imagine a thing. Which isn't that difficult for a young girl. It was easy to imagine a favorite doll in every detail. Or a sweet I particularly liked.

"And it was also easy to imagine things I dreamed of being able to do. Like winning the affections of a handsome boy. Or beating a bully in a wrestling match."

Leiria laughed. "I should have been born a witch," she said. "Bullies are easy. I've whacked more than my share. But I've yet to unravel the mysteries of the male race!"

"It wouldn't have helped," Jooli said, sharing her laughter. "When it comes to men, witches are no better at it than normal women."

Briefly forgetting her worries, Leiria asked. "What was the next thing you learned?"

"The Law of Cause And Effect," Jooli replied as she began mixing the foul-smelling brew in her witch's cup. "Which means, quite simply, every effect has a cause and every cause has an effect. Fire makes heat. So if the effect you want is fire, you only have magically to cause heat."

She indicated the cup. "If I added a drop or two of a certain elixir I have," she said, "we'd get an enormous bonfire." She wiped sweat from her brow. "Although in this awful humidity I don't know why we'd want to."

Gingerly, Jooli poured the mixture into a small clay vial, then plugged it with a little cork stopper.

"And that elixir I mentioned," she said, "leads to the next law of magic. Which is: Like Produces Like. The elixir is made from the root of a plant whose flowers are fiery red and look quite like flame. Also, the root itself is quite hot to the taste.

"Long ago some clever witch figured out that if it looked like fire and behaved like fire it might be the perfect thing to cause the effect of fire."

"It sounds easy," Leiria said. "Although there must be more to it than that. Otherwise anybody could be a witch."

"The theory is simple," Jooli said. "But the practice requires a special gift you are either born with or not. Also, only a few witches have really good imaginations. Which is the most important secret of magic.

"You have to be able to imagine a thing in perfect detail — break it down into all its parts and put it back together again — before you can achieve your goal."

"What about prayer?" Leiria asked. "Most people believe that if you pray to the gods and they favor you, miracles can be performed."

"Most people are deluded fools, my friend," Jooli said. "Because if you are depending on prayer for rescue, you might as well call in the dogs to urinate on the fire for all the good it'll do you."

Leiria nodded. "Safar's of the same opinion," she said. "Except he thinks the gods are asleep and not paying attention. And even if they were awake, he doubts if they'd care."

Leiria's worries flooded back with the mention of Safar's name. "What about this witch?" she asked, pointing at the dead butterflies. "How good do you think she is?"

"Actually, I think we're dealing with a male witch," Jooli said. "I'm only guessing, of course. But my guesses are usually accurate.

"As for his powers, I can't say. His spell was clever enough. He trapped Safar and probably Palimak too with it. On the other hand, this jungle is his home. And even a very weak witch — or wizard — is hard to beat in his own home."

Leiria slapped her sheathed sword. "Then it is my wish and fondest imagination," she said, "that when we encounter this fellow it will be blades, not magic, that'll win the day. And I'm not boasting when I say I've met only one swordsman in my life who could best me.

"Except that was long ago and I've had a great deal of practice killing people since then. So I don't think it'd come out quite the same way."

Jooli's eyebrows arched. "Iraj Protarus again?" she guessed.

Leiria nodded sharply. "The very same," she replied.

"I'd like to see that fight," Jooli said.

Leiria smiled, but without humor. "Consider yourself invited," she said.

Jooli rose, saying, "Enough girl talk. Let's find out what sort of stuff this witch is made of."

She went to the piled-up butterflies and placed the clay vial in the center. Next she got Leiria to help her surround the colorful mass with dry sticks, carefully placing them in the shape of a pentagram.

Then she stood and dusted herself off. "If this works," she said, "we'll only have a few seconds to act."

"I'll get the men ready," Leiria said.

Jooli shook her head. "The original spells trapped two people," she said. "We'll have to strike the same balance. So I'm afraid it's down to just you and me against whatever is waiting."

"That sounds like damn good odds to me," Leiria joked.

She called for the soldiers and filled them in on their plan. They were all disappointed at being left out of the fight. But Leiria cajoled them, stroking their egos, and told them how vital it was for them to remain here and stand guard.

"Ah, then we're expectin' more action, right?" Sergeant Hamyr said, pleased.

Leiria clapped him on the back. "Count on it," she said.

Then she joined Jooli at the pentagram.

"Ready?" Jooli asked, drawing her sword.

Leiria nodded and drew her own. "Ready," she replied.

And so Jooli cast the spell.

A sheet of flame shot up, momentarily blinding them. Then the flame shattered in a soundless explosion. Bursting into thousands upon thousands of fiery bits of color. It was like all the rainbows in the world had been gathered together, then smashed apart with a giant's hammer.

Slowly an enormous face formed within the hot shower of color.

It was the face of a lion. His huge cat's eyes glared at them. And then he roared.

Leiria and Jooli shouted their war cries and charged!

38

SLAY GROUND

Safar stood frozen in the center of the arena as his own son rushed toward him — a spear aimed directly at his heart.

The arena thundered with the shouts of a savage audience urging Palimak to "Kill, kill, kill! Kill Safar Timura!" Underscoring the wild, blood-demanding chorus was the marrow-freezing roar of a mighty lion.

Caught on the horns of a nightmare dilemma, Safar was helpless to act.

The cold, outraged wizard side of him commanded self protection at any cost. Automatically digging for the ultimate, death-dealing spell to cut Palimak down in his tracks.

But in the place where all love dwells another part of him demanded the ultimate parental sacrifice — to die so that his son might live.

And then, from the narrow gulf between death and survival, came yet a third, most desperate voice: *Kill him, brother! cried the voice. Kill him or all we worked for together is lost!*

Safar had the sudden vision of a world strangling in its own poisons. Of corpses heaped to the heavens. Of seas turned into barren deserts littered with bleached white bones. Of howling devils fighting to suck out the last bit of marrow from life itself.

And with that vision came the nearly overpowering urge to slay his son. Ghostly commands shot through his body making his nerves and muscles twitch in reflex.

The killing spell flooded into his mind unbidden — numbing his will to resist.

Palimak was almost on him. So close Safar could hear Gundara crying, "Stop, Little Master, stop!"

But the boy ran onward, eyes burning with murderous hate.

The heavy spear blade was only inches from Safar's heart. At the same time his killing spell coiled like a hissing cobra, ready to launch.

He had no doubt which would strike first. In less time than it took for a heart to beat, Palimak would be lying dead at his feet. And Safar would be standing over him, the bitter victor.

A man whose soul would carry the blackest mark of all: the sin of a father who had slain his own son.

But as Asper once wrote: Between thought and action lies a shadow. And in that shadow dwells the true power of choice. Of free will. The only real blessing the gods of creation bestowed on humans and demons alike. A gift to leaven the curse of this too-brief life.

So, at the last possible instant, Safar snatched up this power and used it as a bludgeon to slay the spell-cobra before it could kill his son.

And as he braced for the thrust of the spear blade, he whispered, "I love you, Palimak."

Then a hot, searing shock smashed into his body.

A thousand painful colors exploded in his brain.

He had a brief sensation of falling and then he collided with the ground.

Soft, leafy ground.

The moist smell of humus and rotting things.

Familiar voices murmuring in his ear.

Safar raised his head, bewildered that he was still alive. And he saw that he was back on the jungle trail. Sergeant Hamyr and the other Kyranian soldiers standing above him.

And a few away was the unconscious body of Palimak, the spear still gripped in his hand.

* * *

Leiria saw the red dirt crashing up at her. She twisted in mid-air and tuck rolled to her feet, sword slashing at a blurred claw reaching for her throat.

She felt the sword strike hard iron, then slip and bite into soft flesh. She heard a lion's soul-satisfying roar of pain and danced to the side as another iron claw lashed out at her.

But then her heel slammed against a ridge in the ground and

she toppled backward, twisting to keep her sword arm free and falling heavily on her side.

The iron claw rang as Leiria parried the next blow. But her fall had left her in an awkward, indefensible position. She caught a glimpse of her opponent as he rushed in, roaring in delight at his advantage.

From the shoulders down he was human — a near-giant clothed only in a loin cloth, which bulged as if he were equipped like a bull. His bare torso rippled with slabbed muscle. His arms and legs were thick as trees. Heavy iron claws were gripped in each mighty fist, one of which streamed blood from her initial blow.

From the neck up he was a lion. His huge cat's eyes glowed with fury. His powerful, spine-snapping jaws were spiked with whiskers like steel cables. All framed by a bristling yellow mane that fanned out like mighty wings.

As the claw came down she rolled to the side just in time and the hooks buried themselves in earth instead of in her flesh. But her back was exposed and she kept rolling, desperately trying to get out of the lionman's long reach.

Then Leiria heard Jooli's shrill war cry pierce the air, followed by the lionman's howl of surprise, and she exploded to her feet — back still exposed but turning, shifting her sword to her left hand so that she could draw her long-bladed knife.

In fighting position once more, Leiria saw Jooli fling herself to the side to avoid the lionman's charge. Blood ran down his bare back, gory evidence of Jooli's lunge to rescue Leiria.

Shouting her war cry, Leiria raced to join her friend and soon they had the lionman pinned between them.

Big as he was, fiercely strong as he was, he was no match for the two warrior women. Only his long reach and ferocity kept them from closing in for the kill.

Gradually, they wore him down. First Leiria would lunge, forcing the lion man to face her. But then she would backpedal as he charged, fending off his blows.

At the same time Jooli would dash in and attack his exposed back. And the positions would be reversed, with Jooli backpedaling as Leiria sprinted into striking distance.

The battle raged for an hour before a strangely silent crowd of savages. They only gaped as their king streamed blood from a dozen wounds, his roars growing weaker with each timed attack.

Then the lionman stumbled and went to his knees. At that moment, Leiria thought she had him. She lunged at the lionman, blade aimed like a spear at his exposed neck.

But it was only a feint and he suddenly exploded upward. She still would have had him, would have buried her sword in his chest, but the lionman had escape — not continued battle — in mind.

He dodged to the side, then bounded away, racing for the big double gates at the far side of the arena.

Leiria and Jooli went after him. Although he was amazingly fast for his size, they were faster and were soon closing on him.

As he neared the gate the lionman roared an order. Leiria saw the gates swing open and thought he was going to try to escape outside.

Instead, she heard bellows of rage and she dug her heels in to stop her headlong charge, shouting a warning to Jooli at the same time.

Both women halted, moving together for protection. Jooli had time to say, "What in the hells?!" and then six strange figures burst through the open gates to join their king.

They were nearly as tall as he, but with broader shoulders and wider backs. From the neck down they were men. But above they sported the mighty horned heads of fighting bulls. They were all armed with huge spiked clubs as thick as a ship's main mast.

The bullmen fanned out around their king. Then, with him in the center, they advanced — their bellows echoing across the arena.

Suddenly, the crowd came to life. They cheered wildly, then took up the chant:

"Kill them! Kill, kill, kill!"

Jooli said, "Looks like we're in for a long fight, sister."

Leiria smiled, then said, "On my signal, we go for the king, agreed?"

"Agreed!"

And so Leiria gave the signal and they charged.

Safar forced a brandy-laced potion through Palimak's lips and he came awake, choking and sputtering. When his son had caught his breath, Safar gave him the flask and he took a long swallow.

Palimak closed his eyes and shuddered as the restorative did its work. When he opened them again relief flooded Safar's veins as he saw sanity had returned.

The young man was pale and shaken from his ordeal. Then, with a start, reality took hold.

He embraced his father, saying, "Thank the gods you found me!"

Moved by the sight of father and son reunited, the soldiers scraped the ground with their boots. Sergeant Hamyr wiped away a tear with a battle-hardened hand.

Then Palimak drew back. "I had a terrible dream, father," the young man said. "I was in this arena. And a man with a lion's head gave me a spear. And you were on the other side of the arena and the lionman —"

"It wasn't a dream, son," Safar broke in. "But never mind that. We have things to do. And they have to be done in a hurry."

Palimak was horrified. "Do you mean it was real?" he asked, voice quivering. "Did I really try to —"

Once again, Safar interrupted. "Please, son," he said. "It wasn't your fault. And we can discuss the whole thing later and I'll prove to you that it wasn't. Just take my word for it right now. All right?"

Palimak nodded weakly. "All right," he said.

"We have to get back to that arena immediately," Safar said. "Leiria and Jooli are in grave danger. Do you understand what I'm telling you?"

Again, Palimak nodded. "I understand," he said.

Safar helped him to his feet. He motioned to Hamyr who stepped in to belt a sword about Palimak's waist. Then he gave him a tunic and a spare pair of boots which the young man hastily pulled on.

"Are you hungry?" Safar asked when he was dressed.

Palimak shook his head. "I couldn't eat," he said. "I'd get sick to my stomach." He motioned at the flask, grinning weakly. "But maybe some more of that."

Safar gave the brandy to him and he drank it down. When he was done he drew in a deep breath, then squared his shoulders.

"I'm fine now," he said.

Safar turned to the soldiers. "Leave your packs here," he said. "Just take your weapons. And the moment we get there, don't stop to think. Or look around and wonder where in the hells you are. Just fight, all right?"

The men all said they understood.

However, Sergeant Hamyr made bold to ask, "Pardon, Lord Timura, but can you tell us exactly who we'll be fightin'?"

Safar chuckled. "The enemy," he said.

Hamyr nodded, smiling. "Ah, the enemy. That's good to know.

Thanks, me lord."

"You're welcome, sergeant," Safar said.

Then he led them down the path to a large black patch that had been burned into the ground by Jooli's spell.

It hadn't taken him more than a few minutes to figure what she'd done and he was quite impressed with her feat. Her action had not only saved him and Palimak, but had also pointed the way for Safar to work some magic of his own.

The spell she'd cast had also weakened the witch's portal so much that he'd be able to return to the arena with Palimak and the entire squad of soldiers. Plus Leiria and Jooli would be able to remain with them, adding two excellent swords to the fight.

Especially Leiria's blade, he thought fondly. She's worth half an army all by herself.

Meanwhile, Palimak was studying Jooli's magical spoor. Gundaree and Gundara also whispered interesting hints in his ear.

After a moment he turned to Safar, saying, "I see how the spell goes together, father. Let me help you."

Safar clapped him on the back. "Sure you can, son. The more we can put behind this, the better," he said.

Palimak raised a hand. "Wait a minute," he said. "Gundaree and Gundara have a suggestion." Palimak said.

He bent his head, listening. Then he grinned. "It's a pretty good trick," he said to Safar. "Something that'll really put a curl in that damned King Felino's mane!"

Safar chuckled, recalling just how evil the minds of the two little Favorites could be. "Wonderful," he said. "The only caution is that I'd rather capture him if we can. I want to find out what's behind all this."

Palimak nodded agreement and Safar got to work setting up the spell. Using his silver witch's-dagger he scratched a pentagram in the ashes. In the center he sketched a lion's face.

He stepped back, raised his arms and spreading them wide, concentrated on his goal. As he did this he felt Palimak's power, backed up by Gundaree and Gundara's energies, flow into him.

And he chanted:

"To fly and fly and grace the skies
In numbers even gods could not add.
We conjure a thing to bedevil a king
And drive a foolish man mad."

Then he clapped his hands together and thousands of butterflies burst up from the pentagram, flying free and high into the towering trees.

"Arm yourselves," Safar shouted, drawing his sword.

Blades scraped from their sheaths and suddenly the jungle vanished.

And they all found themselves standing in the center of a huge arena, a battle raging not far away.

While all around them a thunderous crowd chanted its bloody anthem:

"Kill, kill, kill!"

39
BUTTERFLY STINGS

In their first charge Leiria and Jooli came within inches of killing King Felino.

The lionman and his bellowing cohorts had clearly believed the two women would be so terrified when confronted with such an overwhelming force that they'd squeal in feminine dismay and beat a panicked retreat.

But Leiria and Jooli launched their surprise attack with such speed and ferocity that the lionman and his forces were caught flat-footed.

If he'd had his wits about him, the king would've drawn Leiria and Jooli in by falling back so that his bullmen could fan out on either side, then slam the trap shut in a pincer action. Instead, they wasted precious moments gaping at the two warrior women charging down on them, allowing Leiria and Jooli come to within reach of their goal — the king himself.

Leiria was even thinking of throwing the last dregs of caution to the winds to launch herself and her sword at the lion-headed enemy.

Belatedly, the king realized what was happening. He jerked back, roaring orders. The two bullmen closest to him clumsily lumbered forward to close the breach, mighty clubs swinging up.

Leiria's sharp blade slashed out at her opponent, taking his weapon hand off at the wrist. The bullman bellowed in pain, lifting up his stump to stare at the red life spurting out of him, then toppled to the ground and died.

Jooli made similar short work of the horned warrior she faced, running him through with her blade, then spinning around in mid-stride to free it and continue her charge.

Leiria struck out at the exposed Felino, who barely parried her sword with an iron claw, then roared in outrage as her blindingly fast return stroke nicked his side, drawing blood.

Jooli was only one pace behind and saw her chance. She hurled her knife over Leiria's shoulder. It spun once in mid-flight and she had a momentary thrill when she saw the heavy blade slamming toward the lionman's chest.

But at the last possible moment one of the king's guards threw his big body in front of Felino and took the blade himself.

Then the three remaining bullmen charged in and Leiria and Jooli were forced to retreat to keep from being overwhelmed. But as they backpedaled they made two of the bullmen pay for their crimes by dealing out shallow wounds to them both.

Despite their retreat, the women were in an excellent position for a counter-attack. With three of the six bullmen dead, two others wounded and the uninjured one reluctant to press the advantage regardless of Felino's roars, they only needed to regroup, then charge again.

Dripping blood from his side and his back, Felino drove his dispirited army of three after the women with roared insults and threats. The crowd had once again fallen into a strange silence — as if the sight of their king's humiliation had robbed them of their voices.

Acting as a single unit Leiria and Jooli skidded to a halt. Shouting war cries, they pretended to charge again and their attackers hastily scrambled back, nearly overrunning Felino.

The two women took advantage of the moment to catch their breath and check their weapons. Leiria gave Jooli her spare knife to replace the one she'd lost in the bullman's back.

She grinned at Jooli, eyes savage with bloodlust. "It's good to fight with you, sister," she said — the ultimate compliment from Leiria.

"My pleasure," Jooli said, equally as charged by the battle.

"One question, though," Leiria said. She pointed at the bullmen who were being harangued by Felino. "After we've killed them, how in the hells do we get out of here?"

"I've been thinking about that," Jooli said. She chuckled. "Maybe we can use the lionman's ears for a spell."

Leiria laughed. "Consider it done," she said as she stropped her blade on her leather harness.

Then she gave the signal and they both sprang forward to renew the battle.

King Felino immediately turned and fled, leaving his bullmen to face the warrior women without his help. Leiria and Jooli tried to go after him, but the three bullmen blocked their path.

"Coward!" Jooli shouted after the king, trying to wound his pride enough to make him return.

Leiria joined in, shouting, "What's that bulge in your loin cloth, your highness? Cotton wadding?"

But he paid them no mind and only sprinted harder for the safety of the big gates.

The two women had no choice but to kill the three remaining bullmen first before pursuing their master. It was a short, ugly fight. Trapped between fear of their master and fear of the women, the bullmen were overwhelmed by fatalism. It was as if they could already see their own ghosts wailing and moaning in a miserable afterlife.

They wept while they fought. Bloody mucus spewed from their nostrils. White foam rimmed their mouths. And they bellowed to whatever gods they held dear to spare them. Leiria and Jooli killed them without pity, spilling their innards onto the floor of the arena. And cursing their souls to the hells as they bounded over the still-twitching corpses to confront the king.

Felino was gone, but they knew he couldn't have gotten very far, so they attacked the gates.

Leiria hacking at the rough wood with her sword, chipping away big chunks. Jooli hammering at the raw depression with a club she'd retrieved from one of the fallen bullmen. They were almost through when they heard a rumble. The gates began to move outward and they leaped back, ready to take on whatever Felino had to throw at them.

As the gates parted a foul animal smell poured out. They heard strange noises, as if a ferocious menagerie of carnivores had been unleashed: a blood-chilling chorus of jackal laughter, mixed with hisses and howls and hoots.

"Swords and knives," Leiria cried, backing away.

Jooli dropped the club and drew her main weapons. "Swords

and knives it is, then, sister," she said. "By the way," she added, "I like my sweetbreads with a spicy sauce, how about you?"

Leiria barked laughter. "I like them plain, with maybe a little salt. We'll quarrel over the recipe after we've cut off their balls."

"Agreed," Jooli said.

Bloodlust in check from this exchange — but barely — the two warrior women slowly withdrew, coming together to make a buttress of sharp steel and hard female muscle and will.

Then they heard King Felino's lion roar and six barking creatures marched through the gates in formation and took up position to the left of the opening. From toe to neck they were hunched-over men with black-striped yellow fur. Jackal heads sprouted from their shoulders, soul-chilling laughter spouting from their crooked snouts. Each toe and finger bore iron rings tipped with curling iron hooks. And as they laughed each jackal jaw exposed long curving yellow teeth, stained partly green with poison.

Six more enormous human devils followed. These were men with the heavy jowled heads of great apes, hooting and chattering obscene threats to the women as they fanned out to the right. They carried short spears and wore thick leather vests reinforced with iron mesh.

Then, spearing out like an engorged serpent, came the final six. Tall men — taller even than the giant Felino — with long, big-boned limbs. They were armed with swords and protected by small circular shields made of iron-studded leather mounted on wood. They had the broad-snouted heads of huge lizards with forked tongues that flickered out to taste the air.

"Sixes again," Jooli muttered absently.

Leiria, who was eyeing this considerable force with growing dismay, was startled by this remark.

"What in the hells are you talking about?" she asked, nearly snapping.

"Apparently the number six has some significance in this place," Jooli said. "The first group contained six warriors. And this bunch is also in sixes. I don't think it's coincidental."

"In the military, squads are traditionally composed of six soldiers," Leiria pointed out. "But I won't quibble. If you're right, how does it help us?"

Before Jooli could answer there was an ear-splitting roar and Felino came bounding out, leaping over the lizard-headed center group to take command. He seemed re-energized. His wounds were freshly bound.

"Kill!" he roared. "Kill, kill, kill!"

Immediately, the savage audience that ringed the arena exploded into life. Screaming, "Kill, kill, kill!"

"It was nice knowing you, sister," Leiria said, bracing for the coming assault.

Then King Felino gave the signal and exploded forward — leading his warrior menagerie down the field against the women.

It took Safar only an instant to size up the situation. Some fifty yards away a ring of howling monsters had Leiria and Jooli surrounded. The two were fighting valiantly, but were being slowly ground down. The lionman, King Felino, raced around the outer ring, exhorting his soldiers to "Kill, kill, kill!"

And scattered around the battling mass were many dead or dying animal-headed soldiers — bloody evidence of Leiria's and Jooli's stubborn resistance.

Safar cracked an amplification pellet against the hard red ground. And when he shouted the war cry of his people it thundered across the arena, drowning out the shouts of the crowd.

"FOR KYRANIA!" he bellowed as he raced forward.

"FOR KYRANIA!" came the echoed chorus from Palimak and the other men as they charged after him.

Stunned by the magically amplified cries, King Felino whirled about to stare at this new threat. His lion's jaw gaped wide when he saw his vanished enemies, Safar and Palimak, sprinting toward him backed by the small but heavily armed cohort of Kyranian soldiers.

Some of his soldiers also turned to gape and were punished for their lack of attention when Leiria and Jooli leaped forward to cut them to ribbons.

Felino recovered from his shock and shouted orders. Half his force whipped about to confront the new enemy, while the others pressed in on the two warrior women.

As the Kyranians waded into the melee, Safar leading the way, Palimak held back a little, waiting for his chance to cast Gundara's and Gundaree's spell. He parried blows but didn't press the fight — slowly circling the massed group to get close to King Felino.

A strange sensation of unreality fell over him. While everyone else was fighting for their lives, filling the air with shouted oaths, war cries and screams of pain, he felt quite cool, his mind acutely sharp; soaking up every detail of the battle.

He thought it quite interesting to note that Sergeant Hamyr's face wore a wicked grin that never changed, no matter what fortune might bring him. Whether he dodged a potentially killing blow, dealt one of his own or was hard-pressed by a skilled adversary, the grin remained the same.

It was also interesting, he thought, that although Leiria and Jooli had only met recently they fought like a smooth, single unit — as if they had been soldiering together their entire adult lives.

Most interesting of all was the way his father fought. Safar had always been a skilled warrior. Taller and more muscular than most Kyranians, he was also quite strong and fast. Today, however, it seemed to Palimak that his father fought on a higher level than ever before.

His swordplay was a thing of agile beauty. Far better than it had ever been before. Quite possibly nearly as good as Leiria's swordsmanship, which was so superior to that everyone else that most warriors considered her to be in a class consisting of one. Although Leiria always said there was one man — Iraj Protarus — who was her equal, everyone thought she was only being modest.

But now it seemed that another had entered that rarefied realm. Incredibly, that man was Palimak's father. He wondered how Safar had made such an improvement. Was magic involved? Or was it something else? Palimak thought the whole thing was very strange and added it to the other oddities he'd noticed about his father since his return.

Just then, Gundara whispered, "There's that stupid old king!"

Palimak looked up and saw Felino backing toward the gates, two enormous lizardmen guarding his retreat.

Suddenly, Palimak heard a familiar war cry and Leiria broke through, Jooli protecting her back as she charged the king.

"Leiria's going to kill him, Little Master!" Gundaree cried.

Sure enough, without missing a step, Leiria cut down one of the lizardmen, leaving Jooli to deal with the other as she raced toward Felino. The king raised an iron-clawed fist to defend himself, but Palimak could see it was too little and too late. The lionman was doomed.

"Stop her, Little Master!" Gundara cried, reminding him that Safar wanted to capture the king alive.

Palimak shouted, "Leiria, don't!"

She heard him and hesitated, breaking her stride and sword blow. To Palimak's horror, that moment's pause gave

Felino just enough time. He smashed her sword aside and leaped toward her — great iron claws outstretched to slash her life away.

Palimak cast the spell, fearing the distance was too great and that he'd be responsible for the death of the person he loved above all others — except for his father. Leiria had practically been his mother, caring for him since he was a babe in arms. Carrying him in a sling across her back while she alternately fled and fought the soldiers that Iraj had sent after them.

Perhaps it was that love, combined with the fear of loss, that gave the spell enough strength to collapse the distance. Or maybe it was because he was in a magical arena carved out by Felino's sorcery that gave his own sorcery added power. Or possibly it was only blind luck.

Whatever the reason, the instant Palimak hurled the spell he knew the rightness and power of it. Like most of the Favorites' magic, the spell was dead simple. On their instructions, he'd scooped up a handful of the ashes left over from Jooli's casting. They'd spat in it and had directed him to mold the ashes into a grimy little ball.

It was this insignificant piece of dirt that he threw at the snarling lionman. At the same time he chanted in unison with the Favorites:

"Butterfly wings,
Where have you gone?
Butterfly wings,
Who did you wrong?
Promised honey
And that's not funny!
Sting, sting, sting,
Butterfly wings.
Sting,
And sting,
And sting!"

Palimak's aim was more accurate than he could ever have hoped. The ash pellet struck Felino in the eye and instead of smashing Leiria down, he roared with pain, throwing his iron claws aside to rub his wounded eye.

At the same time there was an explosion of colorful light and thousands of butterflies popped out of nowhere.

They circled the injured lionman, buzzing like angry bees. Palimak saw long, barbed stingers emerge from their abdomens as they were magically armed by the Favorites' spell. Then they attacked, swarming all over Felino, thrusting their stingers into him by the hundreds.

The lionman ran about, flailing the air hysterically. Begging the now-silent audience to help him. Then he fell to his knees, covering his head in a futile effort to protect himself from the painful stings.

Palimak strolled casually over to him, an amazed Leiria several steps behind. He stood over the lionman, repeating the spell chant:

"Butterfly wings,
Where have you gone?
Butterfly wings,
Who did you wrong?
Promised honey
And that's not funny!
Sting, sting, sting,
Butterfly wings.
Sting,
And sting,
And sting!"

Now Felino was completely covered with the beautiful but deadly butterflies. Thrusting their abdomens forward to deliver their poison. Then fluttering away to let another take their place. Felino collapsed to the ground, moaning and barely able to move.

When he was certain the lionman was completely helpless, Palimak waved his hand and the butterflies vanished.

"I don't know what just happened," Leiria said "Except I think you saved my life."

Ashamed, Palimak blushed. "I'm sorry, Aunt Leiria," he said. "Actually, I almost got you killed. I shouldn't have shouted at you like that."

Leiria clapped him on the shoulders and said, "Never mind." Then she directed him to the main battle, where Safar was dealing the last blow to the last opponent. His sword cut through a jackalman's throat, sending the barking head flying across the arena. The rest of the beastmen were either all dead or dying.

"I've never seen Safar fight like that before," Leiria said in her cool professional manner. "If he practices a bit more he'll be good enough to give me trouble."

"I was thinking the same thing," Palimak said. "Maybe he's got some new kind of magic."

Leiria frowned. "I don't know," she said. She started to say more, but then broke off as Safar approached them, wiping blood from his blade and returning it to its sheath. He looked down at King Felino, eyes hard and blue as newly-forged steel.

"Now let's see what this fellow has to say for himself," he said.

Safar plucked out his silver dagger and gestured. Flames burst out all around them. And the blood-stained arena, along with its silent audience, vanished. And they were suddenly back on the jungle trail again. The softly moaning lionman shivering on the path before them.

There came a series of soft popping sounds, like a child making bubbles in his cup of goat's milk, and Palimak saw Hamyr and the other Kyranian soldiers appear.

They all breathed sighs of relief and collapsed on the ground. But they only stayed like that for a few moments. After the men caught their breaths they started rummaging through their packs to dig out rations and wine to stoke up their energies in case danger should once again rear its head.

Palimak didn't see where Jooli came from. She was just suddenly there, walking up to the stricken lionman.

"If it's of any help to you," she said to Safar, "he seems to favor the number six. Maybe it has something to do with his magic. Maybe it's coincidental. Either way, I thought I'd better mention it."

Safar nodded, stroking his chin. With some surprise, Palimak noted the stubble of a golden beard sprouting from his face. Their ordeal had gone on so long Safar hadn't had a chance to shave.

And once again Palimak wondered about the changed color of his father's hair. Previously, he'd attributed it to bleaching by the sun. Now he wondered why a normally dark-haired person would grow a light-colored beard. It didn't make sense. He glanced at Safar's head and saw that what had once been dark hair, albeit streaked with gold, was now entirely blond.

Like the sudden improvement in Safar's fighting ability, something seemed wrong here. On the other hand, maybe it was only his imagination.

Then his father spoke and the doubts were forgotten. "Let's get His Highness aboard the airship," Safar said. "And we can question him at our leisure."

Everyone agreed with his thinking and so he sent up a green flare to signal Biner.

A half-hour passed and there was no sign of the airship. Frowning, Safar shot off another magical flare. Again, there was a long, fruitless wait.

Finally, Leiria said, "We'd better get back to the beach the best way we can. Biner's either asleep or in big trouble."

"Biner *never* sleeps when he's on watch," Safar said. "And neither does Arlain."

"I know," Leiria replied grimly.

A few minutes later they had the barely conscious King Felino tied to a litter and were dragging him along the trail as they retraced their steps through the jungle.

40

GODDESS OF THE HELLS

Queen Clayre paced her cabin, waiting for news from the Hells that her secret plot against Safar and Palimak Timura had succeeded.

From the cabin adjoining hers she heard the muffled sounds of a man moaning in pain. She smiled in pleasure, thinking that in her case the news didn't have to travel very far. Only the door to her suite separated her from one small, particularly nasty corner of the nether world.

Above her came a flurry of barked orders and the slap of bare feet as the sailors raced across the vessel's deck to do the bidding of their officers.

Safar's ship had been spotted and even now her son and his minions were beating windward to catch the Timuras by surprise.

Clayre snorted derisively. She had little faith in her son's ability to bring the Timuras down. Even though the stolen fleet was packed with more than enough soldiers to overwhelm the Kyranians, in her mind Rhodes had failed before when he'd held even better odds.

And then he'd been engaged against the boy wizard, Palimak. Not a sorcerer of Safar Timura's enormous strength and cunning.

Clayre heard more sounds of pain and moved to the cabin

door. It was open a crack and she could peek inside. Spreadeagled across her table was a half-naked sailor, his loins covered by cut-off canvas breeches. Bound and gagged, blood streaked his bare torso and legs as if he'd been lashed.

Some invisible force seemed to be tormenting him and he twisted against his bonds, causing the table to shift a few inches. Then he gave a strangled cry and went inert as he fell unconscious.

Excellent, Clayre thought. The spell is working. She turned away from the door and resumed her pacing, reviewing her plan.

After Clayre's first effort with the tree-beasts had failed she'd decided to seek help from a higher power.

By this, she did not mean the Heavenly gods. In her decidedly less than humble opinion the gods were useless things noted for not sticking to their bargain no matter how rich the sacrifice. The deities who ruled the Hells were much more trustworthy.

Charize, her mentor in sorcery, had speculated that the Heavenly gods were asleep and paying no mind to worldly affairs. Charize had postulated that this was the era for monsters and devils like herself.

Moreover, she'd said, there was an excellent opportunity to replace the gods in the minds of humans and demons with more realistic objects of worship.

"The worlds we reside in are quite cruel," Charize had observed. "Pain is the destiny of all living things. And this pain is not even relieved by death. Note the poor miserable ghosts who wander everywhere, bemoaning their fates.

"As if Fate had ever truly offered anything better. It would be kinder — and more delicious to us — if mortal creatures understood that everlasting pain and disappointment make up their eternal future.

"As I tell all my sisters, your prey's submission is such lovely sauce to be served up with a good, suffering marrow bone."

During Clayre's sessions with the monster queen she'd learned — and gloried in the learning — that during this period of inattentive deities, helpmates such as herself were not only spared misery but also got to feast at the wondrous table of hopelessness.

"And even if Asper is correct and things do eventually change," Charize had said, "and the gods should ever awaken, they have no loyalty to mortals. After all, corporeal beings are mere playthings to be tormented for the personal enrichment and enjoyment of the gods.

"So there will still be much for us to feast upon. But I think we should eat while the eating is good, and be damned to Asper and the gods. The longer we can delay their return, the better. And perhaps we can even prevent it altogether."

In the meantime, Charize recommended regular sacrifice to the Goddess of the Hells, Lady Lottyr. An unholy deity who had no love for mortal kind and who made it her practice to mix beasts with higher life-forms to achieve her aims. As false prophets of Asper, it was Lottyr's praise that Charize and her sisters had sung during their observances:

> *". . . We take the sin, we take the sin,*
> *Sweet Lady, Lady, Lady.*
> *On our souls, on our souls,*
> *Holy One . . ."*

The Lady Lottyr was the hellish shadow-goddess of her heavenly twin, the Lady Felakia. To whom her human and demon worshipers attributed all good things.

Charize had scoffed at Felakia's goodness. She firmly believed that good, as represented by the Lady Felakia, was only the feeble sister to evil, whose cause Lady Lottyr championed.

"Lord Asper was badly mistaken," she used to tell Clayre. "Because when the gods decided to allow the death of the present world it was only because they preferred the heartier taste of evil to the weak soup that the bones of good make.

"Ultimately, only Lady Lottyr can provide such wonderfully tormented souls. Made more delicious by their misery. All aged by their ethereal corpses being hanged on the butcher hooks of the Hells."

Despite the claims of friendship — and the revelation of many magical secrets — Clayre had never believed that Charize had her best interests at heart.

And so Clayre's emotions had been decidedly mixed when Palimak had killed the monster queen — the worshiper of Lady Lottyr. On the one hand, she'd been freed of Charize and her influences. On the other, Clayre's personal magic was much weakened without Charize's assistance.

Kalasariz had provided some of the answers to her dreams. He'd not only defeated but had digested his enemies. Enormous power was in the offing. Power Clayre was determined to control.

The spymaster had first proposed that he enter her own body.

An offer Clayre immediately distrusted and refused.

Let Kalasariz possess her son. She could deal with Rhodes, no matter how much he might be influenced by Kalasariz. She had no doubt Kalasariz and Rhodes were plotting to make her their slave eventually by eating her soul — just as Kalasariz had devoured the demons, Luka and Fari.

Clayre snorted. Let them make their silly plans to betray her!

The main flaw in their plot was that they first had to defeat her enemies. And when the moment came for them to turn against her, she'd be ready. In fact, she was already building the spell to turn the tables on them — as well as widening her contacts in the spirit world.

But it was in the Hells that Clayre had found her greatest source of strength.

The Queen Witch glanced at the slightly open door, smiling at the memory.

The Hell Goddess Lottyr had been more than willing to join her conspiracy. No expensive sacrifice had been needed. Only the pledge of Clayre's immortal soul. A thing she did not value and so was eager to turn into coin for her hellish bargain.

And now, while her son's three-ship fleet closed in on the single Kyranian expedition ship, Clayre had already overreached him.

Somewhere in the jungles of Aroborus the Lady Lottyr's sycophant was confronting Safar and Palimak in a magical arena specially constructed for their doom.

Of course, the goddess of the Hells had also warned Clayre the first attempt might fail.

"As a sorcerer," she'd said, "Safar Timura is as close to a miracle as any of us can imagine. Although he is a mere human, his magical abilities are far beyond those of any being I have ever encountered. Even the demon master wizard, Lord Asper, would pale if put beside Lord Timura.

"Our main weapon is that Safar does not yet realize his full power. He's limited by his own imagination. But each time he tests those limits he overcomes them and gains more confidence and strength.

"I never believed it possible he could escape the otherworld of Hadin Future. But somehow he managed it. And now he is back to bedevil us, with abilities much greater than before."

Since her last session with Lottyr, Clayre had formulated many questions that hadn't occurred to her when she'd first conjured up Lottyr's presence.

For instance, Kalasariz had told her more about Safar's strange love/hate relationship with Iraj Protarus. Although the spymaster had not been completely forthcoming, Clayre had surmised that the unknown whereabouts of Iraj Protarus troubled him greatly. And that he was basing all his hopes on finding and overcoming the former king of kings by capturing and killing Safar Timura.

He'd even let slip the magical term that still bound him to Protarus — The Spell of Four. Clayre had done some research on this spell. But there were few magical texts available to someone stuck in such a provincial place as Syrapis.

However, it wasn't hard to figure out that the spell involved shapechanging. And that four participants were required to form that spell. Obviously, Kalasariz had once been one of those four. But he'd managed to break loose and now two of his spell partners had become his slaves. And the fourth, whom he was desperately seeking, could only be King Protarus.

As she paced the cabin, Clayre wondered where the final, most valuable link could be. At this point it was only a matter of curiosity. But if her attempt on Safar and Palimak failed, the question — and its answer — might surge to the forefront.

Who was Iraj Protarus? What were his aims, his goals? And, finally, where was he?

And if found, could Clayre make a bargain with him that would be beneficial to them both?

Her thoughts were broken by renewed moaning from the adjacent cabin. Her heart leaped in anticipation. Finally! She hurried to the door and slipped inside.

The sailor was a mass of horribly moving color. He was covered with hundreds of butterflies — fixed to him like winged leeches — and he jerked and twitched as their tiny mouths devoured his flesh.

Near the table was a net made of golden strands of silk. Quickly, Clayre picked it up and threw it across the man's body.

There was a single muffled scream, an explosion of intense light, and then Clayre hastily pulled the net away.

Hundreds of bloated butterfly corpses fell to the floor, their wings making a rainbow carpet of death. And the sailor was gone.

In his place was a huge spider-like creature, nearly three feet high. A fabulous form curved out of its throbbing, bulbous body. It had the torso of a beautiful woman, but fixed to that torso were six arms and six heads held aloft by long, graceful throats.

Each lovely face was identical — alabaster skin, high cheekbones and dark, flashing eyes. The mouths were full-lipped and red. And when they parted they displayed sharp white fangs, tipped with emerald drops of poison.

Clayre bowed low. "Greetings, Lady Lottyr, Goddess of the Fires," she said. "And thank you for blessing this worshipful one with your exalted presence. May I be so bold as to ask the news?"

The heads all spoke at once, making a strange chorus of identical voices — all melodious, like royal courtesans skilled in the arts of theater and song.

"The news is neither fair nor foul, sister," said the six voices of Lottyr. "Our first attempt on the wizard, Safar, and the demon boy, Palimak, was only partly successful. We captured them. And engaged them in sorcerous battle."

Clayre was confused. "But that's wonderful news, O Goddess," she said. "If we captured them, then victory is ours. And all our efforts will soon be rewarded."

The six long graceful arms waved in unison, slender hands arcing like posing dancers. "Unfortunately, the Timuras managed to escape, sister," Lottyr said. "And they also captured my slave, King Felino. No doubt they will soon put him to the torture in an attempt to learn our plans."

"Forgive me for suggesting any doubt of your words, My Lady Lottyr," Clayre said, biting back bitter disappointment, "but you said the news was neither fair nor foul. Yet the events you describe seem to have little good in them. Is there something this ignorant one is missing?"

Musical laughter issued from the six mouths of the goddess. Then Lottyr said, "I cautioned you once before, sister, that our first attempt might not entirely succeed."

It was all Clayre could do not to snap. She calmed herself. "You said the Timuras escaped," she said. "Forgive me, but the only conclusion I can draw from that answer is that we had no success at all."

"Oh, but we did, sister," Lottyr said. "As for their escape, you must share some of the blame. It was, after all, your granddaughter, Queen Jooli, who assisted them."

Clayre gritted her teeth. Be damned to that girl! "I'm sorry to hear that, goddess," she said. "And you were correct in saying I am at fault when it comes to Jooli. I should have killed that child long ago."

More laughter from the goddess. "Do not despair, sister," Lottyr said. "You'll have your chance to rectify that soon enough."

She paused, graceful arms waving, then she said. "Also, the man we used for the sacrifice wasn't satisfactory. He was too weak to bear the pain long enough."

Again, Clayre was stricken with guilt. Something she was quite unaccustomed to. The sailor had been suffering from some illness and she'd used the excuse of treating him so there'd be no suspicions of her intent.

"Next time I'll make certain the victim is quite healthy, Lady," Clayre vowed.

"Excellent," the goddess said. "Also try to find someone younger. Virility is the spice of life, you know. And of death."

"I'll do that as well, Lady," Clayre promised with a smile. "As a matter of fact, I've had my eye on some of the younger men in the crew for my own purposes."

"Lovely," the goddess said, giggling musically. "Then we can share."

"Pardon, Lady," Clayre said, when the giggling subsided. "But you said we did meet with some success in this encounter. What might that be?"

"The most important thing," the goddess replied, "is that I found the answers to several questions I believe you were thinking of asking me."

Clayre's eyebrows rose. "Yes?"

"To begin with," said the goddess, "I've learned the whereabouts of a certain king. His name is Iraj Protarus."

Clayre clapped her hands in delight. "That's wonderful news, my goddess," she said. "Wonderful news, indeed!"

An hour later, secure in her new-found knowledge, Queen Clayre sent for her son.

King Rhodes tromped into her cabin, full of protests and bluster. "By the gods, mother," he thundered, "have you lost all your senses? You know damned well I'm getting ready for battle! And yet you insist on interrupting me."

"Oh, the battle," she said, suppressing a yawn. "I'd forgotten about that."

"How could you forget?" Rhodes fumed. "This is the chance we've been waiting for ever since we left home!"

Clayre ignored his anger. She waved a hand airily. "Have you managed to catch up to Safar Timura's ship yet?"

Rhodes thrust a thick finger at her port window. "It's just over the horizon. We're going to heave to for the night, ready our defenses, then attack at dawn."

"How clever of you, my son," Clayre said. "Or should I say, how clever of Kalasariz. You couldn't have done this on your own, the gods know."

Rhodes, thanks to some mental prodding by Kalasariz, kept himself from exploding. He sighed heavily.

"What is it you want, mother?" he asked.

"Nothing much," Clayre said. "Just the loan of one of your younger sailors to help me with a little task here. A nice handsome lad would be best. Someone with a good, virile physique."

Rhodes glared at his mother. "Since when did you start thinking I was your whoremaster?" he demanded. "Get your own bedmate and be damned!"

Clayre smiled, quite unmoved by his words. "If you continue to insult me, son," she said, "I won't lift a finger to help you during the battle. Without my magic things might not go so well as you wish."

Once again Kalasariz had to surge forth to keep Rhodes from losing his temper.

Finally, after an intense internal debate with the spymaster, the king said to Clayre, "Very well, mother. I'll get you your lad. He'll be here within the hour."

As he turned to go, Clayre said, "Oh, by the by. I mentioned that I needed this boy on loan?"

"What of it?"

"I misspoke," Clayre replied with a shrug. "When I'm done with this fellow I fear they'll be nothing left to return."

"Whatever you say, mother," Rhodes growled.

As he exited, he made sure to slam the door.

"Such a temper," Clayre said to herself. "Just like his father."

41

BATTLE FOR THE *NEPENTHE*

Queen Clayre should have had more faith in her son. Although he was no mighty wizard like Safar, he was a skilled general and a cunning adversary.

He hadn't wasted a moment of those many weeks at sea pursuing Safar and Palimak. His men were trained to the highest degree of readiness. And, after consulting with Kalasariz about Esmirian weapons and tactics, he'd come up with several tricks to stack the odds even more in his favor.

And so, as the pearly dawn crept up over the horizon, he approached his task eagerly and with supreme confidence. His first goal was to trap the *Nepenthe* against the coral reefs that lined the Aroborus shore.

With his ship, the *Kray*, in the center he spread his little fleet out windward of the Kyranian vessel to cut off any possibility of escape. Then, working in the half-light, he crammed every launch he possessed with soldiers.

Using muffled oars, the launches moved out ahead of Rhodes' ships, trying to get within easy striking distance before they were discovered.

Although Rhodes wasn't too worried about that possibility. At Kalasariz' urging, he'd asked Clayre to cast a spell that would fuddle the Kyranians' minds until it was too late. From all appearances her spell seemed to be working, for as the longboats approached there wasn't the slightest sign of life aboard the *Nepenthe*.

To the king's immense delight, the Kyranian airship was nowhere in sight. Clayre had warned him that her spell could only creep along the water and blanket the *Nepenthe* and thus would have no effect at all on the sky warriors.

Although Rhodes was fairly certain the airship would show up once the battle commenced, his hope was that his main task would be completed before he had to engage the flying vessel. But even if this hope proved false he was well prepared for the airship's arrival.

Within the king, Kalasariz wallowed in the juices of Rhodes' pleasure. In his mind's eye he saw Safar Timura led before him in chains. He imagined the elaborate torments he'd apply to Safar's body and soul. Whips and racks and bone crackers for the flesh. The sight of Safar's loved ones — the bitch woman, Leiria; the demon boy, Palimak; his mother and father and sisters — all tortured and humiliated most gruesomely, then murdered before Timura's eyes.

Kalasariz' emotions were so intense that his joy boiled over, flooding Rhodes' veins. Feeling his own senses sharpened by the pleasurable turmoil within, Rhodes couldn't help but laugh aloud.

Fortunately, Tabusir and his other aides weren't close enough to hear, but only noticed their king's broad smile. He's in a good mood, they all thought, their own morale lifting along with Rhodes' own spirits.

The king whispered, "Are you thinking what I'm thinking, my friend?"

And Kalasariz lied: *That soon we'll be rid of your mother, my lord, and then nothing can stand in our way.*

"Exactly," the king said. "But I was also imagining some particular tortures we might apply before we kill her. She's such an awful woman. You have no idea what it's been like to be in her thrall all these years. It's kept me from being the true king I deserve to be."

Shifting focus, Kalasariz said, *There's not much I don't know about imposing agony on miscreants, Majesty. When the time comes, perhaps you'd be interested in my views on that most absorbing subject.*

"Oh, I would, I would," Rhodes replied, his imagination running wild about all the things he could do to repay his mother for her hateful treatment of him.

Then he saw the first of the longboats drawing near the Kyranian ship and pulled himself back from the contemplation of such delights. If he wanted to achieve his dreams, discipline was now required.

"Friend of mine," he said, "it's time to concentrate out energies. For I do believe I already hear the sweet song of victory."

Kalasariz said, *You are king and I am your glad servant. Give the signal, Lord, and let us engage the enemy together!*

And so Rhodes motioned to his officers. Who passed the word down. A signalman hoisted yellow flags and the heavy-weapons crews on all three ships went into action.

With a clatter and a rumble big catapults were run out on their wooden wheels. There were ten such weapons per ship — thirty in all, with skilled crews to man each one. Once run out and anchored into place, there was the groan of twisted sinew cords as they were wound down against their counterweights. Followed by the muffled thud of catapult arms settling against thick leather pads.

The next stage, loading the catapults, was tricky. A special fiery material, based on a formula Kalasariz had passed on and which Rhodes thought of as Esmirian Fire, was kept in furnaces placed next to each weapon.

Once the material was loaded into the catapult's scoop it was necessary to fling it at the intended target as quickly as possible, or the weapon itself might catch fire.

Although Rhodes had personally drilled each crew, still there had been several accidents — something he wanted to avoid repeating at all costs once the battle commenced. And so he'd worked out a simple system of signals so that all the catapults could be loaded and fired simultaneously on his command.

When all the crews reported that their weapons were ready and only needed arming, Rhodes took his time before issuing the order. Once again he surveyed the scene. All the longboats were in position — about a hundred yards off the *Nepenthe*, which was still unaware of the danger. There they would wait until the bombardment was over, then they'd rush forward to board the ship and seize it.

The king looked left, then right, noting that his ships were in proper order.

"Very good," he said.

And he gave the order to load and fire.

Immediately thirty furnaces roared into life as their doors were slammed open and the hot material inside hungrily sucked up the salty air. Then came the grind of shovels against coals as the loaders dug their wide-bladed instruments into the green-glowing mass of Esmirian fire.

Followed by a long steady hiss from each catapult as the loaders heaped the sparking emerald flames onto the wet leather pads lining each catapult's scoop.

The moment the fiery mass touched the scoops, the crew captains triggered their weapons and the huge catapult arms slammed forward.

And thirty fiery green balls arced toward the sleeping *Nepenthe*.

Aboard the Kyranian ship Renor was caught in the throes of a nightmare. In his spell-induced sleep he dreamed he'd stumbled into a quagmire and no matter how hard he struggled, it was drawing him down, down, down.

What made the nightmare worse was that at the same time he sensed danger creeping up on him from the outside world. But, as with like the imagined quagmire, the more he fought to come awake the more the spell entangled him.

Nearby, Sinch and the other young Kyranian soldiers were

experiencing similar nightmares. Some of them had been on watch when Clayre cast her spell and now they were slumped unconscious on the deck, twisting and groaning in fear. While their comrades who had already been asleep found themselves mired even deeper in their nightmares.

All around the ship the officers and crew were also struggling against Clayre's magic. The least influenced was Captain Brutar, who'd gone to bed so drunk that the fumes from his heavy load of liquor seemed to lessen the spell's effects.

Instead of a nightmare the pirate captain was enjoying a dream in which Safar and the other Kyranians had been overpowered by his crew and looted of their valuables. Now he was tossing them into the sea. Pausing after each one plunged into the shark-infested waters to enjoy the humor of their frantic struggles.

He was fantasizing about holding Leiria and Jooli back for his further enjoyment when the first fireball struck the ship and exploded.

The impact hurled him out of his bunk onto his hands and knees. He remained there for a moment, fighting the alcoholic fog to regain his wits. Then another fireball hit, although this one failed to explode.

Cursing, Brutar struggled to his feet. It was then that he smelled what every sailor the world over fears the most — smoke!

He raced for his cabin door and hurled it open, practically ripping it from its hinges as he shouted, "Fire! Fire! Fire!"

When he stumbled up on the bridge it took him a long, bleary-eyed moment before he realized that no one was rushing to answer his call. To his amazement he saw one sailor curled up at the base of the ship's wheel, sound asleep. Not far away was the officer of the watch, also asleep.

Brutar lumbered around, seeing several other sailors scattered about the main deck, all sleeping fitfully. Then he saw smoke and fire raging near the center mast, green flames licking up the thick spar toward the sails.

He was too stunned to be angry. Never in his life had he seen such a sight. Slovenly pirates that his men were, no one had ever fallen asleep on watch and lived to tell the tale. To his further amazement he spotted several of the young Kyranian soldiers slumped on the deck, also unconscious.

What in the hells was going on?

Then Brutar heard a loud whoosh! from above and he looked up to see a large green fireball arc over his head to plunge, hissing and steaming, into the sea.

It was then that he became aware of the line of longboats moving toward the *Nepenthe*, all filled with heavily armed soldiers. In the distance he saw three familiar ships drawn up, and firing on the *Nepenthe* with huge catapults.

The ships, he immediately realized, were from the fleet he'd left back in Syrapis many weeks before he'd begun this ill-fated voyage.

Brutar did what any right-thinking pirate captain would do under the circumstances.

He ripped the white shirt from his back and ran to the rail, waving it frantically at the approaching soldiers.

"Ahoy, the longboats!" he shouted. "We surrender, gods dammit! We surrender!"

In what had to be the twentieth time in less than half an hour, Biner shaded his eyes with a broad palm and peered out over the waving green sea of treetops that was the Aroborus jungle.

And the same three questions chewed at his mind like a dog nipping uselessly at fleas. Where in the hells was Safar? Had he found Palimak? And, finally, when would they signal him to pick them up?

He kept telling himself that the constant worrying only made the hours drag on like a closely-watched sand clock, where time was measured by each slow-falling grain.

Safar hadn't really been gone that long, after all. He'd only spent yesterday afternoon and the night in the jungle. It was unlikely that he'd have searched for Palimak in the darkness. Instead he would have made camp until morning. And, now that dawn had broken, Safar, Leiria and the others were probably only just now grabbing a quick bite before resuming the search.

Logical as this line of thinking was, it did nothing to dispel the sense of dread that had been with Biner all through the night. It was one those feelings he'd learned to trust long ago. As the circus ringmaster it was up to him to make certain that all the equipment was as safe as possible. And that all of his people were healthy and concentrating on their performances.

A loose wire could send an acrobat like Arlain plunging to her death. Something as small as a toothache could break someone's focus during a particularly dangerous feat, with disastrous results.

Superb performers like Kairo tended to hide their ailments —

the show must go on, and all that — and it was up to Biner to spot their weaknesses and then convince them to drop the most dangerous portions of their acts.

And then there was the audience — Biner's most important responsibility. Improperly tended fires could set the tent ablaze. Poorly constructed viewing stands could collapse. Children had a tendency to get lost in the marvelous confusion of the circus and then turn up in the most perilous situations.

As Methydia always used to say, if there were a weight hanging from a frayed rope or an untended hole in the ground, a child was certain to wander into the danger zone.

Also, there were always the rowdies, petty criminals and sometimes even cut-throats who preyed on Biner's guests. Which in his mind was the definition of an audience: honored guests to be protected and welcomed into his home, Methydia's Flying Circus.

And so Biner had spent a fretful night worrying about that vague feeling of unease he'd always heeded in the past. He'd driven everyone crazy, snooping about the airship, seeing that everything was just so. Several times he'd roused the crew to repair things that could have waited until morning.

But mostly he'd paced the deck, peering endlessly into the night, searching for some sign of Safar. Chilled by the knowledge that his sense of dread had never failed him before. Wondering fitfully what would go wrong.

As always, when the answer finally came it was from an unexpected direction.

Arlain's voice rang clear in the early-morning air. "Biner! Over here!"

He whirled about and he saw her standing in the aft section of the airship. She was waving furiously at him, smoke hissing from between her teeth — a sure sign of agitation in the dragon woman.

Quickly, Biner tied off the ship's wheel, then raced down the gangway and across the deck to where Arlain stood.

"What is it?" he asked.

She pointed a long talon at the shimmering gray of the distant sea. "I thaw thomething, Biner!" she lisped, great eyes wide with concern. "Thomething really, really thtrange and thcary!"

Just then a huge green fireball lofted high into the air — hanging at the airship's height for a second — then flaming downward like a meteor in a crisp mountain sky.

"Did you thee it!" Arlain cried. "There it ith again!"

Biner gaped at the sight, wondering for a bewildered moment of indecision if both he and Arlain were suffering from delusions because of their worry for Safar and Palimak.

Then another green fireball arced high. And another. And another.

Realization sunk in. "It's the *Nepenthe*!" Biner bellowed. "Someone's attacking the *Nepenthe*!"

And he sprinted back to the bridge, shouting orders to the crew.

Moments later the airship was turned about and they shot off for the *Nepenthe*, magical engines steaming and boiling at their greatest heat.

Jooli hacked at the thorny barrier with all her might. But, just as before, every barbed vine she cut was immediately replaced by several others, shooting off the main branch.

Beyond the barrier was the beach and freedom from this awful jungle.

At least the spiders haven't reappeared, she thought, as she hacked once more at the thorny vines.

Then Safar shouted, "Get back!"

She leaped away, fingers instinctively clawing madly at her hair, thinking that the huge spiders had returned after all.

But then she saw Safar loft a small clay jar into the air. It smashed just beneath the vines. A sheet of flame shot up, scorching the underbrush. Light from the outside world burst in. Then, to her dismay, she saw new vines inching forward to cover the exit to the beach.

In a calm voice, Palimak said, "It's working father. One or two more might do the trick."

And then she noticed just how thin and weak the new growth was. Palimak squatted and started mixing another batch of blasting elixir, while Safar fished a second clay jar from his pack.

Their flight through the jungle had been maddeningly slow. Scores of spells had been hurled at them. But each time either Safar, Palimak or Jooli had cast counter-spells, blocking their force.

Once a troop of enormous apes had threatened them, but Sergeant Hammer and the Kyranian soldiers had quickly driven them off with a barrage of arrows, backed by curses as heated as the obscenities the apes had voiced.

But then night had fallen. Just as Biner had surmised, they'd decided to camp out until first light. Leiria had suggested that perhaps they ought to signal Biner to lift them out, but Safar had been opposed.

Gesturing at their bound captive, King Felino, he said, "Someone very powerful is supporting this fellow. Let's call her Queen X. Although I suspect from the spoor that 'queen' is a lesser title. Maybe a minor deity. Maybe not. Time will answer that. However, it's my guess that if we involve the airship before we escape this jungle we'll be giving our Queen X an opportunity to work even greater magic."

He grinned down at Felino, who was tied securely to the large litter they'd used to drag him through the jungle. He was also securely gagged with a dirty strip of rag torn from Sergeant Hamyr's breech cloth. An indignity the good sergeant had insisted upon. The gag was to keep their prisoner from shouting orders to any of his minions who might have followed.

"Isn't that so, Felino?" Safar said. "Isn't she just waiting for us to let down our guard? And wouldn't she just love to cast her spellnet over the airship?"

Felino could only grunt through the gag. Muffled as his response was, it didn't take a great deal of imagination for Jooli to recognize several filthy expressions.

"My, my," she said. "Such language from a king."

Leiria burst into earthy laughter. "I've known some kings better than I like to admit," she said. "And this fellow is nothing when it comes to royal curses."

Her jibe silenced King Felino for the remainder of the night. A silence he'd maintained when dawn broke, poking silvery beams down through the close-set trees.

The remainder of the trip to the thorny barrier had taken surprisingly little time. This was in the nature of journeys, Jooli thought. Slow to get there, quick to return.

Then she and Leiria and the soldiers had taken turns standing in the narrow avenue, hacking at the regenerating growth. While Safar and Palimak conferred on a magical solution.

Jooli felt left out of their endeavors. She was a witch, wasn't she? A damned good witch, even if she said so herself. Why wasn't she being consulted?

And then she realized there was no insult intended. It was merely a father and son attempting to make some sort of personal contact after a long period of mutual fear for the safety of the other.

The other thing she noticed was that every once in a while a strange tiny creature would appear on Palimak's shoulder. Apparently none of the others could see it. And even through her own sorcerous lens the creature was quite hazy. Obviously it was some sort of magical creature.

Whatever was going on, powerful magic was being discussed and worked. Despite her empathy for a father and his son, this rankled her even more.

By the gods, she wanted to be included!

And then, as she stepped back from her latest attack on the thorn barrier to catch her breath and wipe perspiration from her brow, Palimak rose to his feet and came over to her.

Without one trace of condescension, he said, "Pardon, Aunt Jooli, but could you help us with this?"

Jooli was amazed. And honored, in an odd sort of way, that Palimak had added the honorific of "aunt" to her name. Instead of all those dreary royal terms like Your Highness, Your Ladyship, and so forth.

Leiria smiled at her as if she knew what was running through Jooli's mind.

Hells, Jooli thought, I'm an aunt to this remarkable young man! What could be better than that?

And then Safar said, "I'm really sorry we've left you out of this, Jooli. The thing is, I recognized your grandmother's hand in this. Her spoor is mixed with that of the deity I call Queen X. And I was reluctant to put you in opposition to your own kin."

He grinned, blue eyes warm and friendly. "Will you forgive me?" he asked. "It wasn't Palimak's fault. He urged, but I resisted. I guess I'm just so much of a family person — being Kyranian and all — that I thought it might cause you pain."

"Nothing to forgive," Jooli said gruffly, surprised at the sudden emotion roughening her voice.

"And if you really need help, I'd be pleased to offer it. Especially if it involves my grandmother. Believe me, there's no love lost between us."

She joined them in their efforts, quickly catching the sense of the spell they were working. And also, after some concentration, she picked up the scent of Queen Clayre's magic — a too-sweet perfume underlying the acrid stench of fire.

Jooli knelt down and brushed aside leaves to make a bare patch of ground. As she talked, she made a sketch with a twig.

"My grandmother likes to use a special table for her magic," she said, drawing the table. "It looks like this . . . also, the center is inlaid with golden tiles in the shape of a pentagram."

She sketched in the tiles, making the lines much deeper to give a three-dimensional effect. "Whatever or whoever this deity is that she's made her bargain with, chances are she's been summoned through those tiles."

Jooli looked up at Safar. "If we can break the contact between them — for only for a few seconds, even — we might be able to get through that barrier."

"How do we do that, Aunt Jooli?" Palimak asked.

"Grandmother is a very strong-willed woman," Jooli said. "Even when she's ill, she refuses to acknowledge it. However, there is one thing that drives her mad."

"What's that?" Safar asked.

"Capsicum," Jooli replied.

Safar's eyebrows shot up. "You mean, like pepper?" he asked.

"Exactly," Jooli said. "Pepper. The hotter the better. She doesn't even have to eat it. The mere presence of capsicum dust gives her a horrible reaction. She swells up like a balloon, her sinuses desert her and she gets a terrible rash all over body. She's a very vain woman, you know. So the rash probably angers her more than anything."

"I don't have anything with pepper in it," Safar said. He glanced around the jungle. "Maybe we can find something here . . ."

"It's not necessary," Jooli broke in. She grinned. "When I was a girl and made up my first witch's kit I made sure to include powdered betel pepper in it." She grinned. "It was the best way I knew to keep my grandmother at bay."

Palimak laughed. "That's a great trick," he exclaimed. "If you can't beat them, sneeze them to death!"

Jooli fished out her kit and found a packet of betel powder — it was orange with streaks of yellow. She handed it to Palimak.

"Add this to your next batch of blasting elixir and see what happens," she said.

Still laughing, Palimak did as she suggested, mixing the betel powder into the foul mixture in his portable wizard's bowl. Then he poured it into the small clay container that Safar gave him, jammed in the cork and handed it over to Jooli.

She hesitated. "It's your trick, Aunt Jooli," he said. "You deserve the honors."

Laughing with him, Jooli accepted the elixir. She cleared everyone from her path and held the jar high.

"Take this, grandmother!" she shouted.

And she hurled the jar. This time, the sheet of flame was even higher and hotter than before. A strange giddy sensation overcame Jooli. She had the sudden flash-vision of her grandmother sneezing and was struck with a fit of girlish giggles.

Laughing like a fool, but not caring, she shouted, "Let's go!"

And she charged through the wide opening created by the explosion. The others followed, dragging Felino's litter behind them and laughing with her. Only Safar and Palimak knew what was so funny, but everyone was so relieved they'd finally broken out of that dank jungle that they laughed anyway. Wheezing and gasping as they trundled out on the beach.

But then they heard the thunder of battle and the laughter died.

And they all looked out to sea, gasping in shock at the sudden realization.

The *Nepenthe* was on fire. Its deck swarming with soldiers in enemy uniforms, trying to put out the flames.

Surrounding the vessel were three other ships, all engaged in battle. But it wasn't the *Nepenthe* they were fighting. Whatever had happened there was long over. One only had to witness the prisoners in Kyranian uniforms crowded into the bow and under enemy guard to realize that.

This battle was going on elsewhere. Huge green flaming arrows — each easily twice the size of man — were being fired into the skies. Battery, after battery of them, shooting off in steady time.

And their target was the airship, hovering over the *Nepenthe* and fighting a losing battle. One of the arrows had struck the bow and they could see some of Biner's crew desperately trying to put out the blaze.

King Felino finally worked his gag free. And now it was his turn to laugh.

"You've lost, Safar Timura," he gloated. "Surrender while you can!"

42
DARK VICTORY

Biner was doing his damnedest to outmaneuver the enemy fleet, and to extinguish the fire raging in the bow of the airship. If it spread to the engines the whole airship would explode.

The ringmaster called on his deepest reserves of calm. Never mind that the show was a disaster, he and his people would continue to perform until the last fat clown provoked laughter and the curtain closed.

His orders were issued in his grand ringmaster's voice. A presentation of things to come for the audience, filled with all sorts of subtext for the performers.

"Turn left," he boomed to the wheelman. Unhurried, but crackling with authority.

"Drop the port ballast," he roared to the port crew, calmly demanding their urgent but measured action so the airship could rise above the next arrow shot.

"Put some soap into that water, sir!" he bellowed to the captain of the fire-fighting team.

And the fire captain quickly, but without panic, added soap to the water barrels that fueled the hoses his men were playing over the leaping green flames. It seemed a long time, but soon thick suds shot out over the fire, quenching it.

Biner heard Khysmet trumpet from the aft section of the ship. The great stallion was housed in a temporary stable, waiting for his master's return. The excitement of the battle, plus his concern for Safar's absence, had worked the horse up into a fury and he was kicking at the wooden partition that held him.

To his relief, he saw Arlain running to the stable to calm the animal. Khysmet was much enamored of the dragon woman and would be sure to respond to her gentle ministrations.

He turned back to the task at hand. "Bombardiers, are you ready?" he shouted to his attack crew.

The signal came back that the sacks of magical explosives were set in their bays. The formula for the explosives had been worked out by Safar during their final flight from Esmir. Palimak had later added a trick or two of his own, guaranteed to devastate the most hardened enemy.

These explosives had been the key to the Kyranian occupation of their little piece of Syrapis. During Safar's long exile in the otherworld of Hadinland, it had been up to Palimak to lead the way against all those hostile forces.

Biner had been shocked when he'd realized that hatred seemed to be the natural state of things in Syrapis. This was an emotional environment he'd never understood. In his mind and experience, people — and even demons — were all the same. An audience was merely an audience. Most were sweet, but some were sour. And turning sour to sweet was his life's work.

He was a gentle giant in a dwarf's body. Short of stature, massive in girth and especially in heart, he believed down to his very bones there was no audience he'd ever met whose spirit couldn't be transformed — if only for two hours — into goodness.

And so the vicious, hateful attitude of the natives of Syrapis completely mystified him. Although he'd performed before thousands, possibly tens of thousands of people in his career, the Syrapians were like no others he'd ever met.

Arlain and the other circus performers felt the same and so although they were fighting for their own survival in Syrapis — as well as for that of the Kyranians — they despised this new, anti-human role they were forced to play.

Now they were being called upon to play that role once again. The *Nepenthe* had been overwhelmed by an enemy force. Biner had immediately recognized the uniforms of the attacking soldiers as being those of Hanadu, the kingdom ruled by Rhodes.

Biner could only guess why Rhodes had followed the Timuras to this far-off place. He supposed the king's purpose was to block Safar's mission to Hadinland. Why Rhodes should want to do this, however, was a complete puzzlement.

The only thing Biner knew for certain was that he had to stop Rhodes. At the moment the only way he could see to accomplish this was to bombard the longboats carrying the enemy troops. To bombard the *Nepenthe* itself would be useless, and would endanger the lives of the Kyranians still on board.

However, the huge fire arrows being launched by the three enemy ships were doing a damned good job of keeping him from that objective.

His maneuvers were designed to carry him above their reach, yet still be close enough to assume some accuracy. To maintain his calm, he imagined the action as raising a diving platform to its maximum height, while still giving the acrobat a good chance of hitting his watery target.

He was studying a group of longboats clustered near the *Nepenthe* as a possible target when he heard Khysmet whinny his shrill cry. A moment later Arlain came rushing up.

"Over there, Biner!" she cried, gesturing wildly toward the shore. "It'th a thignal from Thafar!"

Biner swiveled his glass in the direction she was pointing. And there, rising from the beach, he saw a green flare. Fearing some new trick to draw his attention away from the battle, he back-tracked the flare's path until he came to a small group of people standing near the water's edge.

One of them was clearly Safar.

"Hard about!" he shouted to the crew. "Set a course for the beach!"

Leaving his friends to tend to the battle, Safar spent just enough time with Khysmet to let him know his master was back for good.

Then he hurried to Methydia's old stateroom, where Jooli guarded their bound captive, King Felino. While waiting to be picked up by the airship she'd hastily briefed Safar about her magical observations in the arena.

"They seemed obsessed with the number six," she'd said.

That was good enough for Safar to make some quick deductions. Suddenly, he was quite certain of the identity of the mysterious Queen X.

In the cabin he gave Jooli a stick of magical charcoal and directed her to draw a six-pointed star on the deck, with Felino at the center. Each star point, he also told her, should bear the likeness of one of the animal warriors they'd faced. A lion to start with, followed by a jackal, an ape, and so on.

Jooli quickly caught on to what he intended and got to work.

Meanwhile, Safar flipped through the pages of the Book of Asper for clues to the proper spell.

He started with the Lady Felakia, the patron goddess of his people. In the most ancient Kyranian myths it was said that the beautiful goddess of purity and health was once wooed by the god Rybian, the maker of people and demons.

Legend had it that the Lady Felakia spurned Rybian's attentions and during the long lovers' siege he became bored and pinched out all the races of humankind and demonkind from the pure clay of Kyrania. The same clay that had made the Timura potters a modern legend; their work through generations was highly valued all over Esmir.

To Safar, however, the key was Asper's claim that humans and demons were born of "a common womb." In other words, never mind the myth of what Rybian had wrought, but pay close attention to the mother.

The demon master wizard had a theory regarding the subject. It was outlined in a poem that began:

"In the days of heavenly love and lust
A wicked sister of the pure and just
Conspired to win the heart of our maker . . ."

In Asper's scenario, the Goddess Lottyr — who was the Hellsish shadow sister of the Lady Felakia — crept into Rybian's bed one night when he was drunk and through guile got him to impregnate her with his heavenly seed. In the morning, when he'd realized what he had done, the god ripped the seed from Lottyr's womb. Then implored the Lady Felakia to accept it into her own. Otherwise, he said, the creatures he had created would all be condemned to eternal lives of torment in the Hells.

In a night of godly passion, Asper said, Rybian wooed Felakia and she finally relented and accepted his embrace and his seed. From these two unions were born all the creatures of the world, including humans and demons.

Safar had never paid much attention to this portion of Asper's text. In both poetic form and mythical content it was quite out of character for the cynical old demon, who consistently warned that the gods were asleep and that the fate of both humans and demons was of little concern to them.

But when Jooli mentioned her own theory of numbers his mind plunged back to his student days in Walaria. He'd discovered Asper's book in the forbidden private library of the high priest, Umurhan.

There were many other volumes in that library to which his curiosity had also been drawn. One of them was a text on Hellsish magic, whose cover bore the drawing of a strange, six-headed, six-armed goddess of the dark worlds. He'd later learned it was the portrait of the evil Lady Lottyr. Shadow sister of the Goddess Felakia.

Although Safar was adamantly opposed to the practice of black magic, as a scholar he was quite familiar with all of its aspects. He was not only schooled in the spells involved in that terrible art, but was skilled in casting their counter-spells to protect himself.

This was how he had defeated Iraj Protarus and his minions when they had tried to destroy him and his people with the shapechanging Spell of Four. Safar doubted he had the power to similarly defeat the unholy deity that was the Lady Lottyr. But maybe, just maybe, he could slow her down a bit.

Finally, he found Asper's poem on the subject. It was one of his strangest verses. Written as if he, himself, had once encountered the dreaded Goddess of the Hells.

He called Jooli to show her. She smiled when she saw the poem. And with much feeling, she read Asper's words aloud:

"Deep in the Hell Fires I spied
Rybian's false-hearted bride.
Six heads and arms had she,
And beauty enough to bedazzle me.
Through the Sixth Gate I fled,
Soul quaking in fear and dread.
Up, up through the world's core,
At my heels that Hellish whore.
To the unfeeling Heavens I cried,
'Where's the lamp, where's my guide?'
Of all, only Felakia deigned to speak.
And those holy words I now repeat:
'If it's my sister, Lottyr, you wish to smite,
In the lion's eye, seek the light.'"

When she was done, Safar shook his head. "I never knew what Asper was getting at before," he said. Then, grinning, he pointed at Felino. "But there's our lion," he continued. "And what we need to do couldn't be plainer."

The lionman roared in fury, twisting futilely at his strong bonds. "You fools!" he cried. "You poor, weak fools! You'll never defeat the goddess!"

Jooli only laughed. "I'll fetch a torch," she told Safar. "That ought to be light enough."

But as she turned, Felino suddenly howled in agony.

"What in the Hells?" Safar exclaimed.

As Jooli turned back she saw the veins in the lionman's body swelling as if they would burst. His eyes were bulging from their sockets.

Then his jaws fell open and the strange, melodious voice of a woman issued forth. Although it was strong, it had a distant, echoing quality to it — as if it were coming from the bottom of a deep cavern. Neither Safar nor Jooli had any doubt who the speaker was.

"How dare you defy me, Safar Timura?" said the voice of Lottyr. "You have bedeviled me from the start of your puny, mortal life. Asper defied me and in the end I made him suffer for it most grievously. And now you make bold to follow in his doomed footsteps? Beware what you wish for, Safar Timura. For some day I may grant it, just as I granted Asper his wishes."

The voice stopped and Felino slumped against his bonds, dead.

Safar suddenly felt exhausted — as lifeless as those lion's eyes radiating nothingness from Felino's head.

He heard Jooli wail, "What do we do now, Safar?"

But he just shook his head. He was out of answers.

At that moment, Palimak burst into the cabin. "Father!" he cried. "Come and see! It's Coralean! With the whole damned fleet!"

Renewed hope leaped into Safar's breast. He and Jooli rushed out of the cabin to see what Palimak was talking about.

And when they got to the rail overlooking the battle scene it was like a vision granted from the heavens.

Nine ships were converging on Rhodes' little fleet of three. Safar immediately recognized the center ship, the *Tegula, which flew Coralean's coat of arms.*

Safar didn't know where his old friend had come from, or how he'd guessed Safar was in trouble. All he cared about was that the tide of battle had been transformed. Rhodes' longboats full of soldiers were rowing as fast as they could back to their mother ships.

And it was going to be a long pull for them, for even now the enemy ships were turning tail and fleeing, with four of Coralean's vessels in hard pursuit.

Directly beneath the airship, the *Nepenthe was sinking. But he could see one of Coralean's ships converging on it to take off the survivors. Many of whom wore the uniforms of the young Kyranian soldiers Safar had left behind.*

Already Biner was shouting gleeful orders to his crew to lower the airship so they could assist in the rescue effort.

Leiria fell into Safar's arms, laughing with joy. Everyone else whooped in glee, hugging or slapping each other's backs.

Just then, a strange feeling came over Safar. It seemed as if he'd suddenly become another person — standing slightly away — observing the scene. All the happy people, with his other self, his Safar self, at their center. Leiria clasping him tight.

And he thought, in an inner voice that was not his own: *Well done, brother. Well done.*

Then he was back in his own body again, trembling with alarm. He pushed a bewildered Leiria away and ran to the place where he thought his other self had been standing.

There was no one there, only a stack of empty ballast sacks. He looked about, but saw nothing out of the ordinary.

Leiria came up to him, concern in her eyes. "What's wrong, Safar?" she asked.

Still dazed, Safar nearly blurted something about Iraj. But he recovered just time.

"Nothing," he replied. "I'm just a little tired from the excitement, I guess."

She started to embrace him again, but Safar held her off as gently as he could. For some reason he felt that if touched her it would be a violation of her flesh. That if she knew him for what he was, she'd feel sullied. But that, like his bitten off response, also seemed insane.

Safar stood quite still for a moment, the world spinning around him. Finally, the mad whirling stopped and he felt whole again.

What now he wondered. What now?

And then the ghost voice intruded once again to answer: *We go to Hadin, brother. Just as we planned all along.*

At that moment Safar knew the answer to a much deeper question. Now he knew where Iraj Protarus had gone.

The deck of the airship rushed up to smite him. And then all he knew was darkness.

Part Four

Goddess of the Hells

CHAPTER FORTY-THREE

THE TWO KINGS

Safar was trapped in the prelude to the end of the world.

And oh, how he danced.

Danced, danced, danced.

Danced to the beat of the harvest drums.

All around him a thousand others danced in joyous abandon. They were a handsome people, a glorious people, led by their beautiful young Queen who cried out in ecstasy.

Beyond the grove, a backdrop to the Queen, was the great conical peak of a volcano. And he knew that at any moment the volcano would erupt and that Safar, along with the joyous dancers, would die.

Was this real? Was he truly on the shores of Hadinland, destined to be swallowed in a river of molten rock? Or was it just a night terror that would end if only he could open his eyes?

Open your eyes, he thought! Dammit, man! Open them!

And then, with a jolt, he thought, Iraj! Where is Iraj? He tried to look around to find him but then Palimak's voice intruded, calling:

"Father? Father? Open your eyes, father!"

And he thought, Oh, yes. I know where Iraj is now.

So he opened his eyes. Or was it Iraj who opened them for him? Never mind. That was something they would have to sort out later between themselves.

The main thing was, his eyes were open now.

But all he could see was darkness. He blinked, but the darkness stubbornly remained.

Alarm crept in, but he pushed it away. Obviously, there was a reasonable explanation. It was probably night and Palimak most likely kept the room dark so as not to disturb him. He could sense Palimak bending over him.

"Where are we, son?" he asked.

"We're in Hadin, father," Palimak replied.

"So soon?" Safar asked, although he was only a little surprised.

"You were unconscious a long time, father," Palimak said. "You had us pretty worried, what with the fever and all. But that's broken now, thank the gods. Jooli and I took turns treating you during the whole voyage."

Safar nodded understanding. "I dreamed I was trapped in that other world again," he said. "Dancing on the sands of Hadinland. I suppose it was the fever that caused it."

"Do you feel well enough to get up now, father?" Palimak asked. "Coralean has some people waiting to see you. They're all most anxious."

The young man paused, then — with amazement in his voice — he added, "It's a delegation from Hadin. They say you are their long, lost king."

Safar was astounded. "King?" he asked. "How could I be their king?"

Inside him, Iraj stirred in his nest. He said, *I told you long ago, brother, that we were both destined for great things. And here is final proof. We are kings of a people we never even met!*

Safar wanted to tell Iraj to shut up. His presence inside Safar's body was all too disturbing as it was without Iraj prattling in his ear. Safar felt confused, dazed, as if he had not quite awakened from a terrible dream.

He brushed his face with his hand, attempting to wipe away the confusion. Then he realized Palimak was trying to give some sort of explanation about the people who believed Safar was their king. He nodded, pretending he'd heard the answer.

He said, "I'll get up, son. Just bring me some clothes. And some water to bathe in."

Then he chuckled and said, "And please bring me a light. I'm not a cat, you know. I can't see in the dark."

His request was met by a long, frightening silence. "Did you hear me, son?" Safar pressed.

Palimak's voice shook when he answered. "I heard you, father." Another long pause. Then, "But it's broad daylight out, father. You shouldn't need a light!"

Inside him, Iraj jolted in shock. *What's this?* he demanded. *Are we blind? Or is this the boy's idea of some cruel jest? By the gods, I'll have him . . .*

Safar slapped his own breast, cutting Iraj off. He had to think, dammit! What was happening to him? Was he going mad?

"I must have misheard you, son," he said at last. "It's not really daytime, is it?"

He reached out desperately and Palimak clasped his hands in a tight grip. "Tell me it's night, son," he pleaded. "Tell me!"

Safar felt wet drops fall on his cheek. Was Palimak crying?

"Can't you see me, father?" Palimak begged. "I'm right here in front of you. And it's daytime, with a bright shinning sun. Honest to the gods, it is!"

Palimak's panic had the reverse effect on Safar. He became quite calm. If he was blind, so be it. Maybe he'd regain his sight later. Maybe not. The main thing was that there were far more calamitous events than his own personal misfortune that needed to be dealt with.

He patted the young man's hand. "Never mind, son," he said. "I'm probably just suffering from some sort of shock. Caused by the illness, no doubt. I'm sure I'll soon recover my sight. It's a temporary ailment, nothing more."

When Palimak replied, his voice was steadier. "Aunt Jooli told me about Lady Lottyr — the Hells goddess," he said. "Maybe the illness was something she caused."

"That's the answer," Safar said, hope growing. "Lottyr's at fault. Well, then. Now that we know the cause all we have to do is come up with some sort of spell to counter her. Couldn't be simpler."

He struggled upright, Palimak putting an arm behind his shoulder to help. After a brief moment of dizziness, Safar felt amazingly strong and full of energy. That was an incredible relief, for deep down he'd worried he'd be physically unfit as well as blind.

"If you'll help me wash and dress," he said to Palimak, "I'll attend to this delegation you mentioned."

He grinned. "Can you imagine?" he asked. "*Me, a king! Nothing could be more amusing.*"

Palimak told him to wait in bed while he went to fetch the things he'd need. Safar listened to the departing footsteps and the sound of the door opening and closing.

When he was sure he was alone he said, "We're going to have to work out some better means of communication, Iraj. I can't just have you charging around with your every thought and confusing matters. Otherwise, they're going to think I've gone mad."

Inside him, Iraj laughed. He said, *You've always been a bit mad, Safar. As have I. Still, you have a point. We'll need to figure out something. However, I must warn you: if you intend to tell this delegation from Hadin that you are* not *their king you'll get no cooperation from me. Never forget, there's not one crown at stake, here, but two. Hadin will have two kings, not one, if I have anything to say about it!*

Iraj's last words hit Safar like a hammer. *Two kings of Hadin! Immediately, he remembered a riddle from Asper's book. He'd always known the answer to the riddle would be crucial. But he'd never guessed just how much he'd be personally affected by it.*

Iraj suddenly found himself awash in Safar's hot-blooded excitement. *What's going on?* he demanded. *Your thoughts are too confusing to make out!*

Safar answered by reciting Asper's riddle aloud:

> *"Two kings reign in Hadin Land,*
> *One's becursed, the other damned.*
> *One sees whatever eyes can see,*
> *The other dreams of what might be.*
> *One is blind. One's benighted.*
> *And who can say which is sighted?*
> *Know that Asper knocked at the Castle Keep,*
> *But the gates were barred, the Gods asleep."*

Iraj thought a moment, then said, *So, we're the two kings, right?*

"That's what it would seem," Safar replied.

Clever fellow, that damned old demon, Iraj observed. *You were always going on about him, but I never paid much attention. Now it seems the old boy had this thing charted from the beginning.*

Safar didn't reply and Iraj suddenly realized he was concentrating on something else.

What are you doing? he demanded? Frantically, he scrabbled for the protection of his sorcerous nest. *If you try to kill me,* he said, *I swear you'll suffer for it!*

Safar's reply came from quite close. Frighteningly so. And he didn't speak aloud, but used a newly discovered inner "voice."

Don't worry, Safar said. *I'm not trying to kill you. I'm just climbing down there so I can "talk" to you without speaking aloud. Funny, being blind made it easy. I sort of turned my eyes inward and found you.*

Iraj didn't believe him. *Don't lie to me,* he said. *I know very well you'd like nothing better than to see me dead. After all, if I were in your position I'd do the same thing.*

That's the main difference between the two of us, Safar replied. *You always thought I desired the same things you did. That's never been the case. You wanted to be Esmir's King of Kings. I had no such ambitions.*

Don't fool yourself, brother, Iraj retorted. *All you ever wanted to do was save the world. Tell me that's not as insanely self-centered as my own wishes. Come on — Safar The Savior! No god appointed you to such a world-shaking role? You did! I was there, remember? And at the same time, boy that I was, I anointed myself the future King of Kings.*

I won't quarrel with you, Safar said. *Arguing about details won't get us anywhere.*

Iraj sneered. *You're afraid to admit I'm right, that's all.*

Safar sighed. *Let's deal with this later, he said. I'll admit you're right about one thing. When I first realized what was happening I decided to figure out a way to kill you, without killing myself. But now I realize we're fated to play this game out together. And the only way either one of us is going to survive, much less realize our goals, is to cooperate.*

Agreed, Iraj said.

Truce, then? Safar asked.

You have my word, Iraj said.

Safar nearly said something sarcastic about the worth of Iraj's word, but bit it off.

Instead he said, *Then let's go greet our new subjects, brother mine. And find out all we can about what's going on.*

Done! Iraj said. *I'll give you my strength and you give me your magic and nothing can stand against us.*

Ever the conqueror, Safar sighed.

I won't quarrel with that, brother, Iraj said. *Conquering is my destiny.*

44

THE ISLAND QUEEN

When Palimak left Safar's cabin he was so stricken with fear and grief at his father's condition that he fled to his own quarters before anyone could stop him to ask when Safar would emerge.

He had to think. He had to get his emotions in check before he told the others that his father was blind. Considering his own reaction, Palimak had no doubt that unless he handled the situation carefully everyone would panic.

Although he'd only recently turned fourteen, Palimak knew they all looked up to him as someone much older and wiser than his years. Despite the fact that demons matured at a faster rate than humans, both emotionally and physically, right now the human side of him ruled and he felt like a mere child incapable of handling such a burden.

He mixed himself a weak solution of water and sweet wine to settle his nerves. But when he took a sip the drink had the opposite effect and he rush to a basin to empty his stomach.

Then he wiped his face, washed out his mouth with mint water and sat on his bunk to think . . .

. . . The voyage from Aroborus to Hadin took many weeks. And although the seas were strange and filled with danger, the journey was without incident.

Even so, everyone kept looking over their shoulders for the reappearance of Rhodes and his fleet. Though they'd only suffered the deaths of two young men in the fight with Rhodes, all the Kyranians were grief-stricken at this loss.

Safar's collapse added even more tension to the atmosphere.

Coralean was all for turning back to Syrapis, reasoning that with Safar in a coma the mission had no head, and therefore no purpose.

Many of the other Kyranians agreed, but Palimak — supported by Leiria and Jooli — insisted that they press on. Safar had undergone such trials before, Palimak said, and given time and careful nursing, would likely recover.

It was Eeda, however, who turned the tide of opinion. Although she was young, her words were wise. She was also quite visibly with child, which gave even more depth to her appeal.

"Back in Syrapis," she said, "we all saw what is going to happen to this world if Lord Timura doesn't reach Hadin in time to intervene. I don't want my child born into the doomed land we saw in Lord Timura's vision. And I don't think you want to condemn your dear families to such a horrible fate."

Coralean spoke for the others when he argued, "That's all very well and good, dear wife. But Coralean must speak plainly when he warns that the chances of success appear small. If Safar doesn't recover — or worse, should he die — where will we all be then?

"Hadin is a land unknown to us all and may be filled with many enemies. If our fates are perilous, wouldn't it better to face those perils surrounded by our friends and families, rather than among strangers?"

"Forgive me for seeming quarrelsome, lord husband," Eeda replied. "But I, for one, would rather die bravely facing the unknown. With some hope — however slight — that we can cure this world of its afflictions.

"For me, the alternative is to cower like some lowly insect while unknown forces drag myself and my child — as well as my dear husband — to certain death. Why, in the vision Lord Timura revealed to us, there might not even be anyone left to bury us and sing our souls to the heavens once we are gone."

A long silence followed this powerful argument. But Coralean, a man who could see all sides, felt it his duty to point out other dangers.

"What of that devil Rhodes?" he asked. "Somehow he has eluded us. He has three ships loaded with soldiers. What if he is even now returning to Syrapis to launch a surprise attack on our homes to revenge himself for his failure here?"

Palimak replied, "I think my grandfather, Khadji Timura, is well able to protect our people against Rhodes. When you left Syrapis to help us, that was the plan you worked out with everyone, wasn't it? And once you'd found us, you told them all that you were to proceed to Hadin, leaving the safety of our people in my grandfather's capable hands."

There was another long silence. No one — especially Coralean — could argue with that statement.

It was Biner who then put paid to the discussion and spiritless mood by rising up from his place and declaring:

"Damn everything but the circus!"

Arlain and the other show people leaped to their feet and joined the ringmaster in a fabulous impromptu performance.

Palimak rushed to help them. And although there were no stretched wires, or tents, or costumes and make-up, they all brought the circus to life on that bare deck.

Incredible feats of acrobatics dazzled one and all. Stirring music from Elgy and Rabix lifted glum spirits. This was followed by a frantic clown chase — with all the circus people joining in — that soon brought roars of laughter to all the people. Laughter that echoed over the endless wine-dark seas, making them seem like a natural and friendly part of the act.

Flying fish leaping high, as if laughing with the crowd. Grinning dolphins gamboling in the ships' wake, playing like merry children in a watery nursery.

It was those people and those actions that kept the voyage from collapsing at the start. And although the cheer was short-lived because Safar remained in his coma, the closer they all came to Hadin, the more determined everyone became to complete the journey.

After Safar's condition, the main worry was Rhodes. Had he returned to Syrapis? Or was he lying ahead somewhere, ready to ambush them?

Biner made several long flights in hopes of catching sight of Rhodes. But the king and his minions were never seen. After a while everyone assumed that he had sailed back to Syrapis and that it would be their friends and families at home who would have to contend with him. This was worrisome, to be sure, but it also meant that Rhodes was no longer their responsibility.

Then, one day, Hadin announced its presence.

Normally, seafarers first become aware that they are nearing land when they notice subtle shifts in the currents. Also, the water color changes as the sea floor gradually rises, or a river makes itself known by the silt carried off by outgoing tides.

These things often present themselves many days before land itself is sighted. There are other signs, such as birds who normally live on shore but which hunt the deeps for food. Also, the variety of fish might change. Even more telling is an abundance of plant debris — floating logs with fresh branches still intact, or clumps of estuary weeds uprooted by a storm and swept out to sea.

With Hadin, however, the announcement was much more stark and more than a little frightening.

As they sailed, the Demon Moon sank lower in the sky until it rested just on the horizon. And there it remained for the remainder of the voyage. Only it seemed to grow larger as each mile passed beneath their bows. And soon it appeared as if they were sailing directly into its grinning mouth.

The color of the moon also changed from blood red to an eerie orange, giving the sky a strange and foreboding cast.

Next came the expected change in the color of the sea. Except that this change came without warning. One morning they awoke to find all the seas were painted a ghastly gray-white. The smell of rotting sea life was intense, coming from the hundreds of dead fish floating on the surface.

One of the sailors dipped up a bucket of water and examined the grayness. Although he didn't know the cause, a grizzled old salt said it was pumice — no doubt thrown into the sky by an erupting volcano.

If anyone doubted his word, they soon sighted huge gray hunks of the chalk-like substance — some as large as great icebergs. But most were the size of small rocks and they bumped along the sides of the ships making it sound like they were moving through a slurry of gravel.

Off to their left they saw a thick column of black smoke rising above the horizon and had no doubt that it was an active volcano — the source of all that pumice.

The fleet captains started to fret that one of the large pieces of pumice would damage the ships, possibly even sinking them, and they urged the Kyranians to turn about.

But Coralean put each captain under guard and forced them to go on.

The following morning the situation improved dramatically. For suddenly they sailed out of the gray waters into sparkling blue seas, full of active fish life. Then the normal happy signs of approaching land made themselves known — floating plant life, hunting birds and several great sea lizards swimming toward traditional nesting grounds.

And two days later, under a bright cheery sun, they sailed into a graceful bay with broad beaches and rich orchards of palm trees waving in a gentle breeze.

In the background of this idyllic scene was a towering volcano. It appeared peaceful, since there were only fluffy white clouds gathered about its conical peak. Terraced farms ran halfway up its sides, followed by lush greenery and then a sprinkling of trees near the top. A winding road cut through the farms, disappearing between smaller peaks.

Palimak was aboard the airship when they came upon Hadin. And when he first saw the beaches, palm trees and the volcano it reminded him of his father's description of the spirit world Hadin from which he'd escaped.

The differences, however, were remarkable. There were no naked dancing people. No resounding shell horns and harvest drums. And the volcano was far from threatening. In fact, it looked like a place where everyone had enjoyed a rich bounty of life for many generations.

Then he saw a group of about twenty people standing near the largest palm orchard. He borrowed Biner's spyglass to examine them.

The first thing that struck him was how handsome these bronzed people were. They were far from naked, much less painted, but their costumes were minimal. Short breeches for the men, with flower garlands decorating their bare chests. And tiny skirts and bright-colored breast bands for the women, who also wore flower garlands in profusion.

Brief as the costumes were, they were quite rich in coloring and design. It didn't take any ponderous thought to surmise that their brevity had more to do with Hadin's hot weather than with how civilized the people were.

A tall, regal woman stood in front of the group. When Palimak focused on her he was stunned by her beauty. Her costume was visibly richer than the others — more colorful and embroidered with what appeared to be gold and gems. A crown of fabulous flowers ringed her brow.

From this, as well as her bearing and the deference the others showed her, Palimak had no doubt that she was in command.

As he watched, the young queen made an imperious gesture and several men lifted large shell horns and blew. A loud but melodious note sprang forth. Both the shape of the horns and the sound reminded Palimak of Asper's magical horn Jooli had given to his father. The only difference was that no spell was created by these horns. There was only the lovely trumpeting music of warm welcome and invitation.

Immediately he rushed to the stateroom where his father was sprawled on a pallet, pale as death. Although he was unconscious, his presence was still powerful. Wild bits of magic sparking in the atmosphere as he twitched and moaned in his sleep. Caught in the throes of a living nightmare about whose content Palimak could only speculate.

He found the shell trumpet and raced back out on deck. There he planted his feet wide and blew an answer.

No magic issued forth, much less the Princess Alsahna — the Spirit Rider — on her magnificent mare, charging into the ethereal mist to confront the enemy. Nor had that been Palimak's intention. He didn't have Safar's power to master the horn, much less cause the appearance of the Spirit Rider. However, he intuitively knew that this was the best way to respond to the call of this island queen.

Palimak was surprised at the pleasing music he made as he blew through the horn. He'd feared that without practice the sound would be more in the realm of squawks and squeaks. Instead, melodious notes poured forth and when he lowered the horn he saw the queen and her court respond — pointing up at the airship in amazement.

"Take her down, Biner," he shouted.

Immediately the dwarf bellowed orders. Ballast was dumped, the engines went silent and at the same time there was the hiss of air being bled from the twin balloons.

They descended. Floating lower and lower to the dazzling white sands of the beach . . .

Palimak dragged himself out of his reverie. Important people were waiting for Safar's appearance. But first he had to explain his father's blindness to Leiria and the others. They'd be shocked, but he had to get them over that shock as quickly as he could.

Queen Yorlain was waiting and history stood in the balance.

45

HADINLAND

Blind as he was, Safar made a striking first appearance before Queen Yorlain and her court.

Dressed in his best ceremonial robes, he rode Khysmet across the sands to where the island queen waited in a portable throne made of rare fragrant wood, decorated with exotic flowers.

Leiria and Jooli walked on either side of Khysmet, their mail burnished to a high gloss. Palimak, dressed in a princely costume, led the way — walking several paces before the snow-white stallion.

Marching behind them was the entire Kyranian contingent. More than a hundred soldiers were spread out in ceremonial procession with Coralean at their head. Mounted on a tall horse, the caravan master was bedecked in flowing robes. Beside him, riding a dainty bay, was Eeda, who was also dressed in her finest. Despite her advanced pregnancy, Eeda looked lovely in her bejeweled gown, her face shining with excitement.

Overhead, the airship circled the beach, stirring music from Elgy and Rabix floating down to enthrall one and all.

Safar held Khysmet's reins loosely, trusting the horse to be his eyes. Once again he marveled at the mystical communication between horse and man. He only had to focus on a thing and Khysmet seemed to flow with his thoughts, anticipating his every need.

Although Safar couldn't see, Iraj's ethereal presence in his body made his senses doubly acute. Every sound was magnified, but not painfully so. Every scent was sharp and clear. The slight breeze fanned his face, making his flesh tingle with increased awareness of his surroundings. He also felt extremely strong and fast, his muscles throbbing with Iraj's added power.

As they approached the queen, Safar heard the murmurs of amazement from her courtiers. Deep inside, Iraj chortled in delight. He said, *They know a king when they see one, brother. But what they don't know is that there are* two *of us!*

Safar didn't need a signal from his friends to know when he was close enough to stop. The knowledge just suddenly came to him — and at the same time to Khysmet — and the stallion came to a halt, tail lashing, flanks quivering in anticipation.

He allowed a moment for drama before he spoke, turning his face this way and that as if his eyes were sweeping the scene. At the same time he soaked up the sensations, building a picture in his mind.

It was all too familiar. The sound of the palms stirring in the breeze, the hiss of the seas. The feel of the warm sun beating down. The smell of ripening palm fruit — and the distant, acrid odor of the volcano, mixed with the heady scent of the queen's exotic perfume.

Inside Safar, Iraj shuddered as he too recognized their surroundings, as well as the identity of the woman before them. He felt the quickening beat of Safar's heart and whispered a warning: *Steady, brother! It was a warning meant as much for himself as for the man whose body he shared.*

Safar nodded, then lifted his head to speak — centering his eyes on the place where the queen's sweet scent was the strongest.

"Greetings, Majesty," he said. "My people and myself will be forever indebted to you for your gracious welcome to your shores."

He heard a surprised gasp, then graceful movement as the queen rose from her throne.

"But why *wouldn't* I welcome you, King Safar?" came a puzzled voice. "Don't you know me? Am I not your sister in misfortune? Have we not danced together in the Vision of the World's End countless times in the past?"

Safar gave a long sigh as answers to questions he hadn't even known existed came rushing in.

"Yes, I know you, Queen Yorlain," he said. "But what I didn't know was that you shared the vision that has been tormenting me since I was a boy."

There was a pause as the queen considered his answer. Then she asked, "You mean, you have sailed from the other side of the world without truly understanding what was happening and what you must do to intervene?"

"What knowledge I have," Safar replied, "comes only from visions, oracles and the Book of Asper." He smiled ruefully. "Wondrous events and learned objects to be sure. But you must admit, none of them are noted for their clarity."

"And yet you came," Yorlain said, voice tinged with awe. "Although you were blind to the world's true needs."

For a moment, Safar thought she'd seen through his ruse. That she knew he was blind, although he'd pretended otherwise. Instinctively, this worried him. He didn't know why, but he felt it was important that he keep his disability from her. But her next words made him realize she was speaking about blindness figuratively and that his secret was still intact.

"Please forgive my ramblings, Majesty," she said. "I'm only happy that you've come at all. That we can look upon one another as ordinary mortals, instead of as slaves of that awful vision."

For an answer, Safar only smiled and bowed low in the saddle. The next question, however, brought him up sharply.

"But where is your brother king?" she asked. "The Holy Lady Felakia was quite clear that two kings would come to Hadin to awaken the gods. Two royal brothers and a child born of human and demon parentage."

Thinking quickly, Safar said, "The child you spoke of is now a grown man. And he stands there before you." He gestured at the place he was certain Palimak stood. "His name is Palimak, my adopted son."

"And the other?" Queen Yorlain pressed.

Safar tapped his breast. "My brother is with us in spirit, Majesty. And at the right moment he will make his physical presence known to you as well."

Inside him, Iraj murmured, *Excellent answer, Safar. But you always were good at turning a lie on its head and making it the truth. Hmm?*

Safar ignored this. Evidently the truce he and Iraj had agreed upon didn't include insults. He still had no idea how he was going to deal with his old enemy, much less present him to Yorlain when the time came.

More worrisome — on a personal level — was how Palimak and especially Leiria would react when he told them about Iraj. Worse still, he hadn't allowed himself to dwell on the living horror inside him. At the moment, the only course of action he could think of was to delay the inevitable as long as possible.

Queen Yorlain said, "I pray your brother doesn't wait too long, Majesty. The time is near when we must act."

"I promise you, Highness," Safar replied, "that we'll both be ready. There's nothing to concern yourself about as far as my brother's appearance is concerned."

"Very well, then, King Safar," Yorlain replied. "Let us lead you to your castle. All has been prepared for the work you must do there."

Safar was puzzled. "What castle?" he asked.

"Why, the Castle of the Two Kings," she said, mildly surprised. "Didn't Lord Asper mention that in his writings?"

Safar remembered the line: "*. . . Know that Asper knocked at the Castle Keep/ But the gates were barred, the Gods asleep . . .*"

He smiled. "Asper only commented on it indirectly," he said. "But I think I understand now what he was getting at. At least in part, that is."

"Will you come with us then, Majesty?" Yorlain asked.

Safar hesitated. "What of my friends and soldiers?" he asked.

"There's ample room, Majesty," Yorlain said. "Actually, it is a castle without inhabitants. A ghost castle, so to speak. No one has lived there since the days of Asper, although it has been kept in good repair."

Once again, Safar bowed low in his saddle. "Lead the way, then, O gracious queen," he said.

There was a rumble of wheels as attendants led a light, two-wheeled chariot across the sands. It was drawn by a matched pair of magnificent ostriches, standing over seven feet high. Safar heard

Leiria and Jooli murmur in amazement and wondered what they were seeing.

Then the queen mounted her chariot. She gave the signal and to the sound of blaring shell horns and rolling drums the ostriches started off, drawing the chariot after them.

"This way, father," Palimak called.

But Khysmet was already moving, following the strange procession. Coralean bellowed orders and the Kyranian soldiers stepped out smartly.

"Do you see the castle?" Safar asked Leiria. He didn't remember one being here.

"All I see," Leiria replied, "is a big damned volcano. Which just happens to be the way we're going!"

Not far away, in the shadow of a small uninhabited island, King Rhodes and his three ships were drawn up in a little bay protected on three sides by high cliffs.

The ships looked different than before. Their hulls and sails had been painted or dyed a grayish blue to match the seas. The figureheads had been removed from the prows and all bright metal objects had been daubed with tar so that they wouldn't glitter.

In short, Rhodes' pirate captains had ransacked their brains for all the tricks of their criminal trade to obscure the ships from casual view.

Even more effective, however, was the spell Queen Clayre had cast with the powerful support of the Lady Lottyr. The spell made the ships completely invisible to prying eyes, such as those of the crew of the airship that had searched for them during the whole long voyage from Aroborus.

The goddess of the Hells had also aided them in other important ways, such as ferreting out the intended route of the Kyranians. And so it was, that when the Timura fleet drew up at the main island a few short sea miles away, King Rhodes and his ships were already hidden in the little bay.

Even now, the king's troops were camped on shore getting ready for the coming surprise attack. Grizzled sergeants strode among them as they cleaned and repaired their weapons and armor. Although their rations were necessarily cold so campfires wouldn't give away the army's presence, the food was plentiful and Rhodes encouraged them to eat their fill and build up their strength.

He'd also captured a native fishing vessel and had tortured

the crew until they'd been emptied of every scrap of knowledge about Hadin that they contained. The four men had then been turned over to Clayre to feed her spellfires and keep Lottyr satiated.

Now, as the Kyranians marched in procession toward the mysterious Castle of the Two Kings, it was Rhodes who saw the edifice first.

In Clayre's cabin, the king leaned forward to study the living diorama of the main island that shimmered on his mother's spelltable. He could see the small figure of Queen Yorlain in her chariot, leading Safar and his people up off the beach toward the volcano.

A road began just beyond a thick grove of palm trees. It shot straight toward the volcano, then wound up its terraced sides — moving past tiny people working in the fields. The road continued through a series of small peaks, then dipped down into a wide, green valley cupped in the volcano's lap. A shallow blue lake filled one side, rippling along a rocky shore.

In the center of the valley — set on a peninsula that jutted into the lake — was a great golden castle surrounded by enormous walls. Within were several domed palaces, surrounding a massive keep that towered over all.

A second, lower wall ringed the castle's outer perimeter and Rhodes could clearly see the six gates that allowed traffic to pass to and from the castle. And a wide road leading past the domed palaces to the keep, where he knew Safar would take residence, since it was the greatest stronghold in the entire castle.

Looking through the king's eyes, Kalasariz examined the diorama with equal interest. Except for the castle, the valley reminded him slightly of Kyrania, which also featured a lake. The plant life was also different and Kyrania was set high in snowy mountains, instead of in the lap of a volcano. But those things aside, the number of similarities were surprising.

Clayre frowned at the scene. "That castle is going to be troublesome," she said. "It may even make our job near impossible."

"Why is that, mother?" Rhodes asked, mildly amused at Clayre's foray into his world — the world of tactics and strategy and fortifications.

She snorted in disgust at her son's imagined stupidity. "Isn't it obvious?" she said. "Once the Kyranians get inside those walls there'll be no getting them out!"

Rhodes chuckled. "That's one way of looking at it, mother," he replied.

"What other way is there of seeing it?" she demanded.

Another kingly chuckle. "That once the Kyranians enter the castle," he said, "they'll have a hells of a time getting out."

He pointed at several places, saying, "We just have to put troops here . . . and here . . . and maybe a few siege engines over there . . . and we'll have them thoroughly trapped."

Rhodes made a fist. "Then all we have to do is squeeze."

Clayre nodded, even smiling a little — pleased at his explanation. "But what about the Queen and her people?" she asked. "They certainly seem to be on Safar Timura's side. Surely she has more soldiers at her command then we possess."

It was Rhodes' turn to snort. "They won't be any match for my boys," he said. "We'll swallow them up and spit them out in no time."

Then he saw the tiny image of the airship rising toward the valley. He jabbed a finger at it.

"That's my main worry," he said. "That damned airship again! It can bombard the hells out of us during the siege while we're sitting helplessly in the open."

Clayre turned to her son, smile broadening. "I've been thinking about the airship," she said. "I even discussed the situation with our patroness, the Lady Lottyr."

"What was the result, mother?" Rhodes asked, hopes growing.

"That we won't have to worry about the airship much longer," Clayre replied.

"That's good news, indeed," Rhodes said.

"I'll need a few days to get things set up," Clayre cautioned. "So don't move too swiftly and give yourself away before it's time to act."

Rhodes shrugged. "No bother there, mother," he said. "I need a few more days myself before *I'm* ready."

Clayre nodded understanding. "You're waiting on Tabusir?" she asked.

"The very one," Rhodes replied.

46

THE HELLS MACHINE

On the surface it was a glorious procession. The beautiful queen, posing nobly in her ostrich chariot, led the way up the long winding road that climbed the volcano. Flower petals covered the road and they gave off a marvelous scent when crushed by the passing parade.

But the higher Palimak climbed the more worried he became. Some of his worries were natural — his father's blindness made him feel he'd once again had to shoulder a burden much too heavy for one so young.

Reason told him this wasn't the case — Safar's blindness in no way diminished his wizardly powers. Nor did his father seem to be affected physically apart from his sight problem. Actually, he seemed much stronger than before.

However, Palimak could not shake off the sensation that something was very wrong — both with his father and with the journey itself. He couldn't get a grip on what was troubling him.

Hadin's air was so full of wild bits and flashes of magic that he couldn't trace the source of what was troubling him. Some of it came from Safar, some from the queen and her courtiers, but most seemed to emanate from the road ahead, and from the towering volcano.

Stirring music still wafted down from the airship, as Biner followed the procession on high. There was more to Biner's choice of music than mere pomp and ceremony. It was also a signal that all was well as far as the lookouts aboard the airship could see. If any danger was spotted, Elgy and Rabix would begin playing fierce music full of trumpets and war drums.

As the procession moved along the road, farmers in the terraced fields stopped their work to see what all the noise was about. Clad in loin cloths and broad-brimmed straw hats to shield them from the sun, they all radiated a feeling of the inner peace that comes from tilling the land.

Then the queen led them around a sharp bend. Along one side were hundreds of nearly naked beggars all crying for alms and bemoaning their infirmities.

Palimak dropped back to tell his father about the beggars — although the loud cries they made surely enlightened him to what was going on. Safar nodded, then called for Renor and Seth who trotted up with large leather saddlebags bulging with silver coins. At Safar's signal they began scattering the coins to the beggars.

Safar had come into the queen's presence well prepared for any eventuality. Although he couldn't have anticipated the journey they were now on, he had guessed that they would encounter the kingdom's poor.

"There are beggars in every realm," he'd said. "And whenever and wherever royalty is welcomed, the beggars turn out to test the visiting king's generosity. So if we want to make a good impression on this queen, we'd better be ready for her beggars."

And ready they were, with hundreds of silver coins being tossed into the air by Renor and Sinch. The two young soldiers went at their task eagerly, as if they were fabulously rich and dispensing their own wealth instead of Safar's.

They joked with the beggars, who all crowded around, blocking the road.

"Here's some for you, pretty lady," Sinch said to an old woman — pushing the laughing mob back so she wouldn't be shut out.

The toothless granny cackled with delight, both at the coins in her palm and the handsome young man who'd given them to her.

"Pretty yourself," the old woman said. "I'd rather have yer warmin' me bed than take your money!"

Sinch laughed with much good nature, giving the granny a kiss on her dirty cheek.

A legless man in a push cart knuckled his way forward, crowding close to Khysmet. Renor stepped in to block his way gently and tossed three silver coins on the beggar's cart.

The man opened his mouth to thank Renor, displaying rotting teeth and a short stump of a tongue. The wet smacking sounds of thanks that came from his mutilated mouth were a horror to someone of Renor's inexperience. Like all Kyranians he'd lived such a sheltered life in the mountains that such things were unknown to him.

Renor suppressed a shudder. Then he felt overwhelmed by guilt for his reaction and pressed two more coins into the beggar's hands.

More horrible noises followed as the legless one pushed in closer. Another beggar stumbled over him, making him lose his balance and reached out wildly, grabbing Khysmet's tail.

The stallion grunted in protest at the rude handling, jerking forward. Several long strands of snow-white hair pulled loose: the legless beggar waved them in Renor's face and spewed more obscene sounds, as if the horse hairs were a fabulous gift.

To Renor's surprise, he heard Palimak shout to him: "Hold that man!"

It was as if all of Renor's brains had run out of his head, because for the life of him he couldn't figure out what Palimak was asking. He gaped about, dismissing the amputee from his mind to look for a man with all his parts.

Then Palimak came rushing up. "The beggar!" he shouted. "The one in the pushcart. Where did he go?"

For the life of him, Renor couldn't figure out why Palimak would be upset about someone so unfortunate that he even lacked legs. But he looked around as he was commanded and to his surprise he realized that the man he'd been ordered to find was gone.

In his stead other beggars were crowding in, crying, "Alms! Alms for the poor!" And, "Baksheesh! Baksheesh!"

Then he heard Safar call out, "Palimak! Get over here right away!"

And then the whole column became a confusion of soldiers and beggars that tied the road into a knot of chaos.

Tabusir was a patient spy. He didn't mind waiting for his prey to come to him. As a matter of fact, he quite enjoyed the wait, planning many plans, anticipating the split second of enjoyment that came when he snatched a secret from beneath the very noses of his enemies.

Then there was the escape to dream about. The greater thrill was to slip away undiscovered and keep the secret of the encounter deep within your breast. Less exciting was to be discovered and to have to wrest yourself from the wrath of the discoverers.

Oh, to be sure, there was the thrill of the chase. But Tabusir had always considered a chase to be the result of his own failure to remain unobserved.

As all spies know, the ultimate value of a secret diminishes in proportion to the number of people who know it. And it is vastly diminished if the enemy realizes his secret has been revealed.

And so it was that when Palimak shouted, "Hold that man!" Tabusir felt diminished. He'd spent three days and two nights waiting for his chance to steal the secrets of the Timuras.

His scant knowledge of the local customs and dialect had only made his planning more exciting. All he knew came from the fishermen Rhodes had captured and tortured. Although Tabusir considered himself a master at language and its local nuances, the screams and groans of men in pain was no way to learn it.

Instead, he'd concentrated on the looks of the men. Ignoring their pain-twisted countenances, he had focused on their thick dark hair and sun-bronzed bodies. One of the men was toothless and his painful babble could barely be understood. This was what had given Tabusir the inspiration for his disguise.

If he pretended he couldn't speak, Tabusir reasoned, then he wouldn't be able to give himself away by using a faulty accent. To make sure people would think he was mute, he made a little device to fit over his tongue which gave it the appearance of being a stump. To further revolt anyone looking at him, he blackened his teeth with charcoal so they looked as if they were rotting.

Then all he had to do was dye his hair and stain his body with walnut juice so he'd look like a native and be able to mingle with the other beggars of Hadin. The cart, which he'd carried with him from Syrapis for just this purpose, had a false bottom that hid his legs.

Tabusir had landed on the island at night and had hidden the little boat among some rocks. Then he'd waited for Safar's arrival. It was the main topic of conversation among all the beggars. There was much excitement and anticipation of how charitable the great King Timura would be. Everyone also knew their queen would escort Safar to the Castle of the Two Kings and there was much dispute over the best place to wait for him.

When the day finally came, Tabusir followed the other beggars up the long road and took his place among them. When they'd seen his mutilated tongue no one questioned Tabusir's right to be with them.

As the grand procession moved past the beggars it had taken the sharp-eyed spy only a few minutes to realize that Safar was blind. It was the way Timura carried himself that'd given him away: a certain stiffness of the head, with the eyes staring blankly forward no matter what happened.

For instance, when he'd called his two men forward to disperse the silver coins, he hadn't looked at them when they came running up. Nor had he looked left or right as the beggars crowded close, crying for alms and singing Safar's praises.

The moment he caught Safar out, Tabusir had realized that even if he came up with nothing else for his king Rhodes would be mightily pleased with the outcome of Tabusir's mission. The spy smiled in anticipation of the fat purse of gold he'd receive as a reward.

Rhodes had also directed Tabusir to try to get his hands on some personal item from either Safar or his great horse. The coins the soldiers had dispensed might not meet that qualification, since there was a chance Safar himself had never handled them.

So he'd gone for the stallion, pretending clumsiness, then grabbing a few long hairs from the animal's tail as he struggled to regain his balance.

But then he'd heard Palimak shout and his perfect mission had been spoiled.

Now, as he sprinted down the road toward the place where he'd hidden his boat, he burned with resentment. What could have given him away? How had his clever disguise failed him? Then it came to him that Palimak — well-known for his powerful wizardry — must have used magic to ferret Tabusir out. Yes, that was the answer: Magic.

Still, it didn't make him feel any better. Perfection was his constant goal and Palimak had marred that perfection. But then, as he pulled the boat from the rocky cove, he wondered why no else had pursued him? It didn't make sense. Palimak had somehow discovered Tabusir's presence and yet he hadn't sent anyone after the spy.

Tabusir pondered on this while rowing toward Rhodes' island hideout. The only answer he came up with was that something more important must have distracted Palimak.

The spy cursed himself for running away so quickly. He should have found a hiding place nearby to see what was so important to the young prince. As he thought about this he recalled Safar shouting something to Palimak. But Tabusir had been too busy getting away to hear what was being said.

He stopped paddling. For a long moment he seriously considered turning back. He could easily adopt some other disguise and again attempt to get close to the Timuras. But then he thought of Palimak's magic and decided against this plan. The young prince would be wary now he knew an enemy had come within assassination distance of his father.

Tabusir started paddling again. He wouldn't tell Rhodes about being discovered. There was no sense in spoiling his king's respect for his abilities.

It would be enough to inform Rhodes that Safar was blind. Then hand him the hairs he'd stolen from the stallion's tail.

Tabusir's failure would remain his own little secret. Thinking of it that way made him feel a whole lot better.

But then the good feeling vanished as he once again wondered why the Timuras weren't pursuing him.

He paddled onward, cold fingers of dread running down his spine.

Rushing to answer Safar's call, Palimak pushed through the crowd of beggars to his side. Renor and Sinch accompanied him, shouting for the other Kyranian soldiers to help them untangle the mess.

"Gundara and Gundaree just spotted a spy, father!" Palimak said. "It's one of the beggars. A man without any legs. Or at least he's pretending he doesn't have any legs. But he's getting away, so we have to act fast if we want to catch him."

"Forget about the spy, son," Safar said. Although his voice was calm, Palimak sensed extreme tension. "We'll worry about him later," Safar continued. "There's something much more important happening."

Palimak frowned. "What is it, father?" he asked. "What's wrong?"

But no sooner had the words left his mouth than he felt a heavy, throbbing presence roil the magical atmosphere. All the wild bits of magic suddenly coalesced into a single deadly entity. An entity that was neither animate or inanimate. It just was. A soulless thing that somehow had a purpose.

"Can't you feel it, son?" Safar demanded. "It's a machine. Just like the one in Caluz!"

Then Palimak remembered that fearful machine from the Hells and said, "Yes. I can feel it."

He looked up at Safar, mouth dry. "What do we do, father?"

And Safar replied, "There's nothing we can do — except go on!"

47

WHERE LOTTYR WAITS

When the procession topped the rise overlooking the Valley of the Two Kings the intensity of the machine's magic struck Safar with full force. He threw up a hand, as if protecting his face from a blazing sun.

In his nesting place Iraj was shaken to the core by the magical storm and its effects on his host. He said to Safar: *Aren't you going to do something about this? You could make some kind of shield, like the one you used in Caluz.*

At the same time, Palimak cried out, "We need a shield, father! But I don't know how to make one."

Jooli too was suffering from the magical blast. "Is this a trick, Safar?" she asked. "Has the queen led us into a trap?"

Meanwhile, Eeda was pushing her mount forward, Coralean at her heels. Her face was twisted in agony from the sorcerous assault.

"Please, Lord Timura," she begged. "We must do something. I fear for the life of my unborn child."

Safar had rarely felt so frustrated. He knew where the machine was. As he turned his blind face from side to side he could easily spot the point of the heaviest magical concentration. But without visual coordinates to support him he was helpless to cast the shielding spells.

"Patience, my friends," he said as reassuringly as he could. "I need to think."

Jooli guessed what was happening. She'd been as shocked as the others when Palimak had informed them of his father's blindness. However, as Palimak had assured everyone, magic rarely required the power of sight. He had said that Safar's wizardly powers were unaffected by his infirmity and they could proceed as planned.

But Jooli's deep studies of magic, plus her instincts, told her this situation presented a unique problem. To build a shield one not only needed to know the location of the danger, but also the location of everyone you wanted to protect. To accomplish this the sorcerer needed eyes.

"Tell us what to do, Safar," she said. "We want to help you."

Palimak and Eeda quickly came to the same conclusion and

urged Safar to instruct them. Meanwhile, the machine's assault was slowly draining everyone of their energies.

Safar realized he didn't have much time to act. If only he could see, the danger could be countered within seconds.

Iraj rose up, saying, *Give me your eyes, brother. I can give sight to both of us!*

Safar hesitated, fearful of allowing Iraj the slightest control over his body.

A bolt of magic struck Eeda and she groaned in terrible pain, gripping her pregnant belly. "Please, Lord Timura," she cried. "Please!"

Safar relented, opening a gateway for Iraj to scramble forward. At the same time Safar's whole body crawled with sensation — like little worms of pulsating energy wriggling a burning path along every vein, every nerve.

And then the whole world became an explosion of colorful light. It was so sudden and painful that he cried out, jamming palms into his outraged eyes. Then the pain passed and he opened his eyes and saw the Valley of the Two Kings for the first time.

At first it was all cool greens and hot oranges, bordered with gray blues and varying shades of purple and pink. Then the image steadied and he saw the golden castle, with its towering keep, sitting in the center of a valley very much like Kyrania.

Except there was more raw orange land than ever existed in the valley of his homeland. It surrounded the castle — earth, hard-packed by hundreds of wagons and feet. Then the green farmland and pines so fragrant he could smell their sharp, fresh scent on the breeze.

And a lake, a lake as glorious as Lake Felakia in far Kyrania. Blue and cool and beckoning. The purples came from the diffused sunlight shining on a bank of coned mountains that fringed the great volcano of Hadin. The lesser purples and pinks radiated from the skies and clouds that framed the whole scene.

Safar tried to focus his eyes on the castle keep, where he knew the magical machine was housed. Instead, against his will, his head bent back — eyes running up the sides of the volcano, where a small dark puff of smoke burst out to mingle with the white clouds that surrounded it.

Panicked, he tried to force his head back down to view the castle. But to his horror he realized Iraj had taken full control of his body. And his head bent back further to take in the airship circling overhead — pleasant music playing as if nothing had gone wrong.

He tried to open his mouth to shout a warning to Palimak. But Iraj only swallowed, forcing Safar's words back down into his gut.

Iraj, speaking with Safar's voice, said, "Apparently my problem has passed. I can see again."

Renewed hope acted as a temporary balm, easing everyone's suffering. Leiria laughed aloud, clutching Safar/Iraj's hand, murmuring, "I'm so happy, my love."

But to Safar, a prisoner in his own body, the sensation of her warm, loving touch came from far away. And her voice seemed even more distant.

Iraj, commanding Safar's body, squeezed Leiria's hand. And, speaking in Safar's voice, he whispered, "Let me feast them on you tonight, Leiria."

Leiria gave Safar/Iraj a startled look. Then, to Safar's dismay, her eyes flashed gladness and she smiled warmly, asking, "Are you sure, Safar?"

And Iraj replied, "Yes, I'm sure."

Then he sent a mental command back to Safar, saying, *Cast the spell, brother. Before this damned machine gets the better of us!*

Despite the growing danger, Safar hesitated. Somehow he had to regain control of his own body.

Sensing his conflict, Iraj said, *Do you want to bargain with me over your friends' lives, brother? And even if I agreed, considering our past history together, do you trust my word?*

Just then Eeda gasped, swooning in her saddle. Coralean steadied her just in time. His big booming voice shattered Safar's indecision. "You must act, Safar!" he said. "Before it's too late for my Eeda!"

Iraj said to Safar, *You see how it is, brother? Now, quickly, tell me what to do.*

And so Safar told him to get out the little witch's-dagger, which was hidden in the right sleeve of his cloak. Then he told him to cut a large imaginary circle in the air. Iraj followed his instruction — a little clumsily since he was unused to such actions. Then Safar fed him the words to the shielding spell he'd used so successfully in the Blacklands during the march to Caluz.

In Safar's voice, Iraj chanted:

> *"Sever the day,*
> *Shatter the night.*
> *Keep at bay,*
> *All sorcerous plight.*

Bedevil the devils
Who speak in flame
And dance and revel
In the Goddess's name."

There was no outward sign of the spell's effect. Only heaving sighs of relief from Palimak and the others as the shield slid silently and invisibly into place — folding the entire Kyranian contingent into its protective cloak.

Queen Yorlain had turned her little ostrich chariot around and was coming back to see why Safar's column had stopped. Iraj leaned forward in the saddle and Khysmet obediently trotted forth to meet her, snorting at the strange feathered steeds drawing her onward.

Iraj gloried in the strong, easy movement of the stallion. A man born and bred to Esmir's Great Plains, there was nothing he loved more than a good horse. But Khysmet was more than just a horse — he was magical. Using his mental voice, Iraj said to Safar, *I once dreamed I was riding Khysmet. Now that dream's come true.*

Safar remembered the dream, which he'd experienced too in that mysterious spiritual connection he seemed to have with Iraj. He said, *Never mind the dream. Let me have my body back. Or I swear I'll make you suffer for stealing it.*

Iraj's answer was a sarcastic laugh. Then he reined Khysmet in as they came up to the queen.

"What is the trouble, Majesty?" Yorlain asked.

Iraj gave her a sardonic look. "You didn't mention the spell," he said, a tinge of accusation in his voice.

Yorlain's beautiful eyes widened in surprise. "But I thought you knew," she said. "Did not the great Lord Asper warn of the killing spell? And propose the protective shield that is its answer?"

Safar whispered to Iraj, *Asper only mentioned the Blacklands and Caluz. He said nothing about Hadin. Tell her you were not informed of the killing spell, but still knew how to counter it when you came up against it.*

Although he was desperate to turn the tables on Iraj and retrieve his body, Safar realized that under the circumstances he had to cooperate with his old nemesis. And as long as Iraj was in control, Safar would have to guide his fingers as they pieced together the dangerous puzzle that was Hadinland.

Iraj gave Yorlain his most charming smile. And although it was

Safar's mouth he was stretching and Safar's teeth he was flashing, his potent personality blazed through.

"I must have missed that part," he said to the queen. "At the time there were some very nasty fellows on my heels. So I only read about the shield, then ran like the Hells for cover."

Then he leaned closer, murmuring, "Visionary that he was, poor Asper must have been a very old demon. For he didn't mention you, my queen. A vision above all visions."

Swept away by Iraj's dash, Yorlain blushed and tinkled musical laughter. "Be careful, Majesty," she said. "Or I might get a false idea about your intentions."

Iraj bowed low in the saddle. "How could I be false," he said, "when confronted with such truly wondrous beauty?"

Meanwhile, Palimak and the others had caught up with them. Leiria overheard the flirtatious exchange and was wounded to the quick. Jooli caught it as well and placed a sympathetic hand on Leiria's shoulder.

"Pay it no mind," she whispered. "He's just sweetening her up because we have need of her."

Leiria shrugged off the hand and straightened — shoulders squaring like the warrior she was. "Safar doesn't say things like that unless he means it," she whispered bitterly.

Jooli said nothing in reply, but only watched with growing disappointment and sadness for her friend as a Safar she'd never seen before preened and postured for Yorlain as if he'd suddenly gone into heat.

Palimak stared at his father, wondering what he was up to. It must be part of his plan, he thought.

Meanwhile, Gundara and Gundaree were chattering in his ear: "Beware, Little Master! Beware!" But he was still feeling shaken and a little dizzy from the effects of the killing spell and found it hard to pay attention.

He gave a cursory glance around, sending out weak magical probes that encountered nothing. Assuming the Favorites were still worrying about the spy, he muttered for them to be quiet until they had privacy to talk.

Once again, Iraj bowed low in the saddle and bade Queen Yorlain to lead the way. Then, just as the queen cracked her little whip for the ostriches to proceed, he glanced over at Leiria, catching her eyes.

He grinned hugely, then shrugged, as if to say, Life has its strange little twists, doesn't it, dear?

Safar saw Leiria's hurt through Iraj's eyes and struggled madly to regain control of his own body. But Iraj was beginning to learn the ways and weapons of his new position and shot a searing inward blast at his prisoner.

Safar jolted as if he'd been struck by lightning. When he recovered, he tried once again to free himself. And the answer was another hot bolt of punishment.

He withdrew into the nest Iraj had once occupied. Nursing his wounds, while his mind ran wild with hate and half-formed thoughts of revenge.

An hour later the castle gates clanked open and Yorlain escorted the Kyranians across the bridge through the cheering crowds of her subjects.

And they all shouted, "The king has come! May the Gods save us and the king!"

Then she took them to the castle keep and Safar had recovered enough to marvel as the huge, iron-bound doors yawned wide to admit them. These were the very same doors, he thought, that Asper had said he'd knocked on without reply.

The old demon wizard's words echoed in his mind: "*. . . Know that Asper knocked at the Castle Keep, But the gates were barred, the Gods asleep.*"

The first thing he saw when the doors swung open was a wide courtyard. Straddling that courtyard was an enormous stone turtle. Flames exploded from its horny mouth. There was a great open grate in its belly and heavily muscled slaves were shoveling whole cartloads of fuel into the furnace within.

Safar noticed that the fuel was similar to the magical stuff the airship's engines used. But just then wild magic suddenly blasted through and he was forced to quickly repair, then strengthen the shield.

One part of his brain noted that he could act without Iraj's cooperation — perhaps even without his knowledge. But the other, larger part focused on a hellish emanation from the Keep itself.

Yorlain whispered orders to her aides, who rushed to open the final barrier — an enormous iron gate with bars as thick as a man's thighs, armed with sharp, spear-like points.

And as they were cranked up, heavy chains rattling against unseen gears, Safar saw a long dark tunnel. A blaze of light, no larger than his palm, winked at the other end.

Yorlain waved them through, getting out of her chariot and walking beside Khysmet.

As they moved into the darkness, both Iraj and Safar heard Yorlain say, "There are those who claim this was once the mightiest fortress in all the world. A thousand years ago, when the last kings ruled, it survived a legendary siege that lasted twenty years or more.

"Ten thousand demons hammered at these gates, but to no avail. If I recall correctly, Lord Asper himself led the last charge and was turned back with terrible casualties."

"What war was this?" Iraj asked. And Safar listened closely for Yorlain's answer.

"My scholars tell me it was an ethnic war of sorts," the queen replied. "Hadin was once populated by people of many races. Also, there was a large colony of demons who lived peacefully among us for centuries. Some say the demons were once so plentiful that one of the ruling pair of kings was a demon.

"I don't know if that's true, since it was so long ago that only the tales survived. There are no records. Regardless, when the slaughter reared its head everyone who was not exactly like . . ." She hesitated, trying to put genocide into passable words. Then: "Well, people without dark hair and dark eyes were condemned and executed as enemies of the state. Of course, the demon king had long since been executed, so that was no bother to these barbarians.

"Then it came time to cleanse ourselves of the demons. It was about then that Asper came to our shores, warning of a cleansing of the entire world. Not just of demons . . . or of people like us . . . but of all living things.

"Naturally, no one listened. We all believed the gods were on our side, just as the demons claimed the gods were with them. Asper, of course, said the gods were asleep and we were all doomed.

"But the words of an old wizard don't amount to much when beings want blood, so everyone turned against him. And they drove him away during the long siege that the demons mounted against the humans.

"In the end, the defenders of the castle keep not only prevailed, but sallied forth to engage the demons in several decisive battles."

Sighing, Yorlain shook her head. "If you traveled throughout Hadinland you wouldn't have to ponder long on the result of those battles. For you would not find a single demon on any island throughout the continent. We killed them all and praised ourselves as saints for the killing."

During Yorlain's history lesson, Iraj's military brain drove him to inspect the tunnel's defenses. Here and there were patches of diffused light coming from above and he looked up to treat himself — and Safar — to a view of heavy grates with enormous iron pots set on swivels hanging over them.

Safar needed no explanation from Iraj that in wartime these pots would be filled with boiling oil or molten lead that could be tipped over to scald and kill anyone daring this passage.

Along with Iraj, he also took careful note of the series of gates spread along the tunnel. Smaller than those barring the entryway, but not by much, these gates were cranked up as they approached. Just beyond each gate were other windows of diffused light, with hot pots guarding them.

It took little imagination to see their purpose. Invaders would be tricked into sending troops into the tunnel. Gates would be slammed shut on each side, trapping them for the boiling oil or molten lead.

Finally, they came out of the tunnel into pure high-mountain light. Yorlain led them around a deep pit that had been constructed only a few yards away from the entrance to the fortress.

Iraj glanced inside the pit and both he Safar saw its purpose. A nest of pointed iron spikes was set in cement in the bottom. Gray, frosted demon skeletons were impaled on many of those spikes. Safar didn't have to hear all of Yorlain's words to know that the ancient bones dated back to the great siege.

At last they came to the keep proper. Iraj dismounted and led Khysmet inside, hooves echoing in the vast interior.

It was then that Safar experienced the strongest blast of machine magic. There was a rumble and a whirl that tore him from his center.

Yorlain said something, but he couldn't make out her words. And the magical storm was so intense that even Iraj was shaken. Eyes moving toward the source, carrying Safar's vision with them. Then fixing on a huge pentagram made of golden tiles.

Like Claire's table, Safar thought. And then that thought was ripped from his mind.

For the magic emanating from the pentagram was so powerful that all his senses were confounded. It was as if a thick fog had descended. A painful fog containing many barbs and poisoned hooks like a deep-sea devil fish.

Once again, he strengthened the shield spell. Putting all his energies into it. Wishing he had Palimak, or even Jooli or Eeda to help. But buried within Iraj he was barred from all contact with them.

Then he got the shield up, took scant notice of the fact that Iraj had also been injured by the spellblast, and concentrated on the colorful work painted within the pentagram.

It was an eight-pointed wind-rose. And on each directional spear was painted the form of one the major gods. Safar sent mental commands for Iraj to investigate.

To his surprise, Iraj caught his sense of urgency and let his eyes sweep from familiar figures such as the Goddess Felakia and the rest. Eyes moving onward, from one god or goddess to the other, until they came to rest on a wide red spear that was turned inward, pointing to the center.

And painted on that spear blade was the exotic, six-faced form of the lady from the hells.

The Goddess Lottyr.

Each face was more beautiful and yet more malevolent than the next. Painted flames shot from every mouth.

And as Safar looked at them through eyes that Iraj had provided he saw the flames bubble and move.

A terrible searing blast shot through Iraj, who moaned and shrunk in his own boots from the fiery assault. Safar felt it too, but quickly turned the attack back against its origin.

Somewhere in the gloom of the castle keep he heard a ghostly shriek.

Then the assault ended. But he knew it wasn't for long.

He mental whispered to Iraj, *This is the center. The center to the Hells. And it is through here that we must attack!*

Iraj asked, *How much time do we have, brother?*

And Safar replied, *Almost none at all.*

48
THE TEMPEST

That night, thick black storm clouds gathered over Hadin. At first they scudded in a few at a time, then they arrived with increasing frequency until even the face of the Demon Moon was obscured.

King Rhodes landed his forces in that darkness, crossing from his island hideout to Hadin on longboats with muffled oars. He ignored Safar's nine ships, which were anchored in the little bay. Tabusir had assured him that all but a few Kyranian troops had left the ships to march with Safar and Palimak.

When Rhodes mounted his planned attack on the castle he also knew he'd have nothing to fear from the pirate captains. Once they saw which way the battle went, they'd be clamoring to join Rhodes in return for a few purses of gold.

As soon as Rhodes hit the beach, he sent shock troops forward to secure the road and silence any stray soldiers or farmers they encountered.

Meanwhile, his longboats returned to the island and began the onerous task of hauling the portable siege engines to the shore.

His mother arrived with the last group, hissing curses at her slaves as they clumsily loaded her magical table onto her royal litter. All the gilded decorations had been daubed with lampblack so they wouldn't glitter if struck by a chance beam of light.

"That's my favorite litter," she complained to Rhodes. "And now you've ruined it with your stupid soldier tricks. You're going to have to commission me another one when we return home."

"You're the only one of us who's not walking, mother," Rhodes pointed out. He'd left all the horses behind for transport after the siege was in place. "You're the one who insisted on bringing your litter along. Plus six useless slaves to carry you!"

Clayre sniffed. "Some people would think you'd show more gratitude to me," she said. "After all, it's *my* magic, not your precious army, that will defeat Safar Timura."

Kalasariz knew hand that she spoke the truth. Clayre had spent hours with the Lady Lottyr casting spell after spell to pave the way for the battle.

He whispered from within: *Please, Majesty. Promise her anything to shut her up! You're never going to have to deliver, remember?*

Rhodes took the advice. Sighing, he said, "Very well, mother. You'll get your new litter as soon as we return home."

"Nothing shabby, now," Clayre warned. "You know how tight-fisted you can be."

"Spend what you like," Rhodes said. "I'll give you a blank warrant on the treasury."

Clayre's eyes narrowed suspiciously and Rhodes realized he'd gone too far. "But half the cost will have to come out of your allowance," he hastened to say. "So don't go wild with the design."

Clayre's suspicions vanished. Rhodes' caveat was much more in character. For a flickering moment she'd wondered if her son had matricide on his mind. But on reflection, that didn't make any sense. To be sure, Rhodes had no love for her. Just as she had none for him. However, they did need each other. One held the hereditary crown, the other the magical means to secure it.

"Don't cheapen your gift by bargaining with me about its price," Clayre said. "I'll pay ten per cent, no more."

"Twenty," Rhodes said.

Clayre shook her head sadly. "You are so mean-spirited," she said. "Just like your father. But for the sake of family peace, I'll agree."

The Queen Witch had her own murderous designs. She'd discussed her hateful son with Lottyr, who had promised to aid her when the battle with Safar Timura was won. Further lessening her suspicion was her own good mood: Many magical tricks had been planned to confound the great Safar Timura.

All she had to do was bear with this barbarian lout who called himself her son for another day at the most, and then the tables would be turned once and for all!

Through the king's eyes, Kalasariz observed Clayre's shifting moods. He knew what she was thinking. He'd had his own private discussions with the Goddess Lottyr and was well aware of the Queen Witch's plans and the agreement she'd made with Lottyr.

But what neither she nor Rhodes realized was the Goddess had ambitions of her own. Ambitions that only Kalasariz could satisfy at this most historic moment.

He laughed to himself, thinking how surprised Rhodes and Clayre would be when they joined Fari and Luka in his belly.

Then he had only to capture Iraj and he'd no longer be the power behind thrones, but the throne itself.

King of Kings. Lord and master of Lottyr's worldly realm. For a single, spine-chilling moment he recalled an old Esmirian saying he had once been fond of quoting: "The deadliest poison ever made came from a king's laurel crown."

But then he dismissed this once-favored saying as nonsense. It was only a thing he used to repeat to soothe his pride when Esmir was ruled by fools like Iraj Protarus.

And as Rhodes massed his troops and organized his siege engineers the spymaster dreamed of powers he'd never held before.

Forgetting another most pertinent Esmirian saying: "When the king's spy plots his own coronation, he must first conspire against himself."

In the Castle of the Two Kings, Safar's warning of impending doom shook Iraj from his kingly posturing. A man of many flaws, he'd been momentarily overcome by his weaknesses.

After a long time of being denied even a human body, he'd reveled in his power over women. Never mind that Leiria believed he was Safar — and it was Safar whom she loved — he'd been anxious to master her with his lust. Never mind that Queen Yorlain thought him her handsome savior, he'd been overcome by the idea of adding another queenly notch to his bedstead.

Once he'd been a man — a princely warrior of the Great Plains — whose very smile and ardent looks could bring women into his bed like nubile mares trotting over the hills to the wild stallion's trumpeting call.

Then he'd been a shapechanger, a creature bound by an evil spell, whose lust could only be slaked by murder and blood. As a great wolf he'd delighted in the carnage of the harem of victims he'd kept. But in those rare moments when his human side had crept in, he'd despaired at all the torment he'd caused.

And yes, on occasion he'd even condemned himself for his betrayal of Safar, his blood brother and friend. But those moments were so rare, so fleeting, that they were easily replaced by rationalizations that it was Safar who was the betrayer, not him.

The saintly Safar who claimed that he never wanted anything but to save the world from itself. The lucky Safar, whose encounters with women had always been marked by a deep friendship and love that had always been denied Iraj.

Nerisa, the little thief who had stolen a great treasure for Safar, only to die at Iraj's orders. Methydia, the beautiful witch who had doted on Safar, only to be slain by one of Iraj's soldiers. And then Leiria — fantastic, lovely Leiria — who had once belonged in the literal sense to Iraj. But he'd given her away to Safar on a whim of false friendship and now she loathed her former master and thought only of Safar.

Thoughts of revenge flooded in. He couldn't kill Safar without taking his own life. But he could make him suffer for past wrongs. Just for starters, he'd torment Leiria by seducing the queen, making her think her lover had betrayed her with another. Next he'd seduce Leiria, then cast her out like scraps from the table.

Deep in his nest, Safar also brooded angrily over past wrongs. He too schemed of ways to strike back at Iraj. His anger was so great that he even considered black spells that would burn Protarus to the core. Only the fact that he would suffer too stayed Safar's hand.

Then he realized that Iraj's madness was stirring up a poisonous froth of bodily juices that were affecting him dangerously and might very well drive Safar over the edge as well.

He had to calm down. He had to focus on the tasks ahead — the *least* important of which was to free himself from Iraj's prison.

And that moment must wait until after he had confronted the Hells awaiting him in the Goddess Lottyr's machine.

Gundara said, "It isn't Lord Timura, Little Master!"

And Gundaree added, "Well, it *is* Lord Timura, but it's not exactly him."

Palimak frowned. "What in the Hells are you two talking about?"

Gundara said, "It's kind of difficult to explain, Little Master. See, somehow Iraj Protarus got inside your father's body. We think he was hiding there and maybe even Lord Timura didn't know. For a while, anyway."

"But then your father went blind," Gundaree came in, "and he needed King Protarus so that he could see and so your father let him out. And now your father's trapped inside his own body and Protarus is in control of everything!"

"We're just guessing about the blind part," Gundara added.

"But it's a pretty good guess," Gundaree said. "Like always."

Palimak considered. Although what the two Favorites had said was very strange, if you assumed their guess was right many things started to make sense.

Like his own perceptions of wrongness about his father, including the odd change in his hair coloring from dark to streaks of gold. If Iraj, who was a blond, had made himself into a magical parasite inside Safar, might not his presence have influenced his father's hair coloring?

It also explained Safar's bewildering and boorish behavior with Queen Yorlain. Which in turn had wounded his Aunt Leiria. His father would never commit either of those acts.

He nodded, accepting the twins' theory.

"What should we do about it?" he asked. "Can we come up with some sort of spell to purge Iraj from my father's body?"

"That'd be hard!" Gundara said.

"Really, really hard!" Gundaree put in.

"And even if it worked, we could kill them both," Gundara added.

Palimak saw his whole world collapsing under him. Everything that was good had turned out to be evil. His own father was trapped inside the body of the murderous Iraj Protarus!

"It would be easier to think of some kind of solution," Gundara said, "if we had something to eat."

"That's very true, Little Master," Gundaree said. "Thinking is hungry work."

Absently, Palimak fished sweets from his pocket and fed the Favorites. In his mind, past moments shared with his father were being blown about by gusts of nostalgia.

Palimak's first memory, so vague it might not even be real but a thing made up from tales adults tell their children, was as a baby held in Leiria's arms.

He was looking at his father over Leiria's shoulder. She was mounted on a snorting, ground-pawing warhorse and Palimak was tied in a sling about her back. Thumping against her chain mail as the horse moved. And there was his father, seen for the first time: tall and dark with fiery blue eyes that melted into softness when they settled on his adopted son.

There were a whole host of other memories: The cheese monster; the battles against the Great Wolf, Iraj Protarus; the flight across the badlands; the race through the Machine of Caluz; but especially the long talks late into the night as Safar patiently and gently taught his son the theory and practice of magic.

Then, with a start, he remembered a riddle his father had once posed. He'd said that if either of them could ever answer this riddle from The Book of Asper then many things might become clear.

It was the Riddle of the Two Kings: "*Two kings reign in Hadinland./ One's becursed, the other damned./ One is blind, one's benighted./ And who can say which is sighted? . . .*"

"I know it!" Palimak shouted aloud. "I know the answer!"

Gundara covered his fangs with a paw and burped politely. "The answer to what, Little Master?", he asked.

"The Riddle of the Two Kings!" Palimak said. "My father and Iraj Protarus are the two kings!"

"Of course they are," Gundaree said, brushing crumbs from his tunic.

"Didn't you know that, Little Master?"

"But don't you understand?" Palimak said. "That means we shouldn't do anything. The last thing that ought to happen is for us to interfere."

Gundara yawned. "That's fine with me, Little Master," he said. "It sounded like a lot of work, anyway."

Gundaree curled up in a little ball. "Wake me when it's time for dinner," he said to his twin. "All this doing nothing has tired me out."

"Thoth cloudth look pretty bad, Biner," Arlain said.

Biner nodded, brow furrowed in worry. "Ain't that the truth, lass," he said. "Some kind of blow brewin', that's for certain."

They were hovering hundreds of feet above the Castle of the Two Kings, the volcano barely visible as the clouds swiftly drew a veil over the Demon Moon.

"We're too clo'th to that thing," Arlain said, indicating the volcano. "If a thtorm whipth up, we could run right thmack into it."

"Maybe we'd better get to ground," Biner said.

He turned to shout orders to the crew, but just then he saw — or thought he saw — movement along the rim of the valley.

"Take a look there, lass," he said to Arlain, pointing at the deeper shadow where the road came over the rise. "Do you see somethin' on yon road?"

Arlain's dragon eyes were sharper even than the proverbial eagle's. This was only one of many reasons for her incredible acrobatic skills. In a darkened tent she could see a thin guy wire as if it were broad daylight. A fire breather, her vision was also unaffected by sudden flashes of the pyrotechnics the circus used to wow the crowds.

She turned her head to where Biner was pointing, dragon's tongue flickering between pearly teeth as she concentrated.

Many miles away, Queen Clayre's litter was being carried over the rise by her slaves. Careful as they'd been to obscure the gilded ornamentation with lampblack, a small speck of blackening had been knocked off when one of her slaves had brushed against it.

Just then, lightning from the gathering storm flared in the sky, reflecting off the exposed gilding. It was only a tiny spark of light, but it was more than enough for Arlain.

She not only saw the reflected light, it helped pinpoint the entire shadowy column coming over the rise.

"Tholdierth!" Arlain hissed. "Lot'th of them!"

Instantly, Biner roared orders to the crew, commanding them to fly over the approaching enemy. And as the airship turned about, he issued other orders to prepare for bombardment.

Meanwhile, Arlain shot off a red flare to warn Safar. But a strong wind suddenly blew up, casting it far away.

Biner grabbed the wheel, steadying it against the buffeting. But he'd no sooner steadied the craft then another heavy gust hit, driving the nose off course.

He started to curse the vagaries of nature, but then a squall hit full force, drenching him with what seemed like tons of water.

The wheel broke free from his strong hands, spinning wildly, and the airship was whipped about until the heavy winds were hitting it square on.

There were *pings!* as cables broke, lashing out with deadly force in every direction.

No one was hurt, but two of the cables snaked up to pierce a balloon and air squealed out as the airbags quickly deflated.

"Get her down!" Biner roared to his crew. "Get her down before she crashes!"

49

SECRETS UNMASKED

When the first spear of lightning struck, Tabusir saw its reflection flash from Clayre's litter and raced to intercept her.

The queen gave him a terrible look as he ran up, so he aped surprise and made a hasty bow as if he'd accidentally stumbled into her presence. Using his sleeve, he quickly smeared lampblack over the bare spot to dull the glitter.

Fortunately, the queen was busy with some task. He caught a brief glimpse of her head bending low over a golden table, then the litter moved past.

When she was gone, he looked up into the darkening heavens and saw the airship swinging swiftly around. The cause of its movements was so obvious that even an apprentice spy would have known that Rhodes' troops had been spotted and the king's surprise attack was now no longer much of a surprise.

Rhodes was about a hundred yards away and Tabusir sprinted forward to warn him. But he'd taken no more then six steps when he heard Clayre shout something in a mysterious language.

The shout was followed by a sudden blast of wind blowing from nowhere. It was so strong that it knocked Tabusir to his knees.

But his heart was full of glee as he looked up and saw the airship spinning out of control. Then it steadied and began a hasty descent to the ground.

The air became still and the silence was as thick as the gathering clouds. Then a whole dragon's nest of lightning snaked from sky to ground in a series of *crack, crack, cracks!* Soon came the shock wave of rolling thunder, so powerful that it felt like a physical blow.

Another long silence set in, only to be broken by Rhodes' roared orders as he drove his men forward. He was so busy that Tabusir had to wait a full hour before he could approach with the news that they'd been discovered.

By then all the men and siege engines were in place and Rhodes only shrugged after he'd heard Tabusir out.

"It doesn't matter now," he said. "All we have to do is wait out my mother's storm, then attack."

And with those words a heavy rain began to fall. Then a steady, driving wind whipped into the valley and Rhodes and his soldiers huddled on the ground, drawing oil-skins over their heads.

Tabusir crouched beside the king, the wind-driven rain hammering against his waterproof hood.

The mud and the storm should have made him miserable. Instead, his excitement grew hour by hour, as he eagerly awaited Clayre's promise of a peaceful dawn.

* * *

Safar and Iraj were also not that surprised when Biner stomped in out of the storm with his news.

"Arlain spotted a column of troops comin' over the rise, lad," Biner said. "She thinks it's that devil King Rhodes. But I don't know. Seems unlikely to me, since we haven't heard one peep out of him for weeks."

Then he stomped his boots and shook himself like a great shaggy dog, spattering water all over the castle's royal chamber.

Iraj started to take offense at his behavior, but Safar hissed a warning that this was a friend of his and Iraj quickly turned an imperious frown of disapproval into a warm smile.

With Safar coaching him, Iraj replied, "We've never doubted Arlain's eyes before, Biner. We'd be fools to start now."

Biner nodded. "Aye, you're right about that, lad," he said. "Nothing we can do to about it now, though. The storm's so fierce not even a giant could stand upright under those winds. We covered the airship as best as we could and we'll just have to hope that the wind lets up enough for us to get outside and keep the fires goin' in the engines."

Iraj poured a goblet of brandy for the ringmaster, saying, "This storm isn't natural, my friend. There's enough magic stink in it to rival a Walarian offal ditch. I think the tempest is the work of Queen Clayre. That's why it's so powerful. And when morning comes we'll find ourselves surrounded by Rhodes' entire army."

Biner snorted angrily. "What's wrong with that rube?" he growled. "He's got more flea-bitten ideas than a circus geek! Why can't he be satisfied with his own kingdom and leave us alone? Why did he have to follow the likes of us to the end of the freakin' world?"

Safar mental-whispered advice to Iraj, who replied, "Maybe we'd better send for the others, so I can explain what we're up against to everyone at the same time."

Biner grunted agreement and went to the door where Renor was standing guard to tell him to pass the word that everyone was wanted in Safar's chambers.

Soon they were all gathered before Safar, the wind whistling wildly outside and the rain hammering a heavy drumbeat on the castle's thick walls. All the shutters had been barred against the fierce tropical storm, making the room uncomfortably warm.

Iraj/Safar gave each guest a warm welcome. There was Queen Yorlain, seated upon a small ornate throne fetched in by her slaves. Also Coralean, immense beside the tiny Eeda. Leiria entered, looking drawn and troubled as if she'd had difficulty sleeping. Jooli was at her side, full of concern for her friend and casting odd looks at Safar, then at Leiria and back again.

Sergeant Hamyr, along with Renor and Sinch, attended as representatives of the Kyranian soldiers. Then there were Biner and Arlain, who came to speak for the circus folk.

Finally there was Palimak, who was pale from worry. The closeness of the atmosphere made the young man feel as if everything might not be quite real — like a dream threatening to spill over into actual life. As he watched his father greet each person, he burned with the desire to shout out his great secret: *This man was is impostor!*

In reality it was Iraj Protarus in Safar's body and he was falsely commanding their respect and rapt attention. But this wasn't totally true and besides, Palimak had promised himself that he wouldn't interfere unless it became absolutely necessary.

With much difficulty, he choked back the words that crowded into his thoughts demanding to be spoken.

Safar, speaking through Iraj, quickly summed up what Arlain and Biner had discovered. Then he said, "It's my strong guess that the storm will end at dawn. And Rhodes will immediately throw everything he has against us."

Queen Yorlain sat bolt upright in her throne. "What a fool this king is!" she said. "Doesn't he know the Castle of the Two Kings is impregnable? We can withstand months, nay, even years of any siege he can mount!"

"It's not quite that simple, Your Highness," Iraj/Safar replied. "To begin with, I doubt you've stocked the castle with all the weapons and supplies necessary to withstand even a short siege."

Yorlain started to protest, then hesitated. Finally, she said, "Unfortunately, your words have struck to the heart of our dilemma, my king. We barely had time to prepare for your coming, much less gird ourselves for war."

Biner thumped his chair arm with a mighty fist. "Never fear, me lad," he said. "We'll get the airship up at the crack of dawn and bombard Rhodes' filthy hide to the hells!"

"As always, your instincts are right on target, my good and trusted friend," Iraj/Safar said. "However, I suspect Rhodes has something planned for the airship. That's what this storm is probably all about. Clayre most likely created it to ground the airship. And it would be most unwise for us to underestimate our enemy and to doubt that he has a follow-up plan to deal with the airship when the storm passes."

"I see what you mean, lad," Biner said. "But I still think we ought to get into the sky as quickly as we can."

"It'th the only plathe the airthip ith thafe, Thafar," Arlain pointed out. "On the ground we're helpleth."

"Then we should take that into consideration in our plans," Iraj/Safar said.

Leiria broke in, saying, "The moment the storm lifts — never mind if it's dawn by then — we ought to hit Rhodes and hit him hard. Nothing big. Just a nasty little in-and-out surprise attack that lets him know we have teeth."

"Wonderful!" Jooli exclaimed. "My father's a good soldier — an excellent general and planner. He also depends heavily on surprise. On the other hand, he's terrible at anticipating his enemy's response. That's his greatest weakness. And if his enemy has some kind of quick reply ready, it rattles him something fierce."

Coralean laid a hand of sincerity across his broad chest. "As all know, I am a great believer in the art of negotiation," the caravan master said in his booming voice. "The weapons of war are most necessary in this sad world the gods have cast us into. However, talk has won more battles than any war. And at the very least, talk has allowed defenses to be strengthened whilst the enemy perused a seemingly weighty bargaining proposal."

"In other words, we strike first as Leiria suggested," Iraj/Safar said. "Followed by a flag of truce to discuss the situation to death while we build up our defenses. Is that what you're thinking?"

Coralean started to answer in the affirmative, but Eeda tugged his sleeve, winning his silence. He smiled fondly at her as she spoke.

"If my lord husband permits," she said, "I can accompany him and cast some small — and quite subtle — spells of confusion to help draw the negotiations out." She patted her rounded belly. "Even that great bitch Clayre won't suspect me because I'm obviously weak from being with child."

Then, realizing the insult, Eeda blushed deeply and turned to Jooli. "I'm sorry," she said. "That was an unforgivable thing to say about your grandmother."

Jooli laughed, waving away the apology. "I've called her worse," she said. "Besides, it's true. She is a bitch of the worst order. And may all the mother dogs of the world forgive me for slighting them."

Meanwhile, Sergeant Hamyr was having a few quiet words with Renor and Sinch. When there was a lull in the conversation, he said, "Me and the lads here," he said, "crave th' honor of first blood."

He turned to Leiria and saluted smartly. "In other words," he said, "we'd be pleased to be in your troop, Cap'n, when the gates open in the morn."

Leiria laughed aloud, her dismal mood swept away by the bright prospect of battle. "Consider it done, sergeant," she said. "We'll all go out together and give King Rhodes' scrotum a good squeeze!"

There was laughter all around, even from Queen Yorlain, who at first struggled mightily to keep her serene dignity. But eventually she giggled, then tittered, and finally exploded in earthy guffaws.

Drinks were poured and toasts were made. Iraj/Safar laughed and drank along with the others — but the whole time each man was considering much deeper thoughts.

Both were finding the war parlay immensely interesting. Their interest, however, had little to do with the nuggets each person in the group had to offer. From Leiria's proposal of a surprise counter-attack to Coralean's idea of false negotiations.

There was an internal understanding that was beginning to take root in each man.

Iraj realized he was deferring to Safar on all matters involving personalities and magic. While Safar instinctively gave way when Iraj was discussing military tactics and strategy.

As the conference reached its climax, to be followed by false pre-battle levity, each man became more impressed with what could be accomplished when they cooperated with one another — without hesitation, or second guessing.

Although neither man asked for a renewed truce, they ceased their internal struggle with one another. Iraj hoisted a goblet of brandy and drank it down. And Safar found himself enjoying the drink, along with the peacefulness that followed.

Then Iraj's attention was gradually drawn to Leiria. Her color was high with excitement, eyes dancing. And then, to Safar's alarm, he felt heat rising in the body Iraj controlled. Legs that had once belonged to him, but now were no longer his to rule, moved toward Leiria.

Leiria looked up as Iraj/Safar approached and through the eyes Iraj provided Safar could see hope and love and pain and fear, all mingled together.

She dared a trembling smile of greeting and Safar could feel words that were not his own ghosting up for Iraj to speak. He did not have to wait to hear them to know they would be soft words, sweet words, and all of them traitorous to the core.

Prisoner though he was, Safar suddenly became aware that he still had a few small powers over the body that had once been his. He frothed up a bitter concoction from his belly and as Iraj opened his mouth to speak, acid flooded into the back of his throat.

Iraj felt the strong bile rise and it was all he could do not to spit. He swallowed hard, tried once again to speak, but only found more acid waiting to be coughed up.

And Safar said, *Leave her be, brother! Leave her be!*

He left Iraj no choice but to turn away. But through his enemy's eyes Safar saw Leiria's face fall and the hurt shoot through her as she thought that Safar had spurned her.

Although he could no longer see her reaction, he knew that most likely darkened as Iraj turned his attention on the lovely Queen Yorlain.

Again he felt the lust rise — even stronger than before. Yorlain smiled up from her throne, eyes full of equal heat and the promise of parted lips pressed together and twined bodies tossing on and on throughout some fated night to come.

Smooth, seductive words came into Iraj's mind — so full of must that Safar could practically hear them spoken aloud before they were uttered.

At the same time Iraj clamped on a more powerful physical control to prevent Safar from blocking him and spoiling his fun.

Except, as Iraj bent low to murmur his words, Yorlain's eyes suddenly hardened.

And she said, loud for all to hear, "You and your people are most clever, Highness. But there is far more to be concerned about than this coming battle with the barbarian, King Rhodes. In the scheme of things, he is nothing compared to with what is about to commence."

As she spoke there was a rumble beneath them strong enough to make the castle sway. And from a distance there came another, stronger rumble, followed by a short, explosive blast.

Then silence. A silence permeated by the gas stench of the volcano coming to life.

Yorlain said, "Did you forget the dance, Lord Timura? Did

you forget the agony that awaits us all?"

And Iraj/Safar replied, *"We didn't forget!"*

For a moment a frown spoiled Yorlain's beautiful face. Then she recovered and her features became blank.

"Two kings are required," she said, "to halt the doom Lord Asper has predicted. I see you — King Safar Timura. But I don't see the other king you promised. Dare I think that you might be lying to me? And if so, to what purpose? For you will die, along with me, your friends — and, indeed, the entire world.

"What say you to that, Safar Timura?"

At Safar's suggestion, Iraj bit back a sneering regal reply. He shrugged as if unconcerned.

"I told you before, Your Highness," he replied, "the other king will be with us shortly."

Yorlain laughed, "Come now, Majesty," she said. "You're toying with me. Why don't you admit it? Why don't you come right out and confess that *he* is with us now?"

Then her eyes started to glow and at the same moment the room darkened so that the only light was that cast by her eyes, framing Iraj/Safar like footlights in a theater.

Outside came another rumble and explosion and the volcanic stench grew stronger.

Safar and Iraj found themselves suddenly frozen by her eyes. And from some place close by they heard drums and horns and the rhythmic slap of bare feet dancing in sand.

Then they felt their wills draining away as they heard ghostly voices lift in song:

"Her hair is night,
Her lips the moon;
Surrender. Oh, surrender.
Her eyes are stars,
Her heart the sun;
Surrender. Oh, surrender.

Her breasts are honey,
Her sex a rose;
Surrender. Oh, surrender.
Night and moon. Stars and Sun.
Honey and rose;
Lady, oh Lady, surrender.
Surrender. Surrender . . ."

The others in the room heard nothing but the rumble of the volcano. But they were transfixed by the strange sight of Safar standing frozen in the pool of light cast by the queen's shining eyes.

Then the area around his body started to shimmer and his form became hazy, less substantial.

Palimak suddenly realized what was happening. He leaped to his feet, drawing his knife.

At the same time the Favorites caught the deadly magical scent and shouted a warning.

But Palimak was already driving forward — sprinting past the startled onlookers.

And then he grabbed Yorlain by the hair and slit her throat!

She fell to the ground, flopping horribly. But not one drop of blood came from the gaping wound.

Leiria cried, "What have you done, Palimak?"

He didn't need to answer — for in the next moment there was a loud thunderclap and the ghostly figure of the Goddess Lottyr rose from Yorlain's corpse.

All her many mouths howled fury, poison dripping from her sharp fangs. Her six arms waved violently as if she were going to attack.

Eeda and Jooli recovered quickly enough to join Palimak's protective spell.

Then there was a bright flash of light and she was gone.

Iraj/Safar suddenly jerked, coming out of their trance.

Palimak stepped over Yorlain's body to confront the strange thing his father had become.

"Tell them!" he demanded. "Tell them who you are!"

The thing that wore his father's body only sighed.

And when it replied it spoke in the voice of Iraj Protarus: "Safar always did say you were a bright lad."

It was Leiria who first understood what had happened. She would have recognized that voice in a cave black as midnight.

She gasped in shock. "It's Iraj!" she cried.

And she drew her sword and charged.

50
PRELUDE TO WAR

Kalasariz never slept. Sleep was something that had been lost to him many years before when he'd pledged himself to the Spell of Four and became a shapechanger along with Iraj, Fari and Luka.

The spell had been broken, but in his new entity as a spirit-world parasite living within King Rhodes' body he was permanently wide awake.

Unlike his former spell brothers, the spymaster considered this a blessing. In his previous existence he'd always hated the moment when the gods of slumber commanded his obedience. His father had been a seventh-generation priest. More to the point: his very name, Kalasariz, was the Walarian term for priest.

His mother had been a temple harlot enslaved to the priests and he had been seeded during a priestly orgy whose purpose was to cleanse sins by sinning. And to create sons for the priests to adopt and rear for their own holy purposes.

Kalasariz had soon learned he was better at ferreting out secrets to use against others than he was at religious scholarship. Better still was to forge those secrets into lies of solid gold. And Kalasariz had eventually sold out his own father with false charges that he was a heretic so that he might win his mantle as the supreme spy of all Walaria.

But deep inside Kalasariz he was still the son of a priest. And when he slept all his subsequent lies and murders sat heavily upon his soul. And so he'd always feared the night, because with it came terrible dreams of his transgressions, followed by imagined punishments for those sins.

Worse still, over the years those nightmares became increasingly and horribly complex because of all the enemies he'd made in his long career.

And so it was that when sleep overcame King Rhodes and he tossed and turned fitfully through the storm, dreaming bloody dreams much like those that had once afflicted Kalasariz, the spymaster was gleefully awake and guilt-free. Plotting his plots and conspiring in his conspiracies.

The best thing of all about his sleepless state was that he could keep constant control of Fari and Luka, who were enslaved in his ethereal belly. He kept their agonies constant and hot, so they didn't have time or energy to conspire against him.

Therefore, when Lady Lottyr came to him, spitting curses about Safar Timura and Iraj Protarus, Kalasariz was bright and alert and well aware that the goddess had suffered a defeat.

She called the incident in the castle a mere "setback," but he knew that this was only a hasty bit of fiction her pride had composed to lessen her humiliation. Failure and defeat dripped from every word she spoke.

"It was that demon brat Palimak who caught me out," she said. "Otherwise I would've crushed those fools who believe themselves to be the two kings Asper predicted would come."

Her six visages were terrible in their murderous beauty. And even though her visit to the spymaster was meant to be made in secret, she was so agitated that Rhodes would've been alerted to her presence if he had been awake.

Surely he would've caught the internal roiling Lottyr's frustration caused when she spoke to Kalasariz. The spymaster's ambitions might have been badly harmed by this royal realization.

In all his days Kalasariz had never met another person — except for himself — as rightfully and unerringly on target as Rhodes was when he became suspicious.

Well, maybe more: There was Queen Clayre. Whose own suspicious nature made her son look like a naï ve peasant. But Lottyr had made her own false bargain with Clayre and had also cast certain spells that had dulled the witch's wary senses.

Lottyr laid out all the plans she'd heard the Kyranians discuss while she'd commanded Queen Yorlain's body.

"They'll attack the moment the storm ends," she said. "They're hoping to wound you severely, then withdraw. Negotiations will follow — all aimed at drawing things out long enough for them to strengthen their defenses."

Kalasariz asked, "Have you informed Clayre about their plans?"

"No," Lottyr answered, "but I intend to the moment I leave you. And when Rhodes awakes, I want you to instruct him."

A canny master of lies and half truths, Kalasariz knew very well that Lottyr had sworn to another bargain with Clayre. The goddess admitted as much when she spoke her puny lies, saying her pledge to Clayre meant nothing, while her promises to Kalasariz were solid as gold.

But which bargain would the goddess keep? Kalasariz knew better than to trust to chance for the outcome.

And so he said, "I have the advantage of long experience with Safar Timura. And also with Iraj Protarus. They've never been defeated — especially when the two of them put their minds together."

Lottyr was angrily abrupt. "What of it?" she asked harshly. "They are nothing compared to me — the greatest goddess of the Hells!"

"Forgive me, Holy One," Kalasariz said, "but I'm only trying to point out that in any physical fight Safar Timura and Iraj Protarus are the likely victors. That is their history. Neither one has ever failed — even against each other. Timura defeated Protarus at Caluz. But Protarus, from what you say, now rules Timura's body. Tentative though that dominance may be.

"From what you've also said, they've made a pact with each other to oppose you. Isn't that so, Holy One?"

"Why are you spewing all this defeatist sewage at me?" Lottyr demanded, her twelve eyes burning with suspicion. "Do you *want* Timura and Protarus to win?"

"Absolutely not and forgive me if I gave you that impression, Holy One," Kalasariz hastened to say. "However, you have asked my best advice. And it is my sad duty to say that my advice is for you to prepare for Rhodes' and Clayre's failure."

Lottyr pealed chorused laughter, her six voices echoing so strongly that they resounded through Rhodes' bones and the king kicked and swore in his sleep.

She waited until he rested again.

Then she said, "Know this, Kalasariz: when the dawn commences, it will be not one, but two battles Safar Timura and Iraj Protarus will have to fight."

And then she was gone. There was not even a flicker between her presence and her absence. One moment she was there, the next she wasn't.

In the distance the volcano rumbled into life. There was a heavy blast and an intense, fiery light poured into the king's pavilion.

Rhodes suddenly sat up, rubbing his eyes. Sleepily, he asked, "What's happening? Is there an attack?"

Kalasariz replied, "Go back to sleep, majesty. There's no reason for alarm."

And so Rhodes fell back on his soft pallet and slept.

* * *

Despite the tempest, Clayre was resting peacefully when the Lady Lottyr came to her.

But as soon as the Queen Witch sensed the goddess's presence she bolted up from her pallet.

"Is everything all right?" she asked.

And Lottyr said, "All is ready, my dearest one. I've only come to you to make assurances."

"What of my son?" Clayre asked. "Are we ready for him as well?"

Lottyr replied, "It's just as we planned, Clayre. At the dawn, when the first enemy arrows fall, your son will die."

Reassured, Clayre smiled. "It'll be good to be rid of him," she said. "He always was just like his father."

Despite his demon strength and speed, Palimak was no match for the infuriated Leiria.

He jumped in front of her to stop her charge against Iraj/Safar, but she only ghosted to the side and kicked his legs from under him.

Worse still, Jooli was on Leiria's heels, her own sword in hand to back up her friend. But Palimak snagged out a hand, demon claws scything out, and caught her by the ankle to bring her painfully down.

None of this mattered. The instant Leiria came within striking distance, she fed all of her hate for Iraj into the sword blow she struck.

Except, in mid cut, she saw that it was Safar she was also about to kill. One part of her wanted to halt the deadly blow. The other demanded that she ram her blade through Iraj's guts.

Between Palimak's feeble intervention and Leiria's hair's-breadth hesitation, Iraj stepped in, taking full command of Safar's body.

Safar almost used his own powers to slow Iraj down, but then he realized Iraj was only using his half-empty brandy goblet for a weapon and released all of his physical energy.

In that moment of hesitation he had three questions that were answered swiftly.

The first was the question of his own survival. If Leiria killed Iraj, Safar would die as well. However, that was of little importance to him. After all he'd experienced and all the people he believed he'd made suffer, death would be welcome. He ached for Leiria's slashing blade as a release from his guilt.

The second was that if Leiria succeeded the whole world was doomed. Except now Safar found himself beyond worlds and the fate of all living things. Let it happen, he thought. We deserve whatever comes!

The third cause of hesitation was that Leiria would never be able to forgive herself for what she'd done. Safar thought, She loves me! And then he thought, by all that is holy, I love her too!

And so Safar let Iraj have his will.

The killing sword came in and Iraj, moving like lightning, stepped lightly into its sweeping arc, crashing the brandy goblet against the blade.

The goblet shattered, the sword went to the side, but all this was nothing to Leiria. She only shifted her grip, so that both her hands were on the sword's haft. Then she swung with power enough to cut a stone column in half.

But Iraj only continued his forward motion, stepping within the blade's path and grabbing Leiria by the throat with immensely strong fingers.

He squeezed and brought her choking to her knees.

"I am the only mortal — man, woman or demon — who can best you in a fight," Iraj said to her in his own voice. "Now, please remain quite still while I explain my intentions."

Leiria's answer was to drop her sword and draw her knife, thrusting it at his exposed belly.

With his free hand Iraj caught her attacking wrist, putting so much pressure on it that she had to let it fall. Then he maintained the pressure there, just at the bone-breaking point.

And Iraj said, "Leiria, I love you more than I have ever loved another." Then he laughed bitterly. "That's not saying much, as I'm sure you understand. But I beg you, not because of my love but because of Safar's, to hear us *both* out!"

Leiria, face purpling from the grip Iraj had on her, nodded. And both Safar and Iraj understood she was making a promise.

Iraj released her and she fell back. And he said for all to hear, "Speak to them, Safar. Tell them what we have planned."

Then he relinquished all control over his brother/enemy and Safar found himself standing in his own body again, while Iraj curled up into the spirit nest he'd vacated.

But as before, Safar was quite blind. He knelt down beside Leiria, guided by her perfume. He reached out to touch her face. She flinched, but then relented as his blindness became apparent.

"Is it really you, Safar?" she asked, voice tremulous.

"I swear it is, Leiria," he replied. "And if you don't believe me, think back to the last time we saw each other in Esmir. Do you recall how we parted?"

Leiria nodded, then remembered that he could not see. And she said, quite softly, "Yes."

"I told you then that I planned to get Iraj's help to stop the machine in Caluz," he said. "Isn't that right?"

"I thought you were making a dark-humored joke," Leiria said as the memory of that sad day came flooding back. "I thought you were just sacrificing yourself to save us."

"As you know now," Safar said, "I did win Iraj's help. Although it was against his will. Well, only partly so. He wanted desperately to break the shapechanger's spell and escape Kalasariz and Fari and Luka. And I gave him the means to do that."

"Is that how he ended up in your body?" Leiria asked.

"It's not so simple as that," Safar said, "but it's close enough. The main thing is, I didn't realize then that I truly did need Iraj's help. Not just to stop the machine in Caluz, but to end what is happening here."

"But how did he end up controlling you instead?" Leiria asked.

"I let him," Safar said. "We both need eyes to do our work. And he can give us sight." He smiled. "Of course, being Iraj, there were lies involved. And betrayal."

"And you're going to let him take over your body again, aren't you?" Leiria said.

"Yes," Safar replied. "I have no other choice. To awaken the gods and end this misery, Iraj and I must enter the hells and face Lady Lottyr. And we'll need eyes to do that."

Then he embraced her and kissed her, murmuring words of love. Leiria wasn't certain whether he meant them, or was only trying to comfort her.

Finally, Safar rose to his feet. Palimak came to him, hugging him fiercely.

"Isn't there something I can do, father?" he asked, tears welling up.

"If you mean about Iraj," Safar said, "there's nothing you can do. But he and I will need every scrap of your strength to face the coming day."

Then he pushed Palimak gently away. He waved blindly to Coralean, Biner, Arlain and the others. And gave them a crooked smile.

"I won't say goodbye, dear friends," he said. "Because I'll be close to you until the end. I only ask that you trust me. And you must trust Iraj as well."

Everyone was weeping, but they all murmured that they would do as he said.

Then Safar opened the gates to Iraj, who once again assumed control. Iraj/Safar blinked his eyes as sight returned and light flooded in.

"Now it's my turn to address you all," Iraj said in his own voice. A voice that made them all shiver. "And the first thing I have to say is this:

"In the morning we'll have not one, but two battles to fight!"

Part Five

Into the Hells

51

THE BATTLE BEGINS

Clayre and Lottyr brought an end to the storm just before dawn. Rhodes immediately sent his men out to gather up any farmers who had survived the tempest and had them put to the sword.

When first light came it revealed that the whole valley was in ruins from the storm: trees ripped up by the roots, farmhouses roofless or smashed, the fields and crops a muddy mess.

The lake was filled with debris, including thousands of dead fish, white bellies turned upward to greet the red Demon Moon as it rose over the volcano, grinning its ghastly smile.

As for the volcano itself, a large gash had been ripped from its cone by the previous night's activity. Small black clouds puffed upward, looking like storm clouds; from his hilltop command post Rhodes could smell the acrid stench drifting in with the breeze.

The volcano made his men nervous, so Rhodes called for his priests and they cast the bones to show that all was well. This relieved Rhodes as much as his men. For although the Lady Lottyr had promised him the volcano was no threat, he was not entirely convinced the goddess didn't have plans which might not necessarily include his own survival.

What convinced him even more than the casting was that, just as Lottyr had predicted, the Kyranians kicked the castle gates open not long after the first rays of the sun spilled into the valley.

As they came screaming out to confront his men, Rhodes chuckled in delight.

Did he have a surprise for them!

He signaled the counter-attack and at the same time passed the word to his engineers. And as he sprang his trap on the attacking Kyranians, the bombardment of the Castle of the Two Kings began.

Jooli burst through the castle gates, Sergant Hamyr and a contingent of twenty men right behind her, shouting their fierce war cries.

Just past the bridge she saw a bristle of pikemen surging forward to meet her. Behind them were archers and she could hear the *twang!* of their bows as they fired.

But she and her men were moving too fast for the archers and as the arrows lofted she waded into the pikemen, cutting men down left and right as Hamyr and the other Kyranians bunched in around her, then muscled outward to break the pack apart.

As she'd expected, her father's soldiers broke ranks too easily and began to retreat. But it was an orderly withdrawal. Not a flicker of panic as the pikemen moved back and the archers threw down their bows and drew swords.

They weren't true archers. None of their missiles had found a mark. But they were excellent swordsmen and they gave Jooli and her men a vigorous fight as they backed up along the road.

Far off, she saw her father's command-post banner waving in the morning breeze. She aimed for it, shouting orders to Hamyr and the others to redouble their efforts.

They overran the retreating men, stopping only to cut the throats of those who had fallen. As Iraj Protarus had warned, most of the men were feigning wounds and were only waiting their chance to leap up as Jooli passed so they could attack her from the rear.

Despite these precautions, with every step Jooli took she could sense her father's trap closing, pinching in from the sides, while leaving the way open to the fluttering command flag.

Any minute now the men she knew were lying in wait on either side of the road would spring up to overwhelm her. Even as she cut a man down she cast a spell of confusion to addle the brains of her hidden enemies.

But she knew that however great her efforts, soon it would be a case of too little and too late.

And she thought, Where's Leiria? Where's Leiria?

In the courtyard of the Castle Keep, the circus folk were desperately trying to get the airship aloft. Huge siege arrows fell all around them, sheeting green flame in every direction as the crew laboriously filled the twin balloons with hot air.

The axiom of all balloonists is that anything that can go wrong will strike in threes. And Biner's difficulties were further proof of that already well-worn prophecy.

First, the fierce storm had forced them to take refuge in the castle. The couldn't tend to the airship's engines and without fuel, the magical fires had gone out. In order to refill the balloons Biner had to waste an enormous amount of time heating up the engines.

Secondly, as the huge balloons slowly filled, straining against the lines, several cables snapped. They'd been badly stressed by the previous day's battle against the tempest and everyone had been so tired that they hadn't checked the obvious danger points.

Thirdly, the rudder had been damaged — another flaw that had gone unnoticed.

Biner and Arlain blamed themselves, not the crew, for these oversights.

As Arlain said, "I thould have been wat'thing. I'm your thecond-in-command, Biner, and it'th all my fault."

But Biner, a perfectionist to the core, cursed only himself for his shortcomings. Never mind the soul-rattling disclosures of Safar's dual identities. Never mind that he hadn't slept for two days. He was at fault, dammit.

It was the ringmaster's duty to oversee all things, and to anticipate all potential problems. And, by the gods, Biner had fallen down on his job.

So, as the explosive arrows slammed in from the skies, it was Biner who constantly threw himself into the most dangerous tasks. Shoveling fuel into the engines while others fought fires on the decks on the airship.

Dodging the scything release of broken cables, while clamping new ones in place. Once his tunic caught fire while he was heaving new ballast sacks into the airship.

Arlain beat the flames into submission while Biner continued to work, driving the crew to complete a hasty patch-job on the rudder.

Despite the brave and frantic work of Biner and the rest of the airship crew, for a time it seemed that all would be lost. The siege arrows kept falling closer and closer, marching their way across the courtyard as Rhodes' engineers gradually corrected their aim.

One arrow — as thick as a sideshow fat man's waist — slammed into the bow of the airship, igniting the well-oiled deck.

Arlain led a crew of foam-spraying fire fighters into the breach, but the flames became so intense that they drove everyone back except for Arlain. Hot flames licked all around her pearly body as she pumped foam on the blaze.

If it had been a circus act instead of real-life danger, the audience would have been thrilled at the erotic vision she presented. A fantastic female body, clothed only in a modesty patch at her thighs and two tiny dots over her breasts, sucking flames into her flat dragon's belly while she shot foamy spume onto the main fire from the hose that she held between her dragon claws.

But it wasn't an act and the fire drove her back, licking all around her fabulous form as she fought stubbornly on.

Then Eeda appeared, running out of the gates of the Keep, waving her arms as she composed a fire-quenching spell, her pregnant belly swelling her tunic to the bursting point. She looked as if she was going to deliver her child at any moment as she hastily cast the spell.

A fierce cold wind suddenly blew into the courtyard, killing the flames. Then the wind was gone.

"Get up as fast as you can!" Eeda shouted to Biner and Arlain. "I don't think I have the strength to do it a second time!"

Biner and Arlain needed no further prodding and minutes later the airship shot up into the sky just as a new barrage of fire arrows fell.

And Eeda dashed back into the relative safety of the Keep.

* * *

Coralean had a deep sense of foreboding as he waited at the edge of the golden-tiled pentagram. Events were moving so swiftly that he felt he barely had control. Looking at the figures of all the gods and goddesses portrayed in the fabulous wind-rose that the pentagram contained didn't help.

Particularly the portrait of the Goddess Lottyr, whose arrow pointed in a direction opposite to the others — straight at the painted flames of the Hells.

Behind him, six Kyranian pikemen were prodding Yorlain's aides across the chamber, hustling them toward stairs that led down into the dungeons.

Meanwhile, in the center of the wind-rose, tail lashing, muscles trembling in anticipation, stood Khysmet.

Iraj, wearing Safar's body and speaking in Safar's voice, said, "Easy, friend. Easy."

Then he vaulted into the great stallion's saddle. He leaned down to offer Palimak a hand up, but the young man gave a grim shake of his head and jumped up behind him without assistance.

Khysmet whinnied eagerly, stomping his hooves on the wind-rose.

Iraj chuckled to himself when he saw Coralean's worried face. Speaking in his own voice, he said, "There's no sense fretting, old friend. Safar and I were either born for this moment or doomed to it. You just concentrate on Rhodes and leave the Hells to us."

The caravan master sighed heavily and said, "If Coralean had a copper coin for all the times he was advised not to worry, Your Highness, he'd be even richer than he already is."

Iraj laughed. "Why is it that every phrase you speak dwells so much on profit?" he asked, half jokingly. "There's more to this world than money, don't you know?"

Now it was Coralean's turn to laugh. "That was always your trouble, Majesty," he said. "You think of profit as a base thing. A dirty thing. Whereas I, Coralean, know profit to be a thing of the utmost beauty. For profit is at the heart of all mortal endeavors.

"As a merchant sage once said, 'It is profit that drives all civilization.' How true, how true. For isn't it profit that makes kings — and lack of the same that ruins them? And does not profit allow the artist to make art and the musician to make music?

"More to the point — if you and my old friend Safar Timura win this day, why, the whole world will profit from your victory. So don't mock profit, majesty. But, praise it to the heavens!"

Palimak, confused and angry over the dual identities with which he was confronted, broke in,snarling, "Never mind the talk! Let's just cast the spell and get on with it!"

Just then Eeda hurried into the chamber, pale and obviously in great pain. "Forgive me, lord husband," she said, "but our child is coming!"

The news badly shook Coralean and he instantly swept Eeda off her feet into his arms. "We must find a midwife," he cried.

"Nay, nay, lord husband," Eeda said. "I can do this myself — if you will help me."

"Of course I'll help," Coralean said, voice weak. "What shall I do?"

"The child's birth can help the spell," Eeda said. "So, please, just place me on the floor. And let me — and your coming son — do our magic."

Inside Iraj, Safar quickly caught Eeda's intention. He rose up out of his nest, urging Protarus to wait until the proper moment. Eeda's bravery also broke through Palimak's reserve and he, too, whispered for Iraj to hold.

Coralean placed Eeda gently on the floor and ran to fetch pillows and blankets to make her more comfortable. As he pushed pillows under her, she cried out, gripping his hand fiercely.

Then she shouted, "He's coming, lord husband! He's coming!"

As she writhed in the throes of birth agony, Safar gave the signal for the spell-casting to commence.

And drawing on all of Palimak's powers, along with those of the Favorites, then combining them with Eeda's magic, Safar forged these spellwords:

> *"Eight winds blow, eight winds bend;*
> *Is it life or death these winds portend?*
> *And where hides the Viper of the Rose?*
> *And what dread secrets shall we expose?*
> *Into the Hells, our souls cast forth,*
> *East and west, south and north.*
> *North and south, east and west.*
> *The gods awaken, ah, there's the test!"*

Through Iraj's eyes, Safar saw Eeda jump as if she'd been struck with a lightning bolt. Then Coralean was holding up a bloody, crying little thing.

And then the whole floor gave away beneath Khysmet and Safar found himself falling through darkness toward a great, fiery light.

52

SPIES AND OTHER LIES

Rhodes was so intent on his daughter's charge that he didn't notice the airship soar out of the castle grounds. Jooli was sprinting toward his command post, smashing through every defense and cutting down every man that got in her way.

Her shrill war cry ululated up the hill, making his blood run cold. Even though she was still at a great distance, he believed he could see the fury and hate in her eyes. All concentrated on her father.

Running with her, the Kyranian troops were also taking a terrible toll on his men. And although he knew Jooli was only prolonging the inevitable — and his trap would close any second — the ferocity of her attack struck fear into his heart.

Brave though he was, Rhodes was so guilt-ridden by his treatment of his own flesh that for a moment he imagined her hot vengeful blade plunging into his breast.

"Get her! Get her! Get her!" he shouted to his officers.

Panicked by their king's hysteria, they ran around shouting confused orders to their underlings.

Only Tabusir kept his head. He walked quickly but purposefully to Clayre's litter. The spy had a duty to perform that he was looking forward to eagerly.

Clayre saw him coming and smiled a thin smile. Although she not only distrusted Tabusir and disliked him intensely, she'd been worried for some time now that her son was playing her false.

Her mind constantly ran wild with conspiratorial possibilities. Foremost among them was that Rhodes might make a last-minute alliance with her granddaughter, Jooli, and that the two of them would turn against her.

And even if this possibility was only the product of a fevered imagination, what if that was how it turned out? No matter their bitter past history, they were still father and daughter.

If Jooli survived her father's trap and struck a bargain with him Clayre had no illusions about what would happen next. A powerful witch, as well as a superb warrior, Jooli would make certain her grandmother didn't survive the day.

As guilt-ridden as her son over her treatment of Jooli, Clayre became fearfully obsessed with her granddaughter's intentions.

She had to be sure, no matter what the cost.

And so during the storm she'd sent for Tabusir, that most corruptible of corrupt men, and had dazzled him with gold and seductive promises.

Clayre was a beautiful woman and a rich woman who had years of practice in all forms of seduction. She'd only needed a little gold and a few hot-blooded hints of pleasures to come to convince the spy to join her.

And now she was not disappointed when the moment of Jooli's death neared and Tabusir came to her just as they'd planned.

When she saw him, she quickly turned her thin smile of satisfaction into one of erotic warmth. And she bedazzled him with her beauty as he dropped to his knees and made suitable gestures of loyalty and obedience.

"You are such a pretty fellow," she murmured to him in her

most alluring tones. "Kneeling there so handsomely before me you fair make my poor heart leap."

Tabusir knocked his head against the ground, saying, "I am but a man, Majesty. A worshipful man, burning with love for you. If only I dared take you in my arms and kiss you!"

"Soon, my handsome one, soon," Clayre said, only partly lying. "Pray be patient. For I yearn for you as much as you yearn for me."

Then she drew the spy up, looking full into his eyes. Delighting at her effect on him as he seemed to quiver and quake with desire.

She drew a long tube from her bodice and handed it to him. "I've made this for my son," she said.

And he pulled the two halves apart, revealing a sharp dart. Tabusir started to test the point with his finger, but she stopped him, saying, "Don't touch the point, my dear. It's poisoned, you know."

With a brisk intake of breath, Tabusir snatched his fingers away just in time. He glanced down and saw that the needle-point of the dart was smeared with a yellowish paste.

"One prick of the dart will do," Clayre said. She pointed down the hill, where Jooli and the Kyranians were hammering their way through her son's lines.

"If my granddaughter should win through," she said, "there's a good chance she'll try to turn my son against me. If this happens, you only need to get close enough to the king to throw the dart.

"It won't kill him, for, as I told you last night, that is not my desire. But it will immobilize him — freeze his body and his will — until we decide what to do with him."

Tabusir examined the dart closely. Marveling at its hand-worked design. The Lady Lottyr's face had been carved on one side. And the needle's shaft had been lovingly stropped many times before the poison was applied.

"But what of Queen Jooli?" Tabusir asked. "Even if we remove your son, she'll still be a threat."

"Never mind Jooli," Clayre said. "I have plans to deal with her. It is my son who worries me the most."

Actually, it was Kalasariz' presence inside her son that terrified her. The king and the cunning spymaster made a formidable combination. Naturally, she said nothing of this to her new ally.

Smiling, Tabusir leaned close to Clayre, whispering, "I am yours to command, my queen. But might I beg of you one kiss to steel my nerve and send me on my way?"

Clayre thought, Why not? Tabusir really was quite handsome as well as clever. Of course, after he attacked her son, he'd have to be put to death himself for treating a member of the royal family in such a manner. Still, there was no harm in a kiss, was there?

And so she kissed him, full and deep. She was delighted when she felt Tabusir shudder.

But as she gently pushed him away, he whispered, "Here's a gift, Majesty, from your loving son."

And he rammed the poisoned dart into her soft, heaving breast.

Instantly, Clayre become immobilized — freezing into a living statue. Her expression was one of great surprise.

"You see, Majesty," Tabusir said. "After I spoke to you last night, I reported to your son. And he made me a much better offer."

He kissed her immobile face, rudely crushing his lips against hers.

Then Tabusir turned away and strolled off to see how the king was faring against his daughter.

Leiria ground her teeth impatiently as she waited for Rhodes to spring his trap on Jooli. From her hiding place in the rubble of a destroyed farmhouse she watched her friend lead the charge through the castle gates.

Sequestered in other nearby places were fifty Kyranian soldiers, all aching to join the battle.

On either side of her were Renor and Sinch and she heard their gasps of alarm as several enemy soldiers confronted Jooli. Then they sighed in relief when the warrior woman easily cut them down.

"Silence!" Leiria hissed. "You'll give us away!"

Not that she blamed them for displaying their youthful tension. She was damned tense, herself. They'd all crept out into the teeth of the storm several hours before dawn.

Drenched to the bone, buffeted by fierce winds, they'd had to fight a battle with the elements long before they were set to engage Rhodes. In the end they managed to set up a perfect double ambush — finding hiding places on either side of the road that Jooli would use.

And they were well back from the positions Leiria knew the king's soldiers would take when they made themselves ready for Jooli.

She hated to admit it, but the whole thing had been Iraj's idea. A master tactician, Iraj had immediately guessed what Rhodes would do after Lottyr reported back to the king that the Kyranians planned a surprise attack the moment the storm ended.

With Queen Yorlain as her slave, Lottyr had obviously overheard every detail of their planning session in Safar's quarters.

"He'll have a surprise attack of his own planned," Iraj had said, using his own voice. "But we'll be ready for him!"

"With me as bait for the trap?" Jooli had asked, eyes glowing at the prospect.

"Exactly," Iraj had said.

Leiria shuddered at the memory of that odd scene. Iraj's voice issuing from the lips of her lover. It had made her feel filthy all over.

She pushed those thoughts away. This was not the time and place for such weaknesses. But she couldn't help wondering for just a moment if she and Safar would ever have a life together.

Leiria bit her lower lip, using the pain to wipe that question from her mind.

Hells, most likely they'd all be dead by the day's end!

She concentrated on Jooli and her soldiers. Saw them fight their way along the road, leaving dead and wounded men in their wake. Saw the shadowy forms of Rhodes' troops creeping in from every side. Saw the defiant flag of Rhodes fluttering over his command post far up the hill.

Then, as Jooli and her troops reached the bend in the road, Leiria saw the enemy soldiers leap up on every side of her. She heard them shout shrill battle cries as they closed the trap.

"Now!" Leiria cried.

Drawing her sword she leaped to her feet and gave the signal that triggered Iraj's double trap.

Rhodes gaped like a village fool when he saw Leiria and her men suddenly leap up and attack his men from behind.

"Where the hells did she come from?" he shouted.

But there was no one to answer, for his officers were as stunned as their king to see such a perfect plan foiled.

It was all over in a few moments. There were terrified shrieks of surprise from his own men, mingled with the clash of steel against steel as the Kyranians worked their awful will.

And then the ambush site was reduced to a bloody mess of soldiers groaning their last, while the Kyranians stood around, leaning on their swords and laughing or slapping one another on the back, no doubt saying what clever fellows they all were.

He saw Jooli and Leiria meet, embracing like sisters. Then turning to look up the hill in his direction. He saw Jooli point straight at him and had no doubt about what she was saying to Leiria.

Rhodes turned and caught sight of Tabusir standing nearby, as stunned by the turnabout as everyone else.

"Send for my mother!" Rhodes shouted at the spy, all his fears and anxieties spilling over the cliffs of reason.

Tabusir gawked at him. "But, Majesty," he said, "your mother can't come, remember?"

"What did you do? What did you do?" Rhodes babbled, drawing his sword.

"Only as you asked, Majesty," Tabusir replied, edging backward, trying to get out of the king's range. But two officers moved in on either side, grabbing him by the arms.

"Please, Majesty!" Tabusir begged, feeling his carefully built world suddenly crumble beneath him. "I only dealt with your mother as she would have dealt with you. I only did what you commanded!"

"Damn you!" Rhodes roared. "How dare you turn my own words against me? I am the king!"

And with one blow he cut off Tabusir's head.

Then he raced to his mother's litter, his men leaping away when the saw the agony in their king's eyes and the bloody sword in his hand.

Clayre was all alone in her litter. Her slaves had already fled, taking with them every valuable they could find in their haste to escape the king's wrath when he learned that his mother had been murdered.

Her silk robes were gone, rent from her frozen body, and she was half naked. Her purse and jewelry were absent. And her magical table was shattered, the gold-tiled pentagram having been ripped from the very wood it had been fixed into.

Even the litter itself hadn't gone unscathed — gilded decorations and jewels had been torn from their settings.

Falling on her and embracing her, Rhodes cried, "I'm so sorry, mother! So sorry! I slew the villain who harmed you!"

But when he felt her stone-like flesh he leaped back, as if she were a leper.

And he shouted: "I need you, mother, more than I have ever needed you before! Please, please help me!"

But the only answer was the startled look frozen upon Clayre's face. And the poisoned dart sticking out of her chest.

Rhodes fell to his knees, weeping.

Inside him, Kalasariz sniffed the blood of failure and rose from his nest like a great white shark shooting out of the sea's cold, dark depths to seek his moment of gory opportunity.

He had the demons, Luka and Fari, crying in his belly, but he was hungry. Oh, so hungry.

And the Lady Lottyr whispered from someplace close: *You were right, Kalasariz. The king has failed.*

The spymaster said nothing in reply, but only ghosted toward the throbbing souls she was offering him, like pearls set in sweet oyster flesh.

First he gulped down Clayre and, oh, she was good and, oh, she was tasty. He felt the fires in his belly explode with increased power and energy. Then he found the soul of Rhodes, which was still weeping for his mother. And that soul was even more delicious and more power-giving than Clayre's.

He felt strong, so strong. And his mind, which he'd always prized above all things, became all-seeing.

Kalasariz/Rhodes whirled around, bellowing to his men. They fell to their knees before his awful majesty.

And Kalasariz thought, *This is good. This is very, very good.*

Coming up the hill he saw Coralean riding a huge horse. The caravan master was so immense that his feet dragged along the ground. He had a small woman in his arms. And she held a bundle that Kalasariz couldn't make out.

Marching on either side of Coralean were Leiria and Jooli, their armor sheening under the Demon Moon. Their troops behind them — Kyranian troops. Eager for the final kill.

And beyond them, hovering over the cone of volcano, Kalasariz could see the fabulous airship floating free. Ready to move in at a moment's notice and bombard King Rhodes' positions.

Kalasariz felt a flicker of disappointment. He'd come so far. Dared so much. But now, on the eve on his ultimate victory, had he already been defeated?

And the Lady Lottyr whispered, *I promised you two battles, Kalasariz. And it is only the second one that truly counts.*

Kalasariz felt hope rise like a mighty spear in his fist. And, already knowing the answer, he asked, *Who do we fight?*

And the Lady Lottyr replied, *Safar Timura and Iraj Protarus. They're waiting for us now at the gates of the Hells!*

The spymaster's hunger burned brighter at this prospect. And he said, *Let's fight them, then.*

But at that moment he heard a cry, coming from far away. It was like that of a newborn infant demanding new life.

He asked, *What's that?*

The Goddess Lottyr replied, *Only a child, Kalasariz. Nothing to worry ourselves about.*

But he was worried. And as the whole world shimmered about him, slowly dissolving, he heard the child cry once again.

Then he found himself striding along a broad beach, sword in hand. He heard drums throb and horns blow, then the voices of singing people.

Kalasariz found them dancing naked under towering palm trees, singing praises to a beautiful queen who led them in their dance. Beyond he saw the volcano, black smoke and angry sparks sputtering into the skies.

He knew he was still in Hadin, but it was a different Hadin. The armies and the ships didn't exist here. Just these dancing people and the volcano that looked as if it were about to blow.

The Lady Lottyr whispered to him, *Wait here!*

And so he waited, leaning on his sword and watching the people dance. Feeling strong and confident in King Rhodes' body. Powerfully cloaked in the magic radiating from his belly, where his enemies danced a quite different dance than the one that seemed to please the island people.

Kalasariz also didn't need to ask the goddess who they were waiting for.

He knew damned well it was Safar Timura and Iraj Protarus. The spymaster laughed aloud at the prospect.

When Jooli came up the hill, trotting beside Coralean's horse, she was only mildly surprised when her father's soldiers stepped out of the way, bowing to her respectfully.

These men knew her — she'd once been their queen. And if her father finally admitted defeat she'd be their queen once again.

Then she smelled the stink of magic and quickened her pace, moving ahead of Coralean toward a knot of officers gathered around what she knew to be her grandmother's litter.

They were pale and trembling when they saw Jooli, but not out of fear of her. The men parted as she strode forward, Leiria close behind — sword drawn to protect her friend's back.

When Jooli saw what had happened she froze in her tracks. Both her father and her grandmother were dead. Clayre was sprawled in her litter, while Rhodes was slumped on the ground.

One of the officers said, voice trembling, "It wasn't us, Majesty! They did not die at our hands!"

Jooli said nothing, but only shook her head. She knew quite well no mortal had slain this pair.

And then, while she was struggling for an answer, the corpses started to fade and to shimmer with a strange light.

"Get back!" she shouted to the men.

They didn't need her warning and were already scrambling away.

Then the light grew brighter and the corpses became fainter still.

There was a double crack as magical forces split the air — and the bodies were gone!

Jooli turned to Leiria. "It was the Goddess Lottyr who did this," she said, almost in a whisper.

She was keeping a heavy check on her emotions. It was no time to test her feelings about her father and grandmother.

And she added, "But they aren't really dead. Well, not as you and I know death."

"Where are they, then?" Leiria asked.

The ground rumbled beneath them and several soldiers shouted. "The volcano! The volcano!"

Jooli slowly turned, then pointed at the cone-shaped mountain. Thick smoke was boiling forth and lava was flowing down its sides.

"There," she said.

Leiria was bewildered. But then she became even more confused when Coralean called to them in his big voice.

"Eeda wants to speak to you!"

They went to her where she was nestled in her husband's brawny arms, the infant whimpering at her breast.

"Safar has need of us," Eeda said, voice weak but urgent.

"What should we do?" Leiria asked, fear clutching her heart.

Eeda gestured at the volcano. "The airship," she said. "We must get in the airship. It's the only way to save him."

Immediately, Leiria sent a signal for Biner to descend. Meanwhile, Jooli told her father's men to flee as best they could.

"Get back in your ships," she said, "and sail like the hells for Syrapis. I'll meet you there, by and by, and we'll put the kingdom into order."

The men didn't need to be told twice. They ran, shedding armor and weapons and never looking back when another blast shook the volcano.

Leiria gave the Kyranians similar orders. She was only going to keep Renor, Sinch and Sergeant Hamyr with her. The rest were told to get back to the ships and tell the pirate captains to stand far off from the island.

"And if we don't make it," she added, "return to Syrapis and tell our friends what happened here."

Then the airship was down and the others were boarding it.

Leiria ran to join them, praying that this time she wouldn't be too late.

53

INTO THE HELLS

They plunged through hot darkness, the sound of what seemed like heavy whips whirring and cracking on every side. Far ahead of them they could hear the muted boom of big metal drums and the distant wail of hundreds of tortured voices.

Red tongues of flame flicked out at them and Khysmet swerved in mid-flight, dodging most of the hot spears. The big stallion shrilled in fury as one blast hit him, then steadied his course and flew onward at an even greater rate of speed.

Palimak felt a searing pain across his thigh but took heart from Khysmet's example and ignored it, concentrating solely on the transport spell he'd created with his father and Eeda.

They were plummeting deeper and deeper into the bowels of an immense sorcerous machine with nothing except the transport spell to guide them.

Enormous unseen gears groaned somewhere in the darkness. They were driven by what Palimak imagined to be huge clattering chains that powered the hellish machine in its mysterious, yet clearly evil purpose.

Gundara and Gundaree chattered fearfully in his ear, crying, "Look out, Little Master! Beware! Beware!" in a never-ending chorus of warnings.

He couldn't see any of the dangers that were stalking him — he could only sense fierce presences looming up with gnashing teeth and rattling claws and the stink of old carnivores.

Khysmet never stopped, only swerving from side to side like a swift-moving eagle, somehow always avoiding the danger.

All of Palimak's instincts shrieked for him to draw his sword and defend himself. But there was nothing to see except for an occasional cloud of hot sparks drifting up to meet them.

A verse from Asper came to him — leaping crazily into his mind and crowding out the fearful sensations.

Palimak chanted it, adding the old demon's powers to the transport spell:

"Into the Hells my soul did fly;
Not knowing if we'd live or die.
But then it returned with this reply:
No truth in Heaven, only lies, lies, lies!"

Palimak felt his strength return, his fears vanish. And the cold demon side of him opened like a yawning gate.

He felt his claws arc from their sheaths and he felt powerful and ready for any monster that dared approach.

And just then — looking over the shoulder of the creature who wore his father's body — he saw a large red ball of light appear. It was as if they were nearing the end of an incredibly long tunnel.

He'd seen a bright light when the tunnel had first opened, but then it had been swallowed by darkness.

Palimak looked closer, gripping Safar's tunic tighter with his claws. Features began to appear on the ball of light. Familiar features.

It was the Demon Moon!

Iraj gloried in Khysmet's fierce ride through the jaws of the Hells. Blood on fire, body burning with the joy of impending combat, he felt like he could take on the gods themselves.

And when the monsters came scrambling through the darkness, with only the beat of their leather wings and gnashing teeth to give them away, he laughed aloud at Khysmet's swift change in course, foiling their charge.

The awful sounds of the great machine and the distant wails of agony only made his bloodlust burn hotter.

He didn't know what awaited them at the end of this magical ride through the spirit world, but he also didn't care.

His enemy was there, that was enough.

What enemy?

Did it matter?

Never!

Only show me your face, he thought. And you'll curse the day you chose Iraj Protarus for your foe!

Then, far below, he saw the Demon Moon. Khysmet was flying straight toward it.

Is this where my enemy waits? he wondered. Then he thought perhaps it was the moon itself that opposed him.

He laughed, thinking, What a marvelous boast for a man to make: I was the one who slew the Demon Moon!

Buffeted by the storm of Iraj's emotions, Safar kept a tight rein on his own. He didn't care a damn for the dangers lurking in the darkness, nor did he allow himself to marvel at Khysmet's skillful flight.

His whole being was focused on the transport spell. He hoped Palimak was doing the same.

Several times he sensed his son's attention falter and the spell weakening under his grasp.

Safar wished mightily that he could speak to Palimak. He had a good idea what his son was going through. To know that his father's body had been invaded by another, much hated presence. Feeling somehow betrayed, but without reason or evidence to support that feeling. Putting his faith and trust into a stranger's hands — hands that had previously done their best to kill him.

Once Safar almost asked Iraj to let him voice words of comfort to Palimak. Then he realized that this would only make things worse.

For how would Palimak truly know it was his father speaking and not Iraj Protarus?

Then the young man suddenly seemed to become stronger than before. Safar caught a whiff of demonic magic and knew that Palimak had transformed himself — giving free rein to his demon side.

And Safar wondered, At what cost, my son? At what cost?

Then Iraj said to him, *Get ready to fight, brother! We're at the final gate!*

And Safar saw the bloody face of the Demon Moon rear up, with its death-mask grin.

Khysmet trumpeted a challenge and Iraj reached for his sword.

Safar said, *Wait, brother! It's not yet time for steel!*

And at that moment the moon's face burst into a violent sheet of flame. The hot blast smashed Khysmet back and they spun over and over, the stallion fighting desperately to right himself. Iraj and Palimak clawing for purchase.

Finally, Khysmet kicked himself aright.

"Go!" Iraj shouted, digging in his heels. "Go!"

And the stallion swooped toward the hot flames.

Safar hissed, *The trumpet! We need the trumpet!*

Iraj immediately plucked the shell horn from his tunic, lifted it to his lips — and blew!

Safar put all his magical energies into Iraj's breath. And the sound was like a thousand war trumpets shouting in unison.

A pale light bloomed, swelling larger and larger. And then the beauteous Spirit Rider burst out of the light on her glorious black mare.

Princess Alsahna turned in the saddle, waving her sword. "This way, Safar!" she cried.

And she and the mare charged straight into the flames.

Khysmet bellowed lustily at the sight of the mare and charged after her.

Then they were surrounded by a sea of fire. Great boiling waves of flame bursting in from all sides. Bone-scorching spears of fire cracking out of those waves.

The heat and the pain were so intense that it was all Safar could do to keep himself from screaming out, I surrender! I surrender!

Iraj shuddered with the pain, crying, *What's this, brother? What's this?*

And Safar felt Palimak's claws tighten, spearing through his tunic and into the flesh. He thought he heard his son shout, "Father! Father!"

But he realized that Palimak was actually urging them on, crying, "Onward! Onward!" And even in all his pain, Safar felt supreme pride at his son's bravery.

Then he saw the Spirit Rider charging back. The black mare rearing up and pawing the air.

Blue spears of light shot from her hooves, driving the flames back. And opening a passage through the boiling red sea.

Then the Spirit Rider whirled her mount about, shouting once again for them to follow, and charged out of sight.

Khysmet surged forward and there came a *crack! crack! crack!* A series of explosions so loud Safar felt like the bones of his shared body were about to burst.

And then everything became hazy. And everything became quite still.

And the only sounds were the boom of a slow, gentle surf, the rhythmic throbbing of sweet harvest drums, and a thousand glad voices lifted in song:

> *". . . Lady, oh Lady, surrender.*
> *Surrender. Surrender . . ."*

54

THE VAMPIRES OF HADIN

The haze lifted and Safar found himself striding across warm sands. Khysmet was no longer with him, nor was the Spirit Rider.

In the distance he could clearly see the handsome dancing people of Hadinland. And there was their fabulous queen, bronzed hips and breasts heaving in the harvest dance.

Above the whole scene loomed the volcano. Beckoning and threatening at the same time.

Safar felt suffused with renewed hope and energy. His sight had returned and he was once again in full control of his body.

He felt so strong he barely noticed his armor. If the fates decreed his death, he thought, this was how he wanted to meet it.

"Welcome back, brother!" came a familiar voice.

And Safar looked to his left and saw Iraj striding beside him. Bedecked in burnished, kingly mail, Protarus was as young and handsome as when he'd first taken to the conqueror's road. His golden hair and beard glistened in the bright, tropical sun. And his smile was glad and innocent, as if he'd been washed of all his sins.

"The question is," Iraj said, "after all that has happened between us, are we still truly brothers?"

Safar wasn't sure how to answer. Wasn't clear in his feelings.

And even if he had been capable of such clarity at this particular fates-colliding moment, he wasn't sure he ought to answer.

And then:

"I'm here, father," came another voice.

Safar looked to his right and saw Palimak, tall and slender, with shoulders as wide as the spreading branches of a new oak tree. His eyes glowed with demon fires and his claws were ten glistening daggers.

Palimak smiled, exposing long, double-rowed demon teeth. And even as Safar looked he saw his son's face transform, the forehead bulging, the demon horn bursting through. And his skin toughened and deepened in color until it was an emerald green.

The boy sadly flicked out his long demon tongue and asked, "Do you still love me, father?"

Again, Safar was confounded. But for an entirely different reason. How could Palimak ever doubt he loved him? Had he been such an unfeeling father that his own son — never mind he was adopted — doubted his love? Under any circumstances? Demon or human, or half-way in between, what did it matter?

Palimak was just Palimak.

Then it came to him — the same was true of Iraj!

And Leiria, oh, yes, Leiria; he loved her too.

Safar said: "All my words are poor. You ask if I love you, son. Of course I do. I always have and always will. And you, Iraj. You ask if I am your friend. And my answer is the same. Even in my hate I loved you."

Then he pointed at the glowering, fire-spitting volcano.

"There is the doomspell that has driven us all these years. And if we manage to destroy it we'll awaken the gods.

"But I must warn you both it's unlikely that the gods will thank us. I think they'll curse us instead and make us suffer for what we've done."

Iraj said, "Be damned to them, brother! What can they possibly do to me that I haven't already done to myself?"

Palimak snorted agreement. "I don't care what the gods think. They may have created this world but we're the ones who must make a life here the best we can!"

Safar laughed. "Very well, then," he said. "Let's have at it!"

Iraj slapped him on the back. "Good, it's settled. Now, brother, let's hear your plan."

He gestured at the dancing people. Just beyond them, standing behind Queen Yorlain, was the bulky figure of King Rhodes, leaning easily against his sword.

"What's the best way," he asked, "to make these fools beg for mercy?"

Safar grinned ruefully. "Actually," he said, "I don't have a plan. Nor do I have any magical tricks up my sleeve. Just my sword to put with yours."

"And mine," Palimak whispered, drawing his weapon.

Iraj roared laughter. "Then be damned to us all!" he shouted.

And with that he charged the dancing people, bounding across the rolling sand dunes on his way to meet whatever the fates had in store for him.

Feeling as foolish and frightened as he had years before when he charged after Iraj down the snowy passes of the Gods' Divide, Safar ran after him.

He heard Palimak shout something, but he couldn't make out the words. And a moment later his demon son was sprinting past him, closing on Iraj.

Safar put on speed to catch up, leaping over dunes and showering sand in his wake as he raced onward.

Soon he was up with them, Iraj and Palimak only a few steps ahead.

But then he smelled the thick, rusty scent of blood. And he knew it to be his blood and Iraj's blood and Palimak's blood.

The scent was delicious — soul-satisfying. And then he realized he was smelling their scent through the hungry senses of others.

Then the dancers all turned to confront the three charging warriors.

They smiled, exposing long canine teeth. And they shouted in glee as their prey ran into their arms.

And Safar finally realized who the dancers really were: emotional and physical vampires, who sucked out a man's soul along with his blood.

And they sang:

"Surrender . . . surrender . . ."

And all his will left him. To be replaced by a fabulous narcotic-like joy. He wanted to be with them again. He wanted to be ruled again.

Oh, how he ached to dance.

Dance, dance, dance.

Dance to the beat of their hungry hearts . . .

And more than anything else he desired to expose his throat, his wrists, his every blood-pumping, pulsating vein and artery to their fangs.

Just beyond them, Queen Yorlain danced, thrusting her hips, harder, harder. Making him lust for surrender all the more.

But then he saw Rhodes, leaning on his sword and laughing through his thick beard.

Damn you! Safar thought. Damn you!

And he was released from the death spell that bound him and he started dealing out death of his own.

Beautiful people, ugly-spirited people, all dying under his sword.

Evil as they were — long teeth reaching to suck the life from him — Safar cried out in agony with each killing sword stroke. As if each mortally wounding blow were struck at himself, instead of his enemies.

Yet, to his wonder, it was his enemies who died, not Safar Timura.

And they died so easily. Their flesh was soft, their defenses weak.

And they fell away, fell away, with each stroke of his sword.

And blood — so much blood — was released by his blade.

The dancers didn't shout or scream, but only chanted his name as he killed each one of them.

"Safar, Safar, Safar. Safar, Safar . . ."

On and on, dying and spouting his name along with their blood.

Then he was stumbling over the bodies Iraj and Palimak had left in their wake. And mortally wounded men and women — so beautifully formed one and all that it made their wounds and impending deaths seem especially abhorrent.

And they all moaned: "Safar, Safar, Safar. Please, Safar!" Until it drove him mad.

What did they want of him? They were his enemies. They were monsters and vampires and all the evil things a mortal could imagine.

But as he slew them they all begged him in voices he could not resist: "Safar, Safar, Safar. Please, Safar."

"Enough!" he shouted. "Enough!"

But it was too late because he and Iraj and Palimak had killed them all.

He shuddered, thinking he was going to become ill — except it was a spiritual, not physical, ailment. And through his sorcerous eye he saw a thousand souls float toward the volcano.

The black clouds grew thicker and seemed to form lips. And then those lips inhaled and he was knocked to the ground by the resulting tornado.

The twister ripped across the island, sucking up the souls of the dead.

On his knees, Safar looked up and saw hundreds upon hundreds of bright souls being carried into the gaping cone of the volcano.

And they were all crying, "Safar, Safar, Safar! Please, please, please, Safar!"

Finally, everyone was dead — the beach littered with corpses. And Safar saw Iraj and Palimak advancing toward King Rhodes.

Queen Yorlain stood in front of him, her face lit up as if she were finding heavenly glory instead of impending death.

She cried, "Safar!"

And Rhodes shouted, "This is the end of it all!"

Then he cut her in two and she fell to the ground, sighing and crying, "Safar, Safar, Safar!"

And her soul was swept away with the others.

The potter's son felt so small and insignificant at being the cause of all these people's deaths. His own soul withered as if it had been dashed by a freezing wave from the cold seas of the far, far north.

Then Rhodes bellowed defiance.

And he stood up, straight and tall and bearded and barbarian-strong. He waved his sword, shouting, "Come to me, little ones! Come to me!"

Safar ran forward, as did Palimak, but Iraj was many steps ahead of them.

But just before Protarus reached his enemy, lightning stabbed from the sky and the earth rumbled and shook under them.

And Rhodes started to transform, growing larger and larger, until he was the size of giant — three times the height of a man.

Safar gaped, but not at Rhodes' transformation. Because as he grew all his features became a stormy landscape of constantly changing images.

First it became the beautiful, evil face of his mother — Queen Clayre.

Then this changed — bursting apart in a bloody welter — to

transform into the grinning demon features of Lord Fari.

And that face twisted and broke and bled to make the royal features of Prince Luka, the demon prince.

Then a shatter of light momentarily obscured the monstrous figure.

And finally, standing before them, waving a mighty sword, was Kalasariz!

Sudden realization of what was happening dawned and Safar shouted a warning to Iraj, who was almost on the giant.

But it was too late.

55

THE GODDESS LOTTYR

When Iraj saw the enormous figure of Kalasariz towering over him, he knew he had been well and truly trapped.

He struck out futilely with his blade as Kalasariz' gigantic hand reached down to pluck him from the ground.

The spymaster held him at eye level, grinning terribly with that thin, cold smile.

"Welcome back, Majesty," Kalasariz mocked. "Your brothers have sorely missed you."

In the spymaster's eyes Iraj could see the reflections of the faces of Luka and Fari. Flames leaped all around them as they twisted in agony.

"We made a pact once, Majesty," Kalasariz continued. "Do you recall it?"

Iraj remembered it very well — it was the Spell of Four, which had once bound him to these creatures in a foul bargain. He'd escaped it for a time, but now his grievous error of the past had returned to haunt him.

He wanted to cry out to Safar to save him, but he knew there was nothing his friend could do.

"I feel compelled to tell you, Majesty," Kalasariz mocked, "that things have changed since we were last together. Then you were the king and we were your slaves. But now it is I, Kalasariz, who shall rule."

Iraj forced laughter. "Don't be a fool, Kalasariz," he said.

"You aren't fit to be king. You don't have the guts, much less the will."

The spymaster's thin smile spread wider. "We shall see, Majesty," he said. "We shall see. With the Goddess Lottyr supporting me, however, I doubt I'll have much difficulty adapting to my new role."

And with that he drew Iraj toward his mouth, meaning to bite him in two. At the same time, his eyes glowed with magical power as he exerted all his strength to bring Iraj once again under the thrall of the Spell of Four.

Iraj tried to struggle and break free, but the spell slowly spread its force through his body, sucking away his will to resist.

Then he heard Safar whispering to him. Not from without, but from deep within. As if he were once again coiled in Iraj's breast.

And Safar said, *I'm here, my friend! Together, we can fight him!*

A fierce surge of energy burst through Iraj's veins and just as Kalasariz's maw spread wide to kill him, Protarus thrust his sword inward and then up with all his strength.

The blade speared through the roof of the spymaster's mouth and then plunged into his brain.

Kalasariz bellowed in agony, ripping Iraj away with his giant's hand and dashing him to the ground.

A red curtain of pain swept over Iraj. More pain than he had ever felt in his life.

Then the pain vanished and Iraj found himself sitting in the cave of Alisarrian The Conqueror. He was with Safar and they were boys again, swearing never-ending friendship and taking the blood oath.

"Someday I will be king of kings," he told Safar, "and you will be the greatest wizard in history. We'll make a better world before we're done, Safar. A better world for all."

Safar smiled agreement and started to answer. But suddenly he seemed quite distant and he started to fade away. He spoke, but Iraj couldn't hear what he was saying and he became quite frightened.

"Speak louder, brother!" Iraj shouted. "I can't hear you!"

Then once again, Safar spoke from within him. And he said, quite clearly, *Farewell, brother mine. A great dream awaits us. And the sooner we get started, the sooner that dream will begin.*

The words made Iraj feel quite peaceful. And he was content.

"Farewell, brother," he replied. "Farewell, my friend. Until we meet again."

And then the cave vanished and Iraj dreamed of horses — a great wild herd flying across the plains.

He sailed with them, moving at breathtaking speed, the air full of fresh spring currents, the horizon a joyous creation of blue skies meeting lush green earth.

On and on he sailed. Skimming just above the fabulous herd.

Flying toward horizons that would never end.

"It's not over yet, father, is it?" Palimak said.And Safar looked up from his friend's crushed and lifeless body to meet his son's eyes.

Palimak's demon face didn't seem strange to Safar. It was as if that face had always been there, waiting to get out. And now that Palimak had transformed into his true self, Safar only loved him the more.

"You're right, son," he replied. "It isn't."

Then they both heard two horses whinny in the distance. Their eyes rose to see Khysmet standing on a hill. Beside him was the black mare. Her saddle was empty and there was no sign of the Spirit Rider.

"Let's go, son," Safar said, suddenly realizing what they had to do next.

He whistled and the two magnificent animals raced down the hillside. A moment later they were both mounted — Safar on Khysmet, Palimak on the mare — and riding up the side of the volcano.

Soon they came to the ridge overlooking the Valley of the Two Kings. But it was the valley of the ancients, not the place they'd left a few hours before. And instead of being ravaged by storm, it had been destroyed by a great army. Farmhouses were still ablaze. The lake was filled with the charred corpses of men and animals.

And in the center was the fabulous golden Castle of the Two Kings, flames engulfing the domed palaces.

Only the great Keep remained unscathed, still standing defiant against what must have been a very long siege.

Surrounding the castle was a strange army consisting of thousands of soldiers. Half were human and half were demon. Some were mounted — horses for the human cavalry, big catlike beasts for the demons — while others were on foot or manning huge siege engines.

At the gate of the Castle Keep was a knot of soldiers, wielding a great battering ram. Flying over them was the Banner of Asper —

the twin-headed snake with wings.

Palimak gaped at the scene. "Father!" he said. "Nothing's moving."

Safar nodded he too had noticed the strangeness. Not one soldier or beast moved. Even the flames licking at the buildings were still. In fact, the entire scene looked like a gigantic frieze of a long-ago battle from a war museum.

And the only sound was the thunder and grinding of the Hells Machine. And the only movement was the thick cloud of smoke issuing from the rumbling volcano.

"Come on, son," was all Safar said.

And the two rode down the broad avenue that led to the castle.

On either side of them lifelike statues of soldiers stared blankly at them as they passed.

The two moved through that eerie, frozen army for what seemed like an eternity.

Safar expected one of the demon or human soldiers suddenly to come alive at any minute and challenge them. But nothing and no one moved all the way to the gates.

The only change as they approached was the increasing loudness of the deadly machine.

Finally they were crossing the bridge and approaching the main gate where the soldiers with the battering ram were posed in mid-hammer. On one side of them was the planted banner of Asper. On the other was a huge, mounted demon.

Safar stared at the demon commander for a moment. Only mildly surprised that it was Asper, himself, leading the attack.

Understanding dawned for Palimak and he said, "It's an illusion, isn't it, father? Just like in Caluz."

"Something like that," Safar replied. Then, "Are you ready, son?"

Palimak squared his young shoulders and grinned a brave demon smile. "Ready, father."

Safar drew his silver witch's-dagger and chanted this spell:

"If the world by Heaven's decree
Should become a hell for thee and me;
Where devils wear the gods' raiment
And None dare answer our lament;
Look for me by Asper's Gate,
Knock on the doors and meet thy Fate."

Then he returned the dagger to its sheath in his sleeve and drew his sword. Palimak followed suit.

Safar shouted, "Open!"

And that single word boomed across the valley, drowning out even the sound of the Hells Machine:

"OPEN!"

For a moment there was silence then came a grumbling and a groan, followed by a loud shriek of protesting hinges. And then the gate swung slowly inward, unleashing a blast of intense heat and foul air.

Safar sensed what was coming and shouted to Palimak, "Steady!"

A score of hellish creatures rushed out at them, each more terrible than the other. Some of them looked like the monsters Queen Charize had ruled — pale as death with enormous bat wings and long fangs. Others were like the tree creatures who had attacked them at sea, with dozens of limbs bearing snapping teeth.

But the warning to Palimak wasn't necessary, because Gundara and Gundaree had already armed their master.

"Ghosts!" they cried. "Nothing but ghosts. You've already killed them once, Little Master!"

So, like his father, Palimak held perfectly still, letting the creatures swirl all around him, threatening with fangs and teeth until they dissolved into nothingness.

Both Khysmet and the black mare seemed not to notice the spirit-world attack and only flicked their tails as if a few flies were troubling them.

Safar signaled and he and Palimak flicked their reins and entered the Castle Keep.

But now there was no royal grand palace entry to greet them. Even the magical wind rose was gone. Instead, they found themselves in the dim, steamy recesses of the Hells Machine. Iron grating beneath them, the horse's hooves clacking across the metal. Huge gears twice the size of a miller's grindstone turning this way and that with no apparent order or purpose. Wide chain belts, thick with old grease, thundering above them.

Flames and steam shot through the grates as they moved deeper into the interior, following the narrow avenue toward a dim light.

Palimak felt grimy — oily sweat gathering under his arms and streaming down his sides.

Gundara cried, "She's waiting, Little Master!"

To which Gundaree added, "Just at the light! Be ready!"

Palimak didn't need to ask who they meant. He *knew!*

Safar led them toward the light, which grew brighter with every step the horses took. Khysmet snorted at the steam and shook his head, great drops of sweat streaming from his mane.

Safar patted the stallion, comforting himself as much as the horse.

Then there was one more long blast of steam and they were through.

And he found himself in a vast chamber flooded with a strange red light that cast no shadows.

At the far end of the chamber was the Lady Lottyr. Her six hands waved gracefully, shooting out long sparks of magic. Driving the huge machine with their incredible power.

Her lush body moved rhythmically to music only she seemed to hear. The movements reminded Safar of the harvest dance he'd suffered through when he was spellbound.

And her six heads snaked in and out on long, slender necks that somehow made an eye-pleasing whole where they met her shoulders.

She was the size of a tall woman and backed by a miniature of the Demon Moon, which was symmetrically twice her length and breadth. Small black clouds swirled across the red face of the moon, making the goddess seem as if she were floating with them, although she always remained in the center.

A red gossamer gown, thin as spider's silk, draped her body — displaying all her substantial charms in an alluring light.

Despite himself, Safar felt heat stab at his loins. He heard Palimak's sharp intake of breath and knew that his son was also affected.

Khysmet snorted and moved closer to the mare who whinnied, then shied teasingly away. But not too far, Safar noticed. Not very far at all.

The whole atmosphere reeked of seduction.

And then, from a distance, Safar heard beautiful voices lifting in song: *"Surrender, oh, surrender."*

The goddess laughed, her tones silky and promising impossible things.

She said, "That's all I ask, Safar. Surrender and all I have shall be yours."

Then she turned to Palimak, saying, "You can have me, too, boy. I know that is your utmost desire, is it not?"

Palimak was shocked both by her offer and his body's unaccustomed reaction to the goddess. He didn't know what to say, or how to respond.

Safar felt like he was back in Coralean's harem, with one beauty after the other displayed to him. Especially the lovely courtesan, Astarias, who had so beguiled him in his youth.

And he kept hearing that spell song:

"Her hair is night,
Her lips the moon;
Surrender. Oh, surrender.
Her eyes are stars,
Her heart the sun;
Surrender. Oh, surrender.

Her breasts are honey,
Her sex a rose;
Surrender. Oh, surrender.
Night and moon. Stars and Sun.
Honey and rose;
Lady, oh Lady, surrender.
Surrender. Surrender . . ."

So powerful was her presence that for a moment he nearly succumbed. Nearly threw himself at her feet, begging her favor.

Then he fought back, thinking of Nerisa, his little thief of Walaria. And Methydia, a woman above all women who taught him all he truly knew about love, life and magic.

Ah, yes, and then there was Leiria. Lovely, lovely Leiria. Who would throw herself in front of a phalanx of charging chariots to save him.

Who needed this woman?

This goddess from the Hells?

All these thoughts — from seduction to hesitation to rejection — flashed through his mind in a split second. Although it seemed like an agonizing — and most tempting — eternity.

Safar formed a spell, a spell above all spells to cast her off. And these were the words he chanted to the unseen, far-away Leiria. It was song she'd taught him when they were lovers:

"Lovers when parted
From what they love,
Have no temptations
Or troubles to bear.
Outside might be temptation,
Inside only love.
There can be no wanting
For what is not there."

And suddenly the lust ran out of the atmosphere like a flood unleashed and the Lady Lottyr's spell was shattered.

Failure struck the goddess like a lightning bolt. The Demon Moon burst into flames and she rose from her throne, all six hands outstretched to blast Safar from the face of the world.

"How dare you?" she cried. "How dare you mock . . ."

But Safar didn't wait for her to finish. Instead, he hurled himself off Khysmet, straight into her waving arms.

His witch's-dagger was already out and as the Lady Lottyr cursed him and folded those killing arms around him he plunged the dagger into her heart. And kept stabbing, on and on.

Like a holy assassin from the temple of Walaria, killing whatever his mad soul and the imagined gods of murder drove him to kill.

Knife in.

Knife out.

Driving and gutting.

Although the goddess was caught by surprise, instead of fighting him off she wrapped all six arms around him and crushed him to her bosom.

Safar felt his ribs go in a ghastly series of cracks and his life's breath being crushed from his body.

But he kept driving the knife in without stop. On, and on, hoping and praying.

A frozen witness to his father's murder, Palimak hung back for a moment. Then he vaulted off the mare to the ground and charged forward.

The only thing he could think to do was to slash at the goddess with his sword and somehow free his father. But in the back of his brain he knew it was a hopeless effort. "

Lady Lottyr might die. But that was unlikely. More likely, it would be his father who would die and the goddess, although sorely wounded, would kill Palimak as well.

Then Palimak saw Asper's shell horn on the floor where Safar had dropped it during his mad attack.

He lifted it up, thinking to blow and raise any spirit he could to help.

But then the Favorites cried, "Smash it, Little Master! Smash it! It's the only chance we have!"

So he threw the horn to the floor and it shattered into hundreds of pieces.

And the last thing Palimak saw was his father driving his dagger once more into the breast of the Goddess Lottyr.

There might have been an explosion, but even years later, when telling the tale to friends, Palimak couldn't swear that was happened next.

If the truth were known, there was only a flash of golden light.

And the sound of angry voices.

Whose voices?

Palimak didn't know.

All he could say was that for a long, long time he seemed to exist in another world.

He saw farmers reaping harvests of plenty.

He saw forests rising unopposed to the sky.

He saw horses, fabulous horses, running wild across exotic plains.

And he saw seas, wild booming seas, full of flying fish and playing dolphins and sounding whales.

All eager for the promises of tomorrow.

But the sight that thrilled him the most was the sight of thousands of little turtles breaking free from their sandy nests and swimming out to sea.

Where no monsters — human or demon — waited to take them.

56

THE RINGMASTER

It was Leiria's turn at the wheel.

All was peaceful on the airship as they sailed with summer winds to far Syrapis — and home.

Beneath her were the ships of the Kyranian fleet, every man happy at his survival.

Far off in the distance, she could see the destruction of Hadin. The volcano was still exploding, venting its wrath on all who had opposed it.

Hadin was gone, turned to molten earth and boiling seas just as Safar had seen in his boyhood dream.

But there was a difference, as Safar had explained to her after the airship had picked him up. The volcano had rent the very earth, to be sure. Except that now its effect was purely local. Both evil people and good people had died in its blast. But now there was no poison cloud to envelop the entire world.

Innocent or guilty, only the people of Hadin had been destroyed. After Safar's struggle with the Hells and the Lady Lottyr, the volcano's effect had been limited.

The rest of the world was safe. And might even return, Safar had said, to its previous bounty.

Leiria looked over the big wheel to see Safar tending Khysmet, giving the stallion sweet corn to eat. And there was Palimak standing next to his father, offering the black mare the same.

Palimak was now fully a demon — from his curled, dagger-armed toes to his green horned brow. And Leiria loved him just as much as the half-human, half-demon child she'd once carried on her back.

She wasn't sure how all the people she loved the most had come to be with her again. Eeda had directed the airship over the volcano, then she and Jooli had cast many powerful spells.

And then Safar and Palimak, together with Khysmet and the mare, had suddenly been with them. Both men had been exhausted and near death, but Jooli and Eeda had used all their skills to resurrect them.

Now Safar and Palimak — still wobbly in their legs — were feeding their charges and whispering words of comfort to them.

Leiria should have been bursting with happiness. Instead, she found herself glowering at the scene. Maddeningly, since his return Safar had kept her at an emotional distance. He was kind, his words gentle, but whenever they were alone together, he became uneasy and made some weak excuse to part company.

And now there he was, feeding that damned horse again! Talking so tenderly to Khysmet that it drove her crazy. Suddenly, she realized she was jealous. Which was ridiculous. How could she feel jealous of a horse?

She gritted her teeth, not sure who she was angrier at, Safar or herself.

A booming voice came from behind her. "Avast, lass! Can't you see you're steering the wrong course!"

Confused, she turned and saw Biner standing there with a wide grin on his face.

"I don't understand," she said, pointing at the compass. "I'm steering just where you said I ought to."

Biner brushed her aside with a mighty hand and took the wheel. "Maybe you were and maybe you weren't," Biner said. "But the plain fact is, it sure as hells isn't the right course for *you.*"

He pointed at Safar. "There's your setting, lass," Biner said. "Can't you see that he's waitin' for you, but he just doesn't know it yet? Because after all that's happened he's not sure you'll have him."

Leiria need no further prodding. Immediately, she broke away and raced across the deck to Safar.

She grabbed him by the shoulder and spun him around.

"Come here, you!" she said.

Then she kissed the surprised look off his face.

And they embraced for a long, long time.

Biner watched, smiling. Then Arlain came up to stand beside him.

Looking at the scene, she said, "I'm glad to thee that Thafar finally know'th that thomebody lov'th him!"

Arlain sighed, breathing a little fire and smoke. And she added, sadly, "I only wi'th he knew it wath me."

Biner patted her, then spun the wheel, turning the airship about. "Never mind that, lass," he said. "I've set a course for the next landfall. And in one day's time we'll find kids and rubes aplenty and you'll forget all that."

Arlain brightened for a moment, then frowned, worried.

She cast down her dragon eyes, saying "But Thafar thaid the god'th might not be happy. What if they curth our performanthe and ruin everything?"

Biner slapped Arlain on her pretty back and bellowed, "Be damned to the Gods, Arlain! Be damned to them all.

"And be damned to everything but the circus!"

Arlain burst into laughter. And she laughed so long and so hard that she set the airship on fire.

AUTHOR'S NOTE

The character of Safar Timura is loosely based on Omar Khayyam, the ancient Persian poet and astronomer. The son of a tentmaker, Khayyam rose to become the chief astrologer of the sultan, his boyhood friend. Just as Safar, the son of a potter, rose to become the chief wazier of the king, his boyhood friend.

Khayyam (1044-1123 A.D) is best known to us today for his poetry, collected in the remarkable "Rubaiyat of Omar Khayyam." Of all the many English translations of this work, I prefer Edward Fitzgerald's.

Students of mathematical history also know him as a pioneer in algebra and geometry. Experts say his mathematical discoveries remained unmatched for centuries — to the time of Descartes (1596-1650).

I first came across "The Rubaiyat" in a bazaar when I was a boy living on the island of Cyprus. Battered and torn, I only paid a few pennies for it. But the first words I read tumbled out like upturned chests of gold:

"Awake! for the morning in the bowl of night
Has flung the stone that puts the stars to flight.
And lo! the hunter of the east has caught
The sultan's turret in a noose of light."

"The Tales of the Timuras" were inspired by that most fortuitous discovery.

Another major influence on these books — and those that may follow — are the hundreds of e-mails I have received from readers all over the world these past few years.

I'd particularly like to thank Julie Mitchell, who kindly contributed her own poem to "The Gods Awaken," which is printed here with her permission. You'll find the poem in the chapter titled, "Jooli's Song."

Ms. Mitchell, a Texas scientist, was the winner of my "Be A

Hero Contest," which drew thousands of entries. The warrior woman character, Jooli, is named after her.

One of the main villains of this book — King Rhodes — was named for another contest winner, Bob Rhodes, a California engineer. Bob, a lovely fellow, is nothing like the barbarian king portrayed in this book. Another villain, Clayre — the Queen Witch — is named after my kind and gentle reader Clayre Kitchen, who lives in the United Kingdom.

ABOUT THE AUTHOR

Allen Cole was born in Philadelphia in the middle of World War II. His parents parents were restless people, as nomadic as America's earliest settlers. The family moved so frequently that for the first six months of his life, his crib was a series of hotel bureau drawers. By the time he was in the first grade, he had crossed the country several times by plane, train and car.

He writes:

> I was blessed, or cursed, with the knowledge that I wanted to be a writer at the age of five. The light bulb winked on one early evening while I was perched on my father's knee. He was reading "The Raven" to me. My father had a rich voice, perfectly pitched for Poe. Although I didn't understand most of the words, their sounds and rhythms swept me away to other worlds. The feelings I experienced were so intense and pleasurable I determined right then that I wanted to make other people feel the same way. I decided when I grew up I'd be an author like Poe. And from that moment on, I made a point of observing everything closely for future reference.
>
> Shortly after the outbreak of the Korean War, my father was recruited by the CIA (out of the submarine service) and my parents got the chance to wander to their hearts' content. We left the U.S. when I was seven and, except for a few trips home between assignments, I lived abroad until my junior year in high school.
>
> We roamed Europe, the Middle East and the Far East — wherever the drums of the Cold War played the loudest. I loved every minute of it, soaking up all the sensations and details I could for that grand day I was certain would come when I could write it all down for those poor people who lived (I believed) such dull lives at home.
>
> I saw the pyramids, the glories of ancient Greece

and Rome. Was stunned by the art at the Louvre and the magnificence of Sistine Chapel. I roamed the bazaars of Istanbul, Beirut, Nicosia and Tripoli. I marveled at the great statues of Buddha, learned Judo from an Okinawan master, and was taught the beauty of the tea ceremony by Geishas who had voices like bells.

What writer could ask for more?

Readers can learn more about Allen Cole's life and work at his web site: http://www.acole.com